A Green Tree in Gedde

ALAN SHARP

NEL

THE NEW ENGLISH LIBRARY

Copyright © 1965 by Alan Sharp
First published in Great Britain by Michael Joseph Ltd., in 1965

*

First published as a special Four Square edition March 1966
First Four Square edition October 1966
Reissued in this NEL edition November 1967

*

NEL Books are published by The New English Library Limited, from Barnard's Inn, Holborn, London, E.C.1. Made and printed in Great Britain by Hazell Watson & Viney Ltd, Aylesbury, Bucks

A GREEN TREE IN GEDDE

This book is dedicated
to Greenock, to its buildings
and chimneys and streets
and the glimpses they have afforded me
of the river and the hills

'A great tree there is in Gedde growing, and in its branches the hawk it perches with the dove; fruit there is for all to eat, golden and silver globes and purple plums, and all abloss with bloom its brondes. No perdifol is there nor foliomort, and hallards none, but green leaf everlasting.

Know ye not this halidome, this greenheart axle-tree; know ye not Gedde. Its seed lies within us each.'

ROBERT GIBBON
b. 1866. d. 1925

MOSEBY'S BOOK
Here we sit

RUTH'S BOOK
Birds in the wilderness

GIBBON'S AND CUFFEE'S BOOK
Down in Demerara

CHAPTER ONE

Greenock lies along the Clyde littoral and is built up on to the hills behind. Thus it is a long lateral town and the streets rise steeply and provide open view of the river and the Argyllshire hills. In the winter there is snow on them and in the summer their great tawny flanks are charred occasionally by heather fires. They are seen across an expanse of roofs and chimneys, the slates dull purple scales and the ridges presided by clumps of lums, cans churning and smoke pennons flying. The buildings are of sandstone block, greybuffs and occasional reds, and are erected in monolithic tenements, achieving their only rhythm in the flowing lines enforced by the land.

During the day the town channels mind and eye swiftly out to the river and the hills, constantly transcending self by the dynamics of its construction. It is only in the evenings, and especially in the autumnal early nights that it states itself. Then the sky takes on a steely blue clarity and against this in edges of unbearable blue black the buildings inflict themselves, the simplicity of outline fantasticated by the chimney abstractions, castles, chess problems, graveside gatherings, with the smoke in slow upgoing to the enormous empty sky.

At this time there is a heroism in the shapes and the colours, an elemental starkness which attains archetype, a town looking across a river at hills. The river flows, the hills abide and the town ponders these images of evanescence and antiquity, while above, with the disinterest of the truly eternal, the sky endures.

John Moseby had been married to Edna Davidson for four and a half years and they had a daughter of three called Carol, named, as Moseby said, in honour of his mother-in-law, Sarah. On Saturday mornings he took Carol for a walk, to the library to return books and then along the town to Princes Pier to feed the gulls. During this time his wife did the shopping and they met in the Regency Room of the only fashionable café in town. They lived in Dempster Street, one of the highest of the old streets, looking from their kitchen window over the whole town and across to Helensburgh.

It was a warm, rather windy day and Moseby pointed out to Carol a chimney can, turning in fitful whirls.

'Is it gyring?' Carol asked.

'Yes, it's gyring.'

'Is it, gyring?'

'Definitely. Can you see it?'

'No.' Moseby pointed it out, squatting beside her to realize the line of vision. With their heads together they looked in different directions. Pointing her face at the roofs didn't help. The can had stopped revolving and he abandoned the attempt, slightly depressed by the failure, and went on down Mount Pleasant Street. A faint regret tinged his mind, barely sufficient to require thinking about but enough to notice and register the fluttered adieus of several handkerchiefs on a line. The thought of separations, of trains leaving stations. Carol ran on ahead and he snatched at her hand.

'Do you want to get made into mince?'

'What for?'

'For running out on to the road.'

'Mince' – Carol didn't see the point.

'That's right. That's what girls get made into that run out on the road.'

'Why Daddy?'

'For dinner.' That held her for a bit and they crossed over at the West Station and went down Inverkip Street. The station cat sat on a ledge in a great neutered puff. Moseby didn't like to see neutered cats because they reminded him that they had had a cat neutered once and when it still damaged the furniture, put down. That was the only time he and Edna had ever really quarrelled. He didn't like to see neutered cats. The old cemetery looked well through the gate. Inside, on the gravel path, two pigeons, the cock fan tailing and swelling, clockworking around the heedless hen. Behind them they dragged their blue shadow-silks. Cock pigeons always amused him. Dogs made sex ludicrous and pigeons made courtship an absurdity.

'Daddy look at the pigeons.'

'I am looking.'

'What are they doing?'

After some thought he said, 'Nothing.' Everything else was too complicated. Wouldn't do to complicate things on a nice morning like this.

'Where do they live?'

'In a pigeon hut.'

'Is it a house?'

'It's a kind of house.' He took her hand and they went on.

'Is it like our house?'

'No it's not like our house. It's not as nice as our house.'

'I don't know one that is.'

Carol thought for a moment, then, 'I don't know any too.' Moseby smiled down at her hurrying head.

[His parents' house. He always remembered it with a smell. Of polish, all kinds of polish, floor polish and metal polish, wood polish and shoe polish. A dark gleaming tell-tale house free from dirt or disorder. And the rooms empty. Empty and full of dark polished furniture. And dark green plants in dull shone pots. Aspidistras. The name frightened him as a child. Made him think of snakes and spiders. And cobby-webs. But Mrs Moseby never let webs frow. Nothing grew in those rooms but the plants and the aroma-ed reflective silence of furniture.]

'Where's that man going?' Moseby could see about thirty men.

'What man?'

'That man,' pointing at half of them.

'Which one?'

'The one with the lump.' There was a man with a hunch back Moseby noticed now.

'Don't point.'

'Is he going to the doctor?'

'No he's going home for his dinner.'

11

'Will he get mince?'

'He might, you never can tell.'

A shop assistant launched water on to a soap scribbled window. It ran down in quick ruffles, causing a pyramid of canned food to wobble precariously. A dog ran through the water and stencilled clovers of paw print which Carol studied carefully until they faded.

[Wee Joe Moffat and Mary Agnew. He had a stick factory. Sat over the chopping block, his swollen bulging back on top of him, chopping the wood deftly, clean sweet 'chicks'. Mary Agnew, big pale girl woman, bunching with her stumpy fingers, her legs spread and where her garter bit at the thigh showing. Up among the bags of sawdust Joe had her, her dark blue knickers hanging on one instep and his trousers at his ankles. His legs were thin and white. The long pencil pokes of sunlight and the dry harsh noise somebody made. The sweet, damp smell of the sawdust. Joe gave him a sixpence and he promised not to tell. But he did.]

Carol played hide and seek in the library, running around among the book racks. Moseby searched the fiction briskly. Edna was reading David Karp and he found the only one she hadn't read. As antidote to his hygienic craftsmanship he took May Sarton's *Faithful are the Wounds*. In his head he delivered a lecture on the liberal mentality in contemporary American novelists. Like most of his lectures it was more notable for the overwhelming sexual passion it aroused in a superb ash blonde girl in the front row than for any marked originality of thought. This girl possessed in apotheosis Moseby's present sexual fetish, roseate breasts through a white shirt. His obsessions tended to the literary. He had once found a book in a second-hand shop about the Temple rites of somewhere, all he could remember were the occasional images thrown off by the turgid prose, 'the wantons abandoned themselves to their depraved appetites' and one which he still puzzled over, 'shamelessly posturing to their patrons', phrases like these became almost objects in their own right and thinking about them, repeating their cadence became a sexual stimulation. Carol appeared with a pained look which he knew of old.

'Daddy I need the toilet.'

'I'll bet you do.'

'I do Daddy, I need . . .'

'Well hold it in for a minute.'

'I can't.'

'Just for a minute.'

'Daddee . . .' and the look on her face intensified.

He left without getting the history books he needed. Of the three assistants he knew only one. She had been in his year at school. She would have been a gaunt beauty if she had been beautiful. He took Carol into the Gents side of the Crystal Palace, the town's premier public convenience. In the cubicle he noted the unceasing vigilance against wall writers. Several promising drawings had been largely obliterated and most of the anecdotes and aphorisms were too faint to read. The honesty of these unknown commentators commended itself to Moseby, their guilty preoccupation with the primary area of human awareness. All over the country, all over the world they were overstating their case, claiming perversions they would not indulge, making assignations they would not keep and inscribing those eternal female figures, faceless and footless, opposed to the total anonymity of disembodied cocks. Moseby in his position as the first anthologist of public convenience literature had decided that these rampant members would be designated 'Rudi Phalli'. His other major contribution to the world's knowledge of the subjects was a conviction that the Lascaux Caves were Neanderthal bogs. While Carol was standing on the seat to flush the toilet he wrote his own motto high up on the door lintel. 'It's an ever sexpanding yoniverse', a piece of cod joycery he had never had the nerve to put into a poem.

'What are you writing?' Her voice echoed in the convenience.

'How long it took you to do the toilet.'

'Why are you writing that?'

'So I won't have to remember.' He was pleased to note

there was no one at the urinals and the attendant was studying the paper with an intensity that bespoke horse backing.
They went along the town, busy with Saturday shopping.
He didn't mind the numbers on Saturday, there was a faint
festivity in the air with the precious paring of the week-end
still ahead. He had liked it himself when single, meeting
Gibbon in the pub, the sawdust fresh down, Mrs Gerrard in
her black hat talking about how old 'the Rowan Tree' was
and the darts floating in simple plots to the board.

Looking to his right he was confronted by a tiled bathroom and a toilet in the window of a builder's showroom. It
was where the Central Picture Hall used to be. They called
it the Ranch because all the Hopalong Cassidys used to
come there. A plumber's emporium. He felt the sentiment
of nostalgia, a genuine sadness at time and things changing.
He took Carol's hand and crossed the road.

[The foyer and the coal fire they burned and the tall
old doorman and the smell of lysol and the black and
white always asleep cat beside the cash box where the
tickets hung on a roll and the girl tore them off with her
fingers with her hair done the way the pictures of the
film stars behind her on the wall had theirs done. It was
always warm to go through the glass doors and see the
fire behind the doorman's back and stroke the cat and go
up the steps to where somebody tore your tickets in half
and the sound of the guns making that noise that didn't
look like 'ricochet' when he looked it up and inside they
were riding through that well-known country with the
rocks and the trees and the music was going 'dan de
dan'.]

Sometimes through the interstices of events there came
what was almost an odour, something akin to that smell he
smelled from old, condemned houses, derelict now, partially demolished sometimes. Looking into the gutted rooms
with the peeling wallpaper and the bare splintered lathes,
and sometimes there was a calendar or an old picture and
this smell, both acrid and damp, of no longer dwellers no
longer dwelling. It was a bit like that with the old Central

only instead of rubble and dust there were stainless steel sinks and tiled showers. But it was the same. Just the same. Where did the past go, what happened to its reality. In time enough Carol would be where he was and he would be with the Central. It made his heart surge in him, this commonplace terror.

'Give us a kiss.'

'Eh, well what kind do you want?'

'Have you got a sixpenny one?'

'Oh well I don't know, no I've just got a fourpenny one.'

'I'll have a fourpenny one then.'

'All right.' She held up her face with eyes closed and her mouth budded in a rosy purse. He kissed her and lifted her up. Carol opened her eyes.

'That's not a fourpenny one.'

'What is it then?'

'It's a, it's a sixpenny one . . .'

'. . . and you told me you didn't have any sixpenny ones . . .' She screamed as he tickled her and he put her up on his shoulders where she held his hair and his forehead. His daughter, he thought, his own, none other than, daughter. They were related, they belonged to each other in bond. In this world she was his reality, his only reality.

[Amid the smell of books and shaving soap, the rub of woollen underwear and faded photographs of unknown people, in a long buff envelope, opened idly, the document, of crackly yellow white paper, inscribed in copperplate, legalizing the adoption by Thomas Carlyle Moseby and Mary Phelps McGregor Moseby of a male child, John, hereafter to be legally known as John Moseby.]

There was a dearth of gulls at Princes Pier. Carol looked for them. A few drifted over the red roofed buildings on the pier proper. A tanker slipped smoothly down river, great rust cancers on its side. Helensburgh could be seen, sparkling under the faintest gauze of smoke.

'Where's the seagulls, Daddy?'

'I don't know.'

'There's some over there. Make them come over.'

15

'Che-che, pss-wss, che-che, che-che . . .'

'You don't say "che-che" to seagulls. You say "che-che" to pussycats.'

'What do you say then?'

'I don't know.'

'Neither do I.' At that moment a brown-looking gull with one leg came past.

'There's one Carol.'

'I don't like that one. I like white ones.'

'If you give that one a bit the others will see it and then they'll come.'

To Moseby's surprise that was what happened. He sat on the rail and ate a crust watching Carol did not throw herself into the two feet of water below while dispensing her largesse. The tanker was going out of sight round the shoulder. Across in Helensburgh a bus toyed along a few inches. Carol as usual had singled out a gull for vilification as a glutton and was trying to lob bread to her favourite. The whole business got her very excited, the wings beating the air, white flares, and the yawks of the disappointed gulls. Her face shone, miming her delight and disapproval. It made him happy just to see her. He didn't think he could ever have been like her. It was rather difficult for him to remember what he had been like before finding out about his adoption, and since then he had the feeling he had been exactly as he was now, that in some ways he was still the same boy, prowling where he had no right to, still sealed somehow in that capsule of incredulous certainty.

[There had been moments of pure madness; in a sweet-shop a woman's hand, reaching down into a butterscotch bottle, drowned before his eyes, writhing desperately among the candy rocks, while he watched, helpless. Or sitting above the staring, cooked eye of an egg, blindly returning its scrutiny. In mid-sentence his mind would recoil from the gritty articles of speech and leave him stranded, bereft of language. And crowds, moving at silent cinema tempo, their faces flicking past his fixed focus eye, noses mouths ears teeth nostrils hair chins lips in endless permutation, all aping one the other. And

16

once on getting out of bed he saw his foot sitting on the floor like some carapace wrenched from its shell. Quickly he had hidden it in his shoe but he limped all day.]

'Daddy, I'm finished all the bread.'
'All right, we'll go and meet your mother.'
'Will I get ice cream?'
'You'll get a cake if you're good.'
'But I want ice cream'
'Well ask your mother.'

The Regency Room was on the second floor but had been decorated and heated cleverly to convey the impression that it was underground. The wall stripes were maroon and the carpeting cerise. The chairs were painted silver with crimson seats. The fronds of female conversation waved to and fro to the occasional chink of spoon on cup. Laughter like bubbles out of sinking bottles and the thick close smell of coffee and cigarettes and women and women's perfume. Edna Moseby awaited her husband and flicked through a woman's magazine. Her mouth was full and well shaped and she had good eyes. Her nose was too long and too thin but it was straight and gave her an arresting profile. Full on the centre of her face seemed rather empty. She dressed with a kind of purposeful elegance, the severity of her suits always on this side of the practical and the low-heeled suède shoes minimizing her good legs but conveying taste and considerable expenditure. On her lapel there was a celtic cross set with an amber stone. Over her whole public manner there was a veneer, almost a frost, of self-control. She was made up only a little but that very carefully, her eyes delicately lined and her lipstick light and pale. The only eccentricity in her twenty-seven years was Moseby. She was two and a half years older than he and as her mother said at regular intervals, she should have known better. She almost had but there had been in the wry talk and the taut nervous energy an inexorable appeal. When the matter came to a head and she had told her mother they were going to marry, Mrs Davidson, from the centre of her flat rage asked what she could see in him. Edna had said she found him

17

electric. It was not the word she had wanted but it was, despite that, the aptest. For her Moseby had stopped doing nothing and taken a job in the Progress department of I.B.M. and after two years left to study under a Teachers' Training grant for Glasgow University. To eke out the allowance Edna worked three days a week at her old job in a local solicitor's, a state of affairs Mrs Davidson thought disgusting. As she saw it her daughter had married not only someone beneath her but also a man with no sense of responsibility. The rapidity with which she had become pregnant showed it. Mrs Davidson had been married for eight years before her husband had impregnated her, an occurrence without repetition. Moseby had suggested to his wife that even once was too hard to believe and that she was a case of parthenogenesis. Edna had never found it easy to laugh about her mother and this was no exception.

He came in with Carol and sat down opposite Edna, feeling her knee under the table.

'Stop it John, anybody can see.'

'Wait until this afternoon then.' She mocked surprise.

'Why, what's happening this afternoon?'

'What didn't happen last Saturday afternoon. You are going to get screwed.'

'Do you have to use words like that?'

'It's fair comment.'

'Can I have an ice cream?'

'No, you can have a cream cake, a Kunzel cake.'

'I want ice cream.'

'There's no ice cream in here.' To Moseby, 'My mother is coming up this afternoon.'

'Why?'

'She said she would last Sunday.'

'Well if she said it I suppose that means she'll be there.'

'Why don't you like my mother?' Moseby could never be sure why Edna asked this question, knowing as she did better than he.

'Well she thinks you should have married Walter Kinneard.'

'Don't you agree?' That was a good sign when she was skittish.

'He walks as though his arse chewed caramels.'

'Oh John stop it. Things like that are not funny and you seem to think everything vulgar is hilarious. And in front of Carol . . .'

'I want a cake.'

'Yes, you'll get a cake. Did you feed the seagulls?'

'There was a greedy one, wasn't there a greedy one Daddy?'

'There were about fifty greedy ones. Look I didn't get time to look for my history texts, this bladder here had to be taken out. I'll go back now and then pick you up again.'

'I don't want to sit in here all day.'

'Well walk up Nelson Street and I'll catch you up. I'll take the shopping.'

'It's all right, I'll manage it. Are you angry about something?'

'Yes.'

'What?'

'Guess.'

'My mother.'

'Not her existence, her presence, this afternoon when I should have you stretched out all bare and eager.' How does she manage to blush, he thought.

'You're terrible, you must walk along the street thinking things—'

'You're right, I do. I'll catch you up.'

'Don't be angry, there's always tonight.'

'I know that, this afternoon would have just put me in the mood for tonight.'

'You're not angry?'

'No all right. I won't be. I'm going, give me a kiss.' Edna kissed him as lightly as she could on the mouth.

'Give me a kiss plum.'

'What kind do you want?'

'Oh don't start that, just give him a kiss Carol, stop selling your pleasures.'

Moseby smiled at his wife and kissed Carol. Going out he remembered how much he disliked the Regency Room. And how much he disliked meeting Edna here. She seemed encased then, in her mind and her clothes, in this placenta coloured room with the used air and the chit-chattering women with their twin sets and their single strings. He smiled at his wrath as he went out. He disliked cafés with juke boxes almost as much. Almost but not quite. And Carol could get ice cream. It was just that Edna always seemed more her mother's daughter there. Sometimes the music hall cut of the whole thing amused him but for the most part Mrs Davidson was an unfunny event. In a way she was the first person he had had to know that he disliked. But for Edna people like her mother would have stayed where they belonged, somewhere else. But shouldn't Edna be there too, wasn't she another of the same, well dressed, with a set of categories for a mental process and that incredible capacity for seeing only what suited them. Christ's sake Moseby, he thought, you're describing ninety-odd per cent of humanity, leave the old cow be. Just because he was being denied his little gout this afternoon. What was so special about sex on Saturday afternoons.

[First time had been a Saturday afternoon. She lived in Glasgow. They met in one of the large stifling dance halls, speckled with the revolving facets, different colours that all died out on her pale face, the peaky features that bespoke a poverty beyond poorness, her flat empty way of saying things, the gnawed finger nails with the cuticles all raggedy. Their early meetings charged with an electric kind of boredom that preceded sex. They blundered ineptly into intercourse one damp sultry Saturday with the roars of the football crowd surging up through the sandstone tenement overlooking Ibrox. On subsequent Saturdays they persevered, never unclothed, never wholly comfortable until she had a scare about pregnancy. They quarrelled after a while, he only ever saw her once again, from a tram going into a cinema. Showing 'Sands of Iwo Jima' it was.]

He got two books from the library and put in a card for another. The gaunt unbeautiful girl was still on duty. They exchanged meaningless smiles as he left. Ugly people depressed him. Smug bastard. But they did. All the compen-

20

sating they had to do for being ugly. Maybe he was ugly. It didn't matter though because there was something about him. It was true. Sometimes he thought it was sex. It should be, God knows he thought about it enough. If you were as preoccupied with cunt as he was it ought to show. But there was a febrile, sweaty tenor to his obsession that he noted with dismay. His preoccupation was that of the tempted saint rather than of the sensualist. How he wanted to be able to sit and watch up some unknown woman's skirts admiring the formal arrangement of folded limb, not go sick with lust and have to look desperately away. And why was it that when something did ravish the sight, the pink distention of a bared nipple wet with spit, like a snail's horn blindly delicately reaching, why was it to his touch a drab crumple, to his mouth a pencil eraser ponderously sucked. And why was his lovemaking so precariously poised on the verge of orgasm from the very onset; unless he could disengage his mind and send it afoot though the streets. So often had he done this that upon the town there had been superimposed another shape with the aura and texture of flesh. The dullest streets sometimes, as he actually trod them, shivered silkily at his passing, caused his mind without further bidding to secrete the milky images of his prone wife. Coming off night shift, slack with fatigue, the sight of the bulk sugar lorries and their high twin mounds of demerara throbbed in his head until putting his hands around Edna's breasts he remembered them, sweet heaps.

In the small, railed-in public gardens in front of the library two men sat, one with a white stick. Several birds hopped about in front of them. It was one of those places that you forget exist he thought and in a curious way it looked remote and secluded, bordered by the Town Buildings, the library and the car park and a main road. Its privacy was that of the secret thought in company, you saw smiles like it on buses. He wanted to go in, in and sit and have the sparrows sprig about his shoes. Gibbon would come and they'd drink stout like they did in the old cemetery. That was another walled-in place, a sanctuary. He always thought of them sitting in there talking, aimless talk that didn't seek to do more than touch the other, like

21

fingers, stroking, soothing. 'You should have married Harry Gibbon' Edna said once. Maybe he should have at that. That was something about Edna's mind, she thought about relationship in terms of institutions; marriage, family, relatives, pals. That was the nearest she could come to comprehending what Moseby felt about Harry Gibbon. His friend from the days before he was married. You can't love a man unless you're a poof. The irony was that if they had been working class instead of lower and upper middle then there would have been a well-defined institution in which they could have met, the 'mate', the boon companion, all those away trips with the Morton Supporters Club and the smokers and darts matches. Instead they had early morning walks and odd evenings in the 'Rowan Tree'.

[They had gone walking in the hills one summer Gibbon had been on leave from the Army, crossing from Gourock on Ritchie's ferry and walking up behind Kilcreggan. The hills were everywhere around them, behind the ridges further ridges piled, tawn upon tan upon grey upon blue distant outlines. From their long calm cambers an aura of silence, sweetened by the tunes of the streams and the mimic burbling of a whaup. They clambered, wordless in the still of the long summer days, across the great slanting flanks, edging up to the watersheds to sit looking for a moment at the next valley and the next hill, letting their shirts dry and smiling at each other, shy almost at their closeness. And they saw a fox, running red like a flame and halloo-ed it as it sped. Gibbon's broad fair face, perspiration at his temples and running down to his ears. Gibbon gave him the army jerkin he wore. It was still hanging in the cupboard.]

In front of the Unitarian Church on Nelson Street, trees, newly desecrated by pruning, hallowed their bristly crops with a nimbus of intense green leaf. Edna was standing talking to someone. When he got closer Moseby could see it was Mrs Davidson. Carol came running to meet him.

'It's my Gran Davidson.'

'Is it?'

22

'Yes. She can't come today.'

'Oh that's a shame.' He wondered if Edna had put her off. Mrs Davidson was her daughter's mother. She was taller but they had the same features and colouring. The late Mr Davidson seemed not to have had much hand in the business. It only confirmed Moseby's suspicions.

'Hello John.' He had never quite accustomed himself to Mrs Davidson's voice. It had the classical range of refinements common to the west of Scotland, well-to-do matron, those vowel discolourations and arbitrary emphases known as the 'pan loaf', but instead of the effete bleat that usually accompanied it, with Mrs Davidson there was a hard vigorous timbre, not quite mannish, reminding him rather of the speaker at women's Guild meetings, talking about serious issues, the increase in illegitimacy or such like.

'Mother won't manage up this afternoon.'

'I have to visit Mrs Callander in hospital.' It was one of the things which annoyed him about Edna's mother that she constantly referred to people he didn't know as though he should.

'So you have a date then.' Mrs Davidson looked a little off-put by the colloquialism.

'It's one of John's terrible jokes. A date, Mrs. Callander.' Her mother looked unwitting. 'Date, calendar. It's a pun.'

'Not very funny.'

'Now Mrs Davidson, do I look like the sort of young man who would tell you a funny joke?' This, he had discovered, was the only way he could best her within the rules of polite conversation, an inane ambiguity constructed on the lines of formal talk. He let Carol tug him away from them as they made arrangements for Sunday. Getting Saturday afternoon free was dearly bought at the price of a Sunday tea. Still he could say he had to study. God bless the English Revolution and all those who sailed in her.

'I can't, Carol, we have to wait on your mother.' The subtlety was not wasted and after a moment she kissed Mrs Davidson on the cheek and Carol was summoned up for hers. Moseby waved and noted again without regret that her calves had run into her ankles. He smiled at his nastiness.

'What are you smiling about as though I couldn't guess?' She was; poking her face into his, amused herself at the whole charade, probably relieved at her mother's defection; she was at that moment quite beautiful.

[He remembered them running up on to the headland, pulling her behind him breathless and shouting, laughing and stumbling over the sprung short turf until unbelievably the sea flooded into sight, sweeping out of eyeshot, beyond imagination, and joy in a surge like the sea poured over the mind and in that moment was the sea and the turf and a hand and the wind, joy was palpable and was the world worn skin-close, the flesh of his experience, and all there was was the sea and the sun on it and her hand in his and the smell of her short sprung hair and the wind blowing over the turf and trying with gentle unsuccess to prise apart their kissing faces.]

He kissed her on the mouth.

'Oh, I do want to make love to you.' She looked about quickly to see if they had been observed.

'You'd better get them then.' 'Them' were condoms. Moseby bought them in a barber's at the West Station and the man always said something about the weather just as he was handing them over.

'I'll cut round now.'

'I want to go with Daddy.'

'No, you can't go.' Edna said a little sharply. Still feels it's all rather indecent he thought. How many times had she ever allowed it to dominate her, so that she didn't care how she looked or smelled or sounded. He used to tease her when they were making love by asking how she would like her photo in *Scottish Field* now.

'Nice day again today.'

'Pleasant, yes.'

They went up Mount Pleasant Street. In the back green with the handkerchiefs a shift filled voluptuously with wind. 'Shamelessly posturing to their patrons,' he thought.

24

Edna coaxed Carol to an afternoon nap. He did the dinner dishes and went into the room. Carol had a small room and this one they used as a bedroom putting up and down a studio couch at night. Moseby liked the house, Edna kept saying it was too small and Mrs Davidson thought pokey was a better word but he liked it. He put the studio couch together and spread a sheet over it. He was glad of the extravagance of venetian blinds. The sunlight, neatly sliced, toned down to that aqueous dim he liked, taking its hue from the green wallpaper. He undressed and lay on the bed. It was warm and he felt the room lap around him. He shut his eyes and let the drift drift. Edna came in and pretended disapproval. He could hear her undressing and she said something about Carol not sleeping for long. She didn't have quite such a good shape out of her clothes. Having the baby had thickened her and she had never quite got it off. Her breasts were long and had milky blue veins shining up through their whiteness. She lay down beside him in her slip. He rolled it up over her head and smelled its warm silky bunch.

There was nothing particularly impassioned about their love-making. He kept his mind light and drifting, like the room, going as slowly as he could, keeping himself high up on her and not coming very far out. Her eyes were closed and she breathed through her mouth. If he let it float it would be fine, as long as the big dark shapes stayed down, the dark squirming wants that changed everything. Like this, with Edna still and compliant he could stay in control, not trying to kiss her or do anything except move slowly the way she liked it. Times like this he let his mind walk.

[The cluster of old tenements on the hill, the long latitudinals, Holmscroft, Wellington, Dempster and the steep cross gridding of Bank Street and Trafalgar Street, then Ann Street and Mount Pleasant, an area of stone and smoke, chimney capped, long high canyons diced with windows and old women cushioned on the sills. Glimpses into kitchens hung with holy pictures and tinted soldiers dead in their frames. Closes through into back greens, when he was a child he thought the psalm said 'in past oor green he leadeth me' and he had a picture of Jesus ducking under the clothes lines. The little wildernesses left by demolition where the pigeon huts stood and the pigeons clippering round and round. A soft flaking world of stone and soot shot through by surprising lances at the river and the hills.]

He asked her if she was all right and she smiled without opening her eyes. He felt as though he were alone on top of a high hill.

CHAPTER TWO

The old cemetery on Inverkip Street is now kept as a kind of public gardens. The turf is shaved close and there is a small tree in the centre that is trained over into a kind of canopy. There are seats where people may sit. Not many use it, old men in the summer come and look around at the tombstones and smoke pipes and talk to themselves or to other old men. The burials in the cemetery are old and the gravestones are much worn, some of them like tables, low thick slabs set on squat legs, others erect, a little tilted perhaps from subsidence, and set around the walls, tablets; and all, all bearing those legends of bereavement and parenthetic dates. Lives begun and ended long ago, now layered in random rote of their falling, sons lie upon mothers and fathers on their daughters, and all finally upon each in a last interlocking knit, their differences at nought and a lasting affection replacing the frailty of human love. These under earth anthologies pervade the place with the monotony of their content and rise in a slow exhalation, without scent or sight, a breathing of bones, a long suspiration that wears as emblem the tree on a green ground.

The children call it the dead centre of Greenock, but the town no longer turns on it, having spilled in a plethora of living east and west and back up on to the hill. But from its seats the roofs of the older buildings make a sweep in half circle around the horizon, roof slant and chimney stack, tiering up on to the hill and sending on quiet evenings countless purlings of dove dun smoke slowly up into the air. At such moments then the old graveyard does seem a hub, the still centre of the town's slow revolve.

As to burial there is now another, larger cemetery, a sprawling overgrown tract, a vast dump for the dead. The bodies here are still earthbound by the rootings of memory, having not yet divested themselves of the love of created beings, insertions still appear in the *Greenock Telegraph*

27

commemorating their decease, people cut their grasses as penance for being alive and every Sunday, in the good weather, groups may be seen, walking slowly, with flowers and composed faces, to look down on graves in recall of lineaments now dissolved.

Held as they are to the land of the living by such un-reciprocal rememberings the dead invest their domain with a prolix tension of growth. Visitors lose themselves on unfamiliar lanes and with mild terror come upon other sepulchral visitors round evergreen corners. And the sheer volume of death that engulfs the eye, the rows upon lines of plinths and plaques, of glass-domed immortelles, urns in mottled mock marble 'from the neighbours' and the cenotaphs of the wealthy which all, no matter how portentous or how pathetic, make the same piteous utterance to the living gaze, finally to hasten exit, like the pressure of fathoms compels ascent, up to the air and the light, for in the bone ground there is no glimpse of the dwellings of the quick, everywhere grow the gloomy greens of rhododendrons, the nevergreens of conifers and the graygreen gravegrass.

But when at last the threads of memory rot and the rememberers themselves are tombed, then the liberated dead move in silent flit to the old open field of the truly buried, and there in sight of the living they relax and at last rest.

Robert Howell Gibbon came to Greenock in 1853 from Wigtownshire, the son of a Welsh mother and an Irish father, combining their darkness and tempers, but bigger-boned and quicker-minded than his parents, a swarthy handsome man with that inbuilt capacity for excess which renders its indulgence all but acceptable. He worked first in Glasgow at his trade of carpenter, but the dark bunched city with its stews and dense poverty oppressed him and one fine Sunday morning he walked the twenty-odd miles to Greenock with his tools on his shoulder, slept out on the Perch shore and sought work in the morning, fresh from swimming in the Clyde.

He had inherited the Methodist faith his mother had

championed against her husband's tepid Catholicism, yet without the fervent grimness of its essence, rather it was a background to his independence, stressing his individual worth before God and justifying him in his self-confidence. He took lodgings with Mother Sommerville in the Vinnel, a narrow, two-storeyed street at the centre of the working quarter, an area of desperate and abundant energy, milling with births and wife beatings, drunkenness and fist fights. Mother Sommerville presided over six more like Robert, lodging them in the other room of a room and kitchen, feeding them on potatoes and porridge and sharing her favours among them at the week-end, a large huddery woman with mottled legs and a powerful arm.

On Sunday mornings, on the hills behind the town, the quarrels which had survived Saturday night's inflamed tempers were formally settled. The opponents, jackets and waistcoats neatly folded, collars on top, circled each other in the bright sabbath light, fists knuckled, striking and grunting, their blood vivid and the green grass trampling down until a man fell and would not rise. Just such a plebeian duel caused Robert to leave Mother Sommerville and seek less Hogarthian lodgings. Another resident had challenged him to fight and upon being heavily punished promised the arrival of his four brothers from Paisley and immediate satisfaction. With a prudence that was not hampered by any great reluctance to quit the Vinnel and his landlady's diet, he moved himself discreetly back to the Perch shore. Next day he found both abode and employment with Blair the wheelwright at the western end of the town, living above the yard and acting, for no additional wage, as a kind of night watch.

Thomas Blair had five daughters and no sons. His wife had died when their youngest child was fourteen leaving to him the final rearing and espousal of his family. His new carpenter was twenty-seven when he came to work with him and the eldest of the Blair girls, Agnes, was twenty-three. Upon her had fallen some of the duties of her late mother and she was at that age a precise and unsuitably severe young woman, given to a low-worn bun and dark dresses. They met some months after his employment when he came to repair a gate. She had brought him out bread and cheese for his lunch and saw the big shouldery man and the spokeshave moving in his hands, the ribbons of yellowy wood spurling out as he smoothed down the post. Coming to the yard on occasions with her father and Robert moving about at his tasks, dark, thewed and heavy boned, growing massively into his prime. Between them nothing passed, save the anonymous glances of workman and employer's daughter. But Robert Gibbon had no sense of his inferiority and Agnes Blair began to note with disdain the suitors of her sisters and find their shortcomings strangely final. One afternoon she was at the yard and found herself entering his small bare room, looking at the single suit, the razor on the towel, the long hollowed bed. Next day she brought curtains and the next a quilt.

Thomas Blair disapproved from the outset but being a man of honour he did not dismiss Robert, counting on the sight of her younger sisters one by one achieving socially acceptable husbands inducing Agnes to modify her affections. But there was in this slender, restrained woman a certain passion, almost a fierceness, that outstayed her father's attrition. Also, on the long hollowed bed she had let herself be taken in token of her earnest and despite rigorous attempts to prevent its repetition on numerous subsequent occasions all control left her and she gave, and gladly, her body's solace.

The first request for her hand was refused but when Agnes threatened to leave home their stilted and encumbered courtship was allowed at last to pass into the elaborate ritual of walking out. Robert survived its rigours well and in 1860, Mr Blair, recognizing the inevitable, made Robert his foreman and received his proposal with grace. They were married the following year and set up house in Kelly Street not far from her father. Their first years were marred by the several miscarriages Agnes suffered, which caused them to doubt the possibility of a family. In 1865 however she became pregnant once more and this time a normal confinement ended in the birth of a son, whom they called Robert. Her father died that year and Agnes inherited the business which Robert continued, taking into partnership another wheelwright in the town, a man named William Dunstable. The business waxed and the family grew. In '68 another son, Thomas, and in 1870 a daughter Ellen. Robert proved himself a good businessman and he and his partner prospered. Domestic life suited him and he turned his great energy into avenues compatible with his social status, becoming a church elder and at one time thinking of the town council. A third son, Harold, was born in 1872 and two years later a daughter, Patricia. The following year, Thomas, their second eldest died, after a painful illness, of inflammation of the bowels. His death greyed his mother's hair and, in the way that illness affects the strong, angered his father. He was buried in the ground Robert had bought for his name and the first Gibbon was inscribed on the austere, empty stone.

Thomas Howell Gibbon
beloved son of Robert and Agnes Gibbon
Born 1868
Died 3rd of February 1875 aged 7 years

The family went to Campbeltown for a holiday, only Robert remaining in Greenock. It was about this time he first noticed his partner's younger sister, Sarah Dunstable, a coppery-haired girl with a sense of her body she communicated fluently. She was eighteen and Robert was forty-six. His old rutting urge flared and the girl twice let herself be taken on Agnes Gibbon's bed before Robert managed to harness himself. To his great relief Sarah made no issue of his reinforced morality and the deceived wife returned unwitting to her home. Her health was not strong however and all that winter she was ill. In the following summer she went away again, this time to Bute to stay with one of her sisters who had married a country minister. Once again Sarah Dunstable took her place at Robert's unmanageable behest. He did once go to visit his wife and must have found the pale, lined woman he had married a striking contrast to the easy haunched young creature he had so recently lain with.

31

In 1877 Agnes commenced a further pregnancy which almost from the start seemed ill advised. The child was premature and stillborn and caused her a haemorrhage. At the age of forty-six her life slipped away from her with her husband powerless to sustain it by his own untapped health or the love he felt rise in him at her plight. She died without knowing of his infidelity but for Robert this was no amelioration to the agony of guilt he felt and the conviction that it was his punishment for committed sins.

Agnes Gibbon
dear wife of Robert Howell Gibbon
Born 1832
Died 19th of January 1878 aged 46 years
'Called to God'

He still had the business and his children, and within the year he had his mistress again. Sarah Dunstable had baited an old trap with a young body and it required only a feigned pregnancy to achieve respectability as Robert's second wife. In the nine years left to him he managed to sire two sons by Sarah and also to grow old. His conscience troubled him and he rediscovered religion, a factor which greatly influenced his eldest son Robert into choosing the church as his vocation. He went to study at St Andrews when he was eighteen. Like his father in appearance he was for all that a more nervous, intense person, given to moods and sudden outbursts of energy. He, unlike his brother Harold, showed no interest in the business and at school displayed an erratic, wilful brilliance. Harold learned his father's trade, a stocky fair young man, quiet and self-effacing, closer to his young sister Patricia than to anyone else after the death of his mother. He was sixteen when his father died.

Robert died of gangrene of the foot and the last weeks of his life filled the house with the terrible odour of putrefaction. Amputation failed to arrest the infection and in considerable pain, convinced he was being meted out retribution, he died alone, with the door locked, on a splendid early autumn evening in 1888.

Robert Howell Gibbon
Born 1828
Died 10th September 1888 aged 60 years

He had made provision for his children but at the prompting of his wife had left the business as such to her and it soon became evident that this in effect was a bequest to William Dunstable. Robert, having almost finished his studies, suddenly developed a distinct mystical strain and removed himself to live in Greenock on his inheritance and preach in the streets. Ellen married a schoolteacher and emigrated to Canada. Patricia grew increasingly delicate and in 1890 entered a sanatorium. Her whole income, and part of Harold's, went on keeping her there for two years, at the end of which time, the necessary organs for survival damaged beyond repair, she died, the faithful Harold by her bedside while her brother Robert prayed in his little tin tabernacle built in the town's east end. She had been a wan-hope of a girl, almost transparent in her delicacy. Her passage to earth was a long dying fall, suffused with an inevitability which, when recalled by her brothers, moved them to grief.

Patricia Agnes Gibbon
daughter of the late Robert and Agnes Gibbon
Born 1874
Died 5th of November 1892 aged 18 years

Harold completed his apprenticeship and approached William Dunstable as to his future. The man offered him a journeyman's post which as he expected was refused. So he left the yard, strewn with shavings, the wood stacked on skeeds and the new spokes showing bright in the repaired wheels, the trams of the carts raised like masts and the sweet damp aroma of wood everywhere. It was here that life as he had come to know it originated, that his mother had first loved his father and that he had patiently worked to win his employer's respect, and that he, Harold, had been taught his trade. He shouldered his tools and walked to Gourock where a boat-builder's employed him.

Sarah Gibbon reverted to her maiden name and changed

her sons' names by deed poll also to Dunstable. The house the Gibbons had lived in, Thomas Blair's old house, was squabbled over by his remaining daughters and Robert Gibbon lived in his mission hut, reading through the night and being pointed to in the street as a town worthy, no inconsiderable achievement at the age of twenty-eight. Harold took lodgings with a seamstress in Gourock, Mrs Kemble. Her husband was a sailor who had been at sea for fourteen years. In that time he sent money twice, once from Bristol and once from Liverpool. His wife had two sons and a daughter to rear and had, by considerable dint, managed remarkably well. Her house was a starched and burnished place, exhibiting the compulsive cleanth of the obsessed. She was a devout christian woman who refused herself the consolation of a male lodger until it became unimportant. She intended almost from the outset however that her eldest daughter Mary should make a match with someone who was of good stock and who had been, by all accounts, cheated of his rightful inheritance. They were left alone in the parlour at every opportunity and Mary's virtues were extolled in her presence until the girl blushed and protested. Despite this their attraction was mutual and in 1896 when Harold was twenty-four and Mary just turned twenty they were married and returned to Greenock to live, finding a house in George's Square through a house agent who remembered and respected his mother and father. He continued to work in Gourock, walking the three miles every morning. Their first child was born in 1897 and named Martha.

Robert's affairs had taken a turn for the worse. His mission was near 'Wee Dublin', the east end area where a large Irish colony, brought over to help the construction of the James Watt Dock, had been deplorably housed. Their single-room shacks had degenerated into a sty of the most appalling kind and in face of their horror drink and brawling were the accepted solace. The appearance among these people, almost all of whom were Catholic, of a Protestant preacher, unaccompanied, unordained and ununiformed was a source of rancorous hostility. The Salvation Army they treated as a comical charade put on for their benefit but the tall, dark man with the deep eyes and impassioned delivery was something different. He seemed to jeer at them, to castigate their squalor, taunt them for their stupidity. He told them they had managed to make life into a cess and to give a fair imitation of enjoyment in it. He was heckled and jeered at and sooner or later during his stand one or more of the men would attempt to manhandle him. Robert showed no aversion to fist fights and usually resumed his harangue, bloody but undeterred. Although this ability to take care of himself engendered a certain admiration in the end his curious evangelism roused the unfortunate people to genuine anger and his mission was burned down one dark night. Robert himself narrowly avoiding incineration.

He stayed with his brother Harold for a short time until he made up his mind to go to Wigtownshire where his grandparents had lived, and preach the gospel to the countryside. To his brother he confided the error of preaching in the east end slums. The people to whom he had tried to speak were degraded by poverty to such an extent that they were incapable of being reached by his vision of God's purpose. Robert was not a religious zealot in the simple sense of believing all but himself to be wrong but he gave his brother to understand that some minds were, not unworthy, but incapable of being illuminated. In the summer of 1898 he left Greenock on his first tour. Harold gave him some money and walked with him on his way to work. They looked unlike brothers, one dark and taller than the composed, taciturn person Harold had come to be.

He remained in the southern counties for almost two years, walking from village to village, hiring out for a day's work in the fields and then in the evening preaching to the men and women he had worked with, in a bothy or under some tree, occasionally overheard by the farmer or the local constable, concerned for sedition or heresy. But Robert Gibbon's preaching seemed curiously unconcerned with either social injustice or the grim presbyterianism of the Kirk. It was from the outset apocalyptic, but its vision was not couched in traditional mystic terms, not the glittering hallucination of St John, rather the rural dream of a Long-

35

land. He spoke of the earth as a great mothering fecundity and of the humans who tended it as a blessed elect, yet made no attempt to glamorize the monotony and harshness of toil. In his sermons he adopted an incantory rhetoric, using the dialect words almost dropped from the language and producing in his congregation nothing of the religious epilepsy of the Wesleyan evangelist but something of the catharsis of drama. After his meetings a dance was usually held and he joined in, spinning the girls until their hair flew in his face and their free breasts throbbed in their dresses and later in the hedgerows he held some willing one close as the sky swole enormous black and trembled with stars. In the morning he walked on, carrying his day's wages and food given him by the wives of the labourers. Within six months he was known throughout Wigtownshire, Kirkcudbrightshire and Dumfriesshire and within the year his first illegitimate children were born. In an area never renowned for rigid sexual morality these offspring were viewed with equanimity and in some cases with a certain indulgence as being the seed of a remarkable and gifted man.

Harold and his wife had had an addition to the family, James, born in 1899 and more than a year old when his uncle returned, browned, lean and with a prophetic mien that made his little niece hide behind her mother's legs and watch the strange man gesture his large sweeping arms and his voice rise and sweep through their house like a wind, bearing on it scents and sounds of farnesses and people she had never known. Their life was an uneventful, contented one, Harold had gained recognition in his work and was now learning the job of mast-making. Their house in George's Square looked along Nelson Street and gave a view of the town with its roofs going up on to the hills and the spires of the churches pointing fingers to heaven. On Sundays the morning was filled with bells and the family, now with the addition of Uncle Robert, would walk soberly to the West Kirk and soberly back to the cold meat and cabbage and potatoes and broad beans of sabbath dinner. Once Robert was asked to deliver a sermon in one of the several small missions in the town where even more acutely than in the Kirk there could be discerned the protestant paradox of total predestination and the importance of outward forms. His sermon caused both incomprehension and consternation, its remarkable language not quite concealing a strong undertone of what can only be called a fertility mythos. He was not asked to speak again and never did in Greenock. This could hardly be said to trouble him, removed as he seemingly was from the world of men and transported to some sealed religious comprehension. During his stay with them, lasting over a year, he busied himself writing his sermons out and studying Jamieson's Scottish Dictionary and other works on the language. In 1903 he left Greenock again, this time not to return for four years.

That year a daughter was born and called Ellen and the Gibbons' family life thickened in texture. Martha, already a beautiful little girl, delighted her father particularly and they took long walks on the hills behind the town, naming flowers and birds and coming home with the child drooped in sleep on his shoulders. On these occasions Harold's usual taciturnity left him and he talked to his daughter with a gaiety and flow quite unlike his normal manner. His wife, although she did not accompany them, noticed the tendency at other times and could not help resenting, almost without being aware of it, that they shared an intimacy she could not enter. Harold was a fine swimmer and he taught his daughter to swim and they spent a lot of time in the summer in the water off the boat-builder's, while Mary Gibbon sat with the two infants and watched them, swimming together out to a raft and sitting talking before returning, Martha always winning the race to the shore. Perhaps only her ignorance prevented her from being jealous for it did not lie within the bounds of her conception that a man might love his daughter as he would never love his wife, with a rapturous incredulity at the creature he had fathered and a delight at the purity of her mind and the innocence of her caresses. He was in all ways a good husband, devoted to her and the welfare of his home, but with Martha he was something else, almost a lover and almost a brother.

Peter was born in 1907 and a week after the event Robert

returned home. He had changed during his sojourn and was now, in his forty-first year, in his mental and physical prime. Four years of life spent in the open air, save five months in all as sentence for vagrancy, working at harvesting, living on good food, neither drinking nor smoking, walking sometimes twenty-five miles a day in all weathers, this had hardened and browned him and the unending succession of meetings at which he preached to a rapt and fervent audience had given him a stature and a self-possession which were immediately apparent. He now had a following all through the three counties which would have been greater had he but professed some special form of worship, some -ism his admirers could practise in his absence. All there was however was the man himself, standing in his shirt-sleeves in the fields or on some small knowe and speaking to them, words they recognized for the first time, making a song out of his mouth they could not repeat but did not forget. Some of his children were brought to him and he knelt and held their small faces in his large worked hands and smiled and kissed them and their mothers in pride and gratitude gave him again their ardencies in the black burning bushes of the night. The authorities frowned but could scarcely arrest him for being a casual worker with a gift for oratory and if in their manses the ministers disapproved his sermonizing they found its heresy difficult to separate from the christian imagery and the dialect vocabulary. Three times he was arrested for being without visible means of support and given sentences of one month, twice, and three months. This longer sentence was achieved by a plea from a minister that the man was a whoremaster and an immoral influence. On each of the occasions he was released there were people waiting to give him food and sometimes even money and to ask him when he might return.

He stayed in Greenock almost two years this time and at his brother's expense published a small volume containing fourteen sermons and then, from money earned cramming young men trying to enter Glasgow University, he had the sermons published as tracts and upon the completion of this set off again, carrying the pamphlets in a knapsack. It was 1910 and the town was flourishing and expanded steadily. Harold was a foreman and he bought a piano for the sitting-room and Martha took lessons and James played truant and went bird-nesting and swimming in the reservoir. It was a joke in the family that the water in the tap should always be left to run if James had been late home that day. From Canada came news of the death of their Aunt Ellen whom they had never seen. Even her brother thought on her as a shadow figment of the past. In 1912 Peter had whooping cough and nearly died. Martha started wearing her hair up and her mother found Harold sitting looking at a daguerreotype of her as a child and quietly crying. Ellen won a prize for embroidery and James split his head diving too deep into shallow water. Dunstables the wheelwright's went bankrupt and Harold went with quiet malice to hear it proclaimed. Rumours of war spread, were quelled and revived. News reached them that Robert had been put in prison in Stranraer but a letter from him assured them of his release, the charges having been dropped. Martha walked out with Donald Garvie, a medical student, three years older than she. The promised war gathered momentum and broke, patriotism was fanned and the local territorials mobilized. Harold disapproved and James quarrelled with his father bitterly, saying he wished he could go, and if it lasted two years he would.

Robert came back to Greenock somewhat impaired in health. To his brother he confided that his imprisonment had been real and his letter of assurance a device to keep their minds at ease. He had got with child a landowner's daughter and had been jailed for poaching for a year. The girl had been sent away to England and there died in childbirth. This had made him vow chastity and it was to implement this decision he had returned to Greenock before venturing back among what he now termed 'his people'. His tracts were spread throughout the south and people read them aloud in the evening to their families. Robert had decided to devote himself to a translation of the Bible, or more accurately a paraphrase into the special heightened language he had made his own.

Donald Garvie joined the Medical Corps and went to

France. Martha knitted socks and comforters while James fretted at his uselessness. Harold had become almost moody, sitting silent by the window or taking solitary walks in the evening. When Donald came home on leave after a year's active service he was a haggard man of twenty-three. He refused to talk to James about the war and woke several times in the night screaming. He and Martha made love one afternoon when the family were out. Afterwards Donald wept uncontrollably on her breast and she stroked his hair and held his terror tight until the sodden shambles of the war dimmed and they turned to protestations of love. Shortly after he returned to the front James ran away to Newcastle and joined the Durham Fusiliers. They received a letter saying he was embarking for France. There was a photograph of him in uniform looking very young. Five days after he landed he was killed in a bombardment. It was three months before they had the news and in that time Donald Garvie was killed too.

James Gibbon
son of Harold and Mary Gibbon
Born 1899
Died 1917 aged 18 years
Buried in France

Martha was griefstricken at the loss of her lover and the whole family lay under the gloom of the deaths they had suffered. Only Robert seemed untouched. He seemed scarcely aware of anything save his work and the small room he used, with the cami-ceiling and the skylight, was always littered with papers and books and his bed unmade. His sister-in-law had grown to resent him for his prolonged stay and his eccentric manner. He lived on pease brose made in cabbage water and ate the cabbage between dry bread. Harold seemed prepared to have him stay for ever but she wanted him to move, return to the south. At the end of the war the first signs of the depression appeared but for a time Harold was unaffected. His brother decided one morning in the summer of 1920 to be off and left the house after more than five years of occupancy. Peter who was his favourite wanted to go with him but was of course forbidden. Robert was fifty-four and only now beginning to grey. He left his unfinished work with his brother and started back down the road he now knew so well.

In Greenock Harold's yard was one of the first to close and then in quick succession the large firms paid off men and the grass began to green among the berths, the cranes pointed permanently inland and birds nested undisturbed in the roofs of the sheds. Harold found work with a boat repairer in Clynder, going across the river every morning on the Gourock ferry, but that failed after a few months and he was drawing the dole along with the others. Martha was now a tall, beautiful woman, made suddenly mature by her deprivation. She became receptionist to a Doctor Banks, a middle-aged G.P. with a good panel he had bought from one of the town's oldest established doctors. Within a year he had asked her to marry him and she, after considerable doubt, agreed. He was forty-six and she twenty-five. His entry into the family made things easier than would otherwise have been possible in the next four years. Mrs Gibbon approved thoroughly but her husband had reservations, partially out of a distrust of Doctor Banks who tended to drink heavily when off duty, and partially from his fondness for Martha which probably would never have totally approved of any male she might have chosen.

Peter, at the age of seventeen, had never had a job and constantly urged his mother to let him go looking for his uncle Robert. He had taken to reading the Bible and the paraphrase Robert had been working on and at night in his uncle's room he would read the sermons aloud. To his father, who was rapidly moving left in his thought and sympathy, these preoccupations were ill-timed and if he never attempted to prohibit them he showed no encouragement. Just before his eighteenth birthday Peter ran away from home. His parents notified the police who in turn sent his description to the southern counties. The boy was picked up at Girvan and returned home, hungry and enraged. Doctor Banks sold his practice and moved to Glasgow, Martha going with him. Her life in some curious way seemed concluded, she did not love her husband and so far had failed to become pregnant by him. She affected black

41

clothes and wore a veil. Her hair showed silverings and her eyes were distant and sad. Her father and she embraced at the station and held back their separate tears until the train had gone. Then both astonished their husband and wife by the intensity of their weeping. Seven weeks later, without ever returning to Greenock, Martha Gibbon was killed in a car accident. Her husband, who was driving, broke his wrist. At the inquest his sobriety was questioned but without any definite opinion being formed.

Martha Banks
dearly beloved daughter of Harold and Mary Gibbon
Born 1897
Died 18th May 1924 aged 27 years
'Oh thou child of many prayers'

The quotation on the tombstone was from Longfellow and the minister deplored this secular tendency. Harold Gibbon, shrunk into silence, paid nothing heed as he mourned his bereavement. Robert returned that same year and stayed in Greenock over the winter and into the spring. When he went this time Peter went with him, carrying the older man's knapsack and listening to him talk of the people and their hardship and the beauty he had brought into their lives by his preaching. His last trip had been one of his hardest and one of his most rewarding. The war and its aftermath had hit the country badly and a great number of the young men had left or had been killed. Times had been harder than he could ever recall, but people still remembered him and came to hear him speak and if the law was harsher now in dealing with vagrants then it only brought him closer to true humility to pray with the beggars and the thieves, to share his food with the poorest members of society. He felt that for the first time in all his life he had come close to God's will on earth. It was unfortunate that the boy should have had no chance to judge of this for himself for while crossing some wooded land to come out at the sea a gamekeeper, without calling upon them to halt, fired and hit Robert in the leg. He died on the way to hospital from the loss of blood. The gamekeeper was exonerated as having simply performed his duty, Peter's statement that he had heard no call to stand being denied. His body was buried at New Luce, the expense of transporting it to Greenock being too much for the dead man's brother.

Robert Gibbon, preacher
brother of Harold Gibbon
Born 1866
Died 1925 aged 59 years
Buried at New Luce

Peter stayed some months in New Luce having been befriended by a local publican who had admired his uncle. He helped in the pub and listened to the stories of Robert's many visits and his wanderings over the three counties and he had pointed out to him several young men and girls who were thought to be some of Robert's many illegitimate children. This aspect of his uncle's life came as a shock to the boy and it was his inability to accept it that caused him finally to return to Greenock, for the people who remembered Robert Gibbon remembered all of him and would not separate the lover of women from the lover of God. He went up once to the grave, looking out across Luce bay and tried to find something to say to the strange powerful spirit who had achieved his obscure destiny in this corner of the world. But he knew nothing and he could guess little and so he left, puzzled and sad at his incomprehension and his uncle's failings.

In Greenock, as elsewhere, the depression deepened. Harold was now a militant socialist and the house was filled with books on Communist theory and argument. Once an agitator wanted by the police stayed with them until such time as it was safe for him to go to Ireland. In the pitiless boredom of unemployment Peter endured a year and then, much to his and everyone else's surprise, got himself attached to a boxing booth that had suddenly found itself deserted and decimated while passing through the town. Not a violent child and without any particular aptitude for the ring he found himself caught up and fascinated by the ritual of two men loosed upon one another to achieve a dominance. He quickly developed a defensive style, a bobbing, crouching weave from behind which he would unleash combinations of hooks and jabs to the body and then retire into defence. He learned that head punching hurt the hands and that the men who fought couldn't take blows to their undernourished stomachs, that pain has its exhilarations and that winning was a mental condition. For three years he travelled the length of the country, going as far down as Bristol and as far up as Aberdeen.

His father went on the hunger marches and fell ill on the road. He came back to Greenock far from well to find his wife being nursed through pneumonia by devoted Ellen, now twenty-seven and showing every likelihood of remaining unmarried. He was now a noted man in the town and the possibility of work was almost extinct. Peter sent money and they took in a lodger, a slow quiet young man from Campbeltown who had a job on the Greenock police force and whose parents had known Agnes Gibbon, Harold's mother, during her stays there. Peter finally came home, having quit the booths as the fighting got harder and harder. He managed to get a job on the sandboats that dredged the river and shortly after his return met Emma Nesbit, a Salvation Army girl from Port Glasgow. In 1932 Mary Gibbon died of peritonitis, the doctor, when requested to come at once, saying if he couldn't manage, an 'askit' powder might relieve what was almost certainly flatulence. Peter would certainly have gone to jail for assault had not the lodger, P.C. John McCracken, sworn under oath that he had not left the house that night.

Mary Gibbon
wife of Harold Gibbon
Born 1870
Died 1932 aged 62 years
'At rest'

The following year Peter married Emma Nesbit and although the house was a little crowded with the various units in occupation they stayed on at his father's insistence. Emma Nesbit was, as the Gibbon women, married and born, had all tended to be, a gentle creature, soft-voiced and mild-eyed and with a tendency to faint but persistent ill-health which she bore as though it were the most natural thing in the world. In Peter she had married the most volatile of the whole line, unlike his father and without the outlet for his nervous energy that in their differing ways his uncle and his grandfather had achieved. In him was a great latent violence and a frustrated religious mania. He thought of sex as being lustful and of its over-indulgence as a sin, but he loved his wife deeply without ever quite making her feel it. In 1935 Ellen married John McCracken and went to live in Cornhaddock in a police allocation house. The following year a son was born to Peter and Emma and was named for his grandfather, Harold. Work had returned to the town and both Peter and his father were employed in the yards, Harold as a carpenter and Peter as a plater's helper. Harry was a placid fair child much like his grandfather in colouring and appearance, and his birth and infancy to some extent made the old man's life richer and happier. He had never been close to his youngest son and with the loss of his beloved Martha had entered upon a decade of much trial and anguish. In the last five years of his life he grew old beyond his years and found in his grandchild unending pleasure and that strange rapport that the old and the very young can sometimes attain.

The war came and the men went. Greenock was blitzed and ships were built. There was the blackout and the razor gangs and the scarcity of sugar. John McCracken became a sergeant and his wife had a second miscarriage. The rationing became something permanent in the mind. Conscientious objectors went to Barlinnie and were called 'flymen'. In 1941 Harold Gibbon passed away in his sleep. In the morning, his daughter-in-law trying to wake him for his breakfast shook his hand and found it cold. The broad calm face was composed and untroubled. His mouth showed the hint of a smile.

Harold Lewis Gibbon
husband of the late Mary Gibbon
Born 1872
Died 20th of April 1941 aged 69 years
'Together now'

As he was, close to Martha at last. Peter attended a small mission in the east end, sometimes taking deputations to other missions in the town and sometimes as far afield as Paisley. Once the family went on holiday to New Luce and he showed Harry his great uncle's grave marked by a small white stone with only the name R. Gibbon, Greenock, on it. The boy had a good soprano voice and although too shy to sing in public at his father's meetings often did at home in the evenings, above his mother's contralto and his father's baritone. He went to school and showed no particular gifts save in sports where his normal slowness seemed to leave him for a fine natural co-ordination.

The war ended and peace, hardly less grey, ensued. The mass X-ray units, in the attempt to exterminate tuberculosis in the bad west coast strip, came to Greenock and discovered, in their impersonal chilling way, a spot on Emma Gibbon's lung. Knowledge of it seemed to activate its life and in 1946 she went to Bridge of Weir for treatment. After almost a year, with no noticeable improvement she was transferred to Millport where the lung was collapsed in order to rest it. Nothing seemed able to stay the slow inexorable decay of her health however and late in June, 1948 she passed into a coma from which she never emerged. Brought back by steamer she was interred in a new plot close by the Gibbon family layer, now sealed and closed.

Emma Gibbon
blessed wife of Peter Gibbon
Born 1907
Died 3rd of July 1948 aged 41 years
Mourned by the living

Her death left father and son bonded by grief. In the man a whole inheritance of the acceptance of God's will was tortured to near breaking and then released in a great surge of morbid mysticism. 'All the dead are dead and all the living are dying', he culled from his uncle's texts, a preoccupation with the vanity of earthly life that steadily estranged him from the mission halls it had been his custom to attend. The precarious euphoria of their evangelism vapoured in face of his insistence on the inevitability of death, insufficiently leavened by the assurance of salvation.

For the boy his mother's passing was the first great subtraction, as distinct from the blurred erasion of his grandfather's decease; a hole in the world through which nothingness poured. The last memories of her haunted his dreams, the wasted woman burning away, a life tapering down to its zero, her dry lips against his cheek, the sweet smell of dying, the writhing blue veins on her hands. And returning to Greenock on the steamer, the land shrinking away and the light fading over the water, a great cold darkening.

Peter Gibbon's relations with his son grew the more obsessive as other avenues to the world closed. He became, quite unjustifiably, concerned as to the purity of the public drinking supply and with the avowed intent of finding uncontaminated sources he took himself on long walks over the moors behind the town, on which excursions he was invariably accompanied by his son and the small book of sermons written by his Uncle Robert. These he read aloud as they walked, to the boy a strange unguessable flow of sounds, more memorable for the effect they had upon the speaker than for themselves alone. He would grow excited and make wide-armed gestures, and his voice would rise and fall and his eyes quit the earth and the watching, trembling lad to assail the heavens with the words of the dead preacher.

Afterwards they found some burn, chillingly fresh, the water bringing an ache to the teeth as they lay drinking, his father extolling the purity of the water, its elixir power and medicinal worth. The ritual was finalized some ten to fifteen minutes later when the copious draughts affected the bladder and they would stand, man and boy, solemnly pissing upon the ground, Harry eyeing in awe and wonder the majesty of his father's member, holding the timid little droop of himself with effacing diffidence.

To what outcome this somewhat unnatural proximity might have led had time been allotted it was permanently obscured by the death of Peter Gibbon in 1953. Harry had been apprenticed as a carpenter and his father, who had no trade, was temporarily unemployed. He recommenced whilst suffering from a heavy cold and four consecutive soakings laying deck brought him to his bed five days later, close to pneumonia. An apparent recovery was followed by relapse, and the man, still in the vigour of his forty-sixth year, seemed to acquiesce in the declension that ensued, dying three days after the twenty-eighth anniversary of his Uncle Robert's death and a hundred years after his grandfather's arrival in Greenock.

Peter Kemble Gibbon
husband of Emma Gibbon
Born 1907
Died 1953 aged 46 years
'The Lord giveth and the Lord taketh away'

The effect on young Harry Gibbon of this second bereavement was profound. He expressed no open grief but his manner became withdrawn and about his physical presence there gathered a slow, ponderous gravity. He became prone to long silences and developed an inordinate capacity for sleep. But these symptoms of emotional convalescence gradually disappeared and with the commencement of his friendship with John Moseby virtually ended.

Moseby was the adopted son of a local merchant, a slight, dark, young man, with a volatile, nervous manner pitched constantly higher than the broad and amiable Harry. The only fault his Aunt Ellen had to find with this contrasted duo was the total loyalty it summoned forth in her nephew, who, to her way of thinking, would have been better served by someone of his own class, and, of the other sex, for early though it was she remained mindful that in Harry Gibbon was deposited the last, name-bearing seed of their family.

Several graves up a man trimmed the grass with shears. They squeaked faintly. It was warm and overcast and in the rhododendrons a blackbird piped. Gibbon sat looking at the inscription for his father. A bus reddened the corner of his eye going up to the Bow Road scheme. After a time he got up and came down through the cemetery to the gate.

His Aunt Ellen was alone when he got back. She had been reading the Sunday papers and had taken a nap. He woke her coming in. She was a plain, pleasant woman, much improved by age and marriage and saddened only by the fact that she had no children of her own. Gibbon was her only living relative, excluding cousins in Canada of whom nothing was known and whom she never expected to meet.

Gibbon made a pot of tea and she got the biscuit barrel out. The sitting-room looked directly up Nelson Street. From it could be seen five churches and the spires of six more. His aunt said it was the holiest view in Greenock. It was the house she had been born and raised in and she had returned to it after her brother's death in 1953, glad to be home again. Upon it she lavished a care that was akin to love and now as she sat stirring her tea it composed around her, a plain and pleasant woman in a big quiet room, made comfortable by the lives that had used it, worn smooth by the passage of events, feelings and expectations and fears. People now dead had been alive here, and alive with life, no thought of dying in their minds. The room which had contained them now contained further lives and had become in this process a kind of presence, a silent listener, the hush into which secret thoughts can be uttered. Aunt Ellen had indeed acquired the habit of talking to herself when the house was empty, a habit which when she caught herself at it would make her frown and warn herself of impending senility, all without lowering her voice.

'Were there many people at the cemetery?'

'A few. Not many up at the top.'

'Was the grave all right?'

'Grass is getting a bit long on grandfather's.'

'I'll borrow Mrs Foster's shears.'

'Aunt Ellen, why was your Uncle Robert never buried in Greenock?'

'He didn't die in Greenock.'

'Couldn't he have been brought to Greenock and buried?'

'Those were hard times, it would have cost too much.

Your grandfather always wanted to do it but when times were easier they said it would be impossible.'

'Why?'

'I suppose the coffin would have rotted away and there would just be bones. Anyway he spent more time down there than he ever did in Greenock. He was always off and we wouldn't see him for years, then one day there'd be a knock on the door and he'd be in sitting there and Peter, your father'd be taking off his boots and Martha God rest her bringing water to wash his feet and your grandfather smiling all over his face. Mother was the only one that wasn't delighted. Then he'd stay for a while and next he'd be getting ready for off again and if you asked him why he was going he'd just say "if you don't go you can't come back".'

'If you don't go you can't come back ...'

'That's silly, Mother used to say when he was gone. If he didn't go he wouldn't have to come back.'

The china in the cabinet, the heavily brocaded settee and the old embossed wallpaper. Pictures on the walls, of Harold and Mary Gibbon and their children and a coloured photograph of James Gibbon in an Army uniform. A daguerreotype of Agnes Gibbon before she was married, her eyes like dark flowers on a pale pond. Aunt Ellen's certificate for embroidery in a frame. The table made by Harold Gibbon during the 'bad times' an oval lake of gloss in the middle of the floor. Gibbon sat quietly and his Aunt talked about those days.

CHAPTER THREE

They were the only two off the train. As they went over the bridge it began to pull out and smoke reached them, going down the steps to the field behind the station. It had been a bright day, not too warm, and the sky was still high and gradually blanching of colour as the flat Cheshire landscape began to darken and settle, the sediment of dusk drifting into the ground, leaving the air thin and pale and clear; in the trees a weight of darkness gathered and the hedgerows were long processions of smoky pitch. They walked close together and she had her hand in the pocket of his duffle, their fingers laced.

'Do you want a cigarette Ruth?'

'I'll have a draw on yours.' He freed his hand to strike a match. Hers, damp from proximity, cooled, waiting for his return. His face flared yellow black and the acridity of the match wrinkled between them.

'It gets dark all of a rush,' she said; 'makes me think of Holland and the sea pouring over the land.' He handed her the cigarette. She drew its stud bright and felt a little dizzy with the inhalation; fused with the cool night air it dazed her. Her face was close to his shoulder and she smelt paint and tobacco and the musty smell his clothes had and a smell under and through these that was him. He took a mouthful of her hair and let it flow through his lips, then bit on the ends and tugged. Her head went over to his. The kiss was cool and dark and under the taste of smoke their mouth flesh clung wetly, crushed poppies.

'Nice,' he said.

'Nice.' And she put her arm around his neck then took it away.

'Forget you were back in dear old Knutsford, where the natives notice all?'

'Must have.' They walked on and she felt depressed, and knew from experience that nothing could be done with the feeling except to let it wither. While awaiting this she dis-

51

missed all the things that came into her head as conversational. Again from experience she knew that anything she might say would be connected in some manner to the feeling of depression and what had prompted it. She just walked and held his hand in his pocket and took another draw on the cigarette. After a moment she said, 'I hope there is something reasonable to eat, I'm pretty hungry.'

That seemed safe enough and she checked saying 'I always get hungry when I'm with you', or some such intimacy. Funny how you could never leave anything alone when you were with someone you loved. Everything had to be dragged into the vortex.

'I think I'd be best going away Ruth.' It hurt as though she had never been able to conceive of such a thing, as though it fell without warning into a happy order.

'Where?' was the easiest thing to say.

'I don't know. I could go down to London and live with Stolleman.' The cigarette looped brightly and sparked.

'There's a star.'

'Where?' he said.

'There—' Low and large, trembling.

'This way we're just teasing each other.'

'Not teasing. Not just teasing.'

'All right, not teasing. Pick your pick.' He could sound curt and hard. It meant he had decided something and wanted her to agree so that it could sound mutual. But it never was. She had been playing this game long enough to know. Still, it was only her he played it with. That meant something.

'What else can we do?' So much for keeping off the subject.

'Old ground Ruth. Why go again?' That clipped, near jargon that meant he was waiting until she came round to his way. She looked up and for a moment the long face was to her, narrow and deep-eyed, the heavy sneering mouth and the tender plane of his cheek, in a slight gaunt to the knuckle of his jaw, then turned away.

'Because I love you, is that a good reason?'

'The best Ruthie.'

'Oh Peter—' Old useless pains, paining pains. Useless.

'Either I go away, or you go away.'

'What if we both went away?'

'You know what if we both went away. Do you think I want you watching me, wondering who I'm with. And with nothing you can do about it—'

'What makes it now, so sudden?'

'Now, tomorrow, next day. It'll always be sudden. It couldn't be anything else but sudden. Not after twenty-two years. No, I have to go. And the sooner the better.' That was him telling. He was right of course. Nothing else would work except that he go away and she would wait until Mr Right came along to rescue her. Without knowing why she thought of the painting by Ingres of the princess with the dragon on a leash and the knight stabbing and the princess looking at him rather peevishly and Cuffee had captioned it 'you bwute, look what you've done to Towser', and it made her smile and half laugh despite herself.

'What?' he said.

'Oh I was just thinking—' And she stopped, not wanting to sound bitter-sweet, bravely full of memories.

'Tell.'

'A foolishness.'

'Tell me.' They were going up through the lane past the old laundry building and it was almost dark and there was nobody coming so he held her hand she told him why she had laughed and why she didn't want to tell him and he was kissing her as she spoke, her hair, her eyes and, sometimes smudging a word, her mouth and she could feel his hands on her back stroking down to cup and splay on the hips, run up her flanks and catch and grip under the soft crutches of her armpits to lift her up on her toes and with the weight press her breasts together and she had her eyes shut and could see the patterns his caresses painted on her body and she felt that way he could have done anything and it wouldn't have mattered.

He put her away from him, his fingers biting in at the back of her neck, holding her at arm's length and she felt raggedy and limp and hopelessly uncertain. In her was the sweet melting that she knew so dearly. 'And my bowels were moved for him.' That was her favourite love song. He kept calling her 'sister' in it, 'a garden inclosed is my sister, my spouse'. That's what she was, his secret garden, into which he slipped in the night. Now that he was going away, maybe once more, a last time. It would be safe enough. A last time.

'When will you go?'

He relaxed his hold and said, 'This week.' She realized he had kissed her to win her over. It made her angry to be left feeling these throbs of desire when he had been engaged on the merely politic.

'You shouldn't have kissed me like that.'

'Why?'

'Because you just wanted to get round me, stop me from telling you I needed you. You don't like to be reminded I need you.'

'That's true. I'd rather you didn't . . .'

'Would you rather I didn't love you?' There it was, the language of quarrels, that self-sorry rancour she hated to hear in herself.

'Is that something you are in any position to control?' His voice was light and studied as it was when he wanted to prevent a useless argument. She responded to this and almost without thought kissed his right hand, still on her shoulder.

'Sorry. It was stupid of me.' He moved her forward and they continued walking.

'I'm sorry too, if we were in Egypt and it was B.C. we'd have gotten married and the whole nation would have run a lottery on when you had your orgasms.'

They were walking through the band of chestnut trees that ran below their house. Their names were cut in one of them, high up among the branches. She had never seen where because she couldn't climb up to it but Peter had cut them when they were still in school.

'But we're in Knutsford.'

'Many a true word spoken incest.' It was an old joke and she smiled at it but she was glad it was in the dark under the trees.

* * *

As was usual on Sunday evenings Robert Eldman was present for dinner. He was Mr Cuffee's second in the English department of the school in which they taught. He had been second to Mr Cuffee for the greater part of their parallel lives, once having wooed Mrs Cuffee when they were newly out of University, before she left him for his friend. They had never quarrelled over it and when, after an unsuccessful spell teaching in the south, Eldman had secured a post in Mr Cuffee's school, they had renewed and continued their friendship. Eldman had never married, saying that the only girl for him had been Dorothy and now that she was gone he would accept defeat gracefully. He continued in a mild and rather ludicrous manner to pay court to Mrs Cuffee, bringing flowers occasionally and holding her chair for her when she sat down to table. He was a short man, about her own height, with stranded brown hair that had always been sparse, and a small hesitant moustache somewhere between toothbrush and military. Mr Cuffee said he looked like Adolf Hitler which was untrue. He had a good light tenor voice and sang Gilbert and Sullivan in the local operatic society's annual production, played a thoughtful end game in chess and had a pipe smoker's breath. He was a permanent element in the life of Mr and Mrs Cuffee and their children, Peter and Ruth, had known him almost all of their lives.

Mr Cuffee was in his early fifties, a tall heavy man, with the remains of florid good looks that he was well aware of. He had a slight stoop and a habit in conversation of tugging the end of his long aquiline nose, little tugs that threatened to pull him off balance. He was talking, as he always talked, to everyone and no one, a manner of address perfected by teaching hordes of anonymous children. He scattered his words with the certainty and disinterest of a man feeding poultry. His subject was the serious dearth of genuine lyric poetry in the modern writers. Eldman agreed in short expletive grunts, trying to give the impression that it was he who was being spoken to, that in fact it was a conversation and not a monologue. Mrs Cuffee looked up brightly from time to time and nodded, smiling when a poet's name or a line was familiar. Cuffee ate his food with gluttonous absorption. Once or twice Eldman glanced over at Ruth and smiled seriously, implying that what was being said was very cogent, very much to the point. Ruth hardly heard what her father said, having long since come to realize that intelligence and education, if deprived of imagination, resulted in the sterile pedantry that she now automatically associated with Mr Cuffee. She had been at this table countless times and seen the same tableau enacted, the same no matter what the topic. Mrs Cuffee ever impressed, ever amused, ever attentive as the situation might demand. Sometimes Ruth thought she must possess some faculty, a selective amnesia that permitted her to hear a hundredth telling as a first. Her pantomime provoked in Ruth a crumpled compassion and a tepid disgust, shabby sentiments of which she was ashamed.

Mr Cuffee had finished and Robert Eldman asked Ruth what she thought. Ruth said it wasn't something she knew much about. Mr Cuffee said that for someone whose whole world was books it was surprising how little his second child cared about their contents. It was one of his affectations to talk about them as his first child and his second. It never failed to raise Cuffee's head. He winked at her, a blink in an otherwise empty look. Ruth smiled into her crème caramel. Robert Eldman mistook, as he had mistaken on innumerable occasions, Cuffee's expression for one of interest. Did he, Peter, think his father was right in what he said. Cuffee let a long pause lapse until it seemed as though he were considering a momentous issue. Then he turned to his mother and asked her opinion. Mrs Cuffee who looked rather surprised to be consulted gathered her wits and said that lyric poetry was one of Mr Cuffee's best subjects. Mr Cuffee confirmed this by saying, yes, it was one of his best subjects and that he could be considered as something of an expert on minor English lyric poets. He reminded Eldman of the article he had contributed to that magazine that was now extinct and Eldman recalled it clearly, saying 'damn good article' several times. Over coffee this article was quoted in fair detail, drawing forth nods and grunts from Mrs Cuffee and Eldman respectively. Ruth listened with a growing sense of incredulity to the charade. She looked from face to face and told herself that these were real people in a real world, whose actions touched other people and affected them. Had these two people not caused, between them, the existence of herself and her brother. What more fundamental instance of their reality could be asked for. Yet why did they talk like this, behave like this. Why did they enact this travesty of communication, each sealed in a little capsule of self, untouched and untouching, going through the motions of comprehending each other's existence.

Cuffee excused himself and went into the kitchen. Ruth said if everyone was finished she'd clear away. Her mother thanked her and turned again attentively to her husband's voice. In the kitchen Cuffee was sitting on the table searching under the cat's jaw for fleas. The animal lay patiently on its back flicking its tail back and forth.

'The secret in catching cat fleas, which are smaller and more sprightly than their human counterparts, is to chase them on to one of the long underjaw tendons and then nip them up under the nail, later dropping them into a vat of boiling iodine where they instantly perish.'

'Do you ever feel sorry for them?'

'No, I don't. I'm committed to a point of view which places them outside the bounds of my compassion.'

'That somewhat scanty fluid.'

'One has compassion for others only because the act of love is too difficult, it's a quasi emotion, it really says, "you disgusting bastards I wish I could care for you." All compassion stems from guilt. And guilt is for the birds.'

'Do you really believe all that?"

'Not from the sound of some of it, but I haven't thought much about it. One can also kill them by applying pressure to the flanks, causing a rupture at arse and cakehole, much to the parasite's detriment.'

She knew this mood, it was the one in which he prepared himself to disregard everyone else. Only since they had stopped being lovers had she come to see how much like his father he could be. It was something she had never taxed him with.

'When will you speak to him?'

'Tonight, after he beats Robert with a brilliant middle game combination.'

'What do you think he will say?'

'About leaving Art School not so much, he never went much on the idea anyway. You were a great disappointment to him Ruth when you passed up the academic future that was yours by right and became a librarian.' She stroked the cat now released form Cuffee's ministrations. 'About money he will tell me it's time I made my own way in the world, make up my mind about what I want to do and do it. He might fork out ten.'

'I can let you have twenty.'

'Not so second child. He owes me the money for not beating him to a mash years ago. He's very lucky I'm a forgiving son.'

'Will you be coming up with me in the morning then?'

'No, I want to sort some things out for taking away.'

'I thought all your things were up in Manchester.'

'I want to have a rout about here though.' She knew he was hiding something but couldn't imagine what. Why should he want to stay in Knutsford with his mother. He could never think of what to say to her. Maybe he intended leaving without coming back to Manchester.

'When will you be up then?'

'Tomorrow night. I'll meet you out of the library. Tomorrow's a late night isn't it?'

'Yes, seven.'

'I'll meet you coming out.'

'No, go over to the room, save either of us waiting about.' He must be going to get round his mother for money. Where would she get money though. Cuffee put his hand on her shoulder. His smile was quite serious.

'Trust me, Ruthie.' He knew that she knew that he knew. What else could you expect after twenty-two years. She smiled and kissed his hand.

'Love you Peter—'

*   *   *

Mr Cuffee triumphed in a chess game that closely resembled many the two had played. He was a good club player and had once represented Cheshire Teachers at short notice, obtaining a favourable draw after nearly winning in the middle game. In this encounter with Eldman the pattern of play had been predictable as Eldman, black, developed from a cramped opening and had been subject to the usual series of dashing attacks that was Mr Cuffee's forte, this time not very originally directed at the castled king. In the end however he smoked the piece out and rather neatly discovered check by a knight move that then gave mate. Eldman accepted his defeat as inevitable, choosing to ignore the fact that had he remained calm the game would have gone by its own momentum into end play where his more methodical analysis would have undone the other's bravura attack. This was something Mr Cuffee was well aware of and he tended to disparage end game play as a kind of draughts. As Mrs Cuffee put the pieces away he stood before the unlit fire filling his pipe and describing where he had lost a valuable tempo in trying to develop a bishop. Eldman nodded conscientiously. Cuffee came in and listened for a moment.

'So you won.'

'Not one of my best games.'

'Still you'll be in a better mood than if you lost. I want to talk to you.'

'We'll talk . . .'

'This is worthy of your study, come on.' Mr Cuffee chose to invent a conflict of wills out of the moment, something he was prone to since he had ceased to confront his son on any issue that mattered. He brusqued his brows and stared hard.

'What's it all about?' Cuffee said nothing, standing at the door his hand on the knob. Eldman steepled his fingers and studied them, inventing a faint embarrassment to countenance Mr Cuffee's attitude. His wife gazed exactly midway between them, her face prepared for any outcome, a half smile surmounted by a mild frown. Unlike Eldman she could recall times when the scene had not been so hollow. 'Right then.' Mr Cuffee announced and she beamed at their manly outspokenness while Eldman dismantled his fingers and turned to speak to Dorothy.

Mr Cuffee's study was small and possessed a striven-for effect of learning and smoky masculinity. There were a great number of books many of which he had read, a desk covered in green baize, a big upright typewriter which he called his 'gatling', a pipe barrel with about twenty assorted specimens and above the door on pegs a handsome smooth-bore shot-gun. Behind the desk was a high-backed elaborately carved chair; Mr Cuffee sat in this and as though contact with its seat operated a circuit, said, 'Imparts a distinctly Gothic strain to my thoughts this chair.' Cuffee sat on the rush-bottomed chair against the wall, drawing it forward and leaning back on two legs. The light from the table lamp lit them melodramatically and into it Mr Cuffee exuded swirls of smoke.

'Don't do that to the chair Peter, there's a good chap.' Cuffee came to rest. 'Now what do you want to talk to me about?'

'I'm leaving Art School.'

'You've got another year yet, then the teachers' training course.'

'Yes, but I'm leaving. There's no point in staying. I won't get any better in school.'

'What about teaching?'

'You know I won't teach.'

'I know you'd be distinctly unsuitable. Still they might have found you an approved school or something.'

'So I'm leaving. This week.'

'In the middle of a term . . .'

'Yes. And I want you to give me fifty pounds.'

Mr Cuffee had an excellent laugh, he no longer used it in connection with humorous occasions, preferring to reserve it for moments like the present. He did not feel it required any text and after it had passed he sat puffing at his pipe and shaking his head slowly to and fro. Cuffee sat without saying anything and the laugh lay between them. In time it began to appear somewhat ridiculous and Mr Cuffee, slightly disconcerted, halted his head.

'Well thanks anyway,' Cuffee said and got up for the door.

'Is that, is that all. I mean what do you want this fifty pounds for?'

'To spend.'

'To spend on what?'

'Me.'

'And you expect me to give it to you, just like that . . . ?'

'No.'

'Then why did you ask?'

'Seemed logical. You've got money, I need money, I'm your first child. There's a syllogism in there somewhere.'

'Now look here Peter. I think I have the right to know what you are going to do with this money, and if I might add, with your life.'

'Spend them on me.'

'Stop trying to be epigrammatic. Sit down.' These two imperatives apparently obeyed Mr Cuffee seemed re-assured of his own authority and went on firmly:

'Now this fifty pounds, it is to set you up somewhere in order that you can paint?'

'No, it's to take me on a trip.'

'Where?'

'Fifty pounds away.'

'And if you don't get the fifty pounds?'

'Oh, I'll get it all right.' Mr Cuffee looked at his son, half of his face in shadow, the other half without expression, watching him one-eyed, a jack of spades.

'If I don't give it to you how will you get it?' His voice denied the rhetorical.

'Well I may put Mrs Cuffee on the streets and collect it in threepences.'

'I think that's in very bad taste.' Cuffee rose.

'You're right, only Father, the whole thing's in very bad taste, the pleading for money to indulge my sordid appetites, you being revealed as a miserly old bastard. It's all too distasteful for words.' And he went. Mr Cuffee sat for a time and when he next tried to draw on his pipe it had gone out.

Ruth was in bed, sitting up reading. Cuffee came in and sat at the foot. She had on a sweater of her brother's loose enough to lose her breasts and make her look small and orphaned. This bedroom which had been theirs as children always made her feel good when she came back for a night. He lay on the edge of the bed and put his head in her lap.

She combed his hair with her fingers, thick on the nape and at the sides, cut close on top. His head rested warm and heavy on her bone, under his hearing her body made its uterine sounds, shiftings in her liquid deeps. She liked when she was going off to sleep to imagine the dark warms of her interior like some Jules Verne journey, blood red and purply pink and pearly white. She always hoped she would dream about it but never did.

'Did you ever see a film called "Journey to the Centre of the Earth"?' she asked. He shook his head, rubbing against her through the clothes.

'Why?'

'Just wondered.'

'Come off it.'

'What did he say?'

'No.'

'What will you do?'

'Let's not talk about it.'

'All right, tell me something.'

'What?'

'Tell me when you loved me most.' He squinted up at her. She doubled over and kissed him at the corner of his eye and the bridge of his nose.

'I'm not getting soppy. I accept that you've got to go away. Our impending separation makes an honest mistress out of me.' She put quotes in her voice for this last, 'You've never been away before.'

'The army.'

'Ah yes, but then we weren't lovers.'

'We've been lovers since you were twelve.'

'Ah yes, but that was in all innocence.'

'And what was the rest?'

'Incest. I never lusted after you before.'

'Before what?'

'Before you came back from the army. And I didn't lust after you when you were in the army, I just missed you dreadfully. But I never thought of you going out with girls and doing things. Did you?'

'What, go out with girls?'

'Yes and do things.'

'You mean have it away?'

'Yes.'

'No.'

'Good. I'm your first girl then.'

'Don't you remember?'

'No, but I mean since you've liked other girls.'

'Yes.'

'Am I your only girl? No, it's not fair to ask that. Am I?'

'No.'

'Was she better, I mean . . .'

'Please Ruth.'

'I'm sorry. Tell me about the army. Remember that time you deserted. You and that Sottish boy—'

'Gibbon, Harry Gibbon.'

'Yes. Tell me about it.'

'I've told you about it.'

'Was that why you deserted? To see me?'

'Not really. We were getting demobbed in a couple of months. It was just for a laugh.'

'I wish I could have gone with you. I was jealous of him, Gibbon, when the M.P.s took you away.'

'Jealous?'

'Yes, he was with you and you were the same way with him you used to be with me.'

'Well hardly . . .'

'No but I mean, together. Do you remember your first leave? We went swimming.'

'Do I remember. That was the first time I ever had a real lust for you. I kept wondering what would happen, if you would want me to make love to you—'

'I just naturally thought you would. Oh we were wicked Peter.'

'We certainly were. Like hell. That day was the start of all this you know, for me anyway. After that you could never be my little pale sister, my quiet little bed mate who liked to tickle—'

'Oh shut up.'

'Does it embarrass you?'

'No of course it doesn't. What made it change . . .'

'The army, the khaki menagerie. Hearing all that endless

randy talk, and me trying to keep you in a little shrine of purity, keep my mind from taking off your clothes. I think I must have done every film star in christendom twice.'

'Poor Peter. Darling.'

'And when I came home on leave then I knew I wanted you differently than before.'

'I remember that time, it was lovely. But that was really the day I lost you then—'

'—or the day I found you. Before that you were a bit of me that I had to pull up into trees and help over streams, I don't mean you were a hindrance, just that you were another part of me, an extension of my being.'

'I liked it.'

'So did I Ruth. But it had to come this way. This is where you have to come to. To yourself.'

'I know, but I'm just sorry it ended. I don't like to think of things ending. Not our things.'

'The only end I'm worried about is the last one. All the rest are just beginnings.'

'Beginnings of what?'

'Of more endings.'

'Very good. I must remember that.' Robert Eldman's voice was heard calling goodnight. Ruth replied and they heard the front door close and a moment later the car start and drive away. It was a sound they knew very well, she thought. The warmth of him through the clothes and hearing his voice and remembering were all very strong in her. She felt a great languor, a thick milky throbbing. Cuffee sat up and the weight removed made her feel naked and exposed.

'I better go Ruth.'

'You too.'

'Me too.' She pointed to her forehead.

'Chaste as chaste,' she said.

'Goodnight Ruth.'

'Goodnight love.' She switched off the light and lay in the dark. The slack, good feeling was going. In its place she could feel a cold emptiness, low in her body as though she were hollow. In an attempt to assuage this she curled herself up tightly and pressed towards sleep.

After breakfast, standing in the kitchen, Cuffee still thick with sleep, he walked her to the station. Down under the chestnuts and past the old laundry, along behind the village and across the field. The land lying away flat and green had a lambence of unthawed dew. Along the hedges a spangle of sequin, and an occasional bejewelled web. Cuffee stopped to urinate. The crumple of his piss in a yellow steaming stalk. She looked into the ditch, at the trembling still of each blade and bead. Poppies shone in the long coarse grasses, frail smuts of red. Five she counted, black eyed, transient, membrane, the colour of passion. She plucked one and ate it. It tasted of morning. Behind she could hear a distant ruck of caws from the rookery. They went on and across the field. 'Look Peter, a kestrel.' The hawk quivered aloft on twin trembles of wing, they watched, breathless, as it slid sideways, checked, climbed, slid briefly, fixed and started a fresh beat. The train came in, slowing down on the curve, lying over on the camber. They ran, sparking the dew and wetting her legs. She got into a compartment with two business men reading *Guardians*.

'See you tonight,' he said and kissed her face on the mouth then went. The guard fussed along then back and blew his whistle. Jerking twice then rolling heavily it moved out of the station. She leant from the window to watch and could see him going back across the field as the train trundling slowly swung past her. The kestrel still poised, fanned and spread, high hunter, alone in the sky scrutinizing the beneath earth across which walked, quickly and without looking back, Cuffee.

She sat down into the seat, letting herself drop and causing the two men to look up briefly at the impact. What do they see she wondered, a plain little miss on her way to the office, or do they notice the degeneracy of my eyes, the sensuality of my nostrils, the salacious tinge of my mouth. She smiled at the fancy and looked out the window. The line from somebody's poem came to her, 'as hawks in their cages dream of hills and the morning.'

65

Cages. Yes that was true she thought. So often she felt caged. If her mother was a budgerigar and her father a parrot, and if Peter was a hawk and he certainly was, what then was she. Nothing suggested itself with any finality on the journey to Manchester.

CHAPTER FOUR

The Rowan Tree is a small dark pub that stands across from the old cemetery on Inverkip Street. The cemetery is no longer used and the Rowan Tree is a quiet pub as Greenock pubs go. It is an old man's pub. It sells the cheap sweet wine the old men like and it is dim and cool in summer, still with its wooden flooring, the boards arched with age and studded with shiny nail heads that glint through the sawdust. On a mild Monday evening Mrs Gerrard sits behind the bar reading the *Greenock Telegraph*. Her daughter, who also serves, talks to a customer in the public bar and in the saloon an old man sits, watching his wine, his hands folded on top of his stick and his moustache and shoulders drooping in unison. He is sitting at one of the three oblong wooden tables that distinguish the saloon from the public. Above his head on the ledge of the window are three geranium pots, the long, knuckled stems rising to sprout a few leaves and remnants of petal. He contemplates his drink, a small oasis of certainty, and under the shade of the geraniums he rests a while and thinks unreachable thoughts. Unknowable drooping thoughts, a tree in October, each thought a little death, a small dry departure, the foliage of his mind dwindling down, unguessably, irremediably. An old man in an old pub across from an old cemetery, gerontic algebra. Moving his feet in the sawdust, under the geraniumbrage, thinking old thoughts for a first time. Soon, when the sweet cheap wine is finished, he will go home to his single end.

Moseby came in. The place was quiet he noted. An old man under the window. Someone in the public bar. Mrs Gerrard put the paper down to come and serve him. He ordered a pint and turned to see himself in the large square mirror that advertised in gilt letters an Edinburgh Pale Ale. The mirror had rust splotches on it. He looked small and white-faced and somehow anonymous. He drank his pint at the bar. It made him wonder how many similar pints he had downed waiting for Gibbon to come, here in the Rowan Tree of a Monday evening. A clock made small notches on the quiet. How many. It was not an arrangement he greatly cared for but like many other things he had grown used to it. Time wounds all heals he remembered and smiled. Mrs Gerrard noticed it and he doused it in beer. He didn't feel much like a discussion of the antiquity of the pub or the interesting personages at rest in the old cemetery. He took his glass over to a table. The old man said good evening. Moseby said good evening. The old man raised his glass and nodding to Moseby took a short sip.

'Been a nice day,' he said.

'Yes, very nice.' The old man put down his glass, a small emphatic placing, and touched his moustache gently, absently, and under this cover licked his upper lip. Moseby felt slightly uncomfortable and thought for something to say. Nothing came.

'It'll be summer soon,' the old man said.

'Well I hope so, not one like last year.'

'You won't remember the summers we used to have.'

'No,' said Moseby, smiling and again quenching the outbreak in his glass.

'Before the war they were, real summers, before your time—' He thought of them for a moment, long and warm ago. 'They really were summers. The pavements were so hot you couldn't run barefoot. Three old men sitting down the Perch died of sunstroke one summer. Things were different then. People were happier. That was all before the war of course. The war stopped all that. Things weren't the same after the war. Couldn't be. Terrible loss of life. If you'd seen that then you couldn't be the same again. Couldn't. I was in the war.'

'Were you?'

'Yes. The Great War. The war to end war. Didn't end much did it.'

'It did not.'

He reflected for a moment on that monumental inefficiency. Then 'Yes, I was in the war from May 1916 to August 1917.'

'Were you wounded?'

'Gassed.'

'Gassed . . .'

'Yes gassed. Oh Jerry used gas all right. So did we. I got gassed and so did everybody in my battery. Artillery I was. Some of them died. Our number one died, Anderson his name was, from Troon. Oh, they used gas all right.'

'Could you see it coming?'

'Oh you could see it coming all right but that did you no good, not if the wind kept up. If the wind kept up you'd had it.'

'Was there nothing you could do?'

'You could run or you could put on your gas mask. And the officer would shoot you if you ran. So you put on your gas mask.'

'Didn't that help?'

'Not much. Soon as the whiff hit you you were sick. Then you had to get it off. Then you got gassed.'

'Is that how you got gassed?'

'The very same, the whole battery got it nearly and a lot of them died. My mate died, died on the way to the casualty station. Couldn't stop coughing. Coughed his lungs up. I went back to England to a nursing home, then up to Killearn outside Glasgow, then I got discharged. The war was finished then.'

'Did it affect you much?'

'Oh, terrible. Had to keep attending my panel doctor. Could taste it in the morning when I woke up. He was out in Union Street this doctor, Banks his name was. Wasn't much of a doctor, too fond of the drink. I used to dream about it and I'd wake up choking and I could taste it in my mouth. Ruined my health it did. Kept giving me tonics he did. Nice receptionist girl there was there. Was almost worth going to see her.' He laughed at this, qualifying it. 'Oh I was a boy for the women in my young days . . .'

He talked on, his memory uncurling itself in the sun of Moseby's interest, long and involved with the minimum of point and a fastidious care for dates and weather and times. He remembered fist fights and football matches, Morton winning the cup in 1922, and a man who had drowned himself in the East India Harbour by buttoning a causey inside his coat. He talked of fairs that came and an escaper who went into a tank chained to an anvil and he told of a young man who had been to the war and had gone melancholy and had suffocated himself in his old army kit bag. He was telling about this when Gibbon came in. He nodded and sat down.

'He got up on the dresser and got in the kit bag and he had a rope through the holes in the kit bag and then just rolled off and that pulled the neck tight and he just suffocated, couldn't get air, and that's how they found him, hanging up from the pulley . . .' Moseby could see it, the kit bag and the little kitchen, swinging slightly, and finding him in the canvas shroud.

The old man was preparing to go. Moseby offered him another drink but he refused and said good night. He went out rather slowly on painful-looking feet.

'That was a cheerful note,' Gibbon said.

'Strange, listening to him talk, like an old newsreel, I felt, well nostalgic for it although I've never been. Seemed, realer somehow. Maybe it's just because nothing very real has ever happened to me—' As he said it he felt annoyed at the self-indulgence of the remark. He looked at Gibbon but he did not seem to be listening. A tenderness for his friend made Moseby touch his sleeve, and caption the gesture with an irrelevance.

'What are you drinking?'

'John I'm thinking of getting out of Greenock for a bit,' Moseby took his hand away and looked interested.

'When did you decide?'

'I don't know really. I suppose it's been in the air for a while. Yesterday brought it up again. My Aunt was telling me about my grand-uncle Robert, he was a kind of travelling preacher, always going away for years at a time, and they asked him why he went and he said "if you don't go then you can't come back". Does that make sense to you?'

'If he didn't go he wouldn't have to come back.'

'Funny, that's exactly what my Aunt said. But somehow it made sense to me. Don't know why. So I wrote to Cuffee, he's at Art School in Manchester, asked him what he was doing this summer. I could save about a hundred quid by the summer. Thought maybe we could go away somewhere. No good asking you is there?'

'I'll have to get a job over the holidays. Anyhow Edna would hamstring me before she'd let me go roaming off across the county. Can't say as I blame her. It was hard enough getting me this settled.'

'Do you really think you are settled John?' One of his transparent questions through which the implied negative was clearly visible. Moseby didn't really want another bout of analysis of his actions and motives. The thought of the man in the kit bag, closing into coma, came to him and seemed strangely comforting.

'Well I've made my choice. It's the first fifty years is the worst.'

The flippancy was to tell Gibbon to change the subject but he went on, 'I mean do you think this is what's best for you—'

'Oh come on Harry, how do I know what's best for me. Circumstances shape everything. It's better than working in the I.B.M. I'm married and I have a child. The ideal state doesn't interest me. Let me be aphoristic, marriage, like politics, is the art of the possible—'

'But are you really happy?' This annoyed Moseby. It was a very untypical Gibbon question and one, he guessed, he had been asking himself.

'Knock it off Harry, questions like that don't apply. There's happiness in my life. I love Edna. And in her pan loaf way she loves me. And I love Carol. And I'll quite like teaching when I get to it. And I like Greenock. And when I get some time maybe I'll manage to write. So what does it mean, am I happy, unless you believe in Eden, some endless bliss of content—' He suddenly caught himself getting ready to flail Gibbon with words, and stopped, a little abruptly. Gibbon seemed during this to have decided to end the matter. He nodded his imitation of agreement.

'Two pints,' he said and got up to get them. Moseby finished his glass and tried to decide if he really meant what he had said. It seemed reasonable enough. A wife of his

71

choosing and a daughter of his delight, the vigour of his intellect. What was his constraint. Did his constantly simmering lust hint at some volcanic discontent. He did not like to think though of marital fidelity as an unbearable imposition. It would die down in time. He found himself thinking of the long gone suicide, crouched in his swinging sack. He tried to discover the link between this and the main thread of his thought but the associations came to pieces as he pursued them. He knew his mind was hiding something from him and it made him feel as though there was a traitor in his castle. He looked at Gibbon getting the pints and wondered if the same cloak and dagger antics went on in that broad amiable brain. Gibbon's cheerful return convinced Moseby that nothing but harmony prevailed.

'What are you smiling at?'

'Oh, just something Carol said. Strictly doting father stuff.'

'Well, all the best John.'

'Cheers Harry.' They drank.

'When do you think you'll get a reply from Cuffee?'

'Well I posted it tonight. He should get it Wednesday. Maybe he'll reply next week. There's no great hurry though.'

'How long is it since you've seen him?'

'Three years.'

'That doesn't bother you, it having been so long . . .?'

'We were pretty close in the army. And we've kept in touch after a fashion. But I have been wondering about it.'

'Would you go on your own?' Gibbon looked down into his glass. He pursed his mouth in self-depreciation.

'I don't know. Doesn't appeal to me half as much as going with someone. I don't like the thought of being on my own somewhere I was a stranger.'

Moseby could see then, as he hadn't before, what Gibbon had been getting at in his previous questions.

'Harry, do you feel I've let you down?'

'How do you mean let me down?'

'Well things aren't the way they were with us. I mean this, Monday nights in the Rowan. Have I made you feel on your own or something?' Gibbon remained looking into his beer

72

and Moseby watched him. He spoke without looking up.

'You remember that time we went across the other side, that first leave I got, ten days it was. Well that was one of the big things in my life you know. Really. When I went back to the camp. I remembered that and I told Cuffee about it. I used to think we'd all get together after demob and go off somewhere, the four of us . . .'

'Four?'

'He's got a sister he's pretty close to, I used to think we'd come up here, to Greenock and we'd all get somewhere together and he would paint and you would write and Ruth would keep house and I would work and everything would be, well right. Only you met Edna, and well. Now here we are—'

'But I've been married four and a half years Harry. You must have known it couldn't work out like that since then.' Gibbon shrugged and something in his manner caught at Moseby's mind. 'Did you think, did you think maybe Edna and I would split up?' Gibbon said nothing. 'Have you been waiting around all this time to see if I left Edna?'

'No, of course not. There was a time, when you were in the I.B.M. I thought you might do something desperate. But as Carol began to grow up, well I knew you wouldn't ever do anything.'

'So why did you hang on?' Gibbon turned his troubled face up for the first time. His eyes were pained.

'John, I thought you might, well need, somebody and I thought, well I suppose I thought there might be a place, you know, best friend, and all that rubbish, but I didn't know the rules, because there are rules, like families are families and friends are friends, women want it that way, Edna wanted it that way, it wasn't anything personal, just in her mind I was a mate of yours before you got married. There isn't any place for that kind of thing. I was just a bit slow in seeing it, that's all.'

Moseby felt empty and guilty and angry and a number of churning other things. He had told himself though that Gibbon and he shared one of those passionate melancholy friendships so much a part of Chinese poetry, forcibly separated by thousands of miles and making tenuous and tender contact by letter. But this was not enough for Gibbon, more of him was involved. For the first time it crossed his mind that perhaps he did not care for Gibbon as much as Gibbon cared for him. It was a painful, thrust away intuition. What if he asked permission from Edna to go off for a fortnight. What was a fortnight. Another little nugget to be polished smooth by the memory, hoarded and handled with miserly concern.

'I think you should go Harry. I think it's really important that you do, even if Cuffee doesn't, I think you should.'

'Do you think so? Really?'

'Really. There's everything waiting outside Greenock. I mean why be a carpenter here when you could be one in Nazareth.' Odd thing to have said he thought as soon as he had said it. Gibbon seemed not to have noticed the reference.

'Yes, carpentry is one of those things you can do anywhere if you have to. It's universal. I'm sorry about going on, you know. It's all, well I feel like it was the end of something.' The end of something, everything was the end of something. Eschatologies. Like a graveyard.

'The beginning of something more like.' Gibbon nodded and smiled.

'Anyway it hasn't happened yet. Fancy a game of darts?'

'Sure.' And as he got the darts Moseby felt almost glad that he was going and that the little world he was trying to construct would be left, the more insular, the more singular.

They played several games all of which Gibbon won. Then two men came in and they played doubles and Moseby played better. But the men were too good and they lost five of the six. They had a last drink and said good night to Mrs Gerrard. Standing outside in the soft night air Moseby was thinking about the man in the kit bag again, and what he kept seeing was how he was crouched, knees up, like a foetus, unborn, in the dark, mimicking his beginnings in his end. Did it all seem darkly familiar as he was drugged down into oblivion, did it start him kicking again for life.

'I keep thinking about that guy who killed himself in the kit bag.'

'He must have been a dwarf to get into a kit bag.'

'A dwarf. Never thought of that.' But now he did. It seemed apt somehow.

'I have to get up in the morning John so I'll be getting home. I'll maybe see you at the week-end.'

'All right Harry. Look I just want you to know, well you're . . .' and he didn't know what to say.

'Sure John. That's how it is for me too. See you.'

They shook hands and Gibbon went down the hill. Moseby watched him until, as predicted, he turned and waved. Moseby had the desire to rush after him and make him see, make him understand. But what. Did he not understand only too well. What would he say that would alter the rules. Would he say 'I'll come with you Harry', or 'you come and live with us'. There was nothing to say. It was the way things were. The way things were. Mantra for the disenchanted. It's the way things are.

The night was darkly blue and patched with windows. Helensburgh lights made a long fizzing string across the river. The West Kirk clock shone its white face in four directions, out over the west end where the houses stood discreet and aloof, down Nelson Street to the B.B. Cinema where the big picture was half way through, over Walkers sugar house as the back shift commenced another sweet long night, and up to the West Station where the last Glasgow train clapped its doors. A ship moved in slow constellation down river. Two drunk men remembered each other outside the British Legion. The Glasgow train emitted steam and smoke and made sigh. Cats glided as birds, headless and safe, slept. Policemen metronomed their beats. Television blue grottoes. Close coupled courters. Owls riddled the cemetery with hoots. The guard whistled and the train overcame its inertia. It chuffed and smoke lifted, dissolving. A few shards cleared Bruce Street and cleared the waste ground. They swirled over the old graveyard and moved, dwindling, across the graves. A rind of moon silvered their brief dance. For Moseby glancing in, they were almost visible. He stopped and looked in. The tombstones were black against a pale ground. Eschatologies. He stood until a shiver touched him and moved him on.

CHAPTER FIVE

There was one thing she had come to wait for. About half past six when she had got back from an early night at the library the birds came in from the country to roost for the night. They came in from the fields and flew in over the suburbs to doss in droves along the ledges of the buildings. Her window looked out into a well made by the blind gables of other tenements. If she looked directly upwards she could see a square of sky framed by the buildings. Through this the flocks inevitably passed at their day's end. The regularity of this occurrence fascinated her. It seemed each time it could not happen again, until it did. Having found it by chance she now waited for it each evening. The wait had assumed the quality of a ritual. She would sit and watch, her head back and her throat drawn tight until she lost all sense of spatial relation to the sky, whether it was above her or below her or how far from her. Rather it seemed after a time that she was herself the sky, that between them was not the dichotomy of seer and seen, but a kind of transcendent empiricism in which she was what she beheld and in the beholding had her being. As she watched her mind became bare and empty as the sky, became the sky, taut empty space that ached at its emptiness and despaired of the evening flight until magical, they came, a first tickling one or two, then a stream, a pour, a surge, filling her whole vision with flight. In over the roofs they came, like enchanted gusts of leaves, filling the evening and her mind with a chittering fluttering release, a shoaling, falling, rising stream bannering across the passive reflection of her mind and in this moment were the very thoughts of which they were the object. Only birds flew and she with them and they in her until some caged thing in her was free and the sky was empty and she was empty and an acute loneliness filled her, aware once more of her watching self.

'I watch and am as a sparrow alone upon the house top.' She had once asked a Sunday School teacher what it meant but the teacher had said it was just a way of speaking the people who wrote the Bible had. There was for her now a plaintive satisfaction in having come in time and experience to where she could answer that question.

After tea she decided not to wait in for Cuffee but to go to the pictures. She left him a note in case he came round but without really thinking he would. She didn't see much of him through the week unless she went over to his studio which was in Salford. This was an excursion she had discontinued partially because of the effect the district had upon her and also because it was too easy to let herself get drunk on wine and end up in bed, something which, if she did not completely regret it, she would rather didn't happen. The last time had been at the end of October, he had sold a painting and they celebrated with a Chinese meal and the purchase of a bottle of Haig's. They spent the tawny autumn afternoon drinking toddied whisky and watching his cats mating. After each successful coupling, and there were about eight of them, the female abandoned herself to rolling and washings while the tom bestowed a few matching licks upon the salmon pink of his penis, then sat by her, momentarily sated, cleaning her paws for her when she finally curled up. All afternoon it lasted, the light becoming both purer and dimmer, encasing the buildings as though they were submarine and in the room permitting the massing of blue shadow in the corners. They sipped their potent grog, his head in her lap, the euphoria of alcohol and closeness punctuated from time by the low rapturous squall of the cat as the tom's ardence pierced her through, her neck extended, eyes unblinking while behind her, his whole body flexed in clonic urging, he served her will.

When the light had almost gone and the room was perfumed with dusk it was their turn, on the same bed as the cats had used. She stripped swiftly, clothes melting from her body, and they made the silk purse out of her sow's ear a once and a twice and a languorous thrice, his face wet from her sweet drunken kisses, her shoulders and throat bitten delicately red.

*　　*　　*

She came out of the cinema just before eleven. The neons along Oxford Street jerked their persuasions on and off. She was depressed instantly after the mild intoxication of wide screen and colour. There seemed to be no good reason to go back to her room, birdless now and dark. People passed, many many people. All of whom she didn't know. She wondered on which buildings the birds slept. Sleeping up above all this, silent hundreds and hundreds of them. Below people passed all of whom she didn't know. She walked, watching the faces change colour in the neons and thinking of the birds, deep in anaesthetized, amputated sleep. She wanted something to happen to her, something meaningful and totally beyond expectation. The remoteness of such an event lay heavily upon her.

In the blue and fizzy lemon lighting she was small and wan-faced, her pale mouth showing scarcely at all. Only the eyes were distinct, dark blotches under the old-fashioned hang of her hair, parted in the middle and caught low on the nape in a loose knot. She walked with her hands in her raincoat pockets, slowly, letting the passers-by brush her aside. A snack bar blared yellow light against the side of her face, she paused and someone coming out held the door open for her. Not wanting to say no after this courtesy she went in. She bought a tea and sat at the narrow ledge running across the window. She stirred her tea absently. The spoon was made of plastic, it was pink and had a little excrescence at the end of the handle where it had been broken from the machine. She ran the tip of her finger over it. The thought of thousands of millions of teaspoons came to her and made her stir the tea again. Outside people passed. Some looked in, some did not. She didn't know any of them. Not the ones who looked in nor the ones who passed on. She knew very few people when you came down to it. If it was other people's recognition that gave meaning to your existence then hers had hardly any. She thought, inevitably, of Cuffee. It always came back to him. All the rest were spoons, plastic, pink, millioned. She could not begin to understand how it would be possible to know one of them, how she would talk with them, come to discover their origins, the things which shaped them and sometimes she was afraid she might not have the energy to try. Now he was going to sever them and she knew she didn't want it to happen, would rather go on in this way, unsatisfactory and painful though it was, rather than face the fact that she must start searching the crowds for that face, the one whose eyes would understand and whose smile would warm her. Knowing that some people wait all their lives and are still waiting when they die. Castaways who fly ribbons of signal in the Personal columns of the Sunday newspapers. He would never be like that she was sure. He had the remoteness of self-sufficiency. He was resigned to his atoll and looking back it seemed to her that he always had been. Resigned to his parents, adult incomprehension, the brutalities of their father and the stupidities of his wife. It was difficult now to think of them like that, her mother a pallid twitter of nerves, Mr Cuffee rapidly becoming an old bore. But then, then they had been the juggernaut, the agents of a malevolent universe. She could remember her brother after being punished, in a frenzy of impotent rage, throw up their bedroom window and shout out over Knutsford his hatred of God and Mr Cuffee until his father came up and dragged him in. She could guess now that Mr Cuffee was that most unfortunate of things a mediocre man who was obsessively aware of the fact, and that his whole life had been a near comic sequence of near misses and semi-successes. But then nothing was known except the terror of parental anger, the clouds that lay over the house as Mr Cuffee brooded at his desk. She could recall vividly, still with a knot of dread, her father dealing out punishment. He would ask which hand they preferred and when they chose would strike with it, open, flat, thick smacking hand that jerked the head sideways and left ridges on the face, risen red welts with frightening white edges. She still became terror-stricken at the thought of a blow on the face, a girl in the library, miming such a blow had caused her to scream involuntarily, the whole library turning to look. When she had flinched from such punishment she had been beaten over his knee, when revulsion and pain joined in the one sobbing agony. He claimed that his blows were always proportionate in force to the misdeeds which warranted them but she could only recall the stunning impact and the unsuccessful attempt to stem the tears. Peter never cried, not in his father's presence. When they were alone he would sob into his hands with rage and she would hover beside him, trying to stem the tears that came through his fingers. They were left on their own a lot while their parents went visiting and it was then their only freedom in the house began. They kept candles and matches hidden and Peter would go down and steal biscuits and they would sit up in bed and he would tell her stories in which they were pursued by villains of various sorts who were all Mr Cuffee and whom they always destroyed.

For the actual destruction they had to wait until Peter was thirteen. Mr Cuffee had summoned them before his punishment chair and after hearing his wife's complaint asked the rhetorical question and in reply to the terse nod struck the ritual blow. The boy's head tugged round and he staggered. Straightening up he hit out violently knocking Mr Cuffee's spectacles off and bleeding his nose. There was a silence which included all manner of terrible noises, Peter's short, fierce breath, Mr Cuffee's intake of pained amazement, his wife's cry of horror and the sound of the spectacles, knocked on to the table and sliding over the polished surface, while all the while her heart drummed enormously. Then Peter was struck again and knocked to the floor and she was lying over him as the blows fell, on her back and his legs. He had been sent upstairs and threatened with a beating on the morrow. But so far as reprisal went tomorrow had never come and Mr Cuffee never called them before his chair again to choose hands.

As she thought about it and sipped her soapy tea it all seemed petty and little more than nasty, retrospect diminished the terror and some of it even seemed funny. But things do not now appear as they were, the veils of time and the refraction of other events change all but the starkest emotions. Now it was over, and they had, in a sense, survived. Perhaps the ones who had really suffered were her parents, now cut off from their children and left with each other and their pathetic self-deceptions. Two unexceptional people who had fostered each other's caricature, and out of

80

these caricatures begotten children whose lives they proceeded to distort and mould until now, when their influence was negligible, they could be seen to have achieved results that boded permanence. For wasn't Peter's closed universe of self, his personal fascism, wasn't this his father at another remove. And her dependence upon him, could she not see her mother there in narcotic attendance upon her spouse. The wry plausibility of it caused her to smile, unamused as she was.

When she got back to her room she lit two candles, not feeling disposed towards electricity. Cuffee had not been round and she made tea for herself. She shared the kitchen with a girl in the other room but she did not appear to be in. Ruth sat on a stool and waited for the kettle to boil. There was an hour-glass egg-timer on a poker-work board showing a hen looking in surprise at a rather large egg. For some reason she found it quite absurd and began to laugh. The laugh sounded quite strange and she stopped it. It was not an evening for glee she told herself aloud and the word 'glee' made her start again. It seemed a very improbable sort of word. The kettle curtailed further mirth by hooting its temperature.

She made the tea strong and took it into her room to stand. The candles made two puddles of yellow light on the ceiling and left great dubs of shadow around the room. She lay on the bed and watched the wavering pools above her. The candles ran clear cooling tears of wax down their sides from the brimming hollow around the wick. The flame trembled its soft thick tongue speechlessly. Candles meant the past. That was the trouble, everything meant the past. The mirror on the dressing-table reflected the candle and in the background picked up the pale mark of her face. She closed her eyes and thought of her skipping ropes. They were in the bottom drawer of the dressing-table. She had had them since she was a little girl and had loved them intensely, more than anything except Peter. She remembered a long time ago when she had just learned to skip well. Her ropes were new, white and waxed and their handles a creamy colour, shaped like pestles. She carried

81

them to school in her school bag to skip at the break and at dinner time and then to skip home. She would run all the way home skipping, running without effort or thought, propelled by the rope as it circled around her. The world of those long gone afternoons still spelled her memory; the handles, creamy-coloured, that turned themselves, the rope a white all around blur, dark where it hit the ground with a sweet thwick, the pavement warm and springy, each jump and she could see over the houses into the faraway green fields where the brown cows grazed under the sun that shone shone shone upon a small girl skipping, encased in a world of her own creation, shone kindly light, gold upon the gold of her joy as she danced towards death, to hang up her magic ropes until the next miles away day when she would again spin her frail dream and take refuge in it.

She got up from the bed and took the skipping ropes out. In her hands they made her want to start but she restrained herself. Some day she thought, she would go skipping again just to see if it could ever feel the same. After she put them away she undressed for bed. The candles made soft tracings of light around her body and as she turned pearled her upper breasts and the round of her thighs. A juggle of shadows and nacreous pales, trembling chiaroscuro. She felt moved at the apparition and with reluctance blew out the flames. The room swooned with dark.

CHAPTER SIX

When Cuffee woke the child was trying to open a can of beans.

'Give it here.'

'This opener. My mother's got one. They're no good.' She brought him over the tin and he sat up in bed.

'Is there toast on?' he said sniffing.

'No. I lit the toaster bit so it would get hot. It's an awful old bollocks of a stove.' She was eleven. A small sharp-looking girl with rare violety eyes and straight dull blonde hair. She had on a grey gym slip and under it a green jumper. He twirled the wings of the opener and rolled round the edge.

'Did your mother send you out without a coat?'

'It's a nice day. I hate that blazer. It's an awful bollocks of a blazer.'

'Don't keep saying bollocks.'

'Well let me say bugger then. How would you like to only be allowed one bad word.'

'Why don't you say the ones I taught you. Nannyflanger. Fine word that. Nice word for a girl like you.' She took the beans and emptied them into the frying pan and put it on the gas. One of the cats left the foot of the bed to enquire of the tin. It licked a tentative lick and decided against.

'It's not real. Is it?'

'What?'

'That word, you made it up.'

'No I didn't. Heard it in the army. Sergeant called me it.'

'What does it mean?'

'Somebody who flanges nannies.'

'I don't like it. I prefer bollocks.'

'Please yourself.' He teased his shirt out from under the tomcat who looked unpleased. It was warm on his back and chest.

'What's he like?'

'Who?'

'The one that's coming in when you go.'

'He's all right. Don't flirt with him though. He won't understand.'

'I don't flirt with everybody,' with a skittish little toss.

'No, well see you don't. He's a very serious painter.'

'More serious than you?'

'Much.'

'I'll bet he's not better.'

'No that's true.' She cut half a loaf three times and left the heel.

'Ever thought of working in a saw mill?' he asked her. She ignored it and put the slabs under the grill. Cuffee poured himself a basin of water and gingerly washed his cheeks and a part of his neck.

'Mavis Dawson got pregnant by a blackie.'

'That was last year,' drying himself vigorously.

'The baby got adopted. Poor little black bastard.'

'Ah ah ah.'

'That's using the word properly. It's not a bad word if you use it properly.'

'Just you watch it.' There were footsteps on the stairs. They exchanged glances and Cuffee indicated with his head. She tiptoed across and behind the hessian drape that divided the long hut. Cuffee put on a shirt and went to the door. It was Mrs Mullen.

'Sorry to trouble you Peter but is Patsy with you?'

'No, she mitching again?'

'Found her books in the coal hole. She'll get me into trouble that girl. There's a letter for you.' Mrs Mullen was trying to see in and he stood aside.

'A virtuous evening well spent,' he said fishing his letter out of the wire basket. 'Go on in.'

'And get my name all over Salford. Oi'm not one of your bohemy-ens.' Whenever she exchanged badinage Mrs Mullen always assumed what was by now a stage Irish inflection. A tall, washed-out woman, six times mother, twice wed, once widowed, once deserted, now living with a rarely afloat merchant seaman. 'If you see her catch her ear and give us a shout, will you love.' She stepped back on to the wooden landing and Cuffee looking at the postmark came out with her. The morning was bright and in the tenement backs whites tugged at the lines and several windows gave back the sun in fractured flashes.

'Important?' Mrs Mullen asked. Cuffee looked up and sniffed the envelope appreciatively.

'Killer in the slaughterhouse she is, bloody nice girl.' Mrs Mullen laughed and went down the wooden steps, holding on to the bannister. Cuffee went back in and closed the door.

'That was your mother.'

'She found my books.'

'Why do you hide them in the coal hole?'

'I hate carrying them.'

'It's only fifty yards. Watch those beans don't burn.'

'You got a letter. Is it from a girl?'

'No, it's from a friend of mine in Scotland.'

'How much toast do you want?'

'Well that thick two will be enough. Can you eat the other one?'

'I didn't take any breakfast so I'd be hungry.'

'Well get dishing.'

14 George's Square, Greenock.
Sunday 21st.

Dear Peter,

Rather a long time since I wrote. Hope all is well with you. I have been thinking about leaving Greenock this summer and moving around and wondered if you were fixed up for the summer. If not maybe we could go off somewhere. It's been a long time since we met but I imagine you unchanged from the tone of your letters. I am still pretty much my same old self, I suppose it's that which makes me want to leave Greenock. Also there is nothing very much to keep me here. Moseby of whom you have heard me speak is busy with marriage and his studies and unless I just succumb to the time honoured tradition of courting the first pleasant-looking Protestant girl who asks me for a ladies preference I think I should get out and see a few things. If you were going away too that would be great. I will have, come mid-July, in about two months anyway, something

85

like a hundred quid. Please feel free to consider this as our capital. Do I interest you. Write and let me know. My regards to your sister.

Yours, Harry.

Patsy put his beans on toast in front of him and scalded the blue enamel tea-pot.

'Anything interesting?' she asked this with her back to him, waiting for the kettle to boil. Her domesticity made Cuffee smile.

'You can read it,' he said, handing it over her shoulder and starting on his breakfast. Patsy read the letter and put it back on the table. She brought the tea over having to hold the pot with both hands.

'Made too much tea again, haven't you?'

'Nag nag nag.' She settled to her breakfast. 'Will the one who's coming look after the cats?'

'No you will.'

'What with. Costs money to feed cats nowadays.'

'I'll make you an allowance.'

'How much?' Like Cuffee she didn't use a knife, cutting the bread with the edge of her fork, one elbow on the table, supporting her head and talking as she ate.

'Ten bob a week.'

'My mother will keep it.'

'No. We'll send it to a post office in your name and you'll collect it there.'

'Like a pension.'

'Exactly.'

'How long for?'

'As long as I'm away.' She went silent after this and didn't speak until she had finished her plate.

'If I was an orphan would you adopt me?' Cuffee looked up. The serious child's face with the beautiful gentian eyes.

'I might, orphans are a lot of responsibility. I don't like responsibility.'

'Mrs Haskell says responsibility is what makes you an adult.'

'And who is Mrs Haskell when she's at home?'

'I told you. My teacher. You never remember anything.'

'I have a bad memory for teachers' names. Stems from my early training.'

'When you say stems do you mean stems like a flower?'

'Patsy don't be bright with Cuffee, Cuffee gets confused when Patsy gets bright with him.'

'Look at tom.' Tom jetted against the bed cover. Cuffee threw his sandshoe which disappeared under the bed. The cat hurried a few steps, watching Cuffee's other foot, then reassured went calmly out through a hole in the floor. Patsy went to collect the shoe and brought it back. He put it on, resting a hand on the sharp knuckly shoulder. He kept his hand there and said:

'Come on, we'll go and see that post office. I'll go in with you and explain it.'

'Will I wash the dishes?'

'All right, I'll write a letter.'

Harry, forget mid-July. I'm leaving Monday. Raise what money you can, travel light and meet me at Ruth's, 172, Mauberley Road, Manchester, 4. Glad you're coming. Peter.

Then he made the bed.

They went to a post office outside Mrs Mullen's normal district. Patsy made him choose a proper office and not one of the small shops that sell other things as well. The woman to whom they spoke seemed a little dubious but warmed to the feeding of the cats who would otherwise be destroyed and in the end was smiling at Patsy fondly. She gave them her name, Miss Elliot, and told Patsy if she had any difficulty to ask for her. They thanked her and left.

'I have to go down to Knutsford.'

'All right. I think I'll go back to school this afternoon. Will you write me a note?'

They went back in and borrowed a sheet of paper from Miss Elliot and Cuffee wrote

Mrs Haskell,

I was forced to keep Patricia away from school this morning while I attended the infirmary for an abscess on my back. She had to look after her youngest brother who has a sore throat. I am sorry about this but I could not think how else to manage, and oblige,

Mrs Mullen.

Patsy read it over.

'You always put in about illness or something.'

'Teachers like it. They like to think about illness and suffering. Puts hair on their chest.' The thought of hair on Mrs Haskell's chest seemed too much for Patsy. She yelped with laughter.

'Here's two bob.'

'Don't need it.'

'Take it in case you change your mind about school. Then you can go to the pictures. But promise you won't stay out at night without seeing your mother.'

'Promise.'

'Okay. See you.'

' 'Bye.' She went down the sunlit street, a thin, Lowry child, hopping occasionally and casting an elongated shadow before her in gawky parody of her gait.

Knutsford was quiet with early closing, sunny and empty with the occasional booming of through traffic on the Warrington road spreading ripples over the hush. From the primary school, plaintive sing song, children chaunt litanies of learning 'four times eight is thirty-two four times nine is thirty-six' and on an end stress of certainty 'four times ten is forr-ty' then in rising coda 'four times eleven is forty-four four times twelve is forty-eight'. Then a silence. In the great green cathedrals of the horse chestnuts countless candles burned, burned in the green gloom with a still light. A flowering cherry, altar bright, a brocade of blossom. The children started on the five times table. Laburnum hung censers, gamboge dangles. There was a smell of macadam, warming. The children made plainsong of their credenda. Cuffee walked unheeding, barbarian and brisk.

The house was empty, Mrs Cuffee being at the Women's Guild. He didn't go in but went round the back. There was a sun porch built out and he got up on top of it, stepping carefully on the spars. The cat looked up from sunning itself and then away. He lifted the window of Mr Cuffee's study and climbed in. There was the heavy stale smell of tobacco in the room. Cuffee sat in the big chair and tried the drawer. It was locked. He sat back and lit a cigarette. The chair creaked and he bucked it back until it rested against the wall. In the stable, laden air his smoke voluted and milled heavily. He smoked with a rapt care, as though it were a first or a last cigarette. The telephone rang downstairs. It went on in the empty house, unheeded by Cuffee, its re-iterations hopeless, reaching – reaching, until, suddenly, de-feated, it stopped. He closed his eyes and the cigarette, between his fingers on the arm of the chair released a pure long line, vocal in its lyricism. Looking he saw it, blueing out of the dull ash, like a note held and held until the world revolves on it. Epiphany.

He assembled the hacksaw blade into the pad handle, screwing down the stud tight. It went between the drawer and the desk and he sawed through the tongue, brass dust falling on to the foot mat. It took about three minutes and he didn't stop until it was finished. Inside were Mr Cuffee's cheque-book and bank statement along with sundry chits from Her Majesty. Cuffee wrote a cheque for fifty-six pounds and marked the stub 'personal loan to first child'. He signed it briskly, without hesitation and then put the cheque-book back. He closed the drawer and shook the mat out of the window. Then he climbed back, observed again by the cat.

The bank clerk was a white-handed young man who knew Cuffee from school.

'Still painting away.'

'That's it.'

'Selling anything.'

'What, for money?' The clerk smiled at this and smoothed the cheque with his long scrivener's fingers.

'Will you sign the back please?' While Cuffee did he drummed them in rotation.

'Seing much of Merle Curvis,' he suggested.

'Almost all of her,' Cuffee said complicitly. The clerk enjoyed this.

'How would you like it?'

'Well daily if I could, oh the money.' Grins and a half a laugh. 'Fifty in fives, six in ten shilling notes, new if you have them.' The clerk licked his fingers and tickled the money. Counted and passed over Cuffee put it in his pocket and said cheerio. Looking back through the doors he could see the clerk still watching him. He waved and the clerk fluttered a pale palm in return.

On the train back to Manchester he wrote to Stolleman.

Stoll, keep this fifty quid for me until I get down. Next week some time I should think. If anything stops me I'll let you know. Peter.

Merle Curvis modelled afternoons in a small expensive gown shop. There was a delay before she came to the phone. Behind her voice a chintz of female talk.

'Hello, Merle Curvis speaking' – a groomed distant voice.

'Peter.'

'Darling, where are you phoning from?'

'The station.'

'The station?' – her tone pitched a little up.

'I'm leaving Manchester.'

'When, Peter?'

'Now.'

'Peter, darling, why, where are you going?' thinner now, anxious.

'Away,' A pause, then the edge.

'You're, what about me—' her voice got ready to rise, then caught and angry, came low – 'what about this—' pause and the hard boiled —'baby of yours?'

'You're going to get rid of it.'

'And you're going to clear out.'

'That's right.'

'Your parents aren't going to like it when I tell them.'

'No they're not. That's a faultless assessment.'

'Stop playing the cool bastard' – genuine exasperation. Then switch, 'Peter, let me go with you. I could get a job in London easily, it's London you're going to isn't it?'

'Passing through.'

90

'Look I could have it done there better safer, can I come with you, you know how much I hate it here.'

'Get out then. But not with me.'

'You don't love me' – accusation.

'No.'

'You said you did' – after a little choke, hollow.

'I lied' – silence. Then venomous.

'You lousy cruel bastard. You never cared about me, never, did you?'

'I could have gone in the night.'

'You just think all you have to do is run, don't you?'

'Most problems are problems of geography. A problem in Manchester is not a problem in London.'

'Well my problem isn't geography, what am I going to do?'

'Look after yourself.' He put the phone down and stepped out.

The city waited, hazed with light, a diffuse brightness from the palled sun, warren town, the provincial burrow incarnate, where the eye can find no rest from streets of houses, from acres upon miles of built-on land, from the preoccupation of the dwellers with the rigours of dwelling, a great self-centred vortex of stone, scabbily pock parked, deserted daily by the birds and inducing in its denizens a torpor of longing for release. Humans, in their flight to freedom, cannot escape violence.

CHAPTER SEVEN

The Sunday visit to Edna's mother was preceded by a walk over the hill, through the new housing schemes and down into Gourock. This was for Moseby the best part of the whole business. He liked walking and he liked streets. He supposed himself to be a town-dweller. Edna was the kind of person who vaguely felt walking to be morally uplifting and in some unspecified way a substitute for church-going. They walked down from Dempster Street and out past the cemetery and up past the Lady Alice park. Up through the box prefabs and past the Rankin Maternity hospital. This Sunday was bright and almost cold and walking was pleasant. Edna had on a tweedy coat checked in soft greys and browns with patch pockets at the bust, each containing a full, mildly moving breast. The texture of the material over the smooth rounded shape itched the palms of Moseby's mind. Carol ran on ahead, being called back from time to time and after a momentary restraint going off again, running with her legs bending exaggeratedly at the knee and arms swinging for balance.

They passed the Rankin Maternity hospital. The visitors were standing in the grounds waiting their turn to enquire after relations. Moseby remembered Edna's confinement with a small immediate depression, remembered standing outside feeling both unconnected with the event and at the same time guilty of some appalling breach of good taste in his mother-in-law's eyes for having dared to show himself so soon after the proof of his rapacity had come to light. It had all been rather like that, unreal and uncomfortable. He had gotten so used to Edna being immense that he could hardly remember when it had been different. Her sundering and the emergence of Carol's reddish, wrinkled being had been a change in the order of things not completely to his liking.

He had been on night shift in I.B.M. at the time of Edna's confinement and on his way home he had phoned, from the phone booth at the top of the stairs on Dempster Street. It had taken some time to get through and when he did the nurse had gone away to enquire and left him, suddenly grainy with fatigue, looking over the roofs and hearing in his ears the distant mingled sounds of the hospital, feet on floors, metallic clinkings and the occasional noises that might have been laughter or screams of pain. He held the phone for a long time, five minutes, maybe ten, a long corridor of time along which he made no progress, thinking wearily of the atrocities of birth on Edna's soft, vulnerable body, standing rubbing his eyes and looking rawly out, yawning and saying hello every now and then into the mouthpiece and standing so, looking, the town's gravid mid before his tired gaze turned to stone, the planes and pitches of the buildings overlapping, giving the sense of a great hewn rock, faceted quartz, aglint with windows in the slanting flush of the bright cold sun and certain chimneys putting forth tendrils of smoke, spare growths on the slaty slopes. And quite simply he did not care about Edna and the child, looking out of the little cell at the metamorphic rock felt utterly weary of the whole pomp of pregnancy and removed beyond all reaching from its melodrama. He put down the telephone and came out on to the street. The cold air made his eyes water. He went home and sat in the chair and fell asleep. His neighbour, Mrs Allen, wakened him around twelve o'clock with the news that he had a daughter, taking his haggard appearance for anxiety and fussing over him so warmly that, sitting in her kitchen drinking sweet hot tea he wondered dimly if perhaps this wasn't one of those moments when he might have her for the asking out of her sympathy and the strange complicity in the fact of his parenthood. She moved about the kitchen, tidying and dusting and sweet and hot in him the desire to still the constant small shuddering of her breasts. He had of course done nothing. Nevertheless it amounted, along with his withdrawal in the telephone booth, to a kernel of guilt about Edna and the birth of Carol. It distressed him to hear her talk of her labour pains and how for long periods before the final expulsion she had been left on her own in the delivery room, calling his name. Those laughing screams might have been hers. He knew how acutely she felt physical pain and was ashamed that at the very moment he had not wished to alleviate it, for having not suffered emphatically. It came as minor relief to hear her say, apologetically, that when the pain had been worst she had called for her mother and not him. This, Moseby assured her, was perfectly natural.

He visited at nights before going in to work. Of this he remembered best the emergence from the Dettol sweet hospital smell into the freezing brightly mooned October nights. Across the valley the hill, rising free of the lit houses, made a clean, painfully clean edge against the blanched sky. The edge of the hill honed keen on the moonstone cut him, through the swaddlings of recent nearness, leaving him, with an almost exultant relief, small and naked. So this became another accretion to his guilt, this willing surrender to his own, singular, unimportance, as he had felt when phoning, this inverted pride, this self-immolation, all without the leavening of humility, 'did you hear about the lonely prisoner; he was in his sel' ' West Coast joke. And it was about now that he began to understand what being West Coast Scottish meant, with its pre-occupations with guilt and sex and sin and its image of man as a monster, hiding his monsterdom from his fellow monsters. And most characteristic was the emphasis on the disguise, you must never cry your foulness aloud because no one would admit it as common. 'Cleanliness is next to Godliness.' Scrub, scrub, scrub. Like his foster parents, the assiduous dark cleanth. And yet in Mr Moseby's bottom drawer, under his winter underwear, a book, in botched type on soft furry paper, *The Town Bull*, about the adventures of a dwarf whose massive member incapacitated his women for all further sexual experience. The w/c mentality.

He had never told her any of this. Had never told her and now she walked beside him unknowing, safe in her ignorance. The fragility of her peace of mind troubled him but the thought of commencing upon the explanations involved deterred him beyond action. And it was not as if he didn't love her or Carol, and Edna had taken Mrs Allen's account of his distraught manner at face value and was pleased and touched by his concern. The truth is a lie that hasn't been found out he thought.

Once past the Larkfield Hospital they were in a brief stretch of open country and down on the right was the Gourock reservoir and straight ahead, across the river that could not be seen at first, the Argyllshire hills.

The strip of secluded road was a favourite courting spot and on a Sunday the verges carried their litter of pale wrinkled sacs, sodden with dew. Random condoms, countless Carols condomed to death he punned. Edna managed never to see them. Also along the verges and sometimes in the road were the burst bodies of frogs killed by traffic. Their undersides were rather the colour of the contraceptives and Moseby had taken to counting them as in a contest to see which side won. Carol sometimes stopped to examine these objects but was immediately moved on by her mother, who at the same time refrained from comment on these instances of thwarted beginnings and untimely ends. Today the french letters won five-three.

Mrs Davidson lived in a large flat in one of the superior tenement properties on Shore Street. Her husband had died shortly after paying for it and his likeness from the top of the piano looked with dull yearning at the tasteful haven he had bequeathed. Mrs Davidson was one of those women whom widowhood liberates, having never been suited to marriage in the first place, but in a society that despises spinsters intent from her late teens on making a suitable match. Any deficiencies the late Mr Davidson might have had in life had been charitably forgotten by his wife upon his death and she occasionally referred to Alec as having been a 'good man' and having had a 'good life'. These comments and the tone of their delivery conjured in Moseby's mind the image of a house-trained, neuter tom, put down in his twelfth year because of falling hair. Certainly untidiness about the house would never have been tolerated. Mrs Davidson had, in conspicuous measure, that sub-faculty known as 'taste'. She had, within a few years of Alec's passing, gone contemporary and frequent visits to Elder's in Glasgow and the considerable death policy she received saw a complete transformation in the interior decoration of her house. In the sitting-room the fireplace wall was done in simulated brick and the others in bamboo striped wallpaper. There was a chaste grey Scandinavian couch and two Cintique chairs. In the corner a splendid rubber plant and several Dufy prints and two cats from Boots of Chinese extraction.

It was one of the constant discontents of Edna's life that they could not make their two rooms and kitchen in Dempster Street look like the annexe of her mother's house. With its slight slope from front to back which caused the room doors to swing closed and the kitchen to swing open, with its pokiness and mild, thorough disrepair it remained obstinately unveneerable. For Moseby, after the sanctified dark of his parents' house, it was, with its view of the river over the roofs, a delight and a solace.

Mrs Davidson, after Edna's marriage, had taken under her formidable wing her husband's only sister, a thin, angular creature who had married the manager of a large grocer's in the town and came early home one evening unwell from a Woman's Guild to find him and one of his assistants, a woman in her thirties, with two illegitimate children, in the bath, soaping each other's privates. She had fled, shocked as much by the communal bathing as by the adultery. She had exhibited a fraught attitude to sex ever since and thought all-over washing disgusting. Moseby, who had never considered his mother-in-law a charitable woman, wondered often why she brought Agnes Davidson into her well-groomed house and watched carefully for instances of domestic sadism or even for a lesbianism to go with Mrs Davidson's large handsome appearance. So far nothing more than occasional pique at Agnes's aversion to her attempts at continental cookery was detectable but Moseby lived in hope.

There were the usual greetings on arrival. Mrs Davidson kissed her daughter and Carol and told him to go straight in. Not that he would have had it any other way. Carol liked her grandmother more than he approved of but there wasn't much could be done about that. He sat in one of the easy chairs and said hello to Agnes who was knitting something biscuit-coloured and unidentifiable. He asked her if it were a bikini. Agnes frowned at the thought and muttered her annoyance. Moseby found it curious that Agnes didn't like him. He would have thought them allies in lots of ways, with their preoccupation with sex and all. He assumed it to be Mrs Davidson's influence and the fact that he was a male with one of those nasty sticking-out things they make so much of.

They were settled in and Carol was on her grandmother's knee looking at her beads, large amber lozenges, and Edna was talking about how fast she was growing out of her clothes.

'She'll probably get her size from our side,' Mrs Davidson said.

Meaning he was dwarf-like. The man in the kit bag suddenly. Moseby had a vision of it suspended from the roof of Mrs Davidson's sitting-room, only somehow this time he was inside it. To keep himself from thinking about it he called Carol over and when she came muttered gibberish into her ear. To this she kept asking 'what', 'what' in louder and louder tones until Edna told her to be quiet. Carol complained that her daddy wouldn't tell her anything.

'Tell her something,' Edna commanded.

'What?'

'Anything to keep her amused.'

'Your mother's a sexy toot,' he said to Carol. The expected effect was achieved. Agnes's steady clicking halted and Mrs Davidson's face went stiff with disapproval. 'Your mother is one of the sexiest of known toots.'

'John. Stop saying that to the child' – Edna, annoyed.

It's not the child, it's this pair of dried up minges. Every time you say the word it's like earwigs crawling into their heads. He would have liked to test them with a few component words just to see if they would give themselves away. Just as quickly the mood left him and he relinquished Carol from his knee and tried to assume invisibility. A regular randy little dwarf he was getting. And what was this dwarf thing. Five foot eight wasn't midget size. He wished he hadn't come, that he'd stayed home and chortled over the Thirty Years War.

The conversation had moved on to local tattle. There had been a minor scandal over a doctor who had been accused of unprofessional conduct with a patient.

'I always imagined him with a bedside manner,' Edna said, a piece of untypical vulgarity that annoyed Moseby the more when he noticed Mrs Davidson smiling at it. I'd hate to try any unprofessional conduct with that he thought. One of those legs thrown over you and it's a limp for life. Someone mentioned the name Banks. It stirred something in his mind.

'Is that Doctor Banks?' he asked.

'Yes, he's got a practice in Gourock. Why?' asked Edna.

'Somebody I was talking to attended him after he got discharged from the war. The First World War that is.'

'That would be old Doctor Banks, his father,' Mrs Davidson said. 'He had a practice in Greenock when I was a girl. He married a relation of that friend of yours, Gibbons.'

'Gibbon.'

'Yes, married a Gibbon. She was his receptionist.' That must have been the girl the old man mentioned.

'Was she beautiful?' They all looked at him as though he had said something in a foreign language.

'She was a nice-looking girl,' Mrs Davidson admitted.

'You knew her didn't you, Agnes?'

'And her mother. Came from Gourock her mother. She thought she was it.'

'Who, her mother?'

'No, Martha Gibbon. She used to walk out with Donald Garvie, he got killed in the war. He was coming out to be a doctor too.'

'Is Doctor Banks her son then?'

'No.' Agnes said with something close to relish. 'She was killed in a car crash in Glasgow not long after they were married.'

'Doctor Banks married again,' Mrs Davidson added.

Moseby felt quite bleak. That this little thread back into living history should be so abruptly snapped by a frustrated old drab with the curious spite of the quick for the mort.

The old man, he didn't know, didn't know that this memory of his was gone from the land of the living. Still in his mind she opened the door and smiled and made him feel it was good to be alive despite the war and his poisoned body. He kept her, pressed between the pages of his memory, like a flower in an album. And she didn't exist any more. Death is waiting everywhere, behind conversations, under anecdotes, life is built on a great graveyard. In the midst of life we are in death.

'Pardon?'

'I said did Harry ever mention it to you, about his aunt being killed?'

'Harry. No. No he didn't.' He excused himself and went to the toilet.

Since he was there he urinated without enthusiasm or accuracy. He wiped the seat with toilet paper and sat down to dry it off completely. The bathroom had been painted yellow and black and had yellow and black linoleum tiles on the floor. Above the wash-basin was an adjustable oval mirror. He adjusted it. He could see himself sitting on the toilet seat, looking quite unreal in a normal and ordinary sort of way. He stood up and looked at the seat. It was dry. He pulled the chain and waited to see if the paper went away. Strange he should take so many pains to cover the traces of his presence. He straightened the mirror. On the glass shelf was a strange little toothbrush receptacle. It took the form of two little Dutch children sitting against a wall. The wall was hollow and on the top there were three openings into which the handles of three toothbrushes could and did fit. The whole thing was in glazed delf and the colouring was blue, a rather faded blue which seemed in some way to have stained the whole piece with a faint phthisic pallor, the brick work, the faces of the sitters which were set in small smiles, their hands and the white apron the girl was wearing. They sat there under a stunted arbour of toothbrush bristle, the green, red and yellow handles bending over slightly to give them shade. Moseby looked at the tableau and mirth, thin and unamused, leaked out of him. Two figures, Dutch, delf, sitting in the shade of a toothbrush grove, smiling their tubercular smiles. The absurdity itched at his mind, trembling on the brink of revelation. What were they saying, this mute duet. He bent closer to look into their sightless bluey eyes, their shiny mirthless smiles. 'Here we sit, look at us, we are life, almost everybody's life, the meaningless answer to the unasked question; we exist therefore we are. Look at us, here we sit.' Was that what they said, or was that what he, Moseby, said. Or was there no distinction. Was this simply something he knew and of which this ludicrous knicknack was the maieutic agent, a metaphor of his mind among all the other metaphors, the alpha and the omega of Durex and frogs, the doomed foetus in the kit bag, the belly of the town that had turned to stone. Here we sit, we can do no other.

He fled quietly, out, pausing in the hall to mark their talk, closing the front door quietly and down the stairs. At the entrance he stopped and listened but no alarm sounded of his escape.

Gourock was busy with its Sunday promenade, girls passing boys and boys passing girls, walking the rut, ignorant save for smutty words and embarrassed images of the rhythm and purpose they were committed to, that somewhere, somehow they could couple and clasp and clinging to the face of the turning world expend enough energy and illusion and seed to make a final, unwitting sense of these afternoons. He had never been very good at this ritual strolling and now removed from it by age and circumstance and awareness he moved with unease, feeling that at any moment one of them would point to him and call attention to his masquerade. For a moment or two he savoured his illicit pleasures, a transvestite in a ladies' lavatory, eyeing the silken limbs, the sudden buffets of perfume and the giggles. Girls with long exciting legs excited longings with their legs. He tore himself away and into the Ashton café. Through at the back, by the window that ran the whole length of the wall, there was an empty table. He used to come here with Edna. He had written a story about a young man and his girl who came here to watch the sunsets and the young man kept saying he didn't believe in sunsets when what he really meant was he didn't believe in love only the girl didn't know this and kept saying you had to believe in sunsets because there they were right there. It had been like the majority of the stories he had written about that time, static, wordy and concerned with relationships in moments of obscure crystallization. He ordered an orange juice and watched out of the window.

The sun was shining brightly on the water, beating it into countless nurls of light, all moving and flashing. Out on the firth a puffer made a black silhouette against the blaze. Its smoke blew forward over the bows. It reminded Moseby of a woman washing her hair, long dark strands of smoke, wet with wind. He thought of his mother, his unknown, somewhere mother. She must have had black hair. Must have washed it and had it hang dripping over her face. Maybe still did, somewhere, unknown. He should go, try to find her before she snapped off, her thread broke. Unless, as Mr Moseby had told him, his birth had ended her life. Botched beginnings and untimely ends. His eyes winced as he tried to follow the puffer against the river's savage coruscation. He lifted his eyes to the hills for soothe. They fell swiftly into the water, making a small splash of white houses on entering. He watched the hills and behind them other hills and hinted at behind again hills. Some day soon he must go over and walk in the hills, into the vast simplification of those long calm cambers, among the jade jump of frogs, foot free from the pale writhe of love's cul-de-sacs. In the hills, smaragd helgafels. Yes, soon, he thought. The puffer went on down river, blinded by its tresses.

After they got home and Carol went to bed they quarrelled. Moseby always marvelled at this capacity of Edna's for compartmentation. He had known upon returning to Mrs Davidson's, to find them at tea, that Edna was annoyed. Nor had the distant civilities that attended homecoming deluded him. But still, to be able to wait until the room was tidied, that was taking calculation a bit too far. It was her capacity for moral indignation that allowed displeasure to be sustained indefinitely. He spent a fruitless five minutes explaining about the toothbrush holder, 'you see it was this toothbrush holder . . .' until Edna said she didn't see what all the fuss was about a figurine in the bathroom. Which made him sound his hooting laugh of scorn. Figurine, he said, it's an effing monstrosity, instantly regretting the bowdlerization, not that it had done much good as Edna froze and assumed her stiff-mouthed silence, a silence which bothered Moseby not nearly as much as the resemblance to Mrs Davidson which immobility bestowed upon her features. There was nothing left but to go out. Either that or start the long siege of abject attrition. Edna started to make some coffee, pointedly preparing only one cup. Which settled it.

The evening was settling after a flagrant sunset away behind Gourock. It left lingering contusions of lilac and salmon, slowly cooling cobalt, the hills purpling down to black and at a certain pitch of dim releasing the early stars' homing light. The buildings stood around in huge geometries against the sky's blanch, great blue blanks, the chimney abstractions softened here and there by the flowering of occasional smoke. The light died with a passionate slowness, absorbed by the intense dark of the buildings, colours going first until an arrested, stilly poise held, a bright empty clarity that illuminated nothing, so thinly was it stretched. To release the tension and herald the dominion of night, the lamps came on, blossoms on the branches of the Greenock tree.

He stood leaning on the railings at the top of the steep steps leading down to Wellington Street. Halfway there was one of the old gas lamps, its candescence dry among the leaves of a tree, shining through the green phanes, like a light at the bottom of the sea. A man came out of the 'phone booth and holding the door open apologized for keeping him waiting. Moseby, not wishing to appear ungrateful, thanked him and entered, going through the pretence of dialling until the man was out of sight. Then he put it down. He didn't know anyone to phone. He didn't know anyone, period. Now Gibbon was gone. The abruptness of that departure had somewhat disconcerted him, he realized. The imperative note and Harry's unhesitating response. 'Here boy, sit,' he thought and immediately regretted his nastiness. Better than Monday nights down 'the Rowan Tree' anyway, and his resentment fixed on Edna. All her fault. She was really responsible for Gibbon going. If she'd left him more time to be with his friend. What, so they could have Monday, Wednesday and Friday down 'the Rowan Tree'. Irritated by his self-criticism he came out of the booth, only as he did recognizing that it was the one from which he had phoned that long ago morning of Carol's birth. For some reason the thought of her made him want to weep. Down the stairs the lamp exploded into a glistening crystal of green tearful light. He blinked the moist away and started back.

Edna had put the bed down and lay breathing deeply in the dark, intimating sleep. He went in to see Carol. On her back, mouth a little open, one hand outside the covers, palm up, fingers curled. He touched them, warm and slightly damp. Under the lids he could imagine her eyes, the pore of the pupil open, drinking in darkness. He put his head down and listened, through the pyjamas with the rabbits and umbrellas, to her heart budding its unnumbered flowers, systole and diastole. How many times already had it made that soft surge. He stood, bent over a moment, listening to her alive and asleep.

Edna's cup and saucer stood, washed, on the draining board. He put the kettle on. Outside the town looked empty and silent. On the stairs down from Dempster to Wellington the lamp shone through the opacity of leaf, the mantle burning with a white gaseous glow and the light tinging green, stained by the fronds into palest viridescence. Like a melancholy thought it burned through the night. For a time Moseby kept it vigil.

CHAPTER EIGHT

The candles made columns of whiteburn. Gibbon sat on the edge of the bed and Cuffee sat in the deep chair with Ruth on the arm. The candle behind her on the tallboy wet her hair softly and left her face dim. There was a candle on the dressing-table counterparted in the mirror. Another on the mantel-shelf above the gas fire. The light from them did not overlap into wholesale illumination but remained soft-edged zones in a general gloom. They had been drinking and it was late and in their various ways were tipsy. It made Gibbon agreeable and even bigger, hunched head forward listening, his hands clasped between his knees, amiable primate. Ruth felt sad and drowsy and peaceful, her hand on the back of the chair stroking Cuffee's neck from time to time while he, wound up and only gradually running down, harangued the listening Gibbon.

'You live through a series of choices, sustained by the whole of your energies until another choice modifies the first, and a third the second and so on. And this is the only salvation Harry, I tell you, you do as you choose and you accept the consequences, remorse is useless, abandon all remorse, it only hampers the true functions of humans, acting, doing deeds' – his hand slashed in emphasis – 'only fresh choices change old choices, no guilt, no agenbite. You can't control your circumstances but you can alter them, act, then act again and again and again, bearing in mind that every action has an equal and opposite reaction and that you may be called upon to pay for everything you receive.'

'That sounds very christian to me.'

'Ah, but without the metaphysics, no transcendental escape-hatch, no final choice that makes all the other choices obsolete. A world without values Harold my boy. Can you face that?' – Gibbon went to say something but Cuffee swept on – 'Except the ones you erect on Monday and dismantle at the end of the week. Human values and all that it involves. Transience. "All flesh is grass, come drink tobacco".'

Ruth thought of poppies, their quivering meninges, and looked at the long etruscan face, its arrogance and beauty and felt other than him, almost like a severing felt separate, knowing what she knew he didn't know, her sense of the world that was not his. Gratitude and dismay contested her reaction.

'What about our responsibility to other people?' Gibbon was asking.

'That's self-regulating, they're taking care of themselves, accepting the consequences of their actions, while I'm accepting the consequences of mine. I don't have to worry about them because they worry about themselves. We are all at the centre of our own universe. Fascism is everybody's personal politics.'

'You mean we are all out for ourselves?'

'We are all trying to preserve our own identities. All our conscious choices can be clearly seen as attempts to maintain and advance what we believe to be our very selves. We may think of ourselves as kind or brutal, tolerant or cynical, but we all try to enact this conception in life. We had concentric rings of identity round us, race, religion, nationality, county, town, football team, family, friends, but it's always our own arsehole we disappear up.'

'Are women different?' It was a strange question, strangely asked as though he hoped to hear they were and would be relieved if so. Cuffee laughed.

'Ask Ruth.' Gibbon looked at her and smiled. He seemed very young to her mind, or very old. Something. In the way he seemed unconcerned to project himself, sexless curiously, a quiet almost vegetable rhythm. Holding to her newly awakened awareness she followed her intuition.

'I don't know about women as a species, but I don't think everybody is like you say. I don't think Harry is.' And after a pause – 'I don't think I am.' Cuffee was delighted with this.

'You are kidding yourself, the pair of you,' taking her statement for Gibbon as seconded. 'There are as many kinds of selfishness as there are people, we are all attempting to survive. Cats only have to keep body and bone to-. gether, their psyche is unfragmented. But humans have original sin, they know they exist, they are self-conscious. So their attempt to survive moves up a notch. All I'm describing is self-preservation, it doesn't exclude generosity or kindness or heroism or anything else. The man who saves someone from the shark-infested seas, if he acted consciously, is just as selfish as the man who pushed him in for his place on the raft. It's society which distinguishes between one kind of selfishness and another, rewards and condemns. But selfishness is pure, it towers above these strictures, an icy unsullied pinnacle.'

'So anything goes.'

'The very words Harold. Never said truer.' Gibbon smiled. She could not be sure if he were sceptical or not. It was strange how he seemed permanent already, moulding himself to Cuffee's explosive well-being, the trusty squire at the black knight's side. What holy grail would this pair seek. Scarely the same one. That might well be his flaw she thought, his acceptance of other people's quests as his. Every man his own knight, a romance of our times. And what did that make her, the princess in thrall, the sleeping beauty. The aptness of her fancy made her smile and Gibbon noticing it smiled in return. She liked him at that moment very much, a little throb of response to his openness, his seeming vulnerability. Yet it was a liking without any undertone of being for a man, perhaps this was her, being so long out of circulation. But she rather thought it was him. Something he withheld or something he did not have. Whatever the reason it existed, a hiatus she would not have the opportunity to assess.

They were staying the night as someone had already moved into the studio. Gibbon went out to brush his teeth and Cuffee, undressing to his shirt, got into the bed. She sat beside him and took his hand.

'You all right Ruth?'

'Fine. You?'

'Don't like last things.'

'This isn't a last thing.'

'Of a kind it is.'

'It's not fatal though.'

'No, no. Not that. It's just, well . . .'

106

'I know, you hate it that you have to think about my feelings. After all that guff about letting people take the consequences of their own actions.'

'We try to write our own dialogue. It might not be good but it's local produce.'

'You look after yourself. And Harry.'

'Harry. Harry can look after Harry. He was regimental middle-weight champion.' She felt he was conspiring to confirm her sense of female subtlety with this remark.

'I don't mean that. He's an innocent.'

'They say you can wash your hands in molten lead if they are scrupulously and utterly clean.'

'Big deal' – and they laughed at her cynicism. Gibbon came back in the middle of it and to her surprise she felt a little put out that he should have seen them.

'Where are you going to sleep?' – and then he looked embarrassed. 'I mean, will you be comfortable?' – and this made her feel all right, his fetching politeness and the Scottish accent which sometimes in the commonplaces of speech ran into a single, long line which denied her ear for a moment.

'Between the chairs is all right.'

'Look use my sleeping bag. It'll keep you warm for sure.' He pulled it out of his bag and unrolled it, a quilted blue scabbard. The feel of it pleased her, she pressed it against herself, cool and light.

'Thanks. It feels great.' She turned her back while he got into bed and then she blew out the candles. The bag was beautiful to be in, roomy and soft and all around.

'This is a lovely sleeping bag.'

'I got it second hand.'

'Careful, you're talking of the woman I love,' Cuffee said. Ruth smiled in the dark and pulled the bag over her head. The warmth laved round her, fusing with the drink and her tiredness in a drowse of well-being. It had been an odd day. Maybe it was only that Harry Gibbon had been there. He was the first person she could recall having spent time with, other than Cuffee, that was not work or family imposed.

And Cuffee's behaviour. All going down to Knutsford and then telling them to walk about for an hour. She had thought he was trying to leave her and Gibbon together but that seemed pointless since they were going in the morning. They walked slowly through the village after Cuffee left them. It had grown warm and heavy and Market Street had linked girls, strolling in pairs past the gazes of the boys who strutted in groups, raucous and ill-at-ease somehow. There was an air of tedium and excitement in the sultry, enclosed little town, the accumulation of Sunday afternoons, the sappy thickness of the air, while all around them in the fields she had a sense of the unending fruct that was mid-May. Knutsford at that moment seemed more unbearably enclosed than Manchester, a caged bird hung in the branches of a tree. The girls exposing their pale breasts, the boys juggling in their pockets; somehow to both of them, merest acquaintances, it was an unspoken embarrassment. They walked down to the little stream that bounded the commencement of the country. She had shown him the poppies and mentioned eating one. He asked her if he might and they laughed at the oddity of it. He plucked two and they touched them like glasses. The fleshy cool pulp in her mouth, a morning taste. He agreed. They sat on a seat and looked at the rich green Cheshire land. He seemed completely at his ease she remembered, once a gnat tangled in her hair and he picked it out with his big, work-used hands. He was a carpenter he told her, his grandfather had been a carpenter and his great-grandfather before that. She had mentioned his hands as with rapt concern he disentangled the midge. His face was close and glancing up she could see the soft hair on his cheek. She could have kissed him, the way a peach, unwanted, compels savouring by its simple presence. He held the gnat on his palm watching it rearrange its filament legs and hoist its wings. Then it was off, blown gently into the air. They walked back to the house and Cuffee met them at the gate, about turning them back to the station. She asked him what had happened but he only smiled and said Mr Cuffee was in a bad mood. Then he had told her about the twelve envelopes to be posted to Miss Patricia Mullen, one a week. A child who was going to look after his cats. It all seemed unnecessarily elaborate she thought and had her doubts. Was it a maternity allowance he was paying. Or had he run up a bill or a debt. There hadn't been much time to think about it. Gibbon bought a bottle of whisky and they went to the Clarendon Hotel and filled their glasses surreptitiously while the Zenith Six drove stomp after stomp along a predestined path to orgasmic conclusion. Going back Cuffee had developed a game which he called hedge backwarding and which consisted simply of launching himself in to privets backwards from side-on run. The only once Gibbon tried it he went through the hedge entirely and destroyed a small bed of pansies, bringing her a mangled bouquet while Cuffee's laughter woke someone and they had to run while he threatened the police.

The bag drifted around her in a feathery silken warm. Harry Gibbon's sleeping bag. It was a bit like him actually, like his presence, warm yet light, diffuse almost. Sleep was claiming her in soft souses, like waves, coming over her and she submerged, receding and leaving her crystal clear and empty-minded. Into one such lucidity came, with hallucinatory brightness, a total recall.

There was a place they used to swim. The river ran over some pebbled shallows and sank itself in a long scoop into the land. The bank was green to the edge and the water ran head-high deep, slack and clear. His first leave from the army and she was but turned sixteen. They had been apart for six months. She was swollen with happiness and incredulous of the simplicity of his return and their being together. They took food and went early. The world was at work and they were free. He carried the bag and talked about the army and she skipped alongside, laughing at the stories. The river was empty and quiet. They walked down to the pool and sat on the bank. The water was clear and solid with only a slow drag of current. Up at the neck where it ran into the basin it was sinewy and rippled with opaque fibrous muscles. She smoked a cigarette with him, coughing, dizzy with the intake. He threw the stub into the water. It made a small hiss of extinction. He began to undress sitting beside her on the bank. It had been nearly a year since they had been swimming and she looked voluptuously at his body, enamelled in the lustrous light. It was unchanged, heavier in the shoulders perhaps, a little browner but still almost hipless and long of leg. On the inside of his calf the hair was rubbed away by the khaki abrasion. She stroked it and he stood up, the muscle making a hard bevel as it flexed. The dark growth on the bottom of his belly burned in her eyes and the tender droop of his penis made her want to reach out. He dived flat and shallow and twisted upstream to rest on the gravelled bar at the top of the pool. There he lay on his back, gasping at first, only partially covered by the in-flow, it breaking over his shoulders and sluicing down his chest and over his belly floating the black pubic weed and curling up at his feet. She undressed standing at the edge. The air clothed her, transparent cling and its touch engorged her nipples, swelling into pink brown tumescence. She was thrilled at their small independent assertions. He called her in. Looking down her hair seemed black as his, but glossier. She asked him if it were darker than his and dived without waiting for an answer. The water sheathed over her, cold and close, and before she surfaced his arms had found her and for a few crystal, frozen seconds they drowned in near-ness. The afternoon passed in a trance. She lost awareness of her own body in a larger identification with the river and the smooth pebbles on the banks and the sunlight, green sieved by the trees and fractured by the water and his body grafting itself to hers, over and under and through and between. She was a kind of a drum on which the day beat its wet cold warm smooth rough percussions until in the grass sweetly bruised they locked and clasped until she did not know, eyes closed, roseate petalids, whose limbs were whose or where or anything except she touched and was touched, flesh intensified its erogenous compulsion and at its centre made sense luminous, made it stay still and go on happening, a minute orifice dilating to allow all of her to pass through it into a breathless wait that broke, sobbing, full of iridescent joys and a limpid backwash of languor.

The next time sleep came it found her weakly adrift in her cocoon and bore her off in a long comber into rest.

The morning was bright and showery. They breakfasted and crept quietly downstairs listening for the landlady and out into the street. It was still early and in the low-level sun the street was bright and empty and wet. Ruth was in her dressing-gown and she kissed Cuffee and then without thought a surprised Gibbon. She felt tragic and eternal and then a little chill. She waved once and went in. Halfway up the stairs she turned and went down and opened the door again. In her absence another shower had begun and the street was aslant with topaz rain. They were not to be seen. She touched her mouth where their mouths had been so shortly since but it felt small and unkissed.

CHAPTER NINE

The ten to eight into the West Station takes the office workers and the students to Glasgow. It rushes out of the tunnel, it sucks the platform clear and goes on, gorged with smokers and readers and puzzlers, tumid colon. Moseby sat facing the engine. Opposite him a deeply unpretty girl. Behind her glasses pale blue eyes fed on the plankton of *Glasgow Herald* newsprint. Her lipstick had done that scummy thing at the corners of her mouth he hated. He searched the compartment for someone attractive. An atlas of contour maps, pitted and growthed, outcropped with bone and hair and flesh. People's faces. How could they bring those botches against other botches, lip to lip, monstrous close-ups. His too. The pallor constantly darkened by growth. The bloodless mouth. He discontinued his self-criticism. There was a girl at the other end on his side, but he couldn't see her face. Maybe behind that woman's magazine was a luminous beauty, a paradigm, a joy. Next to her was a man with the kind of nose that exposed the septum, raw-looking and with little red veins. A workman, dirty from night shift and with his eyes closed, luxuriously picked his nose. What was it about picking your nose Moseby wondered. And cleaning your ears with matches. Orificial sex. Someone was talking in that public service vehicle voice, pitched audibly low, about the modernity of German autobahns. Average speed seventy. Five lanes each side. The Central Station. No one came in. He had a session with his history lecturer this morning. Maybe he would cut the moral philosophy class in the afternoon and come back. Then there would be Edna to face. She had been bleak enough this morning. These things could take a week or so, never coming quite to a head, held in reserve to be re-introduced in the lulls before bedtime. Did they all play it this way. How did MacIndoe's wife handle him. Wasn't he supposed to be unhappily married or something like that. Not a bad lecturer though. He was going to tear him

112

off a strip about his mid-term paper. It had been a bit of a fiasco. Most of what he had said now evaded him but he had thought at the time that MacIndoe wouldn't like it much. He wondered idly how many times he had travelled like this in the mornings and allowed himself to imagine all the hours totalled and having to travel them again, all at once. The horror of it was too drab even to simulate a shudder. Port Glasgow. The working man got out and two students from the University got in. Unwilling to be separated they stood uncertainly. Moseby got up and took the seat up beside the girl he hadn't been able to see. He still couldn't see her face. He debated the wisdom of trying to get to sleep. It meant waking up with that taste of cinders and sore eyes. But it might avoid having to live through the next forty minutes. Woodhall. A fat man looked in wistfully at the nominal vacancy and passed on. Thank God for small mercies Moseby thought, except if he'd been on the other side he'd have had to crush up against the masked beauty. Forty minutes of distant proximity, thinking sweaty thoughts with his leg. The fat man went past again looking rather desperate. Suddenly Moseby was depressed by his obese plight. This allowed other, more personal depressions, to expand. Primarily it was Sunday. In many ways Sunday had been quite a day. Three more like that and he'd be an old man. Seemed further away than yesterday. At least two years away. Two light years. Heavy days and light years. He remembered something from the *Reader's Digest* about how at the centre of the sun a cubic inch weighed about a million tons it was so intensely concentrated. Langbank stretched its long shelves of silt out to the distant channel. As he looked a seagull rose, white flight reach animate against the tedious sand. It excited him with its brevity and the starkness of the image. Flight. Escape. Freedom. From what. 'I think the world is falling down, falling down around us. Not as buildings or bombs or men fall, but as sea shore castles succumb to the inexorable encroachments of the tide.' Was it. How could you tell if it was or not. Perhaps because when you saw seagulls taking off you thought thoughts like that. At this point the train would go on for ever and he could suspend the necessity for such speculation. He could go on just sitting here, like that pair under their toothbrush tree. His involuntary glance up made him smile. They didn't have such a bad time of it after all. Teach me Lord to sit still. Was that what he wanted. Bishopton and the girl glanced up from her magazine. Her ordinariness was staggering. She had a nose above her mouth. Moseby felt perversely pleased with this development. Showed the world to be of trustworthy consistency. What would he have done if she had been beautiful, if in her eyes there was that translucence that let her soul shine forth, one of those private faces in public places, one of the ones to whom you can say thou. What would you do Moseby. Would you fall in love with her, would you pursue her, would you leave Edna and Carol, write her poems. Or would you let her go out of the carriage and never see her again. Who wants to fall in love. Loving somebody is hard enough without metaphysics getting into it. Of course you'd let her go he told himself. Only it would always be with the feeling that he had shirked something. That he had sat still. In the way he had done about his mother. He hadn't ever really believed Mr Moseby's Victorian melodrama of an explanation. So why not. Because he was afraid she might not be the tragic beauty he longed for, the mother mistress of his desiring. Because she might by her mundane presence place him back among all these other travellers, ordinary as Monday. His mind ached with the frictive rub, he could feel himself unravelling, a bunch of raw fibres. Driven to inertia he came up with a bizarre, apposite recollection. A photo someone had shown him in the I.B.M. It had been taken in the desert during the war. It was a man's leg, wearing a boot and puttees, blown off at the knee. It looked quite unreal and yet unmistakably what it was. A leg lying on the sand. A leg someone used to run on. As he tried to think why this had come back to him he remembered that it looked as though it were stuffed with wool, and bursting out at the end. No blood, no mess, just this dark fibrous bunch at the severed end. It had made him think that perhaps people were not of flesh and blood but of some dry stringy packing. Paisley, and the girl went off. It brought up the question of love again. He really wasn't in any position to talk about love.

114

Other than Edna there had ever only been one woman, the girl in Glasgow, Cathie Marshall her name wasn't it. That hadn't been love. He had been a self-obsessed youth of nineteen and more than anyone he had ever known before or since she had radiated a kind of hopelessness. In the full gloom of her youth as he had said to her in a quarrel. He had been a nasty little bastard when he wanted to be. So had he ever been in love. If you didn't count his attempt to be what Edna thought a good husband should be. Not even with his mother. Poor little Johnny Moseby. Nobody loves him. His sneer mingled with self-pity produced an unpleasant flavour, vinegary custard. The train rattled in over the bridge, the Clyde like dull pewter, supporting ships and the fluid reflections of cranes. The carriage emptied and he was the last to rise. He let the flow take him out into Gordon Street.

He walked round on to Renfield Street to wait for a tram. There was a queue and a lot of traffic. He stood at the end and thought about MacIndoe without great pleasure. Someone said good morning. He looked round. A girl with a university scarf and black stockings. He knew from previous telling who was having sex with her but it eluded him just then. He had a brief impulse to ask. Excuse me but who is getting his end away with you. Fine chap. Know his condom company. Have you heard they puncture one in every gross. British sense of fair play. Yes, it is disconcerting. Never use them myself. The Irish method every time for me. Place a jaffa orange in the left armpit, right if she's Protestant, and start pressing as soon as you introduce old fagan. When the juice runs down your flank, withdraw. If you squeeze the pips out it's too late. Does it work. Well look at Ireland.

She asked him something about Spinoza.

'Pardon?'

'Were you at the Spinoza lecture?' Moseby said yes. 'Didn't you think that was rather a good analogy about Spinoza's philosophy being an inverted pyramid?' An inverted pyramid. Your head's an inverted pyramid you silly cow. Monday fucking morning.

'Oh he was no mug Spinoza wasn't. Inventor of the Dutch

115

cap wasn't he?' The girl evidently didn't think so. 'Spinoza,' she said unbelievingly.

'Yes. Got him into trouble with the church. You ever see any photos of him and he's wearing one of those little skull caps. That's what gave him the idea. Saw it sitting there one day on his desk' – Moseby snapped his fingers in mimic inspiration – 'coitus ergo cum.' The girl looked unconvinced. An Anniesland tram came up. Moseby gave her a smile and made for it. She called out it was the wrong tram. He swung on as it passed and went upstairs. So I'll be late he said to his face that bulged in the stair mirror.

Somebody got out of the front seat up in the cupola. Moseby sat down. The warmth of the leather soothed him. He sat back and put the briefcase on the floor. The tram jolted and rolled and made noises. The conductor took his fivepence and ejected a ticket. He folded it into a spill and poked it between his teeth. Saliva softened it and made the paper pulpy. He stopped poking his teeth and chewed the ticket. Looking out he felt relaxed. The tram staggered on. The heat from someone else's buttocks, fivepence worth of jolting, rolling, noisy comfort. He felt he could sit on for ever. On the streets below everyone moved to work. There were hundreds and hundreds of them, all walking and turning corners and passing one another. He had never seen them so clearly before. The tram carried him high in erratic flight and looking down, slack with comfort, he saw them. They walked and swung their arms, different arms from legs, right arm, left leg and then left arm right leg and then the same over again. This way they proceeded. Some had umbrellas, the girls and women had bags and walked more quickly it appeared, their pale legs flickered as they walked. They all walked quickly though, passing each other and turning corners and tapping their umbrellas and swinging their bags. The streets were full of them. They scurried. Out of the tram window all that was to be seen was this scurrying, filled with purpose and intent. The figures moving and the grey vertical buildings and the sky pasted in a strip along the roofs. There were many more than he could count. There were many more than he wanted to think of counting. As he looked at them they looked quite unreal yet unmistakably what they were, people going to work. There were a great many of them. He wished the tram would go on for ever and he would sit there and later there would be no people and no buildings and the sky would tear itself free from the roofs and float up and up until it got blue.

MacIndoe was one of the younger lecturers. He was in his early thirties with scant frizzy hair and a short compensatory beard. He had married one of his students in his third year of lecturing and she had borne him five children in the next eight, becoming in the process a middle-aged, middle-class slattern of twenty-nine. MacIndoe was currently involved with a physical training instructress at Jordanhill. He was sitting looking out of his window when Moseby arrived. Clenching and unclenching his teeth on the stem of a pipe.

'I wouldn't say you were exactly early,' he remarked without looking round. He had a number of little mannerisms most of which Moseby could trace to the cinema. This was his weary policeman, tired D.A. bit.

'No I wouldn't say I was early either. I'm sorry.'

'You're rather a casual chap altogether' – still watching what Moseby knew to be a remarkably dull set of windows.

'Nobody's perfect Mr MacIndoe.'

'You stole that line from "Some like it hot" ' – swivelling round.

'I didn't see "Some like it hot",' Moseby lied contrarily.

'Excellent example of Wilder's amorality. He's the right man to make the definitive film about poofs. And he has something that's very rare nowadays. A genuine sense of vulgarity.' He liked doing this, MacIndoe, so that when he started on about history he had established himself as being of this age. Moseby didn't dislike MacIndoe. He didn't care about him. He knew no one he cared less about, for whom his feelings were so totally unengaged. He had no objection to the man posing as a contemporary, for all Moseby knew he might even be a contemporary.

'My mid-term paper,' he said. MacIndoe didn't like that.

'I scarcely feel it behoves you to come late and then act as though your time were of the essence.' After this he

117

swivelled away again. Moseby waited for an analysis of Wilder's contribution to the comédie noire. Instead Mac-Indoe spoke of the paper.

'Yes, your mid-term paper. Glanced over it again last night.' Psychiatrist dealing with evasive megalomaniac. 'Curious item I must say.' A pause during which Moseby noted the shape of MacIndoe's skull, silhouetted against the window through the meagre curlings of his hair. 'Tell me Moseby, what do you think history is?' and turned purposefully to face him, secret service chief about to send untried agent into Albania. Moseby returned the gaze earnestly. What did he think history was. Not an epigram in sight.

'I think it's a lot of writings by men who didn't live at the time.'

'Aren't we being a little too undergraduate now?'

'Isn't that what I said in my paper?'

'At much greater length.'

'I thought it was standard length.'

'Perhaps it was the dearth of any significant content which made it seem so long.' Moseby didn't think of Mac-Indoe as being a caustic individual. Perhaps his wife was pregnant again.

'I thought there was a reasonable content.'

'Pray summarize.' Now only a balloon would say something like 'pray summarize', Moseby thought.

'Like I said, I think history consists of writings by men who didn't live at the time. That we can forget about truth, and in some cases even fact, and prepare to be influenced by the skill and sensibility of the writer.'

'History is dead, long live the historian.' Moseby checked the features before him for some hint of the comic but Mac-Indoe awaited reaction to this shaft with utter gravity.

'That's one way of putting it,' he said, and as he did saw that it was.

'Do you really think this is a sufficiently serious frame of mind in which to study history?'

'Well I think it's an honest frame of mind. I mean nobody reads history as though it really happened.'

'I find that a most ludicrous statement from someone of your intelligence.'

'All right then, I don't think anyone reading history cares whether it really happened or not. All they want is to be able to detect patterns and meanings and the elements of life that preoccupy them. We all read history to convince ourselves that we are right. And we read, not history, but writings about history.'

'So history as a study has no objective value?'

'I don't understand that question.'

'The fact that history is about what actually happened doesn't convince you that it is different in kind from say an historical novel?'

'Well I'm not sure history is about what actually happened, not any more than a novel, historical or non-historical, is about what actually happened.'

'Don't you think we should be under the English department?'

'That's where we are as far as I am concerned.'

'You come close to absurdity there I feel.'

'No, now look, does it matter very much that Green was misinformed about the feudal system in England, that he can be proved wrong on dozens of points of interpretation or opinion. Compared to the narrative power he achieves does this matter?'

'Of course it matters. We must hope that someone comes along with Green's literary gifts and a more painstaking sense of research, otherwise we will be fed palatable pieces of false information.'

'But it doesn't matter, short of deliberate falsification. I mean either you're Cavalier or Roundhead, Royalist or Parliamentarian. You can't be in two minds about whether you're pro-Cromwell or pro-Charles.'

'But history is not a cricket match. You don't take historical sides.'

'Of course you do, or else it's totally meaningless. If you can remain detached then either the writer is a dud or the character is without interest. And there is no character without interest.'

'So to discover what actually happened, and why it actually happened is of no importance?'

'Yes, but it is only the beginning. There is a difference

between writing history and reading it. What someone else has produced as an absolute I will treat as a relative. I will come along and experience his work with my own built-in preconceptions and proclivities, and I will see what I want to see. Historians provide you with excellently documented fiction.'

MacIndoe appeared to find this last more than he could take. He swung round to the window again and Moseby sat wondering if the man was annoyed or merely exasperated. When he spoke however there was neither apparent.

'I find it difficult to take you seriously Moseby, yet I know that you are not a stupid person so I can only assume that what you say makes sense to you, that in some way or other history for you is a long cast-of-thousands epic, out of which you choose heroes and villains and allocate blame and credit. I find this quite distressingly adolescent I must say and while it may not prevent you from managing a creditable pass in the subject, I do not like to see anyone treating a noble branch of human activity as their kaleidoscope, to be adjusted until a pleasing design shows up. I think you ought to develop a little self-discipline.' Well now thought Moseby, that's you shot down in flames. He thought it a little unfair of MacIndoe to take quite that portentous tone but he could see the man was sincere and not simply intent upon ticking him off. And he could see also just how dead end his attitude was from a certain standpoint. He couldn't think of anything to say so he stayed silent. MacIndoe seemed engaged in thought but after a moment he said:

'You're married aren't you?'

'Yes.'

'Kids?'

'I have a daughter.'

'Would you say you were happily married?' – and he shot over a glance to see how Moseby was taking this.

'Yes, I would say I was happily married,' again the glance.

'Are you happy, other than being happily married?'

'Not entirely.'

'Do you ever go after other women?' No glance this time.

120

'No.'

'Why?'

'No opportunity I suppose.'

'It's not moral grounds then?' – and he spun himself around looking at Moseby in passing.

'Not really. Like I say, no opportunity.'

'Surely there are plenty of eligible girls at the university?'

'Well I travel back to Greenock each night. I don't want some bit of grope and tickle in the Cosmo.' Once more he went round.

'Are you a Christian?'

'No.'

'I am' – timed to coincide with his coming full in front of Moseby. You phoney bastard he thought. 'Does that surprise you?'

'No.'

'I'm C. of E. Very high church. Wonderful liturgy. Means a lot to me being church. It's about all I have left. That and history. You may appreciate how I feel when I meet your kind of attitude. I find it almost sacrilegious. Did you go through all that to get at me about history he thought. You pitiful, devious little man.

'My paper wasn't directed against the foundations of your life,' he said as flatly as possible. MacIndoe seemed upset by this.

'No, of course, I didn't mean anything by that. It's just, well, I was rather disappointed when I read your paper. I had always looked on you as rather an ally.' What did that mean Moseby wondered. 'I'm not a person with many allies.' Then he changed his tone, if not his manner. 'I'd like you to come to dinner with us. I mean lunch-dinner, not evening dinner. Give your insides a rest from that refectory muck. Will you? My wife would be pleased.' Moseby said he'd be pleased to accept and without saying anything further about it MacIndoe stood up. Moseby rose and was confronted by the lecturer's hand, held out with a jerky unpremeditated-looking movement. He shook it and with MacIndoe saying he'd see him in lecture tomorrow, left, trying to decide whether he had been given the Freemason's handshake or not.

He walked slowly towards the refectory thinking it all over but at the door the sweet sodden smell of mass cooking met him. It made up his mind without a moment's indecision. He went back to the cloakroom and took out his briefcase. As he was leaving the University he saw MacIndoe going through the close. He had put on his gown and going through the cloisters looked strangely medieval and among the great squat pillars a menaced figure. Moseby felt guilty at the sight of him and broke into a run for a bus he had no hope of catching.

CHAPTER TEN

A long swing of road macadamed purple blue. Verge grasses blowing in the windy wakes. Cuffee denim-legged in a black shirt thumbing. Gibbon asquat, shading his eyes under the rake of his hat. Sun adrift on the sky, slow splendid voyager through cloud islands. Gibbon cooling his gaze in the eavebrim. Cuffee striking a long mark on the ground with his shadow. Sun goes galleon among the blendipeligoes. The indigo road ashimmy with heat and over all the blue oceanic loft where solar sailor the sun on full spate of midday its golden argosy goes.

The cars come beetling up and rip past to fade away down the road. Cuffee thumbs only single men in cars, leaving women drivers and couples and lorries to pass unheeded. Gibbon watches into the grass where insects pursue small segments of their lives. He finds a ladybird, orange with black polks, and lets it make its mazy way around his hand, through the columns of his fingers and into the hollow of his palm. Holding his hand close to his face he can see it come suddenly into sight, bright little traveller. The size of his hand close to, turning on the wrist to afford him glimpses, is enormous. It is the ladybird's whole landscape, a hand that picked things up and worked and clenched is now a context, a climate made beautiful by the gaudy bug. Seen from where Cuffee stands thumbing he seems engrossed in some leisurely process of self-hypnosis, intent upon his turning hand.

Cuffee watches up the road, frowning in the glare, spotting his vehicle from afar and singling it out with a terse thumb. As they pass he looks away across the fields to where distant Manchester lours the sky with smoke. Once, at a man who shakes his head as though insulted, he turns to shout abuse, breaking Gibbon's reverie.

'What's a good name for a ladybird?'

'Is it a male ladybird or a female ladybird?' Gibbon seemed not to have considered such a complication. Cuffee came over to inspect it. 'Must be a female. Look at the gear it's got on.' Gibbon nodded in agreement.

'What's a good name?' But Cuffee was concentrating on a Morris 1000.

'Think Ruth would mind if we called it after her?' The Morris ran past then braked fiercely, stopping about fifty yards on.

'Lucky he's not on an aircraft carrier, eh?' Cuffee said to no one, running up.

After a moment he waved to Gibbon who rose and blew the ladybird gently. It uncased its wings and made flight across the road.

'Not much point in taking a ladybird called Ruth to London is there?'

'He's going to Hereford. Thought we might cut over to Tenby for a swim.'

'Fine.'

They moved south through the passive, richening land, the early summer land where green quickenings everywhere masked the brown throb of the earth, in eager spiring the corn quilled and the trees rooted to bunting forth leaf and black and brown mapped cows made munch, summer a silkiness in the air, a thrum of growth, and with them at its own royal rate the sun rode coronation.

At Hereford they ate cold meat and cheese and pickles and drank iced lager in a cool stone basement room where the woman who served them had great white arms, plump as fishes, in a sleeveless black blouse that showed her brassiere straining massively at its twin task. Cuffee couldn't keep from watching and the woman became rather annoyed but Gibbon left her five shillings as an apology.

'Did you see them Harry?' upon leaving. 'Oh breasts like that have a life of their own, you should need a licence for them. They're like, ah like animals, like blind night creatures. Oh I love them Harry I love them. Once when I was in the army we were going to firing camp. Remember, Tonfannau, in a Matador. The one that broke down and we went into the orchard. Yes, well we were passing through this village and there was a woman cleaning a window, she was stretching up to clean the top and I couldn't see her face but as she stretched up her breasts moved, just as if they were alive and I wanted to shout and laugh because I felt all those things about beauty and love. Just from that. Just from that moment. All the good things are like that. They just happen. It's letting them happen's the trick. And not trying to hold on to them. "All life is smoke, come drink tobacco".' Three girls passed, summer dressed, splotched with flowers, mysterious magical creatures, silk-legged, lipsticked, turning to look at Cuffee and Gibbon and converging in a spray of laughter.

'Oh those little red twat flowers blooming in the thickets.' Gibbon looked at Cuffee curiously his face deliberating some issue.

'Funny you should say that—' but Cuffee let out a roar of laughter and wrapped his free arm round Gibbon's neck.

'Oh Harry you are a droll, serious bastard.'

'No but—' only Cuffee's laughter went on, loud and long, causing people to look and Gibbon finally, without comprehension, to join in, until the laughter itself generated its reason and went on and on, raucous in Hereford's sedate streets.

Westward from Hereford the lush vale of Evesham rolls out and up into the great billowing bares of the Breconshire plateau where the sheep look wild and swift and there is a keen to the air. They got the back of a truck for most of the stretch and lay couched on grain sacks looking up at the unbounded blue pend, coming on their journey across occasional cumula, massy floaters. Gibbon remembered the cathedral at Brecon from a two week posting and they went round to see it, leaving their bags under a tombstone outside. It swallowed them whole; leviathan, silent utterance of praise, holy with hush, cool with stone. Into their horizontal of air and sun, of blood and flesh a vertical moment, cross purposed. Their footsteps sounded dropped in wells, their voices awed low. They came out and sat a moment on the tombstone.

'Well,' said Cuffee, 'they certainly know how to make you feel little.'

'I had a grand-uncle, I never met him, he died before I was born. He was a preacher. Wrote sermons. Reminds me of in there. I would have liked to meet him. He said something that made me think. He used to go away on these preaching trips, like a tramp, no money or anything, and when they asked him why he was always going off he said "if you don't go you can't come back" ' – and Gibbon looked at Cuffee to see how he took this.

'If you go far enough you don't have to come back,' he said.

A farmer took them down to Carmarthen, driving a Land Rover with a florid exhibition of wheel and gear manipulation. Once he halted and got out, beckoning them to follow. They went into a big field that sloped away down from the road and that was marshy at the bottom. He plucked a small clover-like plant and showed it to them, saying it made a good poultice for burrowing ticks if the heads were left in. He sent Gibbon to one side of the field and Cuffee to the other. Then he started picking. They looked at each other for a moment and then at the farmer, his shiny leather-patched arse in the air then began to tiptoe up the field, breaking into a run and smothering their laughter in the grass at the top. Cuffee thumbed a clergyman in an Anglia and they got their bags out of the Land Rover and got in. The farmer was still bent to his task as they went on.

A small, dexterous river made its way down the valley, running over pebble beds and plump sandbanks, carving, curving, cool and clear through the passive land, frothing occasionally over changes of level. The clergyman talked to Gibbon about Brecon Cathedral and Cuffee watched out at the passing country, the smooth lush land, stitched by dry dyke-ing and ringed with sheep folds. The sun, though lower, still shone undimmed, sparkling on the river and among the pebbles. The great browsing clouds, herded by the wind across the endless pastures of blue. Once, down through some alders and edge growth, a heron stood its sentry, slatey waiter. Cuffee smiled at the chance glimpse.

They were in Carmarthen by seven and on the road outside the town an army officer going to Manorbier picked them up. He was young and clean-cut and wore his cap raffishly forward. He called them chaps and drove very fast. Around them millioning spores of dusk swoll and

126

sworled and his headlamps tore through the country lanes discovering a sudden, flashing past world, while the fluttering things of the night were transfixed and sucked up the light tubes to extinguish themselves on the windscreen. He took them through to Tenby, refused a drink and wished them a good holiday. They had a fish supper and then made their way down to the shore.

On the dunes behind the beach they bedded down, among the coarse tall grasses that the sand dryly nurtured. The sky was high hung with star lights, the sea repeatedly kissed the prone naked curve of the shore, kissed and hissed satisfaction and kissed again. The grasses allowed the small wind, fraught with salt, susurrous among them and in their bags they slept while the moon, silver meniscus, crossed the night.

They swam next day from a stone spit, diving into ten feet of clear bright water. The sun gained height and warmth. Gibbon was a slow ponderous swimmer, unused to the open sea, moving himself deliberately through the water, content most to float or tread and watch Cuffee's thrusting overarm. After a meal in Tenby they walked back along the sands and up on to the headland. On Caldy the monks moved small and black and beyond them Carmarthen Bay went to the edge of their eyes and smokily, beyond. They lay on the short sward and looked out at the great prairie of water. The grass smelled of salt.

'Moseby came here on his honeymoon.'

'Did he. How long has he been married?'

'About five years nearly.'

'What's she like?'

'She's all right. Bit sort of, I don't know, middle class I suppose.'

'It's a terrible crime I agree.'

'I don't mean that. Moseby's middle class too. By upbringing anyway. His foster parents, I told you he was adopted didn't I—' Cuffee nodded— 'they were always well to do. Mr Moseby owned a couple of shops. He's retired now. They live on Arran.'

'How did he get on with them?'

127

'Don't think very well. Never says much about them. I've only seen them once, at the wedding.'

'You were at the wedding?'

'I was the best man. Gave him a clock, everything, evening dress, the "Lorne", the works.'

'How's he liking it?'

'Hard to tell, he's got a great daughter. Oh, he's all right I think—' Then stopped.

'Better him than me,' said Cuffee and threw a stone hard out to sea. Its long drooping arc failed to clear the cliffs and bounced down among the rocks. Gibbon threw one and it reached the water close to the edge where a riding gull took offence and rose, speeding low over the water out towards the island.

In the evening they got drunk, slowly and steadily, and had a late meal in a small restaurant overlooking the harbour. Small boats wagged their lamped masts, the night was awash with the liquid vocables of sea shore, and Gibbon listened, gravely drunk as Cuffee talked, the long face dark on the side to the window, a renaissance face, made for histrionics its owner never used, always, even when excited, a calm almost bleak face, talking only with his mouth, the eyes looking constantly into Gibbon's, holding him in spell.

'You know incest has its problems Harry. I mean you've got to be pure. You know that you can let molten lead run all over your hands if they're quite completely clean. Did you know that? True. It's like that with incest. You have to be pure, you can't be thinking dirty things, you can't think about other women when you're doing it. You have to be very very pure.' Gibbon believed him. 'It wasn't complicated before I went to the army. But it got complicated then all right. I suppose I didn't really think she existed when I wasn't there, you know, like solipsism. Only when I went back after six months she'd grown up a bit, changed, even her body had changed, we went swimming, and I knew she did exist, even when I was somewhere else. That changed a lot of things. One thing was I fell in love with her, and that was the beginning of the end. You know what love is Harry, do you, it's when you see that somebody is unattainable, not just you can't have sex with

128

them or marriage, but when you see they're another separate person, that's love, that's why I fell in love with Ruth. It was all there was left for me to do. Wasn't enough though. But love isn't.'

Gibbon frowned in concentration. By some personal association Cuffee went on as though in logical sequence. 'I mean we had good lifts coming down but you know how it can be, when you get stuck. You know that feeling when the light's going and you're on a bit of dual carriageway and they're going past like the clappers and you're standing up there thumbing. Thumbing. And you really want to be down praying or waving your arms but instead you just turn your thumb over, and it's getting to be night and you're frightened, just to be out with nowhere to sleep and no money and you know those bastards in the cars don't care and the night doesn't care, nobody cares except you, and you think about everything and it doesn't seem much use. That's where you learn the score, on the verge, you learn that all you can say is "all right, fuck the lot of you, I'll survive", and when a car stops you get in and say thanks and smoke his fags and listen to his rotten chaff until it's time for you to get out again and then if you haven't learned the lesson you get a chance to do it all over again. And if you don't learn it and know you'll survive, well then you're just an animal, just a poor brute.' Gibbon looked out of the window and nodded.

'I wish now I'd brought that ladybird,' he said.

Going back to their beds the wind was blowing the sand in great writhing serpents over the empty beach, swirling around their feet, hissing a grainy wrath and filling their shoes with sand. They walked apart, Gibbon behind and nearer the sea, Cuffee ahead looking away along the deserted shore.

They woke in the morning to a hagger of rain and a sea mist. Tenby was damp and grey and after breakfast in a small workman's café they started back towards Carmarthen. It was a slow trip in. Short lifts and long waits. They bypassed Swansea but had to walk through Newport and spent some time remembering their old army haunts, hanging about till the pubs opened and having a drink in the

'Tudor', pouring the last mouthful of their beer into the tropical fish tank when the barman wasn't looking in memory of Bob Norman who had on his demob done likewise with a full pint, reflecting mournfully that it was 'useless trying to drown one's sorrows because the bastards could swim', which was more than could be said for the tropical fish afterwards.

The evening had grown mild and pleasant by the time they reached Chepstow and after a meal they decided to spend the night. The river flowed muddily through and they sat watching it for a time while the local youth dallied and sallied along the banks. Heavy lorries came down the steep hill into the town and across the bridge, swinging left and up the gradient out of the valley, their lights catching the river and then raking across the wooded rise on the other side. It began to turn chill and they moved off to the old churchyard they had noted. It was thickly grassed and they found a long box vault and settled down behind it, their bags under their heads. Cuffee lit a cigarette. The church made a dim shape against the sky, a lopsily hung moon rind showed the canescence of past and future life and in the clear sky the stars clustered. In the grass and in the air innumerable creatures frayed the still with their small abrasive lives, a stridulant crust upon the mute earth. They lay in their sleeping bags, Cuffee on his back, smoking, the cigarette end casting a cosmetic of soft red on his face as he inhaled. Gibbon cradled his jaw on his elbow, a drum beat of blood in his head. Their warmths reached through and joined them. Above Cuffee's looking up face, far far above, stars, up through an immensity of up to the stars, solitaires. The world wheeled steadily. The stars seemed to be drooping down to earth, without growing larger they seemed to plummet down onto their watching eyes, or else their minds were drawn out and up into those stellar heights.

The roaring of the lorries was growing dim when boots on gravel, the poking white stick of a torch, movements among the tombstones and then the light on their faces.

'What are you doing there?' Cuffee raised himself on to an elbow.

'We're the three wise men, the other one's away for a piss.'

The police station had descriptions of stolen jewellery, of a boy run away from a remand home and a photograph in colour of a Colorado beetle. There was also a pamphlet about foot and mouth disease. The constable who had brought them in was a tall, close-eyed man with the mental dexterity of a windmill. He had informed the man on the desk of the circumstances. This young man had a spare grey face and a clipped dry manner.

'What have you to say then?' Gibbon was reading the foot and mouth pamphlet and indicated that Cuffee was to speak for him.

'Nothing.'

'You refuse to explain your presence on private property?'

'What private property?'

'The churchyard is private property.'

'Who does it belong to?'

'The church.'

'Well I'm C. of E.'

'Don't try to be funny with me chum. If you get funny with me I can get funny with you mighty quick.' Gibbon had a good look at the Colorado beetle.

'Have you got any pictures of ladybirds?' he asked, coming over to the desk.

'What have you got to say for yourself?' he was asked.

'I suppose I must be guilty, I'm Presbyterian,' Gibbon said, smiling.

'Right George, check the wanted descriptions. We've got a couple of smarties here. Real smarties.' George departed.

'You're Peter Cuffee, and you're from Manchester. Ever been in trouble before?'

'No.'

'What do you do?'

'I was a student.'

'What did you study?'

'Art.'

'Oh an art student.' He noted Cuffee's hair and understood much.

'And you're from Scotland?'

131

'That's right.'

'Any previous convictions?'

'No.'

'Any means of identification?' Gibbon got out his wallet from the bottom of the bag. The young constable checked through it and took out the money. 'How much is here?'

'Forty pounds or so.'

'How did you come by this?'

'Work.'

'What are you?'

'A carpenter.'

'Where's yours?' to Cuffee.

'I haven't got one.'

'Where's your money?'

'That's his too,' Gibbon put in. The policeman looked from one to the other.

'He your fancy boy?' Gibbon looked at him a moment and without turning his gaze, said to Cuffee,

'Did you hear about how they were unloading cattle at Princes Pier and one of the cows took fright and jumped into the water and this young constable threw it a lifebelt—'

'No I didn't hear about that. What happened?'

'They were unloading these cattle at Princes Pier and this cow took fright and jumped into the water and there was this bright young constable and he threw the beast a lifebelt.' George came out of the other office and shook his head.

'Nothing in there Tom.' There was a silence and then the policeman behind the desk flicked the wallet and it fell on the floor at Gibbon's feet. Before he could pick it up Cuffee caught his arm.

'Right you two, get going, and get through Chepstow or I'll book you for loitering with intent.'

'You knocked the wallet on the floor,' Cuffee said.

'You heard me, get moving.'

'You knocked the wallet on the floor.'

'Well pick it up.'

'I didn't knock it on the floor.' The other policeman picked it up and gave it to Gibbon who put it back in the bag.

'Come on lads, I'll see if I can get you a lift.'

'Good night Tommy,' Cuffee said but received no reply. They went out and down the street. The policeman wanted to stop a lorry for them but they wouldn't let him and went on and over the bridge. Just as the lights of the town were cut off by trees, a lorry, running fast and high loaded, braked for them. They climbed up into the noisy warm cockpit. The driver said he was going into London through Oxford. Cuffee sat on the engine and Gibbon in the seat. In the lights of an oncoming lorry they looked at each other and smiled.

They swung on through the night, drifting in and out of sleep with the country slipping blackly by on either side of the headlights, the steady roar of the engine punctuated by the ripping noise of lorries going in the opposite direction. On the downhills he switched off the engine and let her run under momentum, the silence exhilarating, the tyres thrumming and the cabin high and remote above the road. Through the long burrow of the night they went, eastwards to the sun.

CHAPTER ELEVEN

The room was small and had a lot of books and several prints. There was a table lamp and two wall lights and five people. They were drinking beer from cups. One of them, wearing a green cord jacket and drinking from a blue hooped mug was talking about the problems the serious writer faced in society today. He said alienation. He said alienation several times. His beard was a different colour from his hair. He leaned on the mantelpiece as he talked. The other two men in the room listened and nodded and the girl with the long straight hair and the trousers said 'yes exactly' now and then. Ruth sat in a wicker chair and looked out of the window. Its blackness resisted the attempt and showed her herself in returned scrutiny. She had only in the past few minutes discovered the depth of her boredom, a boredom that went beyond the people present and their conversation, but concerned the whole day as she had spent it and the remnant as she expected to.

Wednesday was her half day and she had gone back and washed some clothes. Nothing in the pictures seemed remotely interesting, so she read for a time, a bright unfunny book with a sneering syntax and an anti-hero of monstrous unimportance. In an effort to escape its aridities she took herself to the news theatre where for a time, immured in the bestialities of the Three Stooges and then wooed by a fetching Laurel and Hardy, she managed to relax. Four pastelled, tediously drawn cartoons however followed and made her ache with disinterest. She came out and went into a pub she had been to once with Peter. The long-haired girl was there and Ruth knew her faintly from the library. She had been with the others and after closing had suggested they went back to David's place for a drink. He was now approaching her with a brown ale flagon and hairy smile. The others were talking about Ingmar Bergman.

'Some beer.'

'Thank you.' He poured rapidly, from some height, and the ale foamed.

'You seem very abstracted.'

'Do I, I'm sorry. I was thinking about something.'

'Not about what we were talking about,' the young man said and was forced to notice the construction as it hung awkwardly between them until brown ale overflowed through the foam and ran over his fingers. He apologized and cut the head off with the edge of his palm and found himself with froth on his hand. After a pause he somewhat reluctantly wiped it on his green cord jacket where it clung and slowly diminished.

'You weren't thinking on what we were talking about,' he said as a second service. Ruth said she hadn't been, that she had been thinking about something else. A pause swelled into a silence. Ruth felt uncomfortable and said she had been thinking about her brother.

'Oh yes, your brother is Peter Cuffee isn't he? I met him at a couple of parties.'

'Yes he was at Art School.'

'Oh, has he left?'

'Yes. Last week.'

'Oh I didn't know that. I gather he was quite a character.' Ruth offered no comment to this assessment. 'You know Tessa very well?'

'No, not really. I've just seen her in the library.'

'Have you read any of her stuff?'

'Stuff. No. I don't really know her.'

'Her poetry—' his voice dropped and in counterbalance his head came closer. Ruth had an unimpeded view of his nose. She looked into the beard. '—bloody marvellous some of it is. She's got a fantastic sense of language for a girl of her age and background. She comes from Hanley you know and the thing that really strikes you is the brightness of her sounds, her vowel sounds, there's a—' he cast for his word '—a hallucinatory quality about some of it, rather like a female synthesis of Coleridge and Dylan Thomas, if you can imagine that.' Ruth made no attempt to achieve any such comprehension.

'Are you fond of poetry?' When she thought about it she didn't think she was. Would it sound rude to say so, or affected.

'I don't understand it,' she said, 'not much of it. And the stuff I do understand I've thought better myself.' That didn't sound very right either.

'Who do you like then? Eliot? Pound? The Beats? Do you like Thomas?' For no reason she could imagine she thought of the doubting disciple. She smiled at the incongruity.

'I've never read him.'

'I'll lend you a copy, you must read "Fern Hill"; it's a fantastic poem. Bloody marvellous.'

'I don't read much.'

'Well that's it then, you must. What do you want of a poem, what you have to ask yourself firstly. Then when you know what you want of it you can look for that kind of poet. What do you want of a poem?' Ruth tried to think what she wanted of a poem. That it leave her alone she thought. Then she remembered the line from the psalm.

'I want it to say my mind.' The young man wasn't quite with it.

'Say your mind. Speak your mind.' It wasn't the same, or was it.

'Like some things do—' she was thinking of the poppy she had eaten, how in some uncertain way it had said her mind, made her feel more alive, more herself. 'Some things do—' and she didn't want to tell him about the poppy so she thought for another instance. The birds, of course, that was the best one of all. The young man was watching her intently as she pondered and looking at him she noticed for the first time his mouth, which was in his beard, wet and red and she suddenly didn't want to tell him anything.

'I must be going,' she said. He looked puzzled and a little set back.

'Hang on, we were just getting our teeth into this. I'm going to make some coffee. Instant coffee, won't take a minute,' and he smiled at this sure touch of light comedy.

'No thank you, really I have to go.' She put on her coat and said good-bye to Tessa. The young man said he would see her to the corner. She said it wasn't necessary but he put on a scarf and came out with her.

The night was crisp and she felt the cold bloom on her

cheeks. The street was not brightly lit and it was possible to see stars. They were very high and looking up with her head back she had an acute sense of the enormity of height, those distant flinders of glitter, aeon distant each from the other and terror at such spaces filled her, like a vertigo. She stood, suddenly sick with loneliness, with emptiness, with distance, with dread. The young man, also looking up, said, 'It's the earth's atmosphere which makes them twinkle.'

'Twinkle?'

'Yes, you know the way stars twinkle' – he fluttered the fingers of his right hand and pointed up in the direction of the sky where the twinkling stars owing to the earth's atmosphere, twinkled.

'Twinkle,' Ruth said and wanted to laugh but stopped herself – 'twinkle twinkle' – and the feel of the words in her mouth made her giggle.

'I must go home now,' she said, 'good night.'

'Look let me walk you back, I really think I should.'

'No. No. You twinkle off your way and I'll twinkle off my way,' and this made her giggle again. He seemed perplexed, but turned and started to go back, then stopped and was about to come towards her.

'No,' she said, 'you're not twinkling,' and walked away from him.

She looked up as she walked and the stars through the earth atmosphere trembled their distant transmissions. 'Twinkle twinkle little stars,' she said aloud, to no one.

Her room smelled sad. There was a droop of cigarette smell and a soft under aroma of female. She came in and did not put on the light. The window made a regular, faint demarcation. Up through the gable ends the sky scadded ochre from the city lights. No birds flew. No stars twinkled. She sat by the window and pulled it up at the bottom. The well carried up a faint odour of garbage, sweet and putrid and not unpleasant. She could feel her body, slack in the chair, as though it were heavy and thick, weighted on the hips and thighs with soft craving flesh. Sexual desire moved in her, casual and aching, an onrush of soft ingrowing need, an upreaching tremor of lust. She touched her body about the thighs and belly with the flats

137

of both hands. It seemed unconnected with the feeling. Maybe it had to do with the smell from the dustbins, or the smell in her room or that sitting this way she folded her flesh into unpremeditated self stimulus. Again in her it moved, an opening and closing movement, and a feeling from the movement, a tenderest flesh frail flower quivering its petals in mindless joy, out of some dark central pulse of memory's inmost folds, the expansion of penetration, the wet weld of coital dip, the smooth friction of received urgings and the gradual contraction of awareness until only the opening in her body being entered and re-entered had existence and upon this hub she revolved in a whirl of senses that spun to orgasm.

The memory passed and left loneliness, a cold stone in her breast, she could almost touch its presence. She sat wishing to shed tears, to break the stretched ache of it but nothing happened for moments that were not involved in time but existed in the eternities of feeling, unending nows. Then without prologue or debate the simple still wish to be dead. Not to die, not to kill herself, but to be dead. At this moment, sitting at the window, looking at the birdless sky, to no longer be. Not so much the nadir of desperation as a strange zenith of insignificance, a final commonplace.

To terminate the mood she drove herself out to make tea. The gas burner bit its blue teeth up into the bottom of the kettle. She thought of people gassing themselves, the pathetic comfort of pillows under their heads. Poor souls. And then she remembered Cuffee's grim advice to her to learn embroidery so that she might work two pillow cases, 'His' and 'Hers', 'for when we drive them to the oven.' Poor souls all of them. Mid-way through its boiling she had no longer any wish for tea. She went back into her room, putting on the light this time. Her portrait looked palely across the room. She nodded to it and got ready for bed. Naked she had the urge to touch herself, caress the starved warm fleshes that gnawed on themselves, longing feeding longing, cannibal hunger. She appraised herself in the mirror, cupping up her breasts, they had a small full weight all of their own that thrilled her, she fondled them as though they were another's, then closing her eyes let her hands be strangers,

138

doing things to her compliant bareness. She lay on the bed face down, waiting for the sensation to start that she might people it with fantasy. When it did she changed her position, bringing her knees up and apart and putting her hand under her body. She kept her face in the pillow, eyes tightly shut. Afterwards she lay for a moment feeling nothing, neither disgust nor release, and then she began to shiver and got under the bedclothes. The book beside her bed was the *Oxford Book of English Verse*. Mr Cuffee had bought it for her twenty-first birthday. She opened it at random. There was a poem by someone called Christopher Smart. She'd never heard of him. She flicked back and came across Ben Jonson. She tried to read a poem but the words kept getting in the way. She turned back too far and found herself looking at the list of poets. On the fly her father's inscription in his page devouring scrawl. 'To my daughter Ruth. On the anniversary of her birth. From her father, Peter Cuffee.' The extravagant egotism of it touched her and in some curious way made her regret the indulgence she had just taken with herself. She shook her head to rid the impending depression. She who sleeps with her brother should hardly take exception to self-abuse. A small poem, The Knight of the Grail.

> Lulley lulley, lulley lulley,
> The fawcon hath borne my luv away.
> He barc him up, he bare him down,
> he bare him in an orchard brown.
> In that orchard there was an hall
> that was hangid with purple and pall,
> and in that hall there was a bed,
> it was hangid with gold so red,
> and in that bed there lyth a knyght,
> his woundes bledyng day and night.
> By that bed side there kneeleth a may
> and she weepeth both night and day
> and by that bed side there standith a ston
> 'corpus christi' wretyn thereon.

The nurl of the language, its falling inevitable lines and the strangely familiar imagery carried her through the

139

ordered world of the imagination that was, even at a first reading, her world, her imagination, her poem. She read it again and then again and both times it was hers, about her and about Cuffee, hawky brother. Often in the fields they had seen a kestrel on high quivering hang. They would watch it from the cover of trees wishing they could see everywhere like the bird, so that no one could come close to them. His face would be taut with excitement and she would hold his arm and her breath as it swooped. When I die I'll come back as a hawk he used to say. She read the poem again and saw it all.

CHAPTER TWELVE

The town divides along Nelson Street. To the west are the residential streets, wide, treey, high cambered and in genteel disrepair. There are few tenements and further out only the large square sandstone houses of the doctors and lawyers and owners and inheritors, of the clergy and the architects and the retired wealthy. There are no shops and few cars and children play faintly in back gardens. There is quiet and the regular grid of the streets beats a slow drum, the tempo of security. Here the prosperous have always lived and had the message boys come cycling out on big basketed bikes, have walked their dogs and trimmed their privets and the reiteration of these events has given to the place a distinctive brooding aura. It could not be the east end or the centre of the town, nor the houses on the hill, not being built so high and affording none of the surprising swathes through sandstone to the river. It is an area of architectural anaesthesia, an Adamed sedation. Here countless housemaids have acquired their knees, the soft shining of unowned silver has whittled a-many fingers and a hundred Octobers the haulms have sent their blue fragrant drift along the wind. It is part smell and part sound and part feeling and for those people who live there and for those who do not, but with equal power, the awareness of it is immediate. On summer evenings people from other parts of the town come to walk in the west end as though it were a park of some sort, their children running on the broad pavements, their prams creaking quietly as they trundle between the discreet, muslined houses. The trees are lopped to grow at respectable heights and birds do not nest there and the wind finds difficulty in making them murmur. A paralysis of insulation is in the air.

Moseby did not like the west end, not as far out as this. He turned up Forsyth Street, past the school for mentally retarded children. It was known to him as the Special School and it filled him with unease to remember the grey single decker bus, bearing its cargo of addled faces. Before Carol

141

had been born he used to torture himself imagining her a defective, having to care for her botched mind, sick with love and horror. As he passed the gates he stopped and looked into the empty playground, a sloping asphalt embedded with white chips. Something twisted him to visualize Carol running across to him and when she looked up it was with the boggled, stretched stare of the mongoloid. He whimpered in his throat and found his hands clamping the bars of the gate. He released the hold and went on.

The minister came to the door when Moseby rang. He was a youngish man with heavily greying hair, very tanned from overseas mission work and when he smiled his incisors were missing and made him seem a very accessible being. He had married Moseby and given him encouragement in refusing to become a church member at Mrs Davidson's insistence. For a time afterwards they had met to talk on the problem of Christian faith and whether its lack in Moseby could be remedied. These discussions were long over and Moseby only dropped in on occasional Saturday mornings with Carol. They shook hands and went into the front room where the minister's wife was knitting. She looked up and smiled. Moseby said hello. He felt his teeth bony and exposed in the smile he gave her. He sat down and let his body slacken with conscious determination, making his legs loosen at the calf and behind the knee, and allowing his hands to lie along the arms of the chair, palms down and fingers over the end of the arm trying not to hold it. Mrs Maxwell asked him how his wife was.

'And how is your wife, well I hope,' Moseby addressed himself to the question with the certainty that it could not be answered. It quivered with implication and demanded a reply that would commence with Moseby's first memory and move chronologically and in fullest detail to this moment when, asked how his wife was, he replied,

'Fine, she's fine.'

'And the little girl, what's her name again?'

'Carol, Carol's fine too.'

Lies. All lies he thought. Even the truth. The truth is a lie that hasn't been found out. There were the simple lies for the minister's wife when she asks how your wife is and the

142

not so simple lies when your wife asks you how you are and the even less simple lies when you ask yourself how you are. All posing as the truth, and to some extent are except there is always some reservation, some qualification, it is never all true and when it starts to unravel there is no stopping it. The truth is a lie that hasn't been found out.

Mrs Maxwell was saying she had some ironing to do and she would leave them. The minister looked at Moseby. 'Well John, what's wrong, you sounded all scattered on the phone.' Moseby looked at him. He was far away. Far away with his hands clasped under his chin. He wouldn't hear anything. He was too far away. He couldn't imagine why he had come, what had made him think he might be able to talk to this man, this unknown far-away man, who sat watching him, waiting for him to speak, to say words, tell, explain. Well he didn't have anything to say, or rather he had everything to say, if he left out everything he would miss it, miss the thing that was sitting on his heart, somewhere, the toad on the spring.

'Tell you what, it's a nice night, let's take a stroll. Better than sitting in here peering at each other.' Moseby said all right and stood up. The minister called to his wife and took off his collar. They went out. It was soft and the last sunlight lay over behind the hills. There was no one on the street and somewhere very very faintly there was music. They walked down Forsyth Street and the minister, who looked rather curious without a collar, was expressing his pleasure at being out in the mild mid of the evening, taking deep breaths and looking about him as though Forsyth Street were a new experience. Moseby thought of him in his surplice, in the pulpit, or at the church door. MacIndoe in his gown going through the cloisters, small, without allies. They passed the Special School. To keep from thinking about it Moseby started talking.

'Maybe it doesn't get to be like this with you, I don't know, I couldn't guess how it gets to be with somebody like you, so maybe you won't really know anything about all this, about the way I am, only I would like to try and tell you about it only I would like it to make, so you would see it, but if I do that then I'll be, well I'll be putting it my way, the way I see it and I don't want to do that I'd rather tell you it all and then you would know for yourself only I'm getting that I don't really know what is real any more, everything is real it seems, even the things that aren't, I mean when your wife asked me about my wife back at the manse, well I knew it was just a question, a social question but I could hardly answer it because it seemed so, I don't know if important is the word but I felt it demanded the truth and that if I told the truth it would start me explaining and explaining until I had explained everything because nothing makes sense if you say it on its own, no that's not right, it does make sense on its own but on its own it isn't true and that's what I feel is happening to me these days I feel everything is in bits and that whatever I do I'm only doing a bit of a thing and that makes everything a lie sort of only nobody sees that, they think I'm doing the whole thing but I'm not, I'm not telling the truth because, well I don't know why, because I don't really think anybody wants to know, they want to know a bit but not it all, even I don't want to know it all but it's inside me and it wants out and I keep thinking everything is symbolic of everything else, I see things and I think they are full of meaning like these two little delf figures in my mother-in-law's house, in her bathroom, in the form of a toothbrush holder and they're just sitting there and somehow just sitting like that under these toothbrushes they seem, well, it's a rotten word, but symbolic and everything is getting a bit more like that, seems to be, or something like on Monday on the Anniesland tram I saw all the people and they looked, strange, they looked, well they didn't look like me and I felt I had nothing to do with them, nothing to do with people at all, I just wanted to sit on that tram for ever, just for ever and I saw my history lecturer that morning and I realized I don't care for people, I really don't except Carol and Edna but even there I don't care the way I should not the way I really ought only for Carol and I suppose that's only because she's a child and that makes it different but I'm glad I've got her I used to be terrified she would be born mentally backward or something because that would be the worst symbol of all wouldn't it if your child was like that, I would think I would know then what-

144

ever it is I don't know only it's too terrible a way to find out and at night I sit beside her and I get this feeling, I can't describe it not really it's like a pain only I know I'm happy because she's all right but I make myself think things, not always sometimes I just sit and watch her but I know that she doesn't answer the question and my whole life feels like it's becoming a question, right from when I wake up in the morning, I ask myself why in the morning before I get up and sometimes I think if I could just lie on long enough I would know but I have to get up, time and the seven-fifty waits for no man so I never find out the answer because I don't really know what the question is except maybe that it's why, just why, why to my whole life, to everything and I don't know how to answer that. Do you know how to answer a question like that?'

'Yes,' the minister said, 'I think I do.'

'It's God you mean, isn't it?'

'Yes, I'm afraid it is,' the minister said wryly. Moseby noticed this and smiled a little.

'I can see too that God is, well, what's needed. Only it's no good to me. Can you believe that, that God can be no good to some people?'

'No I don't believe that. I wouldn't be a minister if I thought that. I think perhaps the Church is no good to you but God is more than the Church. I think you have to find God.'

'I get frightened, at me, I think sometimes I'm going to destroy everything, even the things I care for, Edna, Carol, you know, destroy it.'

'Why would that happen?'

'Because of what I'm like. I'm not good. That sounds strange, naïve I suppose, but it's true. You always think you are and it's a terrible shock when you find you're not.'

'When did you find out?'

'After I was married I think, really found out I mean. It was to do with sex I suppose. And Edna. Sometimes I think it's all got to do with sex. All of this.'

'Do you have good sexual relations with Edna?'

'Oh well, I don't know, the trouble is Edna's pan loaf and

I'm pan sexual,' and he laughed, amused at the expression. The minister smiled.

'I heard rather an odd joke the other day,' he said, 'about a man who was out having a walk when he heard a shout, "one, two, he's done it again" and when he looked there was a crowd of people gathered round in a circle and he went up to them and just as he got up they all shouted at once "one, two, he's done it again" and he couldn't see into the ring so he asked this big tall fellow what was happening and he said "there's a man in there with no legs" and just then the crowd shouted "one" and the tall fellow said "he's thrown one crutch away", "two" they shouted, "he's thrown the other crutch away, he's done it again" they shouted. "He's fell on his arse.

They were halfway up the Lyle Hill and the sun had gone completely, the hills were violet shapes against the vitreous blayke of the sky. Without a word they turned and started to come down.

'It's like a parable somehow,' Moseby said, thinking of it, 'like something out of Brueghel.'

'It is rather strange,' the minister agreed almost casually and Moseby could see that he had been preached a sermon. Well he thought, that's what I came for.

They walked back almost in silence to the foot of Forsyth Street.

'You sure you won't come up for a cup of coffee?' the minister asked.

'No, I won't, thanks all the same. I'll be getting back. Edna'll think I've gone off on the randan. Thanks again.'

'I'm sorry to have been of such little help.'

'Well you listened.'

'Give my regards to Edna and the daughter. Come around some time soon, we'll have another stroll.' They shook hands. Moseby came down Union Street, walking briskly, his head lowered in thought. Passing the Little Sisters of the Poor Convent on his left, through the gate something caught whitely at his eye. It was a large, life-size crucifix by the door of the convent. In the dusk it hung in a startling pallor, pale as pale. He was sure it meant something to have seen it after his visit to the minister, it

146

was the kind of thing you found written up in tracts, called 'the night I met Christ', which led to salvation and being able to stand your workmates' taunts. The far chime of the West Kirk clock brought him to and sent him home.

It was almost dark when he got in and Edna was watching television. She didn't switch off, but looked up to ascertain it was he, her lawful wedded spouse, and not Mr Allen from next door, mad drunk, with a hypodermic of spanish fly between his teeth. There was a play on the television, apparently set in the showroom of a furniture store.

'Is it good?' he asked.

'Not bad.' He watched it for a moment and gathered it was more dramatic than comic, but that there wasn't a lot in it. He had a brief look at Carol and went into the room. A well spent evening he told himself, lying on his back in the dark. What if she asked why he had gone to see Maxwell. The only answer that would really please her was that he wanted to become a church member. And why not. He'd been married there and Carol had been christened and he had said that bit about bringing her up in the light of a Christian conscience whatever that might mean. So why not and have a good old sing every Sunday. Good idea morning churchgoing really, gave you the rest of the day to yourself.

His strained facetiousness evaporated, leaving him deflated and, curiously, hungry. He was rising with the intent of making a sandwich when he heard the television switched off. He lay back, face down. The door opened and Edna came in. She put the light on, then after a pause, off again.

'You asleep?' He rolled over and she came and sat on the edge of the couch.

'Not watching the play?'

'Oh, it wasn't much use,' and he wanted her, just like that, without touch or smell or word of encouragement. She pushed his hand away, lightly though.

'Here, I want a word with you,' but there was a smile bending the words. He caught her round the neck and pulled her down. After momentary resistance she came, kissing her he startled the fat slug of tongue in her mouth.

The kiss went tepid and he rubbed her breast for a moment then went quickly under her skirt.

'Stop it John, I didn't come through for this.' This, not that, he noted, assessing his prospects. 'John-nn,' the protest elongating with pleasure. He put his face among her warm woollen breasts and thought of Jesus, hanging cold through the night. Poor Jesus, when mere men might lie like he amidst their wives in mortal love. Poor Jesus.

'You better go and get them,' and he rose, leaving her sprawled, white thigh smears above the stocking tops, making the awkward motions of divestment.

Out of the window the river swathed a luminous band between the shores and above the mass of the hill stars made high distant blinter. Nearer home, certain chimneys preached evanescence. Moseby saw but disregarded these images, enthralled as he was by the suddenly vouchsafed prospect of meanwhile oblivion.

CHAPTER THIRTEEN

The traffic came drumming up the Finchley Road to Swiss Cottage. They sat outside the pub and watched the one-way flow, noisy and soothing. The students from the Central School of Drama were all around, acting out their lunch breaks. There was a sun, high up and obscured by the London haze. Their pints shone like pots of gold and the beer tasted coppery sweet. Cuffee watched up the girls' skirts. Above black stockings flesh gloamed.

'I have my first erection,' Gibbon drank to it.

'Wishing it decent interment and a pleasant subsidence,' Stolleman said. Stolleman was tall and going bald and American. He was in his late thirties and wore a washed-out blue shirt and denim trousers. He was smoking a panatella. The air was rich with it and the fumes of the cars.

'There's a lot of twat here Michael.'

'This is cuntown boy,' Cuffee looked steadily up clothes.

'I'm getting very horny here.'

'You're going to come all over yourself on the subway then.'

'Can you see up that ones?' – nodding his chin at a big carelessly crossed girl whose knees made silken glosses as she sat. Gibbon and Stolleman looked. The girl noticed their six-eyed scrutiny and sat round.

'You clumsy bastards. Why didn't you stick your heads in between her knees.'

'Have another pint as consolation,' said Stolleman, rising to get them. He moved through the tables, floppy wristed, with his sleeves buttoned down.

'It's a nice day Peter.'

'Pleasant Harry, pleasant. You tired?'

'I'll sleep when the time comes.'

'We'll go over to Stolleman's studio. You can doss on the couch.'

'No rush. It's nice here.'

'Pleasant, very pleasant.'

149

The traffic surged off again. Gibbon watched it. Cuffee looked over at the big girl who had readjusted and opened for view again. Cuffee watched accurately. The girl glanced to see if he was looking, then away but she didn't alter her position.

'Do you remember that orchard?' Gibbon asked.

'What orchard?'

'That one in Wales, a field it was, remember?'

'Yes, where we all stole apples.'

'We didn't just steal them, we ruined the whole orchard, running from tree to tree shaking them down.'

'This thing wants me to sketch her clout I think.'

'That must be the way foxes get in a chicken coop. All those apples falling down on you. Remember?'

'They were nice. Big hard yellow ones weren't they?'

'Don't you remember them all just tumbling down all over you. It was a great feeling.' The traffic ground down to a halt. 'Never done that before. Never done it since. Have you?'

'What?'

'You'll strain your eyes going on like that, it's not good for them, stands to reason, you're focussed for daylight out here but up there to see anything you have to be focussed for twilight. You're straining your focussing powers that's what you're doing.'

'Oh shut up, you're worse than Ruth.' The traffic started up again and Gibbon waved to no one in particular. Stolleman came back with the drinks. Cuffee raised his glass to the girl who pretended not to notice.

'Have you been in London long?' Gibbon asked Stolleman?'

'Three years. I'm getting past it.'

'You don't like it?'

'You get past places, outgrow them. I outgrow New York, outgrew Paris. I've almost outgrown London. You been here before?'

'Only with the army, the odd week-end.'

'It's a good town to live in, no two ways. But you're not staying are you?'

'Only until I get a passport.'

'Paris you're going to. You'll like it. Pete's been there before.'

'Did you live with him in Paris?'

'He doesn't live in a town, he assaults it. We shared the same slit trench.'

'I've never been. Where will you go after London?'

'San Francisco. I hear it's a great town for rheumatics.'

'No.'

'You don't have to worry then.'

'No, I don't.'

'You wouldn't know her name would you?' Cuffee asked. Stolleman shook his head.

'They're all from the Drama School round the corner. Anyway I want you to meet Gerda.'

'This is your woman.'

'I'd be hurrying you along to meet my woman wouldn't I. No I know her from my early days in London.'

'And she's a hot piece.' Stolleman drew on his smoke and puffed slowly.

'She's a bit more than a hot piece.'

'Okay let's meet her, you ready Harry?'

'I've got a pint here to finish. Let me sit and you can pick me up at closing.'

'You're going to snaffle that bird. I get it all itchy and big smoothy Gibbon collects.'

'That'll be right. Leave us your pen. I'll write Moseby.' Stolleman lent him a biro and they went off through the tables, the American taller by the inch, narrow-shouldered, a slouchy loll alongside the controlled stalk of the dark young man beside him.

The sun shone its filtered shine on the green, beer-ringed tables. The drinkers drank, the speakers gesticulated. The world held promise, fecund quotidian.

Dear John, it was all a bit of a dash and we really didn't get a chance to talk, not that in one way there is a lot to say, I feel we know each more than we've ever needed or tried to tell. Which may or may not be a good thing.

The trip so far has been marvellous and it was nice to meet Peter's sister again. She is very attractive. He hasn't changed much, a bit more aggressive in a way, I don't mean fight aggressive, just more overpowering and sure of himself. I wonder how you would like him, or if you would think he was 'at it'. Well we all are, one way or another, I suppose.

I'm sitting outside a pub with those black and white stripes, and it's a lovely day and there are a lot of good-looking girls round about and anything much less like Greenock would be hard to imagine. I suppose Paris will be. That's where we are going when I get a passport.

I still wish you could have managed, even if only to keep an eye on me, I feel a bit unlike my usual self, whatever my usual self felt like. That's the strange thing, it all seems so long ago and it's not. Time is funny . . .

'How long have you known her?' Stolleman wrinkled his upper lip and recollected.

'Year and a half. Just after I met you in Manchester. Met her through her husband, Terry. Poor bastard. Drinks like four camels. The war got him. One of the walking wounded that boy. He was a pilot, Battle of Britain stuff. He married her during the war, she was in the women's air force thing. They've been separated for years I think though they seem to be friendly enough. I think it happened in bed, or didn't happen in bed. And he drank like I said.'

'She lives alone?'

'Well she lives alone yes but she doesn't sleep alone much. Don't get me wrong. I'm not calling her a name, I'm not saying whore. Gerda's not a whore.'

'She's an enthusiastic amateur.'

'Don't be flip Pete, you know nothing. Terry wasn't the only one the war got to. Oh I don't know maybe she's a nympho but she's a nice person, don't you go being snide to her.'

'You've had it away with her?'

'Sure, I've been there, for a while. Then she got somebody else and I got sore, we're vain bastards you know, we can't stand the idea that some guy might be better at it than we are. I got annoyed but it passed and we started having drinks, just good friends, the truth, I haven't laid hands on the woman in a year.'

'How was she in bed?'

'Kinda nosey guy aren't you. She's a funny one Gerda. It's like she's done it all, she's not bored or anything like that, no, she's just ready, ahead of you. You feel, oh I don't know what you feel, that there's more here than you're going to touch. She's big, there's something big about her, especially in bed. It's like making out with the whole world.'

'Why did you quit then?'

'Look at me Pete. I'm not the cosmic cunt type. I like them very regional, I like them young and hipless, I like them with down on their bellies and fluff on their bums.'

'It's little girls you're talking about.'

'Too damn true it's little girls. I've been up to my armpits in fud since I was thirteen, I'm sick of all that, it coarsens the palate, all those willing broads falling on their backs with thighs like bolsters smelling of last week's talcum. From now on it's girls, slender juvenile willing girls.'

'And after that?'

'Slender juvenile willing boys.'

'You're kidding.'

'I am kidding no part. I've got my painting, I like to drink, I like to smoke cigars. What's wrong with boys? You were a boy once yourself.' Cuffee roared and Stolleman slapped him on the back. 'Honestly though, I'll never go back to affaires, never. All that emotion, that striving. You know what it is. I don't have anything to say to them. Do you understand that. My world's just not theirs. Sure if it was just off with your gear and into pit fine. But it's the talk, the unending talk, before during and after. But especially after. I don't want to talk. I can't talk. I hate talking. To women anyway, the ones you're trying to lay. Now with girls, nice little girls who've just been tampered with in cars and in Regents Park, they're too busy finding out what it's like, listening in case they can hear you inside them. But those others, well they know by now what it's like, that it's never going to be any different and they're bored, bored to death with themselves, with you, with it. And so they talk, and talk, and talk.'

'And there's nothing in between.'

'Sure, oh sure, plenty, but they want love. And I'm not in the market for love.'

'You're never going to get wed and have kids?'

'What's that got to do with it. You're as bourgeois as they come. I just don't want the love part of it. You need an awful lot of energy to love a woman like she wants to be loved, what I've got I need, to paint. Never divide your forces, remember the Little Big Horn; up here.'

Gerda lived in a mews flat above a garage. She let them in and went upstairs and they followed her into the sitting-room. It was medium-sized and painted white except for the back wall with the double divan against it which was dark green. On it a large canvas by Stolleman made a gaudy lateral. The rest of the room contained two tall wooden arm-chairs and a plain wooden desk by the window. The floor was dark-stained and had a dull gold rug. There was a small table in an alcove with an oil lamp on it. Gerda was about medium height or a little more, with loose brown wavy hair around a full, wide-eyed face. She was big in the body, deep breasts and wide-hipped and her hands though small were chubbed with plump. She was wearing a plain yellow dress, round at the neck and sleeveless. The flesh on her upper arms was firm and smooth. Her whole body looked com-pact and she moved well, her hair shifting as she turned, a strand catching on her lip and she put out a tongue to lick it away. They were introduced and looked at each other a moment, Cuffee's upper lip raised in the first position of a smile while she studied his face. Then Gerda looked at Stolleman and back to Cuffee, smiling at him.

'He told me you looked like a Borgia. You do too.'

'He never told me what you looked like but I'm not sur-prised.'

'Good, I hate surprises. Michael get yourself a drink. There's Scotch and there's lager. I'll have Scotch. Peter?'

'Lager please.' Stolleman went into the kitchen and Gerda indicated a seat with a small fluent wave of the hand. He sat in one of the big chairs and watched her steadily. Stolleman from the kitchen.

'Who's giving this party?'

154

'Jane Cowell. Do you know them?' She lit herself a cigarette from a pack on the mantelshelf, offering Cuffee one but he said no.

'I know him. He's a poet or a dog breeder or something isn't he?' She smoked with a certain flair, almost a theatricality but not quite that, taking the cigarette quickly away fom her mouth and inhaling deeply, then releasing smoke from her nose in a long contemplative sigh.

'She's a nice girl really. She worries too much about being Jewish though.'

'One of those, what's the party in aid of, has she just read *Exodus*?'

'It's just a party, she said bring some interesting people.' She sat down opposite Cuffee and watched him, smoking and talking to Stolleman, doing it like a juggler might keep three plates going, implying complexity in the most ordinary of circumstances. Cuffee watched without waver, finding her eyes through the smoke and talk.

'Do you want water Gerda?'

'No, there's some ginger ale in the fridge.' She crossed her legs and the calf muscle was pressed wide, making her neat ankles look even smaller. Turning to look at Stolleman with the drinks the tendon in her throat tightened, the long flexion balanced the line of her jaw. They took drinks and Stolleman standing raised his glass.

'To General Custer,' he said. Cuffee and Gerda looked at each other and smiled. They drank to General Custer.

The place was crowded when they got there and the people were in several rooms. There was music from a tape recorder and fitful dancing. It was warm and the windows were open. Draughts of tepid London air made scarves of the muslins. In the rooms light sprang out of wall fittings and standard lamps. A smell, of perfume and the bodies wearing it and of cigarettes and alcohol. Someone said Edith Piaf was divine. Someone said 'utterly ravishing'. A man brayed, throwing his head back. A woman with much of her spine bared was dancing with an absent-minded-looking gentleman in a dark suit. He had a black patch over his left eye. Gerda was wearing a green sack dress, looking

155

large and cool. Cuffee had on a jacket of Stolleman's and his black shirt. Gibbon was slightly drunk and in a linen jacket seemed very big, making Stolleman thin and narrow in his ivy league suit with a brown button-down shirt. Gerda introduced them to Jane Cowell who was a small dark woman in a white dress, beringed and hot-handed. She took them up to get them drinks and introduced her husband who wore a cravat under a blue denim shirt. While they were getting glasses Jane Cowell took Gerda by the sleeve.

'Is the dark one Jewish?'

'I don't think so.'

'He looks very semitic.'

'He may be, I don't think so or Michael would have mentioned it.'

'He is with you?'

'I only met him this afternoon.' Jane Cowell looked at Gerda, her small beaky face intent for a moment, then she smiled and laughed, far back in her throat.

'Oh Gerda you are a terror. I know you when you have your mind—' and she paused— 'set on someone. We must have coffee some day and you can regale me with details.' Gerda smiled and turned back to the bar.

Stolleman was talking to a young girl with small high cupped breasts and bad breath. He could see down into the fissure through his cigar smoke. It was the kind of brassiere which pushed them up into a ledge and the nipple promised to come into sight if she heaved a sigh. He tried not to be breathed at nor to drop ash on the bare bubs. She was saying that young men were too fresh with their hands, touch, touch, touch all the time.

'And in exactly that order,' said Stolleman waiting for the nipple to dawn.

A woman in a leopard-skin dress was saying what an absolutely marvellous accent Gibbon had. She urged him to say something Gaelic.

'Gaelic. Oh, well, you wouldn't understand it would you.'

'No, but I love the lilt of the true Gaelic. Do say something.'

'Sinkrabootinaweewinger.' She expressed delight.

156

'What does that mean?'

'It's a kind of battle cry.'

'Oh a battle cry, death to the sassenach I suppose,' and laughed as only those who can take a joke against themselves may. 'Do another one.'

'Aye furawull so furawull, naw fur yull naw so fur yull naw.' This one really thrilled her.

'It's so liquid, so musical. What is it, a lover's lament?'

'Sort of, it's more a kind of mouth music.'

'Oh the mouth music, I've heard about that, it sounds fascinating, can you play it?'

'No, I'm afraid I can't, I can't do the fingering. The fingering's very tricky.'

'Is it?' the lady in the leopard-skin dress said and Gibbon nodded.

'Very, handed down it is.'

'Father to son,' she supposed.

'Wrapped in an old semmit,' Gibbon said.

Cuffee and Gerda danced. For a heavy woman she was very light. He held her firmly but not close.

'Did Michael tell you about me?'

'Yes. A bit.'

'And what did you think?'

'I wanted to meet you.'

'And now that you have?'

'I like you.'

'Why?'

'I like the way you move. It's nice to watch.' She smiled, a half-serious smile.

'What?'

'Just people. They exist all over the place don't they. They just come walking into your life out of wherever they've been.'

'Does that frighten you?'

'No it doesn't frighten me, it surprises me a bit though.'

'And you don't like surprises.' She looked at him curiously.

'How do you know, oh yes, when we met. I don't suppose I do, do you?'

'I don't mind surprises. As long as it's not me who gets

157

surprised,' and he smiled. Gerda didn't but she came closer into gentlest contact, her hair against his mouth and their bodies riding, cushy on her bosom.

Stolleman had his girl out into the corridor and had fed her several more drinks. Her name was Lynne and she downed vodka and tomato juice in swift gulps and talked in a bright little Kensington voice about better parties than this one and Daddy's super Bent he wouldn't let her drive and Mummy who didn't live with them while Stolleman kept an eye on her rounded little heavings. In bringing his hand up for his panatella he managed at the apogee of uplift to graze the curve of the left breast and it shuddered like a milky blancmange, quite independently of the other. She noticed this and gasped with delight.

'How fab, do it again.' And he did. 'Do you like them, Daddy calls them by boobies.' Stolleman blew thick smoke into her dress where it mulled and lingered before dispersing. 'Ooh that's nice, like a black man's breath' – and giggled.

Gibbon had escaped the leopard-skin woman and was feeding himself at the buffet. He had had several more drinks and was talking to the man with the black patch about pirates, a subject that had wormed itself into topic relentlessly. The man had asked what part of Scotland he came from and he said Greenock, following that with the information that Captain Kidd was from those parts. The man seemed quite interested and said he'd read a book on Henry Morgan. In the middle of this the woman with the dress open at the back came up and claimed him. The man winked his unpatched eye and said 'off to walk the plank eh', and left Gibbon at the bar. He was now quite drunk and carefully made himself a large anthology of a sandwich and then retired to the bathroom. He locked the door and went to sit on the toilet. There was a small beige turd floating in the pan. He put the lid down and flushed. After the cistern emptied he looked. Spinning around the little toley remained unsunk. He watched this time. It was too buoyant and the inflow merely bounced it up and down without taking it away. He unrolled some ten yards of toilet paper and stuffed it into the pan where it assumed a sodden pink hue, a sinking mound of tissue. He worked the lever and it slumped into a mush and sucked away, taking the dod with it, only to choke on the bend and have the pan fill up with water and then slowly begin to drain away.

'Got you you bastard,' Gibbon said and sat down to eat his sandwich.

There was more noise and the talk was thicker. Glasses sounded constantly against other glasses. The music was louder. Lights had dimmed and the figures in the rooms seemed to have melted at the edges and gave the impression of a large, corporate organism existing its multi-celled existence. That fabulous beast, the Party, was uncoiling itself. A woman laughing at a joke began in the middle of a breath, to sob. Jane Cowell was letting a bearded man dribble saliva into her throat while they danced. Women were gesturing upwards, disclosing the yellow mouths of shaved oxters. Here and there a haunch was handled. Negligently seated women found their thighs scratched by furtive peepings. A coloured girl got up to sing. There was a half hush and she rotated herself through two choruses of 'Love me or leave me' in a droning potent voice. When she was finished a man helped her down from the table and kissed her. When he had finished another man kissed her and then another then several more and she fell from one clasp into another while the women sneered and pretended to look away. The moment lasted scarcely longer than it takes eight men to kiss a drunken negress but it was the core of the evening, its very heart. When it was over the party was over, four hours before the finish. What should have been ritual rape scarcely attained indecency, the tickle and scratch of urban eroticism broke cover, tawdry fugitive, and as quickly went to earth. The anarchy towards which all parties are aimed flared a moment and lit the orgiasts, unwilling agents, then flickered back to burn in certain minds, contained from general conflagration.

Stolleman had his poppet in the linen cupboard bared to the waist and was rubbing his head between her breasts. She was very drunk and had braced herself by holding on to the shelves while he played with her thus.

Gibbon was asleep on the toilet, unheeding the clamour

of strained bladders and flexed sphincters at the door. His sandwich, half eaten, lay on top of the cistern behind him. He snored.

Gerda and Cuffee stood by an open window looking out. A plane tree grew in front of a standard lamp. The leaves were lit yellow and the branches showed like bones in an X-ray. Outside was cool and quiet and the tree made the most of a small wind. A man walked a poodle and while it wet looked up at the window.

'Let's go,' Gerda said.

'Okay. I'll just see Harry knows what's what.'

He met Stolleman combing his sparse hair in a wall mirror.

'Where have you been?' Stolleman looked at him out of the mirror.

'Taking an old Sioux cure for dandruff,' he said.

'Seen Harry?'

'No.' There were several people outside the bathroom. One of the women was making a pained face. A man knocked loudly on the door. Just as Cuffee and Stolleman got to it, it opened and Gibbon, holding his sandwich, came out. There was an outburst of abuse from the group which he seemed not to hear, coming straight to Cuffee.

'I was just thinking about you,' he said; 'forget what . . .' Lynne appeared in the corridor and passed them, a dull far look in her eyes. Her dress seemed rumpled and without her brassiere she had very little bust. Stolleman stroked the top of his head gently with the ends of his fingers. They got Gerda and went.

'I'll walk him a bit to sober him up. You two get a taxi,' Stolleman said. He took Gibbon's arm and they walked along. Under the plane tree Cuffee kissed her, once, on the mouth.

'Please,' she said. Stolleman waved as they passed.

'That Peter an' Gerda?' Gibbon asked.

'Yes.'

'Michael—' a pause— 'Michael, do you know any queers?'

'Sure.'

'What are they like?'

160

'Sexwise?'
'No, I mean, what sort of people are they?'
'Same as other people.'
'Exactly the same? I mean can't you tell them?'
'Sometimes yes, sometimes no. Why?'
'Do you think Peter is that way at all?'
'Cuffee, never. What makes you ask that?'
'Oh it was just something somebody said.'
'They're mad.'
'I think so. Yes. I think you're right.'

In the light from the oil lamp she was taking off her clothes. Cuffee lay on his back, on the bed, naked. He watched her undress. The lamp was behind her and edged her body with light, ambering the tops of her breasts and the cleave of her buttocks; as she bent to take her stockings off, her breasts, swollen with shadow, swung thickly. She threw the stockings away, opening as they went, making sudden chiffons against the lamplight, cinnamon scarvings. Soft they fell, silent softs, two pools of still shimmer on the floor. Their crumpled abandon found response in his tumescence, a sluggish rearing. She was above him, enormous flesh, braced untouching, lowering her breasts to trace pink trails on his face and chest. They swole against his sight, rosy areolas. He caught at one with his mouth but the heavy drag took it from him glistening. In a surge of blood he stiffened and sensing she sought, back and down. Following her breasts he slid away. The nipples were penny large puffs, tight tipped. He whorled his tongue till the tease made her wince and then shifting she swallowed him in unlappe. The smell of her, warm white bread. He kissbit up into the fold, blinded in dark nearness. Slipping down impatient for incus she reached the barb but he pulled her back, this time dragging down between her breasts, his mouth open the lip membrane pulling dryly over her belly, tongueing the sunken curl of the navel, perspiration bitter pitlet, down until the rough scrub above the bone caught his mouth, wiry tangle, and she all the while reaching down to kiss his far below head. Coming up to the surface rubbing his face against her to feel the soft bruise of her breasts and she now spreading and dropping back on to him, almost finding, allowing when he moved and rolled her over on her back, doubling himself to bury between her thighs which clamp on his head and silence all save the pounding of his blood and he straddles high above her and she pulls him down, salival silvering, sweet socketing, till rising in him, a rising feeling rises and he breaks the plump vice and rounds, turns and sprawls her back, pinned, breasts falling in white lolls, both watching the stab, the hovering delayed thrust that bludgeons her body into prone acceptance, up again and again into the under-gulp and hammering, moving her physically on the bed, holding her arms wide kissing all the while a moaning mouth, urging him on as he reaches under and lifts her higher, each calling forth a low cry that tenses into yes, yes wait wait yes oh yes now yes now yes yes yes oh yes oh yes and he tunnelled through by the burning worm screams low and hard, losing control in the violent outgoing spurge that triggers her molten contractions.

He opened his eyes. Her hair was on his face. In the soft light her eyes were liquid and blind.

'Silky red fuck,' he said.

The studio was cold and seemed big with the light on. The bulb hung from a long flex and had no shade. It was impossible to see up past it to the glass roof and through to the trees.

'Like a morgue,' Stolleman said. 'Fill a kettle Harry and I'll get the fire on. The tap is outside on the garden wall.' He went out and found the tap. The water drummed in the kettle and splashed coldly on his hands. The trees moved above making cool sifterings in the night wind. Looking up he could see them darker against the dark sky, moving and moving. Moving on the night wind they moved, London trees in a wind from the west. Several windows were lit in the house in front of the studio. At one of them, looking out, a woman combed her hair, the comely movements of her arm and head in silhouette, looking out into the tree moving night. Gibbon watched her after he had turned off the tap. She stopped combing and stood a moment longer. The trees rushed overhead and inside the studio the sound of Stolleman breaking wood. Gibbon went in with the kettle. The stove was roaring up the long funnel and there was a smell of turpentine. Stolleman had broken an orange box up and had several small branches stacked against the stove.

'There's a lot of people in the world isn't there,' Gibbon said. Stolleman took the kettle from him and set it on the stove.

'Yes,' he said and sat in the wicker chair. 'What prompts that observation?'

'I just saw one of them,' which made Stolleman smile.

'You're a strange one to be friends with Cuffee,' Gibbon pulled the bed nearer to the fire and sat down.

'How's that?'

'You're not Peter's kind at all really. Not that I am but we're painters, or he might be.'

'I knew him in the Army.'

'I know you did but how come you're here now, the Army's a long way back.'

'Oh I don't know, I was fed up with Greenock, I needed the change and Peter was just getting ready to go so I came with him.'

'You've never been to Paris?' Gibbon shook his head.

'I've got a friend in Paris you might like to look up. If I know Peter he'll be too busy chasing tail but you might like this guy, his name's Kimber, he's a poet and a translator. He's' – with the emphasis on the pronoun – 'queer'. Gibbon didn't look up, only nodded.

'There was a queer in Greenock but he was, well he was a pathetic wee bloke.'

'Queers kinda fascinate you, don't they?'

'I can't say I ever thought much about them, not in Greenock anyroads, I just seem to be thinking about them now. What's this fellow, in Paris, like?'

'He's a nice guy. Good poet or he will be. He lived with a man in America who was a fine poet and a brilliant critic. He was a bit under this man's influence, as a writer.'

'What happened, to the man?'

'He shot himself.'

'Oh. Why, because he was queer?'

163

'No, he got cancer and they couldn't cure it.'

'Oh.' The stove made crackling noises and the chimney growled like a dog.

'Has he been queer all, well you know has he always been queer?'

'No, he was married once. Still is I think, never got a divorce. I didn't know him in those days, he's from Chicago. I met him in New York.'

'And he was queer then?'

'That's a moot point. He became this man's secretary and this man was queer all right but he wasn't one of the kind who have to have every man they meet. I think Norman just admired him and his work but of course he kept meeting a lot of homosexuals and a few real queens among them. So somewhere along the line he must have jumped overboard.' Gibbon shook his head.

'Still don't understand it. I mean how it happens.'

'It's difficult if you think of them as freaks. When you've been with them for a while, well—' Stolleman opened the front grill and put in more wood, the light shone ruddy on his baldy part, '—it all changes Harry,' straightening up, 'you meet some of these boys and I mean boys, hipless dark-eyed pieces and after a time you have to admit that as objects, as things, they are just as beautiful as women will ever be. And after that, well it just depends on how you were brought up, how much pleasure you get out of women, whether they fancy you.' He got up and put off the light. 'Bit of a glare that light.' The stove threw out a lantern of yellow red. Their reflections were on the glassed part of the roof. Above them, like thoughts trying to be born, the dark suggestions of the trees. The kettle began to make heating sounds.

'What makes you think you are queer, Harry?' The chimney a dull murmur now, the lid of the kettle lifting and falling back, the wood cracking in the fire. Gibbon looked up at Stolleman and smiled ruefully.

'I don't know that I think that. It's just I know so little about myself that anything might be true.'

'Yeah but why pick on homosexuality, why not wonder about something else, why that?'

'Oh just odds and ends. Peter's sister. Do you know her, Ruth?'

'I've only heard Cuffee mention her.'

'Well she's very attractive, beautiful you might say. I was with her on Sunday, and I liked her, I thought she was attractive, only I didn't feel anything to do with sex.'

'Maybe you don't really find her attractive, just because you can see she's pretty doesn't mean to say you find her desirable.'

'No I suppose not, but it's not like I had a lot to pick and choose from. I mean Greenock isn't exactly brimming with it. Then something that happened when we were hitch-hiking, it's daft but, well this cop asked if Cuffee were my fancy boy, I wondered if Peter looked queer or something. Or if I did. And I was just thinking about it, that's all.' The kettle boiled water over on to the stove top where it danced and spat in bubbles. Stolleman lifted it off with a stick and scalded the pot.

'Christ Harry if you start worrying about what the police say—' he shook his head. 'Let it float boy, you look about as queer as bull to me. Wait till one of those "poules" calls you out of a doorway, "un peu d'amour, chérie", and the lamps are misty and it's half past two and she smells of cognac and garlic and Chypre and sin. Then you won't have any doubts boy, believe me. They're not the same breed as these so-holy tarts London has. A good Paris prostitute is one of the best grinds known to man.' He gave Gibbon a mug of tea. 'Here's to them.' Gibbon nodded and drank. The trees swooped and touched the roof with their very extremities, causing him to look up but they were away, moving high above his head again, almost invisible, like nearly remembered happenings, like the past verging on recall.

'Here's to them,' and the tea was sweet and wersh at once, hot and comforting.

After Stolleman had gone he lay in his bag watching into the stove through the open grill door. Inside a glowing char of stick bones shifted and candesced. Gibbon lay on his side watching into the fire. There was almost no flame, only the liquid bright ash and the red remnants of wood. It burned into itself, its flamboyance past, a fire for the solitary still-awakes, burned softly and inwardly in slow cease.

And above him, in the absence of a wind the tree held itself still in the night, waiting for its call, its urging, its caress.

CHAPTER FOURTEEN

She awoke early and lay in the warm trough looking at the objects that had survived another night and waited in their places for another day. Light had filled up the well of the gable ends into which her window looked and it spilled mild bright into the room. Few sounds found their way in over the roofs and the tenants below did not waken as early as she. It was quiet. The clock insisted. She liked this time better than any other save when the birds came and sometimes even more than then. It was the only time when she felt one with the room, felt in it and of it. She liked to waken as now and feel the soft immerse of her body and the rhythms of the day, echoed in the pulse of her, heart safe as a mole under its hillock, the beatings in her wrists and the soft red pound of blood in her ear. She touched herself without thought, the smooth, almost glossy smoothness of her thighs, the slightly granular rub of her breasts. The nipples melted to her fingers, then firmed and stretched, taut papillaries. She liked to feel them doing that, growing up on her breasts so surely, so swiftly, proud little teats. It must feel wonderful to have a soft gnawing mouth on them, drawing out the milk. She discovered herself in small, absent touchings and thought of uterine stirrings, the manifold divisions and coherings of birth.

Her clothes on the chair nagged at these fecund thoughts. The empty deflated stockings and the pocketed, curious brassiere. Her briefs reminded her of antimacassars. They waited in surreal festoon, giving no sense of the warm lax body her hands searched, alien to the shapelessness of early morning waking, the mindless blind caressing, the small adjustments that swam with pleasure. She did not want to exchange fluid foetal comfort for the encasing identity of clothes. But slowly the bed grew irksome and the hush was flecked and scratched with sound. The clock became king. 'The quietest clock in the world makes the loudest sound in the mortuary.' The line, unbidden, alerted her with its incongruous aptness. It was Sunday, and Sundays were en-tombment, burial in the great sabbatic mausoleum of Man-chester, adhering with methodist grimness to a Sunday of the Lord.

She rose, and postponing dressing wore a brown mohair robe. She went into the kitchen, barefooted cool tactiles on the linoleum. She filled a kettle and set it on the gas. In the bathroom she looked at herself, her eyes pouched with sleep. The small mouth and the long nose, running up into the low wide forehead, the severe classical face of the voluptuary. She opened her robe to show the camber of her breasts. She should have a man in bed waiting for his break-fast. The thought pleased her. Enjoying it in her mind's eye she noticed that the man was her brother. She found this disconcerting and scrubbed it away with her toothbrush.

She ate breakfast by the window, two soft-boiled eggs and toast and tea. With her mouth clean she could taste every-thing sharply. Even with the window open at the bottom there was still very little noise. She sat in her robe, her legs crossed over at the thighs, a sense of flesh on flesh, com-plaisances of Sunday morning; the succulent eggmeat, the butter-rich toast and the thin tang of unmilked tea, the loose comfort of her body inside the robe, the pleasant droop of her unsupported bosom, a fold in her stomach. A second cup of tea, darker, stronger, made sweeter. Somewhere a bell tolled nine tolls, spaced, drifting bronzes, over the roofs and down her well, 'planch'. It made her think of Knutsford on Sundays, full of bells and churchgoers. She smoked one of her seldom cigarettes. From it rose lithe smoke, fluting inflections, blue aubade. Sunday morning. She felt somehow to be on the threshold of something and she felt the world to be conspiring in her favour. A pre-carious peace of mind settled upon her, a coaxed bird on the hand. She would find a man, she did not try to think what he would be like, and she would be happy, nor did she examine happiness, there would emerge a kind of order, no matter what, and her childhood and her youth and her love for Peter would all be resolved as inevitable antecedents to her new, unimaginable content.

Someone knocked. It was Maureen from next door, a

small cloud in front of the sun. The gas had gone out. Ruth found her a shilling. On Sundays she went to have dinner with her boy-friend's family. He was at Technical College and lived in Oldham. She had told Ruth that they wanted to sleep together but he was frightened. Once they had gone to bed but he hadn't done anything, only kissed. It made Ruth sad to think about them. Suddenly the morning was not so promissory, its blithe a little tarnished. She took the dishes out to wash them. Maureen was waiting for the kettle to boil, a lacklustre gaze at the flame. Ruth saw afresh what she knew very well, that Maureen was not a pretty girl, she was not ugly or deeply unattractive, but standing there in her flouncy nightdress, looking blankly before her, she was fixed in Ruth's mind as a drab hopeless girl, trapped without malice in mediocrity. To dissipate the depression she felt Ruth spoke up brightly.

'You're up early.'

'I'm going to have a bath before everyone comes up from downstairs. Then I'm going to Tom's.'

'Roast mutton and two veg during Forces Favourites,' Ruth said, repeating Maureen's caption of her impending Sunday dinner. Maureen seemed not to recognize it.

'Well it's better than staying in this dump. What are you going to do?'

'I think I'll go down to Knutsford.'

'You're lucky, living so close.'

'Yes it's handy.' She dried the dishes and went back into her room. The furniture stood around, dull lumber. Bugger Maureen Proverbs she thought. But that was hardly fair. Her euphoria would certainly not have lasted to the train. And when had she decided she was going to Knutsford. Just when Maureen asked. It must have been the bells. She took some pains with her dressing and brushed her hair out of its bun into a straight short cap, like she wore it in the portrait. The moss green dress had always looked well on her and she lined her eyes, doe-ing them slightly. She had an unfashionable lipstick, too gaudy for the prevalent anaemia and after a deliberation she put it on and was pleased to see how well it flourished against her dark hair and eyes. When she thought of the only males likely to have the privilege of witnessing her appearance it made her smile to herself. Robert Eldman and Mr Cuffee were among the least observant of men. Maureen was coming out of the toilet. Her face told its own story.

'No go?' Ruth said. Maureen suffered from chronic constipation.

'That's two weeks,' she said.

'No it can't be.'

'Bloody well is.'

'You should see a doctor.'

'Oh they just give you pills, ask about your roughage.'

'Well you better do something.'

'Mm, I had hadn't I.' The thought of being two weeks constipated oppressed Ruth all the way down the stairs and into the street. Surely it meant something. Your body was trying to tell you something, give warning. But of what. That there was a famine coming. She giggled at this. But seriously, it was a dreadful thing, and somehow it fitted Maureen's personality. That was it exactly. She was a constipated girl.

There were few people about as she walked along Oxford Street, looking up at the great grimy quiet buildings, their fronts streaked with bird droppings, large unlovely, tired buildings, hundreds upon hundreds of vacant windows, and behind them hundreds upon hundreds of empty rooms, shiny empty corridors, unopened doors. All Sunday they would lie, unentered, unsounding, all existing without use, idly passing the day through their shiny corridors, the still doors, the empty hushed offices. Would an old limping man make his way round, his lopsided steps sounding before him, looking into the arrested silences of countless rooms. And if he did would it make any difference, if no one saw the door swing behind him, heard the irregular metronome of his walk, if his shadow through the pebbled glass never caught an eye, did he exist, all that Sunday, in the empty buildings?

Her terror was none the less real for being barely understood. She hurried through the streets to the station.

During the dull, short journey she watched out of the window, seeing nothing. The wheels made the noises that fit themselves to any thoughts, dinning repetitively away behind hers, repeating the image of the limping man in his great silent hive, and curiously, whenever she forced her mind away from the other, Maureen, ingesting this Sunday's dinner before she had rid herself of last's. The tracks alongside ran swift and bright, tangling with others but coming out as single-minded as before, sometimes apparently slipping under the train and disappearing but always replaced by an identical pair; the lines of her inexorable thoughts. The telephone wires repeated their maddening melody, rising glissandi that never attained crescendo. The poles beat out the tempo. Sunday had resisted all temptation and attained monotony.

When she got out it was starting to rain, a soft smirr. She went down the steps and across the field. She looked for the kestrel but the air was empty save for the rain. 'The faucon has borne my luv away.' The rain spun down all around her, soundless, small as small, a mood of rain falling gently yet relentlessly, wetting everywhere.

Her mother was up, moving about in the kitchen, the clicking of delf and the rattle of cutlery as the drawer was pulled open. There was the smell of frying. Sunday morning. She stood inside the door looking down the hall. The stand with Mr Cuffee's old raincoat hunched upon a peg. There was a mirror with a flaw that had been at eye level when she was about twelve or thirteen. It made your eye into a great goggle. There was a photo of the school she and Peter had attended between the front-room door and that into the living-room. She looked at it. The pupils banked in six rows, the staff sitting in front. Her eye slipped over the serried faces and found themselves, Cuffee thin-faced and with eyes as black as his hair. She was surprised to see herself as always looking very pale and small and with her features scarcely registering. Their father sat beside the headmaster on his left. He looked very much the father of his son. The other faces extended emptily all around. She could hardly remember a name. The boy behind Cuffee had chased her once and tried to kiss her. Peter punched him in the stomach the next day and then kicked him. That girl had become captain of the school. Alison something. The girl in the back row was the one who became a fashion model in Manchester. Merle Curvis. She hadn't been called Merle then. Jane it had been. Robert Eldman looking just the same as he did now, he had always been middle-aged-looking. What would have happened if he had married Mrs Cuffee. One thing, she wouldn't be here now wondering about it. This simple demonstration of the indissoluble bonds of parenthood depressed her somewhat and she left the photo and went into the kitchen.

Her mother was in her dressing-gown, a placenta-coloured candlewick affair. She was wearing a pair of Mr Cuffee's slippers. They scliffed and threatened to fall off as she went about the kitchen.

'Ruthie. I didn't hear you come in. I'm just making breakfast. Do you want ham and egg?'

'No, I've had breakfast thanks. Just a cup of tea. Is father in bed?'

'Yes he's not keeping too well. Peter upset him going off like that. Brought on his migraine.' Mr Cuffee's migraine was something Ruth rather suspected, he came down with it when he was crossed, or one of his articles came back.

'How do you mean "going off like that"? He just took a holiday.'

'Leaving art school like that, right in the middle of term. And the money.'

'What money?'

'He borrowed money from your father.'

'Well he can afford it.' So Cuffee had managed it after all.

'But taking it like that. I thought your father was going to get the police.'

'For Peter?'

'Yes, didn't he tell you. He came down last Sunday and told your father he had taken a cheque for fifty pounds to the bank and forged your father's signature. Oh it was terrible in here for about twenty minutes. I thought you knew, that was why you stayed out.'

'No, he never told me about it. I thought he was going on Harry Gibbon's money.'

'I think your father was very lenient with him. He's too headstrong that boy by far.' Ruth poured herself a cup of

172

tea and went upstairs behind her mother and into her room. It was still raining. She stood at the window and sipped her tea. The crab apple tree in the garden leaned heavily on its crutch. It didn't produce apples any more. She could remember when it had. Small green megs, the taste shrivelling in the mouth. Her face wrinkled in acute recall. On the back lawn the murderous starlings ran rapidly, unearthing worms. She became aware that a blackbird was singing and saw it, half hidden in the crab apple fork. Its pure, fluid song fluted through the rain. It was all too sad for any words Ruth could find. It was like walking in just such a rain as this and suddenly realizing you were drenched. It had been nice when she woke. What had started the decline. Getting up. No it was pleasant at the window. Maureen had somehow been the cause she thought. And then those buildings. And the train and the rain and the school photo and now everything. Maybe she had been sad right from the start but had just taken a little time to find reasons for admitting it. Or was that nonsense. The blackbird had stopped. It opened its wings and made a low swoop across the lawn, fan-tailed, to disappear among the rhododendrons at the bottom of the garden. She didn't like rhododendrons, with their lumbering names and the florid flowers and the smell the ground had under them, damp and deprived by the swarthy luxuriance. She used to hide there from her mother, tearing off leaves and nipping little scallops out of them with her nails, then her fingers smelt all that rank sour way. That smell and the fear of being discovered and the fact that she always needed to wee, all together were rhododendrons for her. Why had she come down to Knutsford. Because she didn't want to spend her first completely solitary Sunday in Manchester. What was down here. Nothing except the past, aching away quietly with its cruel casual memories. Oh the past, the dead empty ghosted past. All those empty faces. All those ghostly feelings. Had she ever, ever really, not in a dream but in real time, crouched, navy-knickered, trying not to wee under the rhododendrons, afraid to do it on to the ground because Mrs Cuffee said if little girls took their knickers off outdoors things crawled up inside them. Childhood was a terrible place. She wondered how anybody ever survived it, or if anybody ever survived it. She left the window and sat on the bed realizing she hadn't taken her raincoat off. Her tea, half left, was cold. The three-quarter profile of Cuffee looked from the wall. He would be able to change this, this feeling, turning over inside her like smoke in a bottle, vaguest shapes forming and changing. He was so ready to act, to do, that things like this never happened to him. She had seen him when depressed and denied any other outlet, turn to sleep, just lie down, cover himself and go to sleep, turning his mood into an event. She was a vegetable and her life had the slow turgid pulse of green things. She had thought that perhaps Harry Gibbon was like her, he was slow and gradual and somehow strong. Or was she romanticizing. Maybe he was just a big dumb Scotsman. The nastiness of her thought was a little surprising. It was because he hadn't thought she was attractive. She could tell, or could she. When his hands were patiently among her hair, the backs of his fingers almost touching her cheek, he had been intent upon the insect, intent on not harming it, wasn't using it as an excuse to touch her. There had been nothing in those careful fumblings that told her she was female. It was ridiculous she thought, what was wrong with her. If he'd done anything she would have jumped in the air. Even if he had kissed her, would she have shied away from that. His face was blurry when she tried to think of it, but she could see his hands all right, big, wide on the backs, with square flat nails. And the palm, hollowed, with the lines like a map of rivers, and the gnat, green little pip, combing its wings with its legs, and then he blew it away. Suddenly his face was quite clear, the spread nose, the solemn look he had under his brows, the square heavy jaw. Who was Harry Gibbon. Someone who passed through and took a midge out of her hair. A knock on the door.

'Ruthie. You in there. Why don't you go in and talk to your father?' Why. How many reasons would you like, she thought. Because I don't have anything to say to him. Her mother looked in. 'Go on. Go in and have a chat with him.'

Ruth got up and heard herself say, 'All right, can you get me a fresh cup of tea.'

Mr Cuffee sat by the window smoking a pipe and reading a paper. He looked up as though cued, his mild, carefully expressed surprise, the way he put down the *Sunday Times* and removed the pipe, the dull purple paisley dressing-gown; Ruth felt she should run to him crying 'Papa'. She sat in the big easy chair with the yellow covers. It was a beautiful chair, the nicest piece in the house and she had considered finding an unfurnished place and begging her mother for it. An empty room and this chair, with her feet curled under her for snuggery.

'Well Ruth, nice to see you. That's a becoming dress.' Mr Cuffee chose his moods like some people choose suits. He was being distinguished this morning. He did it well though she had to admit to herself.

'Thank you. That's a nice ensemble you're wearing – your cravat sets it off to a nicety.' She had forgotten all about the cravat, a royal blue with pale blue dices. Two Christmases ago. What had she bought him last one. A tobacco pouch wasn't it.

'Heard from my firstborn yet?'

'You mean Peter?'

'Who else?'

'No.'

'Wonder where he's got himself to.'

'London, Paris, one or the other.'

'He's told you about his plans?'

'I knew he meant to go to Paris via London.'

'Did he tell you where he was going to get the money?'

'He said he would ask you for it. That was a fortnight ago, when we were over, then I gathered you'd refused.'

'I did. Do you know what he did?'

'My mother told me this morning.'

'I haven't told your mother what he wanted the money for. But I'd like to tell you.'

'He wanted to go on this trip.'

'That's what he told you, and that's what he told me, at first. But when he came down last Sunday he told me what it really was for.'

'What?'

'To pay for an abortion for a girl he's got into trouble.'

175

Should she feel some special way. Was it something that should matter to her. Anyway it didn't. She felt the recipient of some dull, meaningless fact, and one which demanded her response.

'Who was it?' she asked without really wishing to know.

'He didn't say.' Ruth suddenly knew he had taken his father in. The way he had behaved on meeting her and Harry Gibbon. He had spun him this yarn to justify stealing the money.

'Maybe he was lying.'

'About a thing like that?'

'Peter doesn't have your sense of propriety.'

'No. I was convinced it was the truth.'

'Perhaps it was.'

'Why do you doubt it?'

'I don't know. I really don't.'

'You and your brother have always been close. Has he ever mentioned this, or anything about any girl to you?'

'No. What made you so sure he wasn't telling it as a cover-up, so that you would let him keep the money.'

'He already had the money. He didn't have to tell me, he could have just gone without saying anything. I was rather pleased that he did decide to tell me, although his reason of course I found most upsetting. I really don't understand him. There is something about him, something quite relentless. He was telling me about the operation she would have to have, quite calmly I should say, and I asked him what kind of man was he, allowing this to happen to a girl and then letting her undergo a serious and criminal risk. He just said, "I didn't make the rules. It's the rules that women have children. They should know this." Just like that, just as flatly as that.'

'You really don't understand anything about him do you?'

'I'm beginning to think none of us do. Is he just a product of his age? What they say about the climate of indecision, of hostility . . .' It was amazing Ruth thought. He knew nothing. About anything. And he couldn't be told. What could she say that might make him see. Anyway what did it matter whether he saw or not. It was all much much too late. Mr Cuffee awaited her reply for a moment and then went on, 'He seems to be committed to one point of view, his own, and anything else just gets in the way. Sometimes I get the impression he dislikes us, or despises us.' He was leaning forwards and speaking earnestly, questioningly. Ruth was dismayed and incredulous. What right did he have to be so obtuse. He wasn't a stupid man. He should know enough not to have to ask idiocies like that. 'Is there anything your brother holds sacred?' What do you know about my brother, or me. Or your wife or Robert Eldman or anybody. You've masturbated your whole life away and you sit here talking about things sacred. What did he hold sacred. Anything. Nothing. Himself.

'You'd better ask him next time you see him.'

'Well that's what I was wondering. If he's got no money how long will he be, how long can he go for?'

'This friend of his, the one who was here with Peter when you called in the military police—' Mr Cuffee looked a little uncomfortable at this being revived— 'well he's got some money. They'll be living on that. Then he'll get a job I should think.'

Mrs Cuffee came in with a pot of tea and two cups. 'Are you having a nice chat?' she said, looking for somewhere to put the dregs out of Mr Cuffee's cup. She had changed into a summery frock and Ruth noticed she had on make-up. In many ways Mrs Cuffee was an attractive woman in a pastelled, faded fashion, and contrasting now with the dark sculpt of her daughter's face, cameo on the yellow cover. Mr Cuffee remained seated by the window and was re-examining his pipe. Ruth watched the tea coming amber out of the spout and felt trapped, but without desperation, without anything really except the knowledge of being snared, down the wrong end of the telescope, taking the minute cup in tiny hands and sipping. How very small everything was, how distant, how remote. She could hardly convince herself that such iotas as they were could house the tangle of thought and feeling they did.

Here they were, while the tea curved to the cup, while the

177

dottle fell from the pipe, while the worms were plucked from the ground; uncertain of their reality, beset by a pervading doubt, that perhaps nothing, anywhere, meant anything. Sunday mornings of the godless, made sonorous by bells calling the faithful to worship.

CHAPTER FIFTEEN

He didn't know why he was avoiding MacIndoe but he knew that he was. At a lecture last week he had made a point of not being in any position where the lecturer might manage to speak to him on his own. And once he had thought he heard his name called but pretended not to, hurrying on into the refectory. These evasions he felt were noted by MacIndoe and surely in his eyes there was a certain dim reproach, a query as to Moseby's motives. As he settled into the tram seat he reviewed these same but could only assume he didn't want to be asked to dinner. Also he found his image of MacIndoe to be one of desperation and the thought of anyone else's desperation seemed a terrible, near obscene matter, to be discreetly overlooked. And there was this morning's lecture. Constitutional Reforms provoked by the Stuarts prior to the Civil War. Maybe he shouldn't be at university at all. It meant rather a lot to Edna, as well as the security it might prove to her mother that he was a socially acceptable creature and vindicate her decision to marry him. The glow of their last love-making had lasted over the week-end. Edna had menstruated and sex had been prohibited but there was a languor in her caresses that spoke of some released well-being, some acquiescence she had given. Although its manifestations were eminently pleasurable this change or adjustment or whatever it was rather disquieted him. Edna was so completely withdrawn from any possible scrutiny, even her own. Things happened to her the causes of which she did not know and which she seemed to have no wish to understand. She was, he had come to realize, one of the most completely inarticulate people he had ever met, not yet having reached that stage of human development in which she understood the possible value of examining her feelings and impulses. She was almost primitive in her emotional behaviour, except she had none of the primitive's direct access to the world through spontaneous action. Except perhaps in bed, when on a few rare occasions, she achieved a rapport between feeling and expression. Thursday night had been one such.

Thinking about it, along with the joggling of the tram, induced an erection. A common enough phenomenon. Interpose briefcase upon rising. Or point the offending member in the air and wait for blood to drain out. Copulation accomplishes similar end but is not always feasible on public transport. He rose as the tram came up to Charing Cross and got off. This was taking MacIndoe avoidance a step towards the ridiculous. Sauchiehall Street went on out towards Partick. It invited him with its uneventful extent. As he walked out something of the drab monotony of the stretch conveyed itself to his mind, dulling its edge, and even further coming in some way to represent the common place train of thoughts that ensued. His white shirt with the pin through collar was fraying at the neck. Carol's fingernails seemed to grow very quickly. There had been a photo in the compartment put in upside down. What was showing in the pictures this week. Did the buildings release these and other thoughts of a trivial like, or were they waiting to spread like oil upon the troubled surface of his mind and simply using the analogous architecture to emerge. Or were these one and the same. He didn't know and for the moment didn't really care. Not wishing to walk the whole way he took the bus out to the Kelvin Hall and spent a few moments looking over the bridge into the steep-sided densely treed gorge of the river. Then he walked on out to Partick.

He liked it as a district. It was shabby and dark but had some kind of animation in its streets and shops. Just behind were the long grim roads down to the docks but these did not depress like their counterparts on the Govan side, or the settled bleakness of the Parliamentary Road. He wandered along, looking at things he hadn't looked at in a long time. The butcher's windows made large sanguinary abstractions, patterns of blood, flesh and fatty marble, bacon slivered and quartz streaky, the shiny lobes of kidneys and the textures of tripe, trays of pork chops pale commas, while within, mute, heel hung pendicles, the hackered knackered sheep drool black blood and swing to the brush of the shoppers. The greengrocer's with their high angled mirrors spotted with rust, smelling of cool and apples and sawdust on the floor. He trod it experimentally. It gave a nice feeling of crumbling underfoot. He bought half a pound of grapes, seedless, taking off his tie while the man weighed them and tore off a paper bag from a sheaf putting the close clump of jade grapes into it and twirling the corners into little lugs. He could see himself as he went out in a mirror, dark and neat, head held to the side slightly. The grapes were sweet and fresh. Next door was a shop selling second-hand books. They had a large Western section. Hank Larribee. Quirt Jerome. Fargo MacQueen. *Bushwhackers Nemesis. Outlaw Range. The Man from Owl Creek.* And the big-boned faces behind the flame-spiked colts and the ejecting Winchesters. Great. The first grape he threw in the air hit him on the chin and bounced on to the pavement. He caught the next one with a small accompanying thrill of surprise. Women went about their purchasing, in their dark coats with their shopping bags and their purses held firmly in hand, gilded in the early sun, making an animate Daumier of the street, confirmed in their reality by Moseby's affectionate witness. They were like his Edna, dowdier, older mostly, but immersed in life as lived and confident of its order. Married to men as solid and purposeful as themselves. John Moseby, pillar of society, defender of the faith, long distance melodeon player to the late king. Standing in Partick eating seedless grapes with his tie off. He toasted her with a grape, feeling tenderness in his mockery. Dear Edna, he said silently, God protect you from all harm if I can't. And Carol. Bless her. He toasted Carol and felt almost gay. Moving on throwing grapes in the air and catching them in his mouth. An old woman with a loose-knit shawl mumbled something about a madman as she went past. He looked back. She had glanced behind her and their eyes met. He gave a short bow. She turned quickly and went on.

There was a picture hall, small and dirty. It looked so self-effacing he thought it might be closed down but a placard pinned to the door said Mon. Tue. Wed. Apache

Drums. 2.10. 5.25. 8.30. Smugglers Island. 3.50. 7.10. There were stills in the glass panels and he felt pleased at knowing all the players in them. Stephen McNally, Coleen Gray. Willard Parker. It made him think of the old Central with the bullets whining and the music and the same bit where Durando turned off to let the baddies ride past. Jesus Christ how good it was to be alive. The director's name was Hugo Fregonese. The other film had Jeff Chandler in it. They were both in colour. On the placard were the prices. 1/9 and 1/-. A woman came out as he was standing. She looked like a cleaner.

'Is it showing today?' She put a padlock on the door.

'Matinee at two,' she said.

'Do they get many in?' he asked chattily.

'Oh, aye, there's always them with nothin' better to do than go to matinees.' She came out on to the street and looked at him with the sharp intimacy of her kind, West Coast, middle-aged, working-class.

'Are ye no' working?'

'I've taken the day off.'

'What'll the wife say to that?'

'If you don't tell her she won't find out.'

'I've enough trouble watching that bugger o' mine without tellin' about any other body's. It's a good show though. Seen it over in Govan.'

'Do you come from Govan?'

'Over in the ferry every morning bar Sunday, hail rain or shine that God sends.'

'Have a grape.'

'Thanks. Are they seedless?' Moseby was inordinately pleased to be able to say yes. He broke off a small bunch and she took them and went on her way down the street, compact and brisk, her green cleaner's overalls showing under her coat and carrying a small rexine bag. He looked again at the times of the films and went on. A pub was just opening, the barman putting back the concertina grille and looking once at the sky before going back inside. Moseby looked at the sky too, it was pale blue and shimmied with cloudings. He went in. The public bar had yellow varnished panelling. The barman was reading a paper. Moseby stood at the bar and looked at the bottles under the counter and the clean rows of upturned glasses. The pub smelt beautifully, damp and cool, like the greengrocer's only different, unmistakably a pub. The barman came down. He had a purple mark on the side of his face, going under the chin and up to the cheekbone. It was the softest palest purple and looked like where a hand had been cupped to support the head. They said good mornings.

'Tennant's please.' It was a long time since he had been in a pub this early. With Gibbon it was. The Rowan Tree. 'It's nice in the morning,' he said to the barman as he poured the stout.

'Aye, best time of day in a pub. Put me in the notion of a stout you have.' He got himself one.

'Cheers,' said Moseby.

'Good luck.' The stout on his clean forgetful palate was like the very morning, cool and sweet and nutty delicately burnt. The barman went back to his paper and shook his head slowly as he read.

'Some team,' he said. Moseby looked enquiring. 'The Thistle. Got beat by St Mirren on Saturday. St Mirren's five from the bottom. Thistle's five from the top, six. Thistle beat Dundee last week at Dens Park. Then they let a lot of mugs like St Mirren come up and beat them at home. Do you follow the fitba?'

'I'm from Greenock. Used to see a bit of the Morton.'

'They're a dead loss this weather. Been at Cappielow a few times. Last time I saw them was at Hampden against Rangers in the Cup Final. A few years back that was. Good game too. Rangers beat them in the replay but they had some good players. Cowan was the goalie and Big Tommy Orr and Billy Campbell were playing. Great player Campbell. Best right half I ever saw.' Moseby remembered him, a slight dark figure with a characteristic cock of the head and a deadly long lunging tackle. Still lived in Greenock. The barman went on. 'After Campbell went they fell away. They've been down nearly ten years.'

'They're doing better this year though.'

'These second division teams are all the same, up for one season and then down again. There's too big a difference in the standard between first and second. That's whit's wrong with Scottish fitba. Not enough competition right through the league. Rangers, Celtic, Hearts, Hibs, Kilmarnock if they feel like it, Motherwell this year, Aberdeen the next. The rest aren't in the hunt.'

Moseby recalled the colours of their jerseys and sipped his stout, thinking unsadly on the fate of Scottish football. The two brewery men came in, in leather aprons and cloth caps. The barman pulled them pints. They talked of Partick's defeat.

'It was that bamstick MacIllhatton. He missed, if he missed wan he missed five. Five. Sitters.'

'Naw, he wisnae good,' said the other man carefully.

'No good?' indignant at such toleration; 'he was bloody diabolical.'

Outside the sun was shining as though it did not care if MacIllhatton ever scored again, shining and making the heavy sandstone buildings black and enormous. He walked idly, looking and seeing, open to the morning. He stopped outside a draper's to look at a lifesize cardboard figure pulling a vest over his head. He had on Y-fronted pants and had stomach muscles. A young woman was looking in the next window. Moseby glanced to see what at. She wore a headscarf of a similar colour to the barman's naevus. He smiled at the unfortunate MacIllhatton and as he was doing so realized he knew the woman.

'Cathie.' She looked at him, blank and then surprised and then recognition. He felt no surprise, only a small elation. Of course on a morning like this it could happen. 'John Moseby.'

'Well,' he said, content to be conventionally inarticulate, 'well, well. How long has it been. A long time.'

'It is. Seven years. Maybe more.'

'Is it? As long as that . . .'

'Must be. You haven't changed much.'

'Neither have you.'

'Are you kidding? I'm married three years since.'

'Well so am I. You still don't look any different.'

'I just slipped out for a message. I've got nothing on my face. She had changed. There was the small curve of a double chin and her features didn't seem so sharp. And her two top front teeth were false, white, square. And under the head square surely her hair was dyed.

'Well it's really nice to see you. Let's go and have a cup of tea somewhere and you can tell me all . . .' Did she glance at the woman going past? She smiled her false-centred smile.

'There's nowhere very nice about here. I'll get some tea bread and you can come to the house. Better than a café.'

'Fine. Only I'll get the tea bread.'

'My you're terrible extravagant gettin' in your old age.' And it didn't ring quite true, it wasn't as he remembered her.

'Do you have a family?' he asked as they walked along.

'No. You?'

'A daughter.'

'That's nice.' They came to the baker's. 'Look Johnny, I live just two closes up. Number a hundred and sixty-four. Pollock's on the door. Second top. I'll away up and put the kettle on and you come up when you're served.'

'Sure, Cathie. I won't be a minute;' and she went. What was that in aid of he wondered. Maybe she just wanted to tidy up, put some lipstick on. For her old lover. The sophistry of the notion amused him. Women didn't have lovers in Partick. They had fancy men. He hadn't really thought on it that way, that they had been lovers. Maybe it was in the back of his mind but on seeing her all he could think was that there was a simple inevitability about it. All MacIndoe's doing. He smiled at this and bought the buns. The fact that it has happened is the proof of its inevitability. He must tell MacIndoe that. He smiled again and went out.

One hundred and sixty-four was a dark narrow close but clean and there was sun coming in the landing windows and the stairs were pipe clayed, worn down in the centre of the step from feet. Pollock was three flights up and the name plate was small and in clear plastic with the name under it in white. It was set in the middle of the mark left by one of the older, large name plates. She came out almost immediately to his knock. Certainly she had put on make-up he noticed and although he couldn't be certain he thought she might be wearing a different dress, a buttoned-up thing that showed her tendency to the buxom, especially on the hips. And her hair was dyed from its brown to near black. She looked like an older, married sister. The house was a room and kitchen with an inside toilet, the kitchen to the back and the room overlooking the street. They went into the kitchen. It was furnished with furniture that had recently been new. The usual piano polished sideboard with rounded edges and moulding on the front. The chairs heavy-armed, covered in moquette, maroon and tan. The table was in the middle of the floor and had a plain blue table cloth. It was set with cups and milk and sugar. The teapot was yellow and had a metal hood that went over it. He put his icing buns on the table.

'I'll just make the tea, the kettle's boiling.' The sun fell into the room and on the blue table. Looking out he could see the back of another tenement and below a set of washing houses and back greens, some with washing out but none of them green. Beyond the roofs the tops of cranes and somewhere further away a single stack which as he watched was giving off smoke.

Her hands had not changed he noticed, sitting down with his back to the window. The raw-looking cuticles, the nails bitten brutally short. Hurt, unhealed hands. He looked around him. On the mantelpiece was a framed photo of Cathie in a wedding dress. On the other side was a smaller photo of a young man in a peaked navy cap. It was still a good morning filled with sun and simple well-being, but looking at the anonymous face under the white cap Moseby felt his neck tighten and suddenly he wanted to urinate.

'That your husband?'

'Yes. He's in the merchant navy.' Moseby knew it was for him to ask, not for her to have to tell. Lightly, stirring his tea and looking up at the end of it.

'Is he ashore at the moment?'

'No, he's on the Abadan run.' The spoon was one of the small kind with a little saint figure on the top of the handle.

'Well I've thought a lot about you from time to time Cathie.'

'I've thought about you too.'

'Only a few weeks ago I was thinking about us, how we met, all that. Strange how things happen.'

'It's funny. Do you think I've changed much?'

'No. Not at all hardly.'

'You're just the same. It's funny. What's your daughter called?'

'Carol.'

'Carol, that's nice. Was she born at Christmas?'

'No. In October.'

'Oh.'

'If my baby had lived its birthday would have been Christmas.'

'Oh, you lost a baby.'

'Yes. Three months after I was married.'

'Oh.' What else could you say, he thought. Yet 'Oh' sounded half-witted. 'You planning to have more?' and too late thought on it.

'I can't.'

'Oh.'

'It was two months premature. I can't have any more.'

'That's pretty bad for you.'

'You going to have a big family? I was from a big family.'

'No. I don't think so. Still you never can tell.'

'What are you working at?'

'I'm at University.'

'Teaching?'

'Christ no. I've got a grant. I'm studying for a degree and then I'll teach.'

'You have to like kids to teach.'

'Well I hope maybe to get teaching in a secondary school.'

'Oh I see. You always were pretty brainy.' It was warm on his back and the rooms to the back were cut off from the street noise. 'I feel changed,' she said, drinking her tea.

'Well we do change. Inside.' He hadn't meant to say 'inside'. 'I mean our minds change.'

'Oh I don't think my mind has changed much,' and she smiled as she said it.

'I've changed quite a bit,' Moseby said.

'Did you keep on with your writing?'

'Well I haven't given it up.'

'I wish I could write. Express myself. There's a lot of things I'd like to write.' Although he could see it was a fraught solution he took it. Out of laziness he thought.

'What sort of things?' She was looking down into the cup and he couldn't really see her face.

'Oh just what I thought sometimes,' and for a moment it seemed as though she might leave it there, then: 'and what I felt. He didn't want to marry me. Then when he did look what happened. It was his people made him. I tried not to have it before. But I couldn't stop it. So I went to his people. And they made him. And then look what happened. Do you think that would make a good story?' What in the name of Christ do you say to that? He looked at her with what was meant to be sympathetic understanding. 'I think that's what did it. Me trying. It worked all those months later. Funny isn't it?' She looked up and he noticed with some surprise she looked nowhere near tears. Which made the low, unemphatic voice one of detachment. Or did it? He could remember her way of talking, flat and empty saying almost everything, and this habit of averting her eyes until she was finished.

'Has your husband been away long?'

'This trip's been six months.' That surprised him, he hadn't thought they went away as long as that at one go.

'That's an awful long time.'

'This is an eight-month trip.'

'You mean there's longer ones than that?'

'Some trips last a year. Then he's here studying for his tickets.'

'What do you do while he's away?'

'Watch television. Go to the pictures with my sister.'

'Oh your sister lives near you?' He didn't know that she had a sister.

'Yes, well at Kelvingrove Street.'

'That's not so bad then,' he said as though he thought that it were not so bad.

'No that's not so bad. Funny. It's not Tom who's the worst upset. It's his people. He's their only son and they

188

wanted to have grandchildren. They're Catholic and so they don't think about him getting divorced.'

'Does he?' She looked at the photograph.

'I don't know what he thinks. Except that I trapped him. He thinks that.'

'Did you?' Somehow it was easy to ask.

'Did I?' She smiled again as she had when she said about her mind not having changed. 'Do you believe in original sin, Johnny?'

'Why do you ask that?'

'Because I think I do. Only I'm not sure what it means.'

'It's the belief that man is guilty of sin from his birth, because of the sins of his parents, who in turn inherit their parents, and so on all the way back to Adam and Eve.'

'I thought it was something like that but I wasn't sure.'

'And that's what you believe?'

'You have to believe something like that, don't you, to explain all this,' and her gesture took in the kitchen and all that she had told him.

'You mean "Life" and all that class of thing,' he said, brightly.

'Yes, life.' She didn't seem perturbed by his attempt at flippancy and appeared to resign interest in the topic.

'How long are you off for?'

'I took the morning off. I had a lecture I wanted to skip.'

'Are you going back this afternoon then?'

'Well I rather thought I might go to the pictures, there's one just down the street looks quite good.'

'The Lyceum. I go there sometimes. What's on?'

'A Western. *Apache Drums*. Fancy a bit of the old distraction this afternoon?' – and let it go on being an innuendo after he had realized it was. She seemed not to have noticed anything however, and said yes, might as well.

Apache Drums was very good. It was based on a story by Harry Brown called *The Stand at Spanish Boot* and had good locations and colour. There was a man with a beautiful El Greco face who played the cavalry officer and another who played the Indian scout. It made Moseby quite mindless to sit in the dark watching the flow of events, escaping into the ordered familiar images, feeling his identity and the identity of Cathie, beside him, becoming nebulous, to exist for eighty minutes on the screen. When the lights went up he saw she was wiping her eyes.

'What's wrong?'

'Nothing. I always cry in the pictures.'

Moseby didn't want to see the other film because of the time. She was going to come out with him but he told her to stay.

'Will I be seeing you again?' she asked. The credits came up with loud music. An American voice said 'Macao' and a gong boomed. It said 'Macao' several times, adding various descriptions, 'port of intrigue', 'melting pot of the east', 'rendezvous of adventure' and after each the gong was struck. After this ceased Moseby said:

'Nothing much good can come of it.'

'I know. I like talking to you, that's all.' A pause, then – 'Will you tell your wife you met me?'

'No.'

'I'll be home on Thursday if you want to come over.'

'I don't know. I really don't.'

'All right. Cheerio.'

The light outside was blinding in the way he remembered it from the matinees of his childhood. He waited for a tram trying not to think about the layers and the implications. The upstairs ride eased him somewhat only on Argyle Street, looking casually to his right, in a side street, a woman, rather fat and elderly, half-sitting half-lying asleep in a pub doorway. Her legs were buckled in front of her and above a dark brown stocking putty-coloured thigh flesh showed. His open eye came upon it unawares and was taken quickly past yet he had seen it all, the awkward loll of the gross old neck, the features contorted in drunken, daylight sleep, the splayed knees, the stocking, the skin, and almost immediately he realized he had left his briefcase at Cathie's. Disgust and excitement uneasily blended.

CHAPTER SIXTEEN

They shuttled out through London to the southbound roads. It was early but clear and there were workmen about, walking briskly, buying papers and catching buses. They took several themselves in getting on to the Dover Road. Once on it they stopped for a cup of tea. Cuffee smoked a cigarette.

'How far to Dover?' asked Gibbon.

'About eighty.'

'What did you say to Gerda?'

'Don't dig your associations. Just said I'd see her when we get back.'

'Is she in love with you?'

'What gives you a Christly notion like that?'

'I don't know. Just a feeling.'

'Gerda knows her arse from a hole in the ground. She's no mug.'

'Do you have to be a mug to fall in love?'

'Helps.'

'Big kinda cynical guy. She's pretty sad somehow.'

'We're all disenchanted.'

'Sure.'

'We're a sad lot of gets, but never forget, from among us will come the leaders of the future, the statesmen, the footballers, the street-sweepers and the child murderers of the 'seventies. We must take ourselves seriously Harold my boy. Did you hear about the coprophagist who came upon this crap under a bush and said "Diana, I'd know that faeces anywhere"?'

'What's a coprophagist?'

'A turd eater.'

'A toley muncher.'

'Precisely.'

'You live and learn.'

Dover was windy and rather empty. They went down to the pier and bought tickets. There was more than an hour before they were allowed on board. The Channel looked grey and choppy. They bought some soap and toothpaste and Gibbon stole a bottle of bay rum, all from the chemists. The girl was blonde and seemed interested in Cuffee who talked all the time he was buying the soap and the toothpaste. After she put them in a paper bag she asked if there was anything else. Cuffee said yes, that since the shop was empty could he have a kiss. The girl made a face of annoyance. Cuffee said only a small chaste kiss was required to remind him of English womanhood while he was gone upon the continent. The girl tossed her head and rearranged some face flannels. She said he had a nerve coming away with a line like that. Upon my bended knees the erect Cuffee swore, one small fragrant tremulous kiss from her bouche rouge. Gibbon stole the bottle of bay rum. The girl said she didn't go around kissing everyone that asked her. Cuffee said in his case she must be stone mad. He gave her a last chance to obtain a souvenir kiss behind the sanitary towel stand. The girl moved away, near blushes. Gibbon from behind, kissed him on the cheek. 'Come dear, don't fight it, it's bigger than both of us.' Exit camping madly.

The boat wasn't very busy. They stood at the rail and watched for a spectacular late arrival.

'A Pakistani pole vaulter,' Cuffee saw prospects in.

'Two drunk men on a tandem,' Gibbon claimed as a favourite. Failure of both or either sent Cuffee to scout the saloon for crumpet, left Gibbon at the rail.

The boat moved out. The few people on the quay waved their hands and hankies and their features shrank into their faces. A few calls floated across. The water expanded. The gulls planed past oynx-eyed, crying in his watching face. The quay emptied. Someone remained, maybe a woman, still waving. It came fluttering weakly to the ship. The horn brayed. Gibbon waved to the sole watcher. The water grew gulf.

After about an hour it started to rain. It was still raining, and quite heavily, after they docked at Calais. Gibbon put on his duffle and Cuffee a proofed windcheater. They walked out on to the Paris road, following the signs and watching the people who looked quite different. They took up a stand opposite a cement factory into which big, white powdered lorries went from time to time. The rain thickened. Cars went past frequently and very rapidly. They stood and thumbed and got wet.

'Never liked the French,' Cuffee said. 'Not even in history, scabby grandiose bunch of bastards. Hated Joan of Arc. I really set my heart on the fall of Orleans. Not even burning her was recompense.'

'Do you really think they're different? I know they look different.'

'As you know, Harold, I am an expert on the Toynbee theory of historical progress. It is my unpublished opinion, not to say my confirmed analysis that there are only, and ever have been, two kinds of society, ours and theirs. If one has the misfortune to belong to theirs, which by my definition is non-English speaking and European, then immediate immigration is advised. Failure to take this elementary precaution can lead to incurable cases of Frenchitis or Germanotology, a few of which former sorry mob you noticed on your way in. Ye must be born again, and ye must be born British. Après us it will piss down—'

'There's one stopping.' It wasn't but immediately after a truck with a load of sand came coasting up and the driver leaned over and spoke in French. Cuffee said 'Paris' several times and the driver replied 'avee' on each occasion.

'A religious maniac,' Cuffee said, crossing himself and climbing up into the cab. Gibbon handed up the bags and got in. The driver smiled enthusiastically and started the truck off saying 'avee' once or twice more.

'Watch the signposts or he'll have us into some monastery.' Gibbon had a look at a map from the dashboard cubby. The driver grinned enthusiastically and said something ending in 'avee'. The first biggish town on the map was Abbeville and when they reached it the driver pointed at it and said 'Avee'.

'You wouldn't credit it would you,' Cuffee said, getting down.

They walked through Abbeville in the rain. It had greywhite walls and the windows had shutters. It all looked old and recently built and was thoroughly wetted by the rain and had a long slow hill up and out of it. The only people to be seen were many identical old women wearing bowlegged black stockings. They had a cognac in a small tabac near the end of the town. Looking down the hill through the rain-specked glass showed a crowdle of wet roofs and several steeples.

'Campaniles rising out of the plain. Sacred stones of old gall,' Cuffee said. The cognac was good and stood repeating.

Out on the road again cars were less frequent and just as fast. Their wetness moved towards saturation. A travelling butcher's van stopped just as they were preparing to return to Abbeville for the night. They sat in the back and bumped along among several swinging joints while the driver, a butchery-looking monsieur shouted splintered English questions above the engine to which they replied yes and no alternately. It was after nine and getting dark when they reached Poix. The driver let them out, gave profuse and meaningless instructions and drove off. They were in a small square, cobbled and unlit, centred by a drinking fountain and peopled apart from themselves by a slowly approaching, bicycle-accompanied gendarme.

'Can you chat him up Peter. Get a night's kip.' Cuffee went towards the policeman who upon marking this stopped and rested his weight upon his bicycle seat. He was a broad, unsurprised-looking man and he nodded shortly to Cuffee when he got up. Cuffee commenced in and at his normal conversational tone.

'Bonsoir, mon homme, que est le chance pour la bunkup, dormir tres tres, pour nous avons fatigue et il est pluie et non para avons nous. Aussi tres faim, desirons a mange et dormons dans un auberge. S'il vous plaît.' The gendarme waited stoically through this atrocity and then, without mounting completely but standing on the one pedal and pushing off, rolled across the square, found an incline and disappeared down it.

'Did that lot mean anything?' Gibbon asked as they hurried along behind his rapid red light.

'Well it said food, kip, weariness and rain. Can you think of anything else?' Down at the bottom of the hill there was a street with houses on one side and a small river on the

194

other. Trees, tall poplar plumes, at intervals. The rain regretted nothing. The bicycle was standing unattended outside an inn called 'l'Espagnol'. The gendarme looked out and waved to them. Inside was warm and had a stove and several Cézanne men sitting round playing cards. A small aproned woman was waiting and smiled hesitantly at them. The gendarme who seemed eager for a second broadcast of Cuffee's borstal French gestured to him to go ahead and waited.

'Une chambre pour mon ami et moi, madame. Est-il possible. Aussi déjeuner pour deux.' The woman said yes and the gendarme looked a little disappointed.

The room was large, long rather than square and contained a vast bed, a wardrobe with a mirror on the front of it, a table with a jug and basin and several wooden chairs. The wallpaper was heavily flowered and above the bed there was a water-colour of a woman in a silk garb standing beside a sundial.

'Très bien, madame, merci beaucoup,' and she smiled and left them. They changed and dried themselves and then went downstairs. The gendarme was still there and they all had cognacs and he, at each sip, looked to Cuffee and nodded as if to say he knew but he wouldn't tell.

They ate at a table set back in an alcove. The woman showed them to it then left to serve the meal. The soup was thick, hot and strong, slippery with onion flesh. The meat was veal, pale closegrained fillets, medium cooked and succulent, with small quartered potatoes deep fried and a lettuce and cucumber salad. There was a carafe of metally red wine. They both ate without talk, drinking between mouthfuls. Along with the cheese was crusty bread.

'That was the best meal I ever had,' Gibbon said, sitting back and smiling in appreciation at the woman who smiled warmly in return.

They had coffee and Cuffee lit up. Gibbon closed his eyes and smiled.

'What you smiling?'

'Remember?'

'Remember what?'

'See how quick it comes back.'

'What?'

'Summer.'

'Summer.'

'Summer, hot, a pub, me, you. Getting close.'

'The Army.'

'Where?'

'Pembrokeshire.'

'Yes. Wooden tables, sitting outside, dipping your finger . . .'

'Map-reading exercise.'

'And writing Ruth. Wonder where that ladybird is.'

'That was a good day. What made you think of it?'

'This.'

'Yes, idylls. They last in the mind for ever. Oh idylls I love you, brief little, sweet little, beautiful little idylls.'

'They do don't they. Pity they don't last a bit longer at the time.'

'It's the nature of idylls to end. If they didn't they wouldn't be idylls.'

'Kinda philosophic big guy.'

'People take refuge from the world in idylls, the big organised idylls like religion and politics or psychology, the big orders. They won't admit idylls are like my woman at the window in Wales, shaking her breasts like a treeful of apples.'

'Remember those apples.'

'Harry it's great to be alive, to be me, to be here, to be with you. Great.' Gibbon opened his eyes. Cuffee was sunk behind his smoke.

'Thanks,' Gibbon said.

'Mention it not Harold, come comfort me in bed with your sweet presence.'

They said good night and went upstairs. The bed was large and cool, the sheets smooth with starch. They got in and lay in the dark. There was no noise and only the faintest of lights from the window. The mirror quivered on the threshold of vision.

'Wonder what direction Greenock is . . .'

'Going to sleep with your head pointing?'

'Ever wonder just how some place lies that's far away. I

feel as though I'm lying parallel to Nelson Street, my head down to George's Square. Should be able to figure it out, the Clyde is like that and the French coast is like that. Would you say we were parallel to the French coast?'

'Hold on, I'll fart out the window and see what way the wind's blowing.'

'You foul-mouthed get. Don't you know a nice word for it?'

'My mother used to call it "pooping", the crud that she was.'

'You don't like your folks much, do you?'

'No.'

'Funny. Funny to think on somebody not, well maybe it isn't. Moseby doesn't like his folks.'

'You said they weren't his folks.'

'Well, he doesn't know his real folks.'

'Lucky bastard.'

'I think I'm more like my grandfather. I'm not like my father much, and I'm not like my grand-uncle. I'm the last of the Gibbons, did I tell you?'

'I'll see about getting you into Whipsnade, you'd be a celebrity, wanking through the bars at women.'

'Why didn't you take Ruth with you on this trip?'

'I can see the way your mind's working. Don't be a mug. What Ruth needs is not to see me for about a year. What she needs is somebody like you.'

'I'm sure.'

'Well you need somebody like Ruth.'

'What makes you say that?'

'No loss what a friend gets.' Gibbon smiled in the dark and turned on his side.

'Good night, Peter.'

'Good night, Harry.' The quiet lay on them in softest quiltings of hush, the room filled with their breathing, waves on an empty shore. Once a dog drew a long curve on the still and distance faint another dog put up response, parenthetic howls within which silence attained purest cadence.

Gibbon woke first in the morning. The sun was barely

197

bright but came in making the whole room clear. He rose and went to the window. A long narrow garden ran down behind the house and beyond its wall there was an orchard, the trees brown-trunked and woven with ground mist. Beyond the land went flat and unfeatured towards the converging sky. The window opened inwards. The balustrade was wet with dew. A cockerel crowed an incredible mimicry of itself. The call crackled terra cotta on the silver pink dawn. There was a smell of damp land and earliness, of earth and dew and morning, begenesings. Scrollings of birdsong unwound. He stood breathing deeply till the chill made him shiver.

He had prepared his shaving before Cuffee awoke. There was hot water in the bathroom outside. He filled his wooden bowl and set it on the table and searched for a nail for his strop. The heavy old Kropp opened out of itself smoothly. Its thick tonguing on the leather was in the room. Against his hearing its edge feathered on the testing thumb. He soaped slowly, working the lather up heavy and rich, white white, the brush like a snowy oak. Watching himself in the mirror he began, with care and skill, to shave. The blade cut smooth and close, leaving the skin clean and almost dry. He shaved the planes of the jaw first in long firm sweeps, then pulling firm he shaved the upper lip, the growth yielding crisply to the blade's insistence. Pulling taut as he went he shaved under his jaw and finally his chin. At every stroke he wiped the curds on a piece of paper. He shaved slowly, with movements of the wrist, the elbow held high and still, the razor making a right-angled figure in his three-fingered hold, the head inclined, the left hand in attendance, tensing the skin and touching for smoothness. When he had finished he washed in cold water from the jug and after drying himself rubbed in bay rum. It smelled nicely and tingled a little.

Outside the sun had strengthened and dried the mist out of the trees almost completely. In the fields beyond figures had commenced work. Gibbon sat looking out on the low bluish horizon. Cuffee came to the window wearing his trousers.

'How are you, Harold my boy?'

198

'Very well uncle, and yourself?'

'Very well Harold my boy.' They sat for a while and Cuffee smoked his first cigarette, coughing a little. The smell of coffee came up.

'Can we have coffee up here?'

'Why not?' Cuffee said. 'Who won the war anyway?' He put his shirt on and went to see the woman. Gibbon sat on.

'Here's to you, little idylls,' he said.

CHAPTER SEVENTEEN

Ruth sat on a high stool and drank an orange squash. Opposite, on the wall, a brunette in a bikini bathing-suit leaned
against a Coca-Cola bottle. Ruth wondered if she should
have put on lipstick. She waited for some feeling about the
evening ahead to show itself but nothing except the doubt
as to whether she would recognize him or not. She hadn't
known who it was when he phoned and there had been a
few moments' incomprehension as he went on with his chat
and she sifted back to identify him. Finally he had mentioned Tessa and she remembered. Would she like to go to
the pictures. Would she? She didn't know. For a moment
she stood with the phone in her hand trying to remember
his face and he said 'hello are you still there', and she was
embarrassed that he might have thought she would hang
up on him so she said yes she'd love to. And now she was
waiting for him, whoever he was, waiting and trying to feel
like a girl going out on a first-time date, trying to feel the
lightness and the casual bright feeling she always imagined
it must have for those who were good at it. But it would not
happen and around the vacuum her mind traced its angular
doodles, coming back to its prevailing discontent, the vague
persistent hangover that Sunday had caused, Sunday with
its dim terrors and the re-entry into that household where
her very nature had taken shape. All day it had rained and
she looked out on the back garden, dark wet green, with the
crab apple black and the rhododendron rubbery shining
bushes, till her mind was saturated with memory, the num-
berless sunken Sundays of the past she had spent looking
out on this scene before they were called for tea. Sunday tea.
'Children's Hour' and Welsh Rarebit. Uncle Mac. They
were all with her, clamouring in her mind for justification,
for explanation of how in time she had come to again be
looking out at the rain and the lawn and the crab apple and
the rhododendrons, on a Sunday before the call for tea. And
when it came, unchanged in form or timbre, 'tea Ruthie, it's

on the table', which of course it wasn't, when it came it was with a strange gratitude that she yielded to its demand, and washed her hands and went downstairs. Mrs Cuffee said grace and the clock struck five. The knives cut, the cups clicked and Mr Cuffee talked about the mentality of modern youth and she allowed it all, 'the longest running farce in the history of the theatre' he had called it, allowed it to sedate her, and thus lobotomised her evening had passed, augmented by the figmental appearance of Robert Eldman who brought Mrs Cuffee some tulips, unreal waxy-looking things.

The brunette in the bikini grinned at her steadily, her arm round the great phallic bottle. Ruth recalled lesbian perversions the authenticity of which had always somehow seemed dubious. Somehow looking at the couple before her it all seemed much more probable, and she was half smiling at the ingenuity when a young man tapped her on the shoulder.

'What's going on in that head? I've been watching you for about a minute. You were miles away,' and only at the end of this did she recognize him.

'Your beard, what happened to it?'

'I shaved it off.'

'So I see, why?'

'Oh, I was fed up with it.' Without it his face looked odd, a sharp chin and wide jaw muscles and where the beard had been was a different colour, pallid and blue from the heavy growth. 'Did you prefer the beard?'

'Well, no, I mean it's just that I didn't recognize you for a moment.'

'I suppose it would be a bit of a surprise if you remember someone only with a beard and he turns up without one. I wasn't surprised, I'd seen me before.' She smiled. 'Do you want something else here, I'm sorry to be late but my beard, or my non-beard held me up.'

'That's all right. I don't want anything else thanks, let's go.'

They saw *Baby Doll*. It depressed her steadily, the low key photography, the strangely stylised landscape and the brooding emotions of the central characters, sluggish pulsings under the minutely observed performances. She had her wrong end of the telescope feeling again, except once when Baby Doll's husband, a large sweaty-faced man, stood outside the house after being humiliated by his wife and her lover, stood beaten and near tears and in a casual unthinking gesture offered his bottle to a silent negro. This moment suddenly brought tears up into Ruth's eyes which she restrained by wiping her nose.

They came out with the crowd and he took her elbow to guide her through.

'Let's go for a coffee,' he said. As they walked along he talked about the film, how it was an allegory of disintegration and decay. 'I mean it's not a real geographical location as Williams sees it, it's about pastoral creatures and predators, how some take and some get taken from' – and she thought of Harry Gibbon and her brother, the hawk and the, the what, what kind of bird was he, with his big slow wingbeats, the hunch of his head between his shoulders. The pelican, as in her psalm.

'What was the man called who played the husband?'

'Karl Malden. He's from the Actors' Studio. Did you like him?'

'I think that time he gave the negro a drink was beautiful. I thought that was the most beautiful thing in the whole film.'

'Didn't you like it, the film, then?'

'I don't know, I thought it was sort of, unreal . . .'

'Ah, but it was, you mustn't think of it as a realistic film, it's not at all, Williams is a symbolist writer,' he said, and more.

The coffee bar they went to was the students' one. Ruth felt rather nondescript among the sweatered, jeantight girls. Her escort identified the music as Brubeck. They sat in an alcove and were served by someone who knew him, commenting on his bare face. The record suited her mood, the saxophone had a dry cool sound and extended long lines of thought above the piano's mutterings.

'That's a very enigmatic look.'

'Is it, it's not meant to be.'

'You were in a strange mood that first time we met.'

'Was I, yes, well I was a bit upset about something.' My brother you see, with whom I was having an affair, was going away.

'I remember you saying something about "twinkle, twinkle little star".' She was about to correct him but let it lapse as being of no consequence. Rather like the whole evening. To prevent an aftermath of depression she thought of her birds, teeming back from the countryside. 'I am as a sparrow upon the house top alone.' She looked at him, watching her with his head on one side. What was he, a jackdaw? Sensing her interest he smiled his naked smile.

'What bird would you say I was?'

'Pardon?'

'What bird, am I like?'

'What makes you ask that?'

'I was wondering, that's all.'

'Funny thing to be wondering.' Anger, at him. At herself, annoyance for having asked.

'Shall we go?' she said and regretted the brusqueness immediately. 'I'm feeling a bit tired' – as a sop.

'Sure. I'll just finish my coffee.'

On the way back she felt uneasy over her continued silence and it was partly to assuage the feeling that she asked him up. Partly too because she didn't know how to terminate the evening decorously, to stall or reject the request for a further meeting, to say thank you and make it sound sincere. She just didn't know the technique of it. She showed him into the room and went to put on a kettle. Maureen's room was in darkness she noticed. When she came back he was looking at the small portrait of her by Cuffee.

'Who did this, your brother?'

'Yes. Quite a time ago though.'

'It's nice. Could you tell me where your loo is?'

'Oh yes, it's the first on the right down the stairs.' He smiled a little sheepishly and went.

Black hair water falling jetly down, wan face, shadow-eyed, erogenous faint smear of mouth. Under the sloehang the nostrils incised and the pale lips palps, a wintry face, delicate as birches in snow. He always said it wasn't a good painting but she liked it, even if it disconcerted her to see the pallor of its gaze some mornings. The cistern sounded and a moment later Dave, his hair combed.

'I think your kettle's boiling,' he said.

She made the tea slowly wondering how long he would stay afterwards. He didn't have to catch a bus did he. No. She could explain about Mrs Pendleton being strict about visitors. Someone coughed, it sounded like a man and she wasn't sure whether it was from her room or not. It was no surprise to note that the tea was weak. He was sitting by the window and smoking. Who are you she thought, what are you doing here.

'Seen much of Tessa lately?' he asked.

'No, no, I haven't.'

'It was Tessa who gave me your telephone number. Pretty decent of her, really.' The 'really' meant something, positioned and phrased as it was.

'I don't know her very well.'

'No. Not your sort of person I shouldn't think. Very dominant sort of person. Always making a conflict out of everything. I don't mind that, I think a relationship needs conflict, don't you?'

'I suppose it does, yes' – and stirred his tea.

'Tessa and I, we had, well a sort of thing going. Only lasted a few months. Very complex girl. I think her trouble was that she resented sex or something, basically she resented it.' Didn't take us long to get round to it, she thought, handing him a pallid cup.

'I'm sorry about the tea, it's a bit on the anaemic side.'

'That's all right. Mind you she's had some rotten experiences in the past, a lot of trouble with her climaxes. Bit screwed up sexwise.' Ruth felt this was her cue to assure him she was nothing of the sort, but the kind of straightforward poke good potty training ensures. The recoil found her wondering just what sort of poke she was. Maybe she too was screwed up sexwise. Dave leant forward, putting his cup down and his arm against her knee in the process.

'I suppose you know I fancied you rather strongly that first night, but I noticed you were a bit upset so I didn't push it.' He was going to make a pass, or whatever it was. What

204

should she do. She didn't want to offend him. Yet again politeness had its frontiers.

'I don't want you to think I'm trying to crowd you, but I still feel the same way.' She'd better get in the bit about Mrs Pendleton. With a curious rising and stooping motion he was standing by her chair and kissing her beside the nose, her involuntary jerk having spoiled his aim. She still had the cup in her hand. While he was working down to her mouth, an elaborate pretence to cover his inaccuracy, she reached it on to the table, trying to keep her face still so that he wouldn't think she was drawing away. Something however disturbed him for he stopped and knelt beside her. They looked steadily at one and other and she realized his was a meaningful gaze, though her own was simply a fixed stare accompanied by a blank expression, behind which it crossed her mind that she hadn't called him by his name once that evening and that now would be the most inopportune moment to begin.

'I think you know I want to make love to you,' keeping his eyes on hers. He was a great one for thinking what she thought. Wasn't he going a bit fast considering he'd only kissed her once and even that hadn't been a total success.

'Yes,' she said vaguely, wondering how one said 'but I don't want you to', and why should it seem such a monstrous thing to say anyhow, then realizing that 'yes' was almost as dangerous as calling him Dave.

'I mean I know you do,' which wasn't the right thing to say either. 'Only, well, it's not really possible.' His expression inclined to disbelief. What was it to be. Did she have a boy friend somewhere, or was it the curse. But then he might not mind that. What was that complaint, cystitis. No, she couldn't go on about that sort of thing. The whole thing was ridiculous.

'Maybe I should have told you, but well, I didn't think . . .' and paused to imply he had been a bit hasty.

'There's somebody else?'

'I'm afraid so.'

'At the University?'

'Oh no, no a friend of my brother's, from Scotland. He's with Peter now.'

'Oh. Is it a serious thing. I mean have you been to bed with him?' And she almost felt angry at the prying but the preposterous side of it caught hold and she lowered her head to conceal the possibility of a smile.

'Actually, I think I'm pregnant;' – and she heard him suck in breath and after a moment the crack of his knees as he got up.

On the way downstairs Mrs Pendleton's door inched open and after Dave had gone, huffy and uncomfortable, she came out to meet Ruth. She was a short broad woman with a plasticine face and hair that seemed perpetually in curlers. Tonight it also sported a yellow snood.

'You know the rules about visitors Miss Cuffee.'

'Yes, I'm very sorry Mrs Pendleton, I'm afraid his watch stopped.'

'Eleven o'clock is the time.'

'Yes, his watch, and we didn't know the time . . .'

'It's now nearly twelve.'

'I'm very sorry. I'll make sure it doesn't happen again.'

'No. Well. It's just that we have these rules and they're as much for your own good as our convenience.'

Several more apologies were required before she managed to escape upstairs. As she was going in Maureen's door opened.

'Did she catch you?'

'Yes. I thought you weren't in.'

'She just missed Tom. I sent him down on his own, but I heard her door.' There was a certain vivacity in her manner Ruth noticed, uncharacteristic.

'Oh she's an old wart.'

'We didn't disturb you?' Maureen said, her voice and face pleading for interest.

'No. No, I didn't think you were in.'

'Yes. Yes we were. Oh Ruth I'm so happy—' and as she came closer it was possible to see that she had been crying. Still, that didn't necessarily mean she wasn't happy. The prospect of the whole narrative being unfolded was averted by Mrs Pendleton's voice from the hall, reminding once more of the proximity to midnight. Before Maureen could suggest they go into her room, Ruth sprang to her own door and whispered good night. Then she got in and turned the key in the lock. She heard Maureen's door close and then, fainter, Mrs Pendleton's.

As the farcical element of Dave faded and Maureen's pathetic gaiety congealed she felt somehow cheap and tawdry for not having been able, in some way, to have met these frail needs. She wouldn't have had to go to bed with him, that particular lie hadn't been necessary. And would it have been so awful to listen to Maureen reeling off her precious, hopeful tale. Oh, the damn. It was all a stupidity. Everybody wanting to touch, reach through to. Behind their words simpler things waited, great clumsy things that could not trust their own voice but waited to see how their glib emissaries fared before maundering forth, yokels of feeling. She had been wrong to go out with Dave, harmless though the evening was. She couldn't manage the necessary mien, suspend judgement on the eventual outcome, knowing in advance as she did what it must be. At that moment she couldn't see how someone else, some strange other someone, could ever mean anything to her. Someone whose whole life had taken place elsewhere, who, while she was being woven into her brother's life, had been absorbing his own special origins, becoming unknowably himself. What of Harry Gibbon, her imaginary impregnator, was he any different? Even if there was love? Love. Maybe not even then. Perhaps this was a truth, a dimension of reality, upon which all lovers, in that insatiable ache for union which is their vocation, would sooner or sooner, later or later, in the fullness of their foolishness, be broken.

If it knew an answer the face gave no hint, but looked out with its cold candour, and past her.

CHAPTER EIGHTEEN

The sun shone on the blue table-cloth, it was a bright soft colour, unlike sky or sea blue, the fabric blue of dyed cloth, smooth now and regular, entirely lit by the sun. Moseby, through the half-drawn curtain of the set-in bed, watched it. With his eyes open it was a blue table-cloth on a table in the middle of a room, but closing almost closed it shone in his dim sight like a piece of blue precious, glowed bluely, lapis lazuli, a diamond square of shapeless hue, burning pale and vivid.

It marked the simple axis of the world and he was very close to it, still centred, hub held. In the slow spin of his thoughts it was all like a dream, with a dream's unfolding inevitable progress.

He had arrived before she was up and she came to the door in her slip with little blue forget-me-nots worked on the hem, face smooth and puffy from sleep and let him in with a small unsurprised 'oh', and went back to bed where she lay with her eyes closed. After a moment, and without looking at him she said 'come on Johnny'. He undressed looking out of the window, looking out over the back courts. The tall chalk of the chimney wisped a faintest smoke. He thought as his trousers came off what might be observed from that vantage. Perhaps a man at a window, taking off his clothes, going into someone else's bed beside someone else's wife. He passed the far afloat gaze of the husband and went among her prone, complaisant fleshes, thinking not of adultery or lust but of the childlike gratuity of warmth and bareness and truant thrill of being out and free while others were confined by self-imposed disciplines. All this lent to the event a certain remoteness that made it seem devoid of consequence.

There was not much to say, it was not a complex matter really. He had done it because the opportunity presented itself. In a way it had nothing to do with Edna. He felt he could almost explain it to her so that she would see, it was a weightless, amoral act, simple as the blue sun on the yellow table-cloth. He thought of his wife, shopping or washing Carol's clothes, and loved her, loved her without remorse or stint, inconsequential man at the centre of his universe. It was not necessary to prove or disprove, words will kill it, let it lie, think of anything, anything will make sense in his crystal bright empty mind. The table-cloth bluemed, magical, commonplace, like the below sky above a country sleeper.

It had been a seldom occurrence in his life, this lucidity, this certainty of existence, with its unasking acceptance of well-being, no matter how precariously poised it might be, how soon to crumble. It was a little idyll of the mind, like that ride in the tram car, based now as then on physical comfort. Strange that such profound mental states should depend on the well-being of the body. Why did he never feel this way with Edna with whom he had so much to share. Perhaps just because of that, perhaps this was a condition that needed a solitude, was even the acceptance of isolation. He half remembered lines from Wallace Stevens, 'the human reverie is a solitude in which . . .' what was it, 'composed the eccentric propositions of our fate'. Something like that. This was the reverie, only he had no eccentric propositions to compose. Unless it was something that involved those two little squatters in his mother-in-law's bathroom, and that legless man of the minister's, and the dwarf in the kit bag, and what about that white Christ. That was the point, it would have to include everything, and suddenly as though it had never been away his life was with him again, pressing close, irking him with its innumerable goads.

A cloud quenched the sun and dulled the blue and Cathie came in with groceries and Moseby got up and without knowing quite why washed his hands and face. Cathie sat watching him as he dried himself. He could see her through his towelling hands and wondered what he would say when the time came to say something. What did she think she had done, how did it word itself in her mind. Adultery. A bit of stray. An affair. What was she waiting to hear him say? Thank you. Goodbye. I love you. What was he in the midst of that he hadn't been in when he woke this morning, that hadn't existed when he lay in bed five minutes ago. What would she say, and what would he reply.

'Do you want a cup of tea?'

'Fine, that'd be fine.' She seemed casual, as though he should be here in his trousers and bare feet, drying his neck on her towels. Was she waiting for him to say the first words that would define them in their roles. This can't go on. This mustn't stop. What are we going to do?

'How many do you take?'

'Two in a cup that size.' This was the first cup since it happened, since he had been unfaithful, acquired a mistress, or could you call her a mistress, a fancy woman was the expression. It tasted stewed. He put another sugar in and sat facing her. She put her face between her hands and looked at him. He must say whatever it was that needed saying.

'Are you all right?'

'A bit tired. Funny how too much sleep makes you tired.'

'Were you surprised to see me?'

'No, not really. I wasn't really expecting you but I wasn't surprised. Know what I mean?'

'I think so.'

'When did you decide?'

'To come?'

'Aha.'

'This morning.'

'I usually go over to my sister's in the afternoon. You don't mind if I go today. I didn't tell her I wasn't coming. I didn't know . . .'

'No, sure, I've got a lecture at the university.'

'Tuesdays and Thursdays I go to her place. Saves her trailing out with the wean.'

'No, that's O.K.'

'Can you come tomorrow?'

'Tomorrow. I don't know.'

'Any morning though is fine.'

They went to bed again before he left, without taking off all their clothes. It was rather erotic this time with her

210

stockings on and the suspender straps twanging slackly against her as he plucked away.

MacIndoe met him as he came out of the refectory.

'Where have you been getting to for the lectures?'

'Oh I'm sorry. I missed the last one.'

'The last two. You going into class now?'

'Twenty minutes.'

'Hold on till I get a sandwich and we'll take the air.'

Glasgow spread, palled in dun smoke, away before the university. They walked slowly down the hill, MacIndoe glancing quickly at the girls who went past and returning greetings by raising his right hand, palm spread.

'When are we going to have you over for that meal?'

'Well, really any time suits me.'

'You don't know my wife do you?' – and Moseby tried to recall what he had heard.

'No.' She had been a student hadn't she. His student. One of his allies presumably.

'She's rather a remarkable woman.' Moseby had the sense of walking slightly to one side, or else everything was just a little tilted. MacIndoe spoke without looking at him, his hands behind his back, stooped so that he was at Moseby's height. Funny, he never thought of MacIndoe as being taller than him. 'I think you will like her.' Isn't she supposed to be some sort of hag Moseby tried to recall. Half a dozen kids or something. 'She's read a few of your papers when I've had them home.'

'Oh.' Passing a building, its gable gilded with sun, in the grounds a tree grew, a wind surged through it, moving it into Moseby's casual tilted glance, reminded him of something, some time. What was it. Something disturbing, past and frightening.

'She thinks you have a brilliant mind.'

'That's very nice of her.'

'I tried to dissuade her.' Joke. They laughed their respective laughs. It was in Glasgow wasn't it, whatever it was. A tree blew into the corner of his eye. Looking up. He was small. What was it. The mood had almost gone, its ominous tinge fading. He stopped and tried to think. MacIndoe went on a few paces, then turned.

'What is it?'

'I'm trying to remember something.' Don't talk about it, he warned. You'll smother it. It's so small and weak and it's trying to get out, out through that gable and the sun and the tree and the angle.

'Something you forgot?' This idiocy upset the calm he was trying to make. He caught up.

'Nothing really. What were you saying?'

'About my wife, she thought your papers were pretty bright. Undergraduate cleverness I told her.'

'Probably.' Things must be trying to get out all the time, buried things, waiting for accidents of juxtaposition to unearth them, then trying to catch the attention of the mind. But weren't they in the mind already? But forgotten. Forgotten things crying to be remembered, 'My God, My God, why has thou forsaken me?' Poor old Jesus. They got to him where he lived. 'Come unto me all ye that labour and are heavy laden and I will give you rest.'

'Some promiser.'

'What?'

'Oh I was just thinking something—' MacIndoe hooked the dead bird out of the verge. It was stiff and its eyes were dusty little beads and it rolled over like a piece of wood might, rolling on parts of itself never meant for rolling. Under its exposed wing was a dark clotted hole and in it a madden of maggots. MacIndoe flicked it back. 'Thrush,' he identified. 'Used to be a bit of an ornithologist when I was a boy. Not here of course. I was brought up in Inverness. Do you know that part at all?'

'No. No, I don't.' The old woman in the street, her grey flesh. A dead bird, seething with life. A gable and the sun and a tree. His mind, lurking in its labyrinth, seizing the passing image, being carried a little further towards, where?

'Where are we going?' he asked MacIndoe.

'Yes, we'd better get back.'

'Go round this way.'

'Can I tell the wife then some afternoon next week?'

'Yes. Fine.'

'When?'

'Well, make it, oh Thursday.' A girl came towards them down the hill and Moseby realized MacIndoe was walking to meet her. She was short and rather stocky, with wide calves and low-heeled shoes. She had on a Jordanhill Training College blazer. She must be MacIndoe's bit of stray. He remembered Cathie and was surprised and pleased he could have forgotten it so quickly, and then in the subsequent instant, like a body released in its due time, floating up into recognition through the gable and the tree and the putrefying thrush, a funeral, an aunt he had scarcely known, in Glasgow, attended with his parents, hushed in the mourning house, they had to keep the coffin screwed down, decomposition had set in, sprayed with a sweet sweet scent, the rotting box on trestles, covered with a purple cloth. He had been so young he hadn't been sure of everything, why they were there and what was in the box and he never asked but wondered about the smell and the lugubrious faces.

'Look John, if you don't mind I'll leave you here.'

'Oh sure, sure.'

'Some day next week then.'

'Fine.' He didn't even notice the girl's face. He was drained suddenly, tired and rather sweaty from walking in the sun. The morning seemed a long time ago. He remembered thinking heady wonderful thoughts in the bed, and couldn't be sure what they were. About Edna. Yes Edna. She wasn't part of this, this stench, this corruption. She was keeping the house clean and washing Carol and changing her underwear daily. He could go there and wash himself and lie down in the cool green room and she would come with her nipples roseated on milky breasts and soothe away his ache, plout his pain, lull his gnaw.

Oh Moseby, be careful he told himself, be careful, sit still, the more you move the more the world trembles. Sit quiet, sit still. Wait for the peace to descend, the down dove of calm to come. Be careful Moseby, oh take care.

He got back a little early and walked along from the Central Station, through the town, quiet on a Wednesday half day. Edna would be with her mother at Gourock. The thought of Mrs Davidson shivered him with dread. It was

213

comical but only too true. She would have him stoned for adultery. Funny how being in Greenock made it all seem quite remote. He thought of Edna's father. Clever move that of his, dying. Imagine trying to hump Mrs Davidson. No wonder there was only Edna. She hadn't done any too well getting him. He remembered the wedding, a distant, white affair, full of unnatural gestures and poses. The photographs, him looking like a tubercular Jew. And poor old Harry, standing like a huge dwarf beside him. How long had he been gone now. Years. He turned up Argyle Street and was tempted to go into the B.B. Café. That was where he had proposed. Between ordering and the girl bringing the Bovril. Edna had to wait to say yes but he could tell by her eyes and he had regretted asking. Dear Edna. Strange that it should have this effect. Cathie seemed quite unreal. What was he going to do about her? Don't think about it and it'll all go away. As he crossed over George's Square thinking his thoughts he glanced right, up Union Street. It lay long and empty, muted slatey blues, brown buff sandstone and the roan red road, going glissando, rising smooth until at the end of it the Argyllshire hills danced a short tawny jig. He and Gibbon walking. The fox fleeing like a fire. The largeness of everything and their smallness, forked twigs, slowing crossing the hills. 'I to the hills will lift mine eyes,' wasn't that how it went, 'from whence doth come mine aid.' The West Kirk clock struck half past and he had a last look and went on up Nelson Street.

After tea and before she went to bed Carol wanted to be told a story. She sat in her pyjamas on Moseby's knee.
'Well you must for to tell me one.'
'Maybe I must for not to know any.'
'Oh yes you do, you've told me them before.'
'Told, not telled,' Edna said.
'You must for to.'
'Why are you so ignorant and can't read?' Carol put on her expression of tolerance.
'Because I'm just a wee girl and wee girls can't read.'
'That's because wee girls get telled too many stories by their fathers.'

Carol had a system for arguments. She pinched Moseby's lips firmly together and held her other hand over his eyes. 'Well you must for to tell me one now' – and after making sure any protest would have withered in the sealed-off head, released him.

'Will I tell you about your mummy when she was a sexy toot?' Edna pursed disapprovingly and went on knitting.

'No, tell me a proper story, about people.'

'All right, once upon a time—'

'I don't like once upon a time.'

'Be quiet and listen or you won't get any.'

'Well don't say once upon a time.'

'One day there was a man out walking, is that all right?'

'Yes, where was he walking?'

'He was walking up this hill—'

'Was it a high hill?'

'Pretty high.'

'Was it a mountain?'

'No, it was just a hill, just a high hill and he was out walking and singing to himself—'

'What was he singing?'

'A song. And he was walking along and do you know what he heard?'

'Yes.'

'What?'

'I don't know.'

'He heard a big shout. A big shout he heard. One. Two. He's done it again. That was the big shout he heard.'

'Was it?'

'Yes. So he looked up the hill and do you know what he see-d?'

'What?'

'A big crowd of people and just as he looked they all shouted at once. One. Two. He's done it again. And they all threw their hats up in the air when they shouted "He's done it again".'

'What for did they shout it?'

'Well the man didn't know so he runned up the hill to the big crowd, but he was just a wee man, he was a wee totie man and he couldn't see over all the people's heads and as he was running round the edge of the crowd trying to see they all shouted "one", "two", "He's done it again" and throwed their hats up in the air so the wee man asked this big tall man that could see right in, he asked him what was happening and the big man said "there's a man in there with no legs".'

'No legs.'

'No legs and he's got two crutches that he stands on.'

'No legs.'

'No, just two crutches and the big man said he was standing on these two crutches and then the crowd shouted, "one" and the man said he's throwed one crutch away. "two" he's throwed the other crutch away, "he's done it again", and all the hats went up in the air, he's falled on his bum.'

Carol considered this story briefly and decided against it.

'I don't like that story,' she said.

'That's a fine story to tell a child, do you want her having nightmares?'

'Our Lord taught in parables.'

'Tell me another.'

'No, time for your pit;' and handed her to Edna after getting his kiss. Edna carried her through and Moseby sat in the chair and closed his eyes. Guilt, pure blazon of remorse. At having projected his fantasies into Carol's world, and behind that at the morning's doings. He thought of telling Edna everything, trying to explain like he had felt it would be possible to explain lying in Cathie's bed, make her understand so much at one and the same time, of what he was like, really like, and how he loved her, and how he wanted her love, and how attractive she was. This last made him stop. He could tell her nothing. She was not ready, would never be ready to hear things like that. She was Edna, wanting to be happy, to buy Carol new shoes, to get her hair styled, be thought pretty, wanting to love and respect her respectful husband. She had been of late, dating from the night he had returned from the minister's, more relaxed, happier, more ardent in her embraces, less worried about money. For him to say anything would be worse

216

than futile. It would be selfish, egocentric in the extreme, and could lead to nothing but her hurt.

'What's wrong?'

'Nothing. I was just thinking.'

'What about?' She came and sat on the arm of the chair.

'I was just thinking I wanted you to be happy.'

'You couldn't have given much for my chances'; and slid onto his lap. He kissed her and looked over her shoulder.

'Sometimes I worry I'm not very good for you.'

'Why's that?' she said looking at him. Moseby shrugged, 'Oh I don't know. Sometimes that's what I think.'

'That's silly. I love you.'

'And I love you, just I sometimes think, well we're, well we don't know much about each other.'

'How do you mean? I've known you nearly, nearly six years.'

'Oh I know, I just meant, well compared with how your mother knows you . . .'

'Honestly you say the daftest things. What's my mother got to do with it?'

'Nothing. I love you.'

'Good. You don't tell me enough' – and they kissed.

By mutual, unspoken consent they retired early. He lay in bed waiting for her to come through. As she opened the door she switched off the light. That meant she wasn't wearing her nightdress. He reached up for her and encountered the warm droops of her breasts. His hands traced the long, practised patterns.

'What's this?' making his tone mock surprised, 'sex rearing its ugly head?'

'I feel like being made love to, do you mind?' She said it with that jaunty manner she used to get over her faint ineradicable embarrassment.

'Such boldness' – putting his face to her breasts and touching with his finger.

'Am I wet?'

'M-m.' They kissed, her open mouth squirming with tongue. The thought was with him that he was going to have two different women in one day. He tried to put it away but he couldn't. Her hand was fondling him. He went under the clothes, kissing her body, working down but she held his head and brought him back.

'Where are you going?' she asked not wanting to know. He was between her legs coming up and he pushed in. Edna held him off,

'Have you got them?'

'You don't need them, you've just finished.'

'Are you sure?' – letting him. He tried to think how it had been with Cathie. She didn't make any sound hardly but moved herself much more.

His mind was suddenly inflamed with a rush of comparisons, he quickened his movements and spoke into her ear—

'Say fuck me.'

'Don't say that word.'

'Say it.'

'You know I don't like that word, it's a horrible word.' It's what I'm doing, don't you know Edna, don't you know it's what's happening now, on your body.

'Say it.'

'Oh John why' – pleading.

'Because I'm doing it and you want me to, don't you, don't you. . . .?'

'Yes, yes, do it.'

'Say it then.' Her arms tightened round his neck and her mouth came close to his ear.

'Fuck me darling, oh John fuck me;' trying to please with her voice sounding strange on the unfamiliar, distasteful word. Please forgive me, Edna, he thought. For what I'm doing to you, please forgive me for there's nobody else who can. He realized she was almost ready and flailed away jerkily inside her. He was left lonely and sickened, staring into the pillow. His mind seethed, maggoty, like the thrush that he remembered now in a violent contraction of nausea that he incorporated into the male sounds of sexual relief. He pressed into the pillow, biting his eyes into the white glaze. Forgive me, forgive my sick, putrefying mind, my hunchbacked crippled mind. An inaudible scream in his head. No tears would come and if they would it would be as creeping white maggots. He tried to drag his mind away from its fester, all he could imagine were the distant hills at the end of Union Street.

'Oh darling, it was wonderful,' Edna said, somewhat breathless from his weight upon her.

CHAPTER NINETEEN

The morning sky faded mauve and in it the sun, pallid yolk. Between the buildings people went, swimming in a gelatin light. Colours out-wave lengths. Cloudy sounds diffusely drift. Cool lookings bathe sight. Far from them a clock chimed, lemon drops on palest greenings. The sun's thin shine evokes shadows nigh blue. Paris made a noise like cars and feet and water all at once. A girl passed, breasts jumbling in a blouse. The fleshes of a croissant tore, layered tissues. Coffee on a central spittle spun. Fragrance of a cigarette. Smoke flutes. A catkin of ash, flaky fall. The bowl of brown sugar crumbled quietly.

'Delicate old morning.'

'Have to do something about that bed, Harry.'

'Like what?'

'Like not sleep in it.'

'Profound. Very profound. Concise too.'

'Pithy.'

'Very pithy. You expecting that girl?'

'Annie?'

'The very one.'

'I have hopes.'

'How, on a delicate morning like this, can you find time for carnal things?'

'You pose a rare puzzle, Harold.'

'Oh, I'm a rare puzzle poser.'

'You have posed many puzzles I presume?'

'In the golden days before the fall.'

'Ah yes, the golden days before the fall, I remember them well.'

Annie came. She had on a white shirt with two buttons undone and a full denim skirt. Her hair was short and several shades lighter than Gibbon's.

'Hi you guys, up early.'

After she and Cuffee had gone Gibbon sat on. The sun gained height above the roofs and the air dried, parchment bright. The black and white cat from the 'Monaco' came out and rolled at his feet. Reaching down under the table he scratched its throat. It rolled and purred. Its teats were palest milky pink, extended in gestation. 'Kittens coming, heh puss?'

He sat loosely in the chair, his right leg over his left, one arm hung down the back, the fingers loose; the other capped on his right knee, his head a little back and looking out from under the brows, the soft flesh of his neck pulled and the bone of the jaw showing, the line up to the small close-set ears. His hair cut short but lying full on the nape, a dull dark blond, bleached at the temples to fade with his eyebrows, faint streaks above the small, wide apart eyes in the broad face, flat-nosed and full-mouthed; the head and features of a prize-fighter, of a tree-dweller, of a fruit-eater.

They found a café with tables out front. The sun shone down through the spread of a large lime tree and made soft edged shapes on the table, blurry amoeba movings, constant commingling divisions and reunions, plasmics. Cuffee watched.

'I'm like you,' Annie said, 'I don't know what I want to do.' She made a wrinkled face and sipped her drink. 'I guess I'm a lost soul or something.' Viscidities, blimpings, shadow-morphoses. Pictures of lymph, protographs. 'I mean what is it all about for god-sake. I don't believe in God any more. All that stuff, sometimes I wish I did. Know what I mean?' He nodded. Shapes without colour, transparencies bounded by opacity, still a moment then reorganized from above. 'I think I'd like to express myself in dancing. Modern ballet you know. There's something about dancing, using your body to express yourself. I've got a good body for expressing myself.' She smiled and her eyelids swole and something in her throat throbbed, made a small pulsation. A big leafy tree tremored by the wind, letting through its branches the source light to play in smears and blears below, mimic chemistry. 'Have you slept with many women?' Cuffee shook his head, exhaling smoke. 'Liar. I bet you think you're pretty sexy, eh?' Long-nosed, renaissance face, uncommitted to its smile. A tree above a café table, the wind coming across the city from the south-west, the sun reaching zenith, late in May. 'Would you like to sleep with me?' – and without waiting for a reply put her hand to her body below the left breast and faintly surprised, said, 'My heart.' He reached across and felt for its quiet patting. 'That's the first time you've ever felt my heart beat,' she said, leaning herself against his hand. Particular, general and universal, their collusion complete, made image of life in venereal weather. Later they stood in an alley, in a deep doorway, dim out of the sun, his face above hers turned slightly, looking down at her eyes closed mouth parted, reaching blind inches, moist trembles crumpling softly, gaping red ring round the thick flexion of his tongue.

Norman Kimber had a smooth, carefully made face, well shaved and with large exact teeth. He had his hair very carefully cut but casual and it gave his head a nice shape. His cuffs were buttoned down and his peaks turned up and he had a mocha-brown cardigan in cashmere round his shoulders. He had an agreeable, modulated voice, a contralto that was not at all effeminate.

'I think this the best room I've ever been in in Paris. I was in several before I landed this. Saw plenty more. Then one day I was on the Ile de la Cité, came up here to the point and saw this place. Water through trees. Coming from Indiana like I do that's quite a thrill.'

'Aye, it's a nice place,' Gibbon said.

It was a long room and had a big window that looked on the river over and through the trees. All around, fitted in a blue grey mosaic, the roofs of the city, and away down, faint, the spike of the Eiffel Tower. The tops of the trees, solid-looking from the window level, budged at the wind's suasion and in so let flitters of sunlight through to play beneath. The room was sparsely furnished. A large knee-hole desk under the window. A bookshelf on the right hand wall. Two tall, spar-backed chairs and a large wicker one and against the other short wall a black vitreous stove. In the middle of the back wall a door went through to the bed-room and the kitchen and the toilet. The walls were pale blue and had three paintings and a map of Paris. On one a guitar hung, a large dark brown female shape.

'My wife used to play the guitar. She was a singer. She sang folk songs. Polly loved folk. She didn't care much for people but she loved folk.'

'You're still married to her?'

'Well yes, but it's been over a long time now. Before I met Stolleman . . .'

'You met him in New York?'

'Yes. He had his first exhibition there. This man whose secretary I was bought a painting and invited Stolleman to a meal. I liked him because he took the trouble to dress respectably. My wife's friends were kind of socialist beatnik people. I've kind of grown out of all that dressing down. What do you think of Stolleman?'

'I liked him. He seemed very happy in a way.'

'I think that's because he's a good painter and that's what he wants to be. Did he tell you much about me?'

'Just about this man, this poet whose secretary you were.'

'Have you read anything by him, Samuel Cleeves?'

'No, I don't read poetry much.'

'He was a very remarkable man, and an artist of quite unusual distinction. I think that before I met him I had no idea whatsoever as to what the poetic function might be. But being with him for those two years, reading his poetry, his essays, talking with him I began to see what poetry might become—' Kimber broke off and smiled. 'I'm sorry, this is not a subject I can talk conversationally about.' He rose and went across the room to the guitar. It hung by the fret, eyeing him out of his middle. He ran his thumb across the strings. The sound filled up the room, not music but fraught with music.

'Does it bother you that I'm homosexual?'

'No.'

'It was difficult in America. My family was pretty well respected. My father's in publishing and all the family, right back, were right as rain. When I was just beginning to sweat it out I dug up all I could on my family. Said I was thinking of writing a family history, just to see if I could find some-one with "tendencies", don't know what good it would have

223

done me even if the family tree had been fruity as an orchard. My trouble was so American it invites disbelief.' He reached to the guitar again, thus urged it responded an identical response, and while the thrill of sound held, turned, smiling in annoyance at himself 'Come on, let's go find some place to eat, you can see Paris from the sidewalk.'

There was a sound in the room, the sound of rain slicing down through the tired warm air and its soft splats on the roofs, and there was their breathing and in the dusk they passed a cigarette between them. As she leaned over to let him have his draw the waxy lemons of her breasts rubbed smoothly against his face, he was lying flat and she was half sitting up. Once she put her hand down to touch him but he put her away.

'What's wrong, you shagged out?'

'I'm smoking.'

'Can't you get a raise when you're smoking?'

'Just learn to do one thing at a time, you'll enjoy it better.'

'You think I don't enjoy things?'

'I don't know.'

'Didn't you think I enjoyed what we did?'

'Here, smoke.' Under the rain sound and their breathing there was traffic and somewhere music, as from a wireless, but faint.

'You mad at me or something?'

'No.'

'Kiss me then' – and when he did she pressed herself to him. He kissed her and withdrew his face.

'What's wrong with you? You worried in case you don't ever get it again?'

'I like it.'

'How many men have you had?'

'In my whole life?' He nodded. 'Gee, I don't know for sure. A lot. I got raped once.'

'Where?'

'I was hitch-hiking in Spain. Me and another girl. She was pretty ugly I guess. And four boys gave us a lift. Anyway two of them took her and two of them took me. There wasn't anything we could do. She screamed and one of them

224

hit her. I could hear her crying. She was in the back and I was in the front. It's pretty damn awkward getting raped in a car. Specially in the front.'

'What happened, afterwards?'

'Oh hell, nothing really. They just took us where we were going and dropped us off. And this girl wanted to go to the police. But I talked her out of it. We didn't have the number and they would have blamed us anyway. So we just got a hotel and had baths and then got into bed. And you'll never guess what, this girl, I woke up and she was all over me, kissing me and all that pretty stuff. I really beat the shit out of her, I can tell you. I'd rather have got raped by all of those guys than had that lesbian at me. Strange how I never noticed it in her before. I hate that kind of thing.'

Cuffee got up and went to the window. It opened outwards. The wet night loudened. The cigarette stub was extinguished in mid-flight. He watched out into the night, thick with the smells of wet and people and buildings and food, throbbing moistly in innumerable erogenous zones, like a great tree swollen at every nodule, burgeoning everywhere in the wet, flesh-redolent night. He flexed and broke wind noisily. Prrraatt.

'I beg your pardon,' Annie said.

'Granted. Granted.'

Gibbon woke up some time in the middle of the night and Cuffee wasn't back. He went out to the toilet which smelt badly and made a long hissing in the cistern. When he got back into bed he lay for a long time listening to it. After it ceased there was a night sound in the room, a city night sound, a kind of buzz, a kind of drone, a kind of hum. It sent him to sleep. When he woke it was morning, greyer and without the sound. He got up and put on his sweater and a duffle coat of Cuffee's and went out. It was very early and no one was about. The buildings looked etched on bread. He walked slowly down round the 'Monaco'. It wasn't cold. He saw several cats. Later he saw a man going through a litter bin. There were several of them as he walked. Dark, whiskered, double-coated. They paid no heed to him and he did not stare. Far away part of the skyline achieved silhouette. 'That'll be the east,' he said to himself conversationally. The pavements were wide and had cambers and there were two steps down into the street. He found a marble. It wasn't possible to see what colour it was. It was one of the kind with a little opaque curd sealed into it but it was impossible to tell the colour of this either. He put it in his pocket. It was quite light but there was no sign of the sun. Everything was in shades of grey. At the metro entrance people were beginning to go down, ashen-faced and introspective. A man slept on the gratings above the underground, lying in the familiar S-bend of sleep as though he were in a bed and not on a main street. Now and then a car made a lot of noise going past and there were several cyclists, silent dark pedallers. A man and a woman passed, coming from some party by their clothes. The woman's shoes made a noise, a clacking sound that seemed loud. Her face was flat with tiredness, the mouth almost invisible. The man was about half a pace ahead of her and seemed unaware that he had a companion. There was a café opened on the other side. The chairs were still on the tables but the bar was serving. Gibbon crossed over. There were two men with railwaymen's caps, off nightshift, drinking coffee, their lips bright in dirty faces. Their bikes leaned against one and other outside the café. Gibbon said 'coffee', then 'café au lait' adding 's'il vous plaît' and the two railway workers looked at him then away. When they had finished their coffee they shook hands and left, mounting their bicycles and going in different directions. Gibbon had a look at the marble. The little sealed-in tongue was pale red. The glass seemed faintly green. Gibbon drank his coffee, blowing on it between sips, and looked into the closed unchanging sphere of the marble, rolling it slowly at the ends of his fingers, watching the arrested silence of its coral heart. After a while he went back. There was more traffic now. Looking up into the paling sky he saw streaming across the roofs a great many birds and could hear a distant high twittering. They flew like an enormous gust of leaves. He stopped to watch them for a time but they seemed unending, a tide of blown leaves. When he got back he went into bed again, taking off only his shoes and the duffle. He started a letter.

Dear Ruth, I never really thought on your name before, not until this morning. I was out very early and I found a glass marble, in it there is a little thing, you know the things they get inside marbles. This one was red, shaped like a fish or a bird or like a kind of leaf. Anyway that made me think about your name, it was the right colour and it was somehow although it was very ordinary like most names are, I mean Harry is, but because it belonged to you it seemed special and not ordinary. Anyhow that is what I felt like. Paris is strange.

After he wrote 'Paris is strange' he didn't write any more, becoming sleepy and drowsing off with the biro and pad still in his hand.

Cuffee was sitting outside the 'Monaco' when Gibbon got down.

'I looked in. You were sound.'

'Where did you get to?'

'I spent the evening with Annie. We pleasured ourselves. Delightful expression don't you think? Pleasured ourselves.'

'Delightful.' Cuffee sat back, smoking and looking at women. Gibbon ordered coffee and stared until he turned round.

'You know Harry, if a man had enough character he might well make it the most satisfying of the art forms.'

'How's that because?'

'Well, all an art form is is a stylized method of imposing your will upon the world, an attempt to create order in the chaos. Sex, or call it what you will, relationships, love, whatever, well it's the same thing at a purely existential level. Of course you'd have to have courage, and an enormous capacity for erotic experience. But if you had, and you were honest you might well discover the true existential art form. The truest expression of the pagan mind. Confrontation by an aspect of the world that seeks to modify you while you seek to modify it. And in your artist's mind you're organizing it into an aesthetic experience, savouring it at the very molten moment of its occurrence, the place you meet, what the weather's like, what she says and what

227

she means, what you say and what you think. When you walk does she touch against you, is it accidental. And when it happens what's the room like, do you have to talk, is she embarrassed, how she undresses, does she disrobe, or denude herself, tear off her clothes or shed them, does she watch and how, and how does it feel, does she cry out or lie still, what sounds when it's coming. And after, when you're looking into the pillow feeling like the hero in the fairy tale who has woken up on the hillside with the moon shining and his enchantment over. Alone again to recall the whole fable. Oh, it's here to stay Harry, mark my words.

'Why are we so different, Peter?'

'I don't know Harry. Sometimes I think you believe in salvation, you think you need to be saved.'

'Maybe it's how I was brought up.'

'Do you think sex is wrong or something?'

'No, I don't think it's wrong. Only when you talk it just seems like some kind of contest, with a winner and loser, a conflict . . .'

'And you don't think it is?'

'Well, I hope it's not.'

'Well, I hope so too then.'

'But you don't believe so.'

'Harry it's a poor thing but my own. I think we're all on our ownsome, that this state is permanent and we all act as though the sun shone out of our arses. Everything we do we do to further the image we have of ourselves and that there is no right and no wrong, only events. When there is no God everything is possible. Only all these God deniers won't accept the implications of their freedom from absolutes, they still want moral priorities, they keep elevating their prejudices into doctrine. Well, I like to think I'll accept the outcome of my philosophical position. Abandon all remorse, anything goes.' Kimber had come along towards the end of this. He smiled at Gibbon as Cuffee finished.

'Shakespeare and Cole Porter,' he said, 'impeccable sources. You must come along to my place this evening, I know someone who might interest you. Philosophically speaking.'

228

'Nobody interests me philosophically speaking.'
'Kinda big philistine guy,' Gibbon jeered.

There were about twenty people in the room when they got there. Someone had taken the guitar down and was strumming it. There were the usual groups and French and English were spoken. A man with a bald head and a long cigarette-holder studied the map of Paris, going in close every now and then to pinpoint somewhere. Kimber was by the window talking to a girl in an olive-drab dress. Her back was to them and her spine showed almost to the waist. The dress made a long flaunt up under the arms and collared her neck. She turned as Kimber waved to them, flexing the dorsals and pulling tight the tendon in her throat, so that she strung taut, acquiver. She had a small head set on a long neck with a swift jaw-line and a wide band of forehead, the eyes set apart under straight brows and the nose short and with a hint of a bridge. She was smiling and had dull reddish gold hair. She looked like a bullfighter, or a huntress or a kind of exquisitely made machine. Kimber introduced them. She was called Uta and her friend, Yani. They were German. Uta spoke a precise, perfect English and she looked at them directly as she shook hands. Kimber took Gibbon off to get drinks.

'And what are you doing in Paris may I ask?' – smiling at him as she said it.

'I'm on a visit.'

'And how long will you stay?'

'Until the money goes.'

'What is your profession?'

'I don't have one.'

'What do you do when you are not waiting for your money to run out in Paris?'

'I paint.'

'You are an artist.'

'No. I paint. What do you do?'

'I live.'

'All the time?'

'Almost all of it,'

'Good.'

229

'Yes, I love it.'

Kimber had been drinking a little but was quite sober under a certain flush.

'I should have unstrung that guitar. There's always someone who knows the chord sequence of "The Foggy Dew" at any gathering. I'd like to work out what proportion of the world population have that unhappy faculty. I don't like "The Foggy Dew". It was a big number with Polly, her hair falling down over the strings. Very fetching. What do you think of Uta?'

'She's a bomb.'

'Peter better know how to punch his weight with that little girl. She's a very hard piece.'

'How do you mean hard?'

'She's a man-eater. She's fast, hooks well and jabs like Kenny Lane. I've seen her take boys apart like they were old clocks.'

'I'll give you odds on Cuffee.'

'You'll lose your money, make it drink.'

'Done.'

'Within the month.' They shook hands.

Uta danced erect, a supple vibrance. She smiled at Cuffee as she danced. Around him she made space and in the space she made shapes, using him as a foil, a column of reference which permitted this indulgence. He kept himself close to the music's pulse, injecting his posture from moment to moment with a small rhythmic adjustment allowing her to improvise around him, floridity checked by the lissom tension of her body and the succession of lines she made of thigh and hip and arm, the whole governed by a total self-possession, that accomplishment of will beside which everything seems stale.

When the music stopped she bowed to him and prepared to return to Yani. He held her hand lightly.

'Now maybe you will dance with me,' he said.

The number was a George Lewis, a stomp progressing with relentless monotony towards orgasm. Cuffee frowned a little as he felt for the rhythm and holding her two hands jogged her to and fro, then as the acceleration commenced he spun her and leaning back let her snap out on their extended arms. In his dancing there was almost no footwork, only a sequence of interlocking turns on hand links carried out interminably at the music's insistence. It required a form of abandonment quite different from her prior exhibitionism, its momentum excluding decoration and demanding a rapt concentration upon the dynamics of movement, always threatening to sunder from the centrifugal energy they engendered; she submitted to the discipline, becoming not two dancers but a dance, her smile thin and exultant while Cuffee gazed down in complete commitment, unaware of his partner save as counter poise.

Yani watched them, a pale face owned by two dark throbs of eyes, inscrutable, yet in that transparently jealous.

'She looks like a photograph of my great-grandmother,' Gibbon said to Kimber. 'Is she a friend of Uta's?' Kimber tapped his nose knowingly.

'She is indeedy, yes indeedy is she. Well established gossip has them lovers.'

'I thought you said she was a man-eater.'

'Ambidextrous Harry, gifted girls both.'

'Greenock was never like this.'

Paris, May 27th
a Wednesday.

John, how goes the war? I wrote you before but as we weren't permanent anywhere I didn't post it. I don't like the thought of writing if the person can't answer back. Anyway now we're settled.

I don't know how long it has been since I left, time goes all out of shape when you start doing new things I think. It's all the things happening and you notice more which must prove something about time only I can't think what. There are a lot of things happening I'd like to talk to you about only I don't know that a letter is much good for these things. Cuffee is one of them. Perhaps even the biggest or most important. He's not at all like me and he's not like you either, certainly he's not like me, in fact we are opposites and in a way that makes me realize what I am really like. For instance Peter has this terrible sort of concentration, everything he does absolutely and I mean completely

231

trivial things like brushing his teeth or running upstairs. The nearest I can think of it is like in American musicals when they start dancing on buses and things like that. I mean he expresses himself in everything he does.

Well I've come to the conclusion that I don't express myself very much, one of the reasons being that I don't really know what I'm like, while Peter certainly knows, or maybe he doesn't really know but he thinks he knows. Anyway I think it's very good for me to be with him, it's sort of defining my boundaries so that I can see where other people leave off and start. For instance I think I know now that I'm pretty puritan about sex. I really believe it's wicked outside of marriage, or at any rate love. Peter said I believed in salvation. I took him to mean I was a Christian and although I never thought about it before I suppose it's true. Be queer if it wasn't when you come to think on it.

Enough of all that. Paris is quite a place, to look at as well as the people. I suppose it's because so much has happened here and you know it has even if you don't know what it is. In Greenock you know nothing has happened nor ever will happen, in the historical sense I mean, so you look at it differently or maybe don't look at all. I have met an American here called Norman Kimber and he gives me that sense of things having happened in his life and that there are dates and landmarks. Compared with him I feel nothing has ever occurred to me or in me since I was born, and yet I know that is not true. So I hope this trip will help to sort it all out.

The food is nothing special and I don't like the bread, it's all crusty with not much bread. The water is terrible, you can't imagine how bad, it gives you the shits if you drink it. I don't think I could live in a place where the water was bad. Inside my mouth gets sore from the crusty bread and drinking wine with meals. Kimber makes tea though, but even in tea the water tastes bad.

I hope you are keeping well and Edna. Give my love to Carol. You can write me at 24 rue Monsieur le Prince, St Germain des Prés, Paris. We'll be here for a while, a few weeks anyway, time for you to get a letter in the post anyway, so let's be hearing from you. Love, Harry.

232

'Love Harry. Big kind of poofy guy,' he said, smiling. He put the letter on the table and went to put out the light. The marble was on the mantelpiece above the boarded-up fireplace. He looked up at the light through it, the red in the middle stained his sight. He put it into his bag, switched off the light, and got into bed.

Cuffee woke before she did. It was barely morning. Annie lay on her back, mouth a little open, snoring slightly. She looked very young. Cuffee watched the face, there was a very fine blonde hair on the upper lip and on the temples. Her eyes showed like pale blue contusions through the lids. At the base of her throat there was a large starry love bite, purple, magenta and yellow. There was one on his body that itched slightly. She looked like a boy, a blond American boy-child woman. He got up quietly and found matches. The gas had a good pressure this early and roared. He put his shirt on and sat at the window waiting for the kettle to boil. Outside there was no sun, grey and quiet the roofs went on without let. A cat on the flat roof below moved delicately along the parapet. Cuffee opened the window to watch and the noise caused the cat to look up. Cuffee nodded. It jumped smoothly on to the dividing wall and looked back, then out of sight. It was cool at the open window and it let noises in. Distant sound of the metro gathering speed. Somewhere the faint unmistakable clangour of an alarm clock. Away to the left birds were starting out of the city, rising and falling over the roofs. He could see into the window opposite. A chair sat, bearing garments. On a small balcony of the next but one window, a table with a goldfish bowl and one goldfish, dull reddish gold silver of fish, swimming and pausing, mandarin mobile cased in clear. He came in and searched for a cigarette. There was a packet of 'Lucky Strike' under the bed with a 'Gitane' in it. Cuffee looked at her and smiled. He lit up and dragged the strong reek down into him. The sheet had slipped down from under her chin, he pulled it lower to expose her breast. The small tight nipples pipped with chill and as he watched the teat stretched, yearning mamelon that he flooded with smoke. The kettle was beginning to rumble.

Annie coughed at the cigarette smoke and nearly woke. He covered her up and went to make the coffee. He poured two cups, sugared, milked and stirred them. Then he got back into bed. He kneed her softly till she opened her eyes.

'It's morning. Here's some coffee.'

'Christ, what time is it?'

'It's morning, have some coffee.' She sat up and without thought covered her breasts. Cuffee got out and fetched his sweater. She looked small and lost in it and still dopey from waking up. Her hair at the back had been pressed flat from lying on it.

'Thanks,' she said, keeping the coffee cup close to her mouth and taking small sips.

'I found a "Lucky Strike" packet with a "Gitane" in it. How come?'

'Huh—' Cuffee looked at her and smiled.

'Want a draw?'

'No, is it a French cigarette?'

'A "Gitane".'

'I hate French cigarettes.'

'Is that why you keep them in "Lucky Strike" packets?'

'Huh?'

'Skip it;' and he watched out of the window, leaning on his elbow. She put her head beside his.

'You all right?' she asked and spilled coffee down his chest, a long thin dribble that he let run.

'Sure, I'm fine.'

*   *   *

'I have this friend in Greenock, his name's Moseby, John Moseby. He's a lot different from Peter. He thinks too much, least that's the impression I get, I met him before I went into the Army. He was adopted, I think it was that made him so, inwards, you know. He and I went around Greenock together. He didn't have any other friends, he argued with them all. He could be a sarcastic sort of bloke. Only he couldn't argue with me because I didn't know anything, and we were both orphans, my folk had died. We used to talk about getting a place of our own and living there, of course we didn't.'

234

'Why not?'

'There isn't anything like that in Greenock. My aunt doesn't mind so much my going away but she'd be insulted if I moved to a place of my own.'

'What did he do this friend?'

'He was a writer. He wrote poetry then.'

'Was he any good?'

'Oh, I don't know. He said he wasn't but he would be. I can only remember one poem, a bit of it only, "I think the world is falling down, falling down around us, not as, eh, not as buildings fall or men fall but as seashore castles succumb, to the, something, encroachments of the tide", I always remember that bit.'

'And what happened to him?'

'Oh I went to the Army and he met his wife and they got married. I was the best man.'

'Were you jealous?' Gibbon laughed.

'Yes,' he said, and laughed again.

'Why are you laughing?' Kimber asked.

'Well, when you said was I jealous and I said "yes", I realized that I had never really admitted that before, to myself. I mean John was my "mate" and being jealous isn't allowed.'

'Did you like his wife?'

'Edna? She was all right. She's a wee bit posh actually, not that that means anything only she had very definite ideas about how things should be. Oh, she was all right. What was your wife like?'

'Oh, well, that's a horse of a different shade' – and Kimber smiled and stretched. 'Polly was an American woman, and that's a very special sort of an animal.'

'Did you know you were homosexual when you married her?'

'My psychiatrist in New York said it was Polly who triggered off my homosexuality, actually he went further, he said it was Polly who made me homosexual, but he was talking from a committed point of view, that I wasn't essentially queer. I used not to think so either but I've changed my opinion.'

'Why's that?'

'Well, I could see what he was talking about as with Polly, but I realized that in many ways I was relieved to be out from under the load of having to be a big deal in bed. You see I'd always had a kind of casual success with girls, I dressed well, and I had money, and the petting system is really foolproof as far as finding out about your sexual prowess is concerned. You can't. I'd had sex with a couple of girls before Polly, but they had no more way of knowing how good or bad it was than I did, it was more a kind of social experiment than an emotional event. Then I met Polly. She was singing at some concert for a socialist poet who'd been jailed and they were raising his bail money. I was really taken with her. It was a barn-storming tour they were on and I just followed them. They had come down from Chicago and were doing all of Indiana. I just got into my car and went with them. After I got to know her she travelled in my car. She held me off for nearly a fortnight, not that I took much holding off. Then we had it one night in a field after the concert. I thought the world blew up that night. I never knew sex could be like that was. My semen was in the sky that night, boy. So we got married when the tour was over. She did a lot of singing, all with this left, liberal slant. I wasn't against that except she wanted me to write poetry for their magazines and I couldn't explain they wouldn't print my poems and I wouldn't want them to, so she didn't like that much. But it was the sex side of it that really killed us. No matter how you wrap it up it comes down to the fact that I couldn't satisfy her. I'm not going to say she was a nymphomaniac although she couldn't have been a kick in the ass short, no it was me, because when I found the pace too hot I just went impotent. God it was funny in an unfunny sort of a way you know. Polly was one of those girls who wanted to screw everywhere but on the bed. On the floor, against the wall, over the table, anywhere but in goddam kip, any fucking place two mortals could get to within genital distance was all right by her. Bedsex, she called it bedsex, was one of the deepest instances of bourgeois immorality, it was there they smothered it with coverlets into a fetid ritual. She said it was necessary to take it out of bed and put it back into its proper surroundings, which wasn't outdoors, or on the grass or in the woods, that was false primitivism, no but in the house, among the ordinary things of life, like your relations and friends. Anyway, she soon knotted my cord. Then she put me through a couple of months of cheapjack psychoanalysis, after I couldn't manage my erection we'd talk about it for two or three hours and try again. This all may sound pretty nutty to you Harry, but for me it was the great American tragedy. My New York psychiatrist says if I had married a woman with a normal, or better still a sub-normal sexual appetence, then I would have been able to preserve my male image and proceed with normal life as a heterosexual. Well, he might well have been right, but think-ing about it now it all seems a bit of a powder keg, it's all to the good that I married Polly whom I can think back on without feeling I lost anything very much. And that lets me get on with the serious business of coming to terms with being queer.'

'You wouldn't rather be, well, normal?'

'I'd rather be happy. The real difficulty about being queer, I've found anyway, is that all one's fellow queers are the most volatile of people, relationships, which are hard enough at the best of times, are almost impossible among all the distracted bastards one meets. I've known a lot of queers who were mad for respectable family men, and I think it's this desire for permanence, an escape from the tantrums and camp of so many of the lads, that explains it. If "true love" is a rarity in the "normal" world then it's virtually impossible on the other side. One is doomed to a series of demented liaisons, or straightforward seduction, and neither is the answer. The nearest I ever came to an answer was with this man Cleeve. Only then I was still in the throes of doubt and horror and fascination, I was one of the very screamers I've been talking about, and Sam wouldn't influence me one way or another, or he tried not to, him being that way himself was a tremendous factor in itself because I admired him so much, as an artist, and a person. But I remember him saying to me once when I was really in the pit, he said, "don't fight it, this thing is smaller than both of us". Took me a long time to be able to see that

237

was the only solution, if there was a solution, to get it clear in your head that you were, and be it, and then get on with the other things.'

'What other things, I mean if you're homosexual I can't quite see, I mean what else matters?'

'I know what you mean all right. I used to ask myself that. The answer is not very much matters except art I think. I'd hate to be a queer if I wasn't committed to the idea of being a poet, I don't know how the ones that aren't keep their balance.'

'I wish Moseby was here, he'd know how to put it, this is something we've both thought about although we never talked of it. But we both used to wonder just how far we could go before we were, well before we were more than "mates". I remember when we went walking in the hills on a leave of mine from the Army, at night we used to stretch out our hands and hold hands, just like that, without saying anything. We didn't have to say anything. It was all, well it was all there. Looking at it it's funny how clear it all is now. Wasn't then though.'

'That never fails to surprise me.'

'What?'

'Just how long it takes to learn anything, anything you can use, that is.'

Gibbon nodded his big fair head in agreement, pouty with thought, then looking up and nodding again, briskly. Kimber smiled his careful contained smile and fitted another cigarette to his holder.

'Why do you always wear the collar of your shirt up?' Gibbon asked.

'Hides the wrinkles in my neck,' Kimber said.

*   *   *

Uta had on a large purple sweater and washed out denims. Her hair was loose and came shoulder length. She sat outside the 'Monaco' sipping a drink and reading a newspaper. Now and then she looked down the street. The morning was thickening into midday. She read with a slight frown of concentration between her eyes, reaching out slowly for her drink. Once she could not find it and when she looked it was because Cuffee had removed it. She put the paper down and smiled.

'Such unpunctuality.' He sat down and looked at her.

'You are very beautiful.'

'Yes, I know. It is very pleasant to be so beautiful. But then so are you.'

'The beautiful people, eh?'

'Yes. That is true. It always has been true. That is really what made Hitler so successful. His theory was right, only his application was chauvinist.'

'Let's not talk about Hitler.'

'No, I agree, only some people do not believe that there are higher and lower humans. Usually they are lower ones themselves. Enough however. What did you think of me?'

'That you were exciting.' Her eyebrows were slightly darker than her hair. Cuffee ran his finger along. The hair was smooth and almost slippery.

'What happened to your nose?' There was on the bridge of her nose a faint line.

'I had an accident. You can see the other scars in my eyebrows if you look.' There were, pale filaments, threading among the strong curved hair of her brows.

'What happened?'

'I was skating on ice, on a frozen pond. There was an iron post in the middle of the pond and I was skating very fast when my ankle turned over and I went with my head into this iron post. At first they thought I would lose my eyes but they were saved. Then they thought I would be disfigured very much. But I was lucky. I healed very well, do you not think?'

'Beautifully.'

'So you see, I was nearly not one of the beautiful people.'

'It's rather a precarious position.'

'Oh yes, it would be nothing if one just inherited it, like a title. You have to work very hard at it. I have, very hard. What is your philosophy, do you have one?'

'I think the world consists of a great number of choices, and that one should choose.'

'No laws, are there no laws?'

239

'No human laws, natural laws but no human ones. Only choices.'

'You talk like an existentialist.'

'That's what I am, I recognize the description. A Cheshire existentialist. There's very few of us left.'

'And what is your choice about me?'

'I want you.'

'You mean my body, to make love with?'

'Certainly that. But more, you, I might even want you.'

'But you cannot have me.'

'No, but we are not talking about what I can have, only about what I want.'

'We will see how much you want what you want.'

'And what of you? What is your choice about me?'

' "For every action, there is an equal and opposite reaction," is that not written?'

'Yes.'

'Well then, I must wait until you act.'

'That's a very traditional role, the passive woman awaiting the male's approach.'

Uta smiled, a bright intense glee, and clapped her hands together like a small girl.

'Oh it is very good to be here, now, in Paris, to be beautiful and young and awaiting the male's approach.' And her laughter rang like silver scatter among the tables, and in the swaddle of her sweater Cuffee saw her breasts jump.

CHAPTER TWENTY

The half day was a mixed blessing. She was glad enough to get away from Miss Armitage telling her thirty denier was best for their kind of work, 'so many things sticking out' was her freudened phrase, and how to sapple caridgans so that they wouldn't mat. She hated Miss Armitage until she was free of her, then felt sorry for her. Once, one half day it had been, she accepted an invitation to afternoon coffee. The memory of it made Ruth grit her teeth in embarrassment. Miss Armitage had a basement flat in which she had assembled a great amount of furniture and ornaments and a budgerigar in a large gilt cage which had been her mother's and had been stuffed by a friend of hers. And so it had. Coffee had been in small, tall cups that made a mark on the nose. The basement was damp although Miss Armitage denied it, and smelled of books of which there were many many hundreds. The place mats were crocheted and there was an album of faded faces all of whom might have been her hostess. They talked of the library and the books that were being published nowadays and the best holidays Miss Armitage had had. It wasn't the sadness of it that bothered Ruth, it wasn't sad particularly, nor the boredom, hideous though it was, but the slow succession of seeping smells that Miss Armitage must have been emitting, and which she must have smelled and which she must have known her guest smelled and identified and to which she carefully refrained from alluding, which omission flavoured the whole afternoon. 'My,' she had said at one point, 'it is stuffy in here', and cleared the table.

She would never make that mistake again, better to wander around Salford with toothache. She remembered she had one of Cuffee's weekly letters to post. Perhaps she should go and meet this Patricia Mullen, find out just what sort of child it was feeding the cats. Cuffee had never struck her as the cat-loving type, not to the extent of spending money on them.

The whole house felt empty. She went up the stairs slowly, hoping to meet someone from the other rooms but no one appeared and there were no sounds. 'If a tree falls in a forest, and no one hears it, is there any sound.' What was that. She'd read it somewhere. Her room awaited in familiar dolour. She stood at the door and looked at it. If that damp, crowded, empty basement was Miss Armitage's life, was this characterless cubicle hers? She went into the kitchen to make a cup of tea and imagine her ideal room.

A long white room, with almost no furniture and a window that had a tree outside, so that the sun shone through it and made the room greeny. And she would have a cat and a view of Fuji and music, self-contained music so that everything would be like Chinese boxes one inside the other, her in the music and the music in the room, she would sit and watch the cat pad tack-tack on the wooden floor and the tree full of sunshine. Just one chair and one couch and one low table and one rug. A lamp with a poppy-coloured shade. And one bed. Would she live with a man? Not in a room like that. She'd sit alone and read a poem or peel an orange or talk to her cat, in the music, in the room. Who would visit her? Peter would be away somewhere, if he was about it couldn't be. Who would come? Harry Gibbon. He would be good, he'd bring flowers, what kind? Carnations, dark red tattery carnations. Would he be her lover? What would he be like. Not quick and dark like Peter, but gentle behind his careful clumsiness, with large cupping hands. She remembered his sleeping bag, how it had felt inside it. What did it feel like for a man to be inside her? It was impossible to imagine what it must be like for them. And they wouldn't know what it was like for a woman. There was that time on the river bank when it all seemed the one thing, or the time they were drunk in Peter's studio, after the cats and she had three orgasms and she was only half awake. But it wasn't the same as knowing.

Oh come on Ruth girl, get off this bus. If she stayed in this afternoon she'd be a goner by tea time. The pawing nangs would get her. Now if she had her room, her long cool white room, she might be able to survive. But rooms like that were just places in your head where you tried to order everything

242

and let only the trusted, tested few in. Only life consisted of other people, that was the trouble, those strange prowling creatures, other people. Like Mr and Mrs Cuffee, and Robert Eldman and David and Miss Armitage. She'd better get out, she knew it, where was that determined downwarding feel to her thoughts, she was going to end up lying on the bed trying to burst into tears and getting a headache out of it. Maybe her period was due. Was it? Now that she didn't have sex she never bothered to count. What was wrong with that gas. Needed a shilling in the meter. That settles it, she thought.

There really weren't very many choices she told herself on the train. Walk around Manchester looking at all the girls better dressed than you were, get stared at, somebody would try to pick you up, go into a café to escape, have a coffee, eat a cake, suddenly find you were grimy, go to the pictures, come out at half seven into the daylight feeling drugged and unreal, go back wash your hair, wash your drawers, wash your bra, wash your suspender belt, wash your handkerchiefs, wash your stockings. Talk to Maureen, read a book, listen to the radio, write a letter (who to?) go to bed, think of Peter, think of the hero of the film, think of a Man, end up restless and unable to sleep. Besides, she didn't go to Knutsford all that often.

She was at the door when she remembered Wednesday was her mother's day for the Guild. The house had that faint pressure empty places can, as though sunken under fathoms. She called out to it, her voice falsely expectant. The photograph in the hall, their two empty faces among the others. How long was it since she had been in the house alone. She couldn't remember, yet she knew she had, often. She walked through the kitchen and unlocked the back door into the garden. The crab apple tree seemed much smaller than she remembered it. She went on down to the rhododendrons. Close to they smelled, dark and green, a rank odour of growth. A bird rattled out from them and as she turned to catch sight, confronted, the view of the house her childhood remembered best. From the bottom of the garden where she had hidden with her skipping ropes and her

243

doll while the adult world took place indoors, Mr Cuffee's broods and Mrs Cuffee's pantomimic placation. All in there, written on the walls, hiding in the cupboards. Yet not so, empty, without memory or thought. All in her head and escaping into the empty rooms. As she started to walk back the phone rang. She hurried in and through the hall.

'Hello. Knutsford 71129.'

'Daisy, what's wrong?' – a man's voice, surprised.

'Hello, this is Knutsford 71129.'

'Is that you Daisy?' – and only the second time did she remember her mother was called Daisy by her friends.

'This is Ruth Cuffee, who is speaking please?' There was a pause and then the voice, sounding distant,

'Oh, your mother's not home?'

'No, she's at the Women's Guild on Wednesdays. Who is that please?'

'It's Robert Eldman, how are you Ruth?'

'Fine thanks. Was it anything special you wanted to see mother about?'

'No, no. Nothing important. What are you doing down in Knutsford?'

'Oh, it's my half day.'

'I didn't know it was a Wednesday.'

'Oh, it changes about. Are you speaking from the school?'

'Yes. From the school. Well, I'd better be getting back.'

'I'll tell mother you called.'

'All right. I'll see you soon.'

'Yes, cheerio.' And she put down the phone. Funny, she thought and didn't know quite why. What was it he had said, 'what's wrong, Daisy.' Maybe her voice sounded like her mother's only different. Surely Robert Eldman knew her mother went to the Guild on Wednesdays. Still, if she forgot, Robert Eldman could. It was turned three. She could go into Coleman's Coffee House and meet her when she left the Guild. Daisy. Funny to think of her mother answering to Daisy. The house seemed even quieter than before. She went to lock the back door and saw the rhododendrons move in a wind and loose several petals from the great pink corollas, to tumble down to the ground, and without knowing why she was afraid, like a child in an empty house is afraid, of everything, of nothing. She went out, closing the door quietly behind her.

Coleman's Coffee House had wood panelling and wall brackets with lanterns and the cushions on the chairs, flat rubber pads, were covered in mock tapestry material upon which were depicted red-suited huntsmen following hounds into copses several times. There was no fox Ruth noticed. All of the cakes were made on the premises. She had a currant slice and a coffee. Several women were in and Ruth found she knew them all. This rather depressed her. She was becoming of late rather an expert at unravelling the skeins of her melancholy and she applied herself to it, cutting small segments from her currant slice with the fork edge. The house of course, and it being empty. And the scufflings of the bushes. And that phone call. Robert Eldman. She'd never thought much about Robert Eldman. She had seen a photograph, where was it, her mother must have had it, of herself and Eldman in tennis clothes and Mr Cuffee in a blazer and flannels, standing in front of a club house of some sort. Robert Eldman, one of those strange prowling creatures. Which made her smile. 'Penny for them.' A familiar, unfamiliar face with the hair piled on top.

'Oh, hello. I didn't recognize you for a moment.' She knew it wasn't Jane but the name refused to come, until as the girl tugged single tugs at her five glove fingers, saying, 'Do you mind if I join you?', it came back and in relief she used it: 'No, sit down Merle.' She had an off-white suit, boxy, with large shell buttons and at her throat a navy chiffon. She smoothed her gloves out on the tablecloth and offered Ruth a cigarette.

'That's a lovely suit you're wearing.'

'Yes, it's nice, belongs to the shop. It's not this year's, else yours truly wouldn't 'ave it on' – the last in Mancunian. Her nails were painted the same colour as her buttons. Ruth tried to remember the condition of her own. It came as a surprise to realize she couldn't. Which day had she clear varnished them. And had she cleaned it off?

'What are you doing back at the dump? Not living at home are you?'

'Oh no, just my half day, came down to visit my mother.'

245

To explain her absence: 'Forgot this was her Guild day.'
She raised her coffee slowly and noted with relief that her
nails were unlacquered. The middle finger of her right hand
had a fairly obvious ragnail.

'Are you living in Manchester?'

'I did have a flat, some of the girls from the shop, but it
wasn't a good idea. You know when you started to bring
men back it all got rather complicated. Wasn't big enough.
And privacy is quite quite essential,' saying it as though
Ruth should agree. She drew on her cigarette and nodded.
'How do you manage yourself?'

'How do you mean?'

'About your dates. Can you bring them back?'

'Yes. You have to sneak in though.'

'Oh. That's tricky. A girl in the shop got knocked up by
her landlady right in the middle, can you imagine it, right
in the bloody middle. It's enough to give you a trauma. I've
been thinking of going down to London.'

'Oh. There should be plenty of work for you there.' Merle
screwed out her cigarette and recrossed her legs. Ruth tried
to analyse the subtlety of her eye make-up.

'Well, I've been trying to make some contacts. I'd like to
go down to a house, not start looking about once I arrived.
Damn dear London though. What's your brother doing this
weather?'

'Oh, he's away just now. He went off with a friend, I think
they were going to Paris.'

'Marvellous;' and she was lighting another cigarette. 'Still
painting is he?'

'Well, yes.'

'You don't sound too sure.'

'I'm not very sure of much with Peter,' Merle laughed.

'He always did go his own way.'

'Yes. I suppose he did.'

'Have you heard from him?'

'No, not yet.'

'Will he be coming back to Manchester?' Ruth smiled
embarrassment.

'I really don't know.'

'You must miss him.' And she felt herself flush with apprehension.

'Well, yes.'

'You were always pretty close.' She tried to see past Merle's handsome, achieved features, but they resisted her scrutiny, the obvious preparation that had gone into her appearance acted as a barrier, Ruth felt a panic in her at the elegant mask that smiled, asked the barbed questions without committing herself to the enquiry.

'Yes, especially at school.'

'Oh, I can remember you at school.' She stubbed out her cigarette. Only a third smoked, the paper tube buckling in the ash tray, lying in an ell, one end bevelled black, the other tinted with Merle's mouth. 'You were a right little waif.'

'Was I? I suppose I was, yes.'

'Always behind Peter. I always think of you carrying flowers. And Peter with a stick.' Somehow the way she called him 'Peter' annoyed Ruth.

'Yes. We were very close,' she said, meaning it as defiance.

'I rather had a crush on Pete in school. He was different from all the other boys.' Then in another tone – 'I rather like your style now, Ruth.' She was surprised, and her curiosity overcame the irritation of 'Pete'.

'What do you mean, my style?' Merle waved a sketching hand.

'I mean how you've projected yourself. Maybe it's something modelling makes you notice, that's really what modelling is, projecting a certain kind of image that'll match the clothes. And people do it all the time. And for women it comes down to a style, of dress, of hair, of manner. So that whoever wants to buy can see right off the kind of goods and the quality. All that.' She smiled, pleased with analogy.

'So what's my style?' Merle adopted a purse of assessment.

'You're serious, sensitive, soft. That range of thing' – and lit herself another cigarette, offering Ruth, who refused. 'I mean I'm obviously the smart, shallow,' and she searched unavailingly for an alliterative adjective, 'hard-boiled.'

247

'Are you?' Ruth asked, a little puzzled at this self-depre-
cation. Merle gestured with her cigarette.

'That's what I'm trying for. But you, we were talking
about you. I mean, your hair.' Ruth touched it automatically. 'Now your hair is very clever, really, I mean it. That
low bun and the centre parting. Now that's hair that's just
asking to be loosed out and stroked. The bun is so obviously a temporary state of affairs. Look at mine. Mine
says, it was very difficult to get it this way in the first place
so just don't dare to muss it up. I mean it puts a man in a
defensive position right from the word go.'

'And is that where you want him to be?'

'Obviously. Oh and there's something else I missed out of
your description, sisterly.'

'Sisterly?'

'Yes, you appeal at that level, too, I imagine, idealized of
course, but as a sister.' And Ruth was sure now she was
being taunted, carefully and coldly.

'Well, that's just how you see it.'

'I should think that's how men see it. I rather envy you
actually. The kind of men I know are all rather terrible
actually. It's a calculated business right from the word go.
They're after one thing and the rules are clear cut. You have
to play them for as much as you can while they're in the
process of getting it. That means from meals right up to
marriage,'

'If you don't like it why don't you do something about it?'

'You always need someone to help you, somebody to
break the pattern. Somebody different. Anyway who said I
didn't like it. It's got its risks but so has everything else. And
once you've learned the rules then you know pretty well
where you are. It's when you get involved with someone who
doesn't know the rules that you're in trouble. Don't you
find?' And Ruth wasn't sure any more whether she had
been right, whether Merle Curvis knew about her and Peter,
or whether she was talking it all out of herself. Across the
room she saw her mother come in, and notice her sitting,
and come over.

'Ruthie, you didn't tell me you were coming. You could
have come to the Guild with me, there was a very good talk

by a Child Welfare woman.' Ruth caught Merle Curvis's eye and she winked. Somehow the wink, common and familiar in the glossy face, reassured Ruth. As she rose and put on her gloves Ruth smiled at her.

'It was nice meeting you again.'

'Yes, I enjoyed our little chat. Remember me to Pete when you come across him. Good-bye Mrs Cuffee.'

'Oh, are you off, Jane. Yes, bye bye.' And she went, her high heels defining the rhomb of her calves in the long, expertly fashioned legs. Ruth felt a simple stab of envy, it was girls like Merle Curvis who made girls like Ruth Cuffee look like stumpy little women. And this made her laugh and her mother, unwitting, looked at her and smiled vaguely.

'Well, tell me.'

'Oh nothing. Except Robert Eldman phoned you.'

'Me. Phoned me? When?'

'This afternoon. I went over to the house, forgot it was your Guild day. And he phoned.'

'It would be your father he wanted,' Mrs Cuffee said fishing a compact out of her bag.

'What would he do that for with him in the school beside him?'

'Oh, was he phoning from the school?'

'So he said;' and watched her mother patting away at her nose.

'You're putting too much on.'

'Oh dear, I could never manage make-up. Now tell me, what were you and the Curvis girl saying? Exchanging secrets?'

Ruth looked at the bright, empty face and this time, perhaps because it was not as well made up, or because she had known it for a longer time, this time she could see past the chatter, see that it was only chatter, see that her mother was hiding something. That known she knew, because there was, when you thought about it, nothing else it could be. Knew and couldn't really understand what it meant, beyond the phrase and a single, unavoidable and unthinkable image.

'Remember you showed me a photograph of you and Robert Eldman, in tennis clothes. With my father beside you. Outside a kind of club house.'

249

'Yes. Yes. We'd just lost the third round of the mixed doubles. Your father didn't like tennis.' And Mrs Cuffee looked down at the ash tray where two of Merle Curvis's long butts lay across one and other, bent at the knee. The silence drew out between them until Ruth knew she must break it, but she didn't and it went on into that purest eloquence which when attained and understood allows the necessary admissions, no matter how enormous.

'You won't say anything to your father, will you?'

Ruth didn't say anything, but only shook her head, trying to prevent tears in her throat from escaping into her eyes.

She wrote to Cuffee that night. Without an address there was nothing she could do with the letter but she felt impelled to communicate her knowledge, to release its tension and in so doing make it real in a more mundane way than it was at present, locked in her head, turning and writhing, frantic with disbelief and aghast with certainty. There was no one else to whom it might make any sense, or rather any non-sense, for the commonplace thought, 'my mother has a lover', seemed in no way to encompass the incredible fact that for the past three years Robert Eldman and Dorothy Cuffee had conducted an affair almost in the house that she and Peter and Mr Cuffee had inhabited. It meant that the three years had to be looked at afresh, re-examined in the light of her discovery, re-processed by the now witting imagination.

Dearest Peter, writing to you when I have no address to send it to is a rather odd thing to be doing, but I feel I have to. Something happened today which I must talk to you about, and since I can't I must write to you about it and hope for a chance to send it later. Since there is no way to put this gradually I'd better just tell you straight out that Mother and Robert Eldman are having an affair and have been for more than three years. If I know you this will raise a roar of something akin to laughter. For me, however, it is not so simple to find a response.

When you think of it, going on all that time and none of

250

us knowing, or even guessing. When I think of all the chess games Robert Eldman played with him, and knowing what he knew. Don't think I am grieving over Mr Cuffee's cuckoldry, I'm not. It's just the whole mixed up mess it all is, the horrible defeated way Mother talked about it. I don't really know why she is doing it, for I don't think she loves Eldman and she has no intention of spiting Mr Cuffee by letting him find out. I think, and it is an awful thing to say, that she is doing it because she is bored, right in her very soul she is bored to death and this business is a kind of distraction from just how bored she is.

I found out by complete accident. I had gone down to Knutsford on a Wednesday, that's today but God knows when you'll get this, forgetting Mother went to the Women's Guild. While I was there the phone rang and it was Robert Eldman. He didn't say anything then that made me suspicious, I just wondered what he was phoning about. Then afterwards I met Mother and mentioned it. The way she reacted I just knew, she couldn't bluff it out and then she told me. Three years, although he had pursued her for much longer than that. It was only after you came back from the army that it started. I asked her how often she saw him. Do you know what she told me? She had seen him twenty-eight times in the three years. Nine times a year. Always on Wednesdays. He has his free periods on Wednesday, when he comes out of school he phones and if she hasn't gone to the Women's Guild she goes over to his place. Which gives them about two hours of uninterrupted illicit love, or whatever it is. I suppose even that is something in Knutsford. But he is really a pathetic little man. Mother says he loves her and always has, once she was going with him steady until our father came along. I suppose in a way he's had his revenge.

But what really troubles me now is the feeling that I'm involved somehow with my mother. After all these years of apathy now I'm looking at her as though I'd never seen her before, which is only true. Now she's real, a real person with a real life and feelings, and I feel that I owe her something. I know you think all we owe them is a kick in the head but we've been outside them until now. In that shop today I

251

suddenly felt I was the mother and she was the naughty girl and if I was doing right I should report her. So I don't know what to do. She really is just a child, I don't believe she knows what she's doing, socially I mean. There isn't any self-justification, or any sense of having proved anything, that she's a woman or attractive. I asked her why it started, in the first place, and she said they were alone in the house, Mr Cuffee was in Manchester, and they were talking about old times and Eldman started to cry, just cry, and she took him upstairs. When she told me that I think I loved her, for the first time a real feeling for her and I don't know what to do with it. I wouldn't think you'll have any ideas but I thought I'd tell you about it. It's a funny sensation after so long, and not wholly an unpleasant one. So there it is.

When and if I get your address I'll add a postscript,
                                    for now, with all my love, Ruth.

—

CHAPTER TWENTY-ONE

Bunce's second-hand book shop was a deep dark room with floor to roof shelves and several tables in the centre on which the paperbacks were displayed. It was not a regular student shop for text books but Moseby had picked up the odd item from time to time. He was sure Bunce ran a pornographic lending library, occasionally men, sometimes well dressed, came in with books wrapped in paper and handed them over, getting similar-looking parcels in return. Bunce himself had the aura of a smut lender, his hair had gone white in patches and in the middle of his frowsy face he wore, in an obscene little rosette, a baby's bunched mouth which he kept moistly tended with his tongue. Once, with a little spate of lip licking he had started to show Moseby, whose occasional purchases qualified him as a regular customer, a set of old sepia photographs in which two men ravished a plump brunette, who wore, throughout the proceedings, a fixed, goitred smile. The entrance of another customer had shuffled them away out of sight, not before he had seen enough, however, to inflame his mind. These worthies haunted Moseby's sex life for weeks, mentally superimposed on his and Edna's decorous couplings and leading to a condition of almost immediate ejaculation and against which no amount of interior street walking was proof. Now that Cathie had occurred he had hoped Bunce might produce them again for with her passive acceptance he felt anything might be permitted. Apart from the odd dirty joke, however, Bunce had remained stolidly unperverse.

Moseby was looking along the sixth shelf, standing on the step ladders and had come upon a thick brown book with the imperative title, *Haeckel's Monism False*. At a cursory glance at the wide margined, small type pages, the book appeared to be about somebody called Haeckel whose Monism was False. Who was Haeckel anyway? Ought not he to know him? There were neat margin notes and once, under-

lined and exclamation marked the words 'but of course!'
The line singled out for this approbation was 'whereby we
find ourselves committed to grossest solipsism, that inde-
fensible pseudo-concept'. Moseby put the book back and as
he did a page fell out and swooped to the floor. Bunce wasn't
watching but he took the book down to replace the page. It
was not from the book however, being a folded foolscap
sheet, printed on both sides. There was no author's name
or nom de plume. Under the title the text began straight
off.

Sermon IV
Text: Psalm 24, V.1.
The earth is the lord's, and all that therein is; the compass
of the world and they that dwell therein.

Dearly beloved, we are gathered here together in the loving
sight of God to give thanks to Him and to refresh our toiled
souls in His praise. All day we have been in the fields, and
all day we have laboured for our wage, all day we have fed
the earth with our flesh and now we lift our backs and look
up to God, as into the branches of a great tree where sings
some bird of praise. And that my brethren is as it should be.
Man was born upon the earth to labour for his wage, to
sweat in the sun and turn at cool of eve to God, for God has
made man in His like, and that like is not a stranger to
work. God has laboured mightily. His handiwork is here,
about us, we but sow and reap God's toil, He sowed this
world and reaped it in the beginning, the first cappilow was
God's, against that other swift reaper, time, and just as God
won His race and rested upon the Sabbath, so shall we, if we
but at godrate go, in time earn our Sabbath, our ease in His
eyes. But until that cease our lives are here upon His earth,
this body from which we win our bread, and between it and
us there is a bond that nothing can sunder, we are the flesh
of the earth, we are its spirit and its life, we are all gauds-
men heredown. To be as God is no lightness. His work is no
play, His labour is no sport. When we bend in the fields,
when the blood baubs behind our dusty eyes, when the
sickle seems a leaden ache, then and truly then are we come
in the kingdom of God, of toil that tests our bodies' will,

that wracks the marrow of our bones. It is then and firstly then we are in the likeness of our Creator, weary in His fields, bringing in His harvest. For this harvest is not grain, it is not barley nor corn nor oats nor rye, this harvest is in us, we are its stalk, our soul its ecker, and what we reap by our life's labour is life, for shall not our souls be made one as corn is made one in bread, shall we not indeed be the bread of life that God will feast upon, for God needs His sustenance and we are it, we shall become as finest dust, we shall die, verily pass from this earth as the grasses of the field, but we shall be born again, white as flour, sweet as bread to grace God's table and find favour in His sight. Dearly beloved we are by God's wisdom in the midst of His promise, for that is what this world is, God's promise to us of His will, it is His book in which we may read His purpose. He has writ in it what we are to Him and what He is to us, it is for us to study it and come to see His meaning. The world is a great bible, a holy book in which we read. Each day is a sentence we must serve, and in serving come closer to the Word. In the beginning was the World and without it no Word was, each acre is a text and each field a prayer, each knowe and downan chapter and verse. And we are the readers of his holy book, for without readers no book lives, but lies in binding, blind and blank, we are the fingers that follow each line, mark each word. And this we are as back birned and bronsed, with thieves evil rent, we stoop and stalk, stack and stound under the sun. We cut the corn and read the Word, on every page it is writ clear, the earth is God and all good comes from it, death is but return to Him, our acherspyre is but brief, as chesbols are that gleuin through gorsk a fauch fud. This is the book and it never lies, its truths endure as earth as earth they are. Look and ye shall see, seek and ye shall find. It is writ large that we come and that we stay awhile and then we go. It is in the rhythms of the year, it is in the turnings of the earth, night following day, winter the summer, we sin that deny this for all sins all widdersins, against the levin light, we may not struggle but only rejoice in God's will in which we are prime, for to us He has given the surety of our souls that we may see His will, not endure it out like brute beasts, but truly live in His like, making flesh of His law. So now we see what each day means in man's life, it is both lesson and sermon. Each morning gerniss with dew is genesis, a beginning of the Word, as you go across the fields you are opening the book and all the long day you both read and preach the Word. For you are to God both congregation and minister, you stand before God in praise for you are God's handiwork, you are God's grain, you are God's seed, and God has given you His word it is so, and God's word is His world and the world does not lie but ever constant is. So brethren, we work in helm of weet or burn of sun under God's pend, thains and windlestraes we are, from bairns to bevars in briefest dwine but we are of that which endures, of God Himself, as flowers and grass are of earth and to them return without pine or pain. So look upon the land and see your surety, your promise of life everlasting, hills are all the breasts of all the buried bodies, the sun warms them, the rivers slake their thirst, the tender touch of grass grows upon them. From day daw to day dwine is allaris, till all our nows are knowes and all our prayers beneath a pray are, each burdalane begrauin and ecker braird is brerd, then though devall take us old erd shall deisheal our schouris, life late lyflats through whose hair the houin drunes. Die we do and all we will and mortmumlings shall accompany us, above our graves merrydancers in the sun will sway and sworl and world without enday shall be ours. For ever and ever, Amen.

Outside, Glasgow. He had never really seen it before, he realized. Not really, not clearly. Coming from the rhythms and the hues of the tract it blockaded the mind, fractured vision on its multiple baffle walls, repeated itself endlessly, the great inarticulate sprawl, saying stony, grimy words, sentences, whole pages of a prose reduced to drabbest utterance, an epic of the herd, sweltering in proximity. Through its streets the mind might wander for ever and not come upon a single image of transcendence, buildings and more buildings, monuments that echoed buildings and buildings that echoed monuments. Green squares sewn into the city's monochrome, in which the old sit and watch their feet. The river, drabbed by commerce and sewage, no sense of its source in the hills remaining, no omen of outcome in the firth presaged. A city demanding to be loved, in default of alternative, allowing its sons and daughters no glimpse of the world beyond, preforming their minds to an acceptance of the human landscape as being of brick and stone, slate and cement, making such words as he had read almost incomprehensible, an alien rhetoric.

It made him see something he had known but never quite focussed before. About Cathie and himself. That their affair was, in this new sense, Glaswegian, it had this incarcerated, ailress aura to it, this unease that lay upon the city-dweller, that beyond what they had something unguessably better existed, that corroded the pleasures of the present without promising future recompense. Was it that yearning for the garden genesis, old green eden, wherever and whatever it had been. Was that why his room was green, why he liked to lie naked and let it swim around him, under the green aquarial light of the mnemonic tree of life. He wanted Edna suddenly, so that standing waiting for the bus, he was suddenly sick with the pang of it, the swift, in-eating long of mute love.

Edna went to her mother's most afternoons. By the time the train got in and he had read the piece again he decided to take it over to Maxwell's for a reaction. There were things in it that a second reading impressed, beyond the incantory flow and the archaic inflexions. For one the formal logic of composition, statement, exegesis and coda, almost musical in its development. And the words he didn't know. Cappielow for instance. The Morton football ground was called 'cappielow'. 'The first cappielow was God's.' What might that mean? And who was he, the author, why was there no printer's name on the sheet. He had searched the *Haeckel's Monism False* right through but there was nothing that might suggest the owner of the book had been the writer of the pamphlet, or whatever it was. Perhaps Maxwell might know something about it, might have read it before.

He was in the back garden working on an outshed. He came down from the step ladders, smiling and wiping his face.

'Hard work's no' easy,' he said.

'I hope that is biblically proportioned,' nodding to the structure. Maxwell winked solemnly.

'Woolworth's ordered me a special rule marked in cubits. What brings you this way?' He took Moseby's elbow and walked him down the garden. 'Just in time for tea.'

'I found this in an old bookshop.' Maxwell glanced at it.

'Well, do you want me to read it now?'

'It's not very long, if you have the time . . .'

'Well, I'll read it and you can try your hand at social chatter. And don't worry, the way Christine does it you hardly feel a thing.'

Nor did he. It was rather pleasant to sit outside in the deep basket chair and sip lemon tea which he'd never tasted before, lemony and tanninish, and masticate a macaroon whirl, noting the way Christine Maxwell's hair grew down in a point on her forehead, a widow's peak wasn't it, and against the wall the forsythia burned countless little yellow peeps and once a blackbird's beak matched them exactly as he ran and stopped, stopped and ran across the lawn. A thick furry bee drew a line through the afternoon. Moseby found himself thinking of his foster parents in their retired cottage. Were they sitting out drinking tea, listening to a bee plunder the fat peonies? Peonies had been Mrs Moseby's favourite flower. Those two strange people he had assiduously forgotten. They should go this summer, if the weather was good it wouldn't be too much of a grind. Arran could be nice in the summer. Maxwell he noticed had finished the piece. He held out his cup for more tea and looked at Moseby while he phrased something in his mind.

'I've never quite decided what the relationship between heretic and poet is. But I'm sure it exists. And it's demonstrated in your man here I'm certain.'

'What do you think of it?'

'As what? A piece of literature or a piece of doctrine.' He sipped his tea and watched Moseby across the cup.

'Both. Whichever you like first.'

'A bit florid for my particular taste, all rather cadenced, King Jamesish, marzipan prose my lecturer at St Andrews used to call it. Still, as I said, that's a personal point of view.' His wife extended a hand for the matter under discussion and Maxwell handed it over. 'As doctrine it's about as relevant to Christianity as most mysticism, which is, in my opinion, not at all.' Moseby felt curiously upset, as though it were a work of his that were being criticized.

'Why is that?'

'Well, I think he, whoever he is, avoids the whole heart of the problem of evil.'

'Maybe he doesn't believe in evil.'

'Then he's a fool.'

'Maybe he thinks the world is basically good and evil is just a concept we use to understand certain phenomena.'

'Maybe he does, but that's not a Christian attitude. Evil is at the centre of the moral question and it's the ability to answer that question, and firstly the ability to phrase it, which is the beginning of Christian practice.'

'Christianity is the attempt to behave in a Christly manner in this world. Or is it the preparation of one's soul for the next?' Maxwell sat up straight and put his cup on the grass, a certain combativeness in his movements.

'Both, the preparation of the soul is the attempt to behave, as you put it, in a Christly manner. All this man offers is a kind of pantheistic trance.'

'I would have thought he put forward a kind of metaphysic of the individual, that first paragraph for instance.' Maxwell turned to his wife who gave him back the paper. He read it quickly, returned it, frowning.

'That's all very well, yes, but his argument could go half a dozen ways from that. It's an extended metaphor, and rather a good one, but in itself it isn't saying very much, just heralding all the rest, and it's all the rest I disagree with. For one thing I find all this fecundity a bit suspect, all this earth worship and harvest festivity. For one thing he would be virtually unintelligible to about ninety per cent of any congregation in Scotland, or England for that matter—'

Moseby, impatient to get in, 'Exactly, that's what I was

259

thinking, just how esoteric such a vision is, simply because we live in towns.'

'I hardly think it's . . .'

'No, a moment, I agree about the pantheism, about the shadowy sort of way he refers to God, by shadowy I mean there's something imprecise about how God is being defined. Maybe that was because his readers knew all about God, maybe they weren't in any doubt about the definition.'

'I don't see your point.'

'Well, just that maybe he was speaking to a very specific congregation, and a congregation for whom the Christian fundamentals, and possibly a thorough scriptural knowledge, were basic. Maybe he wasn't preaching to city dwellers at all.' Maxwell seemed disinclined to this, he sat back and steepled his hands in front of him.

'You're making too big a thing of this country, city, thing. I mean human beings don't alter value because of where they live.'

'No, but your environment shapes your mental resources. You wouldn't argue but that this thing was rural, even agricultural, in its tenor.'

'I'd be inclined to be nasty and say it was a city man's vision of the country.'

'I think you're right, but that makes it even more cogent, does it not?'

Maxwell seemed to have decided something, for his tone was brisk and definitive.

'I think this man's a mystic, he has that disquieting ring I have learned to beware. I don't trust mystics, all but the greatest of them are megalomaniacs pursuing themselves in the likeness of God. Still, that's their business. But primarily it's the fact that people's minds today are complex things, I don't mean they are very much more intelligent, just that there are more things they know about, and this kind of vision is too large, too specious, and in this case too abstruse. When you are trying to relate Christian doctrine to the twentieth century something like this is anathema.'

Moseby found himself wanting to say something snide, about the 'Sunday Break' mentality, about the cosiness of the epiloguians, but checked and shrugged.

'Would you not rather preach him than, "Ecclesiastes" say?' he said.

'If you're asking me do I prefer mystics to nihilists the answer's no, I don't. Nihilism's a dead end, you get into it and come up against certain facts, that life is without meaning for instance, but mysticism's a maze, an endless maze of ever decreasing circles until you end up disappearing in the time-honoured tradition.' Mrs Maxwell smiled at her husband and rose to take the tea things in, giving Moseby back the sheet of paper. He felt depressed that Maxwell should have come down so emphatically on his little treasure. Silence lay between them in the bright garden and after she had gone in it stretched, allowing them both to guess the other's thoughts.

'I must sound pretty het up about it, eh?' Maxwell said.

'No. I mean you feel strongly about it, so that's it.'

'I don't think you quite understand my position, John. I'm a Presbyterian minister. That's not like being a shipyard worker, or a coalminer. It's more like being a doctor, or an artist. Only more so. I'm a Presbyterian minister all of the time, I think on the people I meet as being souls, souls to some greater or lesser degree in search of God, and my obligation to them is always the same, to help them find God. You are a soul, you are struggling with the Devil for possession, you are locked in the battle against evil, against sin. You may translate these terms how you will, but that's what I read in you. I am a busy man. I don't see enough of you, you don't come to church and I have no wish to ask you to come, but I recognize that I am dependent on your whim for our meetings. I am not authorized to seek you out, I have responsibilities to my parishioners, it is one of the severities of my calling, I must enact the dispassionate equality of God's passionate concern for each soul. So to gain some idea of how I feel you must imagine a doctor who has diagnosed cancer in a patient and the next time he sees him he is brandishing "the Lotion", Shake well and rub in.' He stopped to see if his point was taken. Moseby watched him gravely, allowing no expression. 'I don't want you going off into the wilds of mystical experience or comparative religion. You're not looking for an academic understanding of the religious impulse in man, you need religion, existential, here, now, daily religion. And I don't think this man, charming fellow as he no doubt was, can supply that.'

It rather surprised Moseby to think of him as having such a deliberated point of view as that, in which he, John Moseby, existed as a soul to be saved. Struggling with the Devil for his soul. Was he? Was that the concept he needed to make sense of his existence? But would it stand up, stand up to his world of illusion and counter illusion, where no appearance could be trusted, where the very reality of the world itself was jeopardised. Still, it was rather touching that Maxwell should be like that, but it also let him see how far he was from anything approaching a Christian. This made him wonder about something.

'Remember that story you told me, about the man with no legs?'

'Yes.'

'What did you mean by it, I'm right in thinking of it as a kind of parable, aren't I?' Maxwell grinned as though caught out.

'I suppose it was a parable of sorts, well I know it was. It meant, that he, the man with no legs, was trying to do something impossible, stand up, and he was trying to do it without his crutches which was, if you like, the sin of pride.'

'And the people laughing?'

'The world, cheering him on.' Moseby shook his head.

'Just shows you. I thought on it quite differently, his deformity was his handicap and his attempt was a kind of heroic, absurd task he had set himself, to transcend his limitations. That one time when he threw away the crutches, he wouldn't fall down. Funny, that we could be so far apart.'

'Well, it wasn't such a very good example of the secular parable,' Maxwell said lightly but Moseby had the sense that in some way he had let the man down by his interpretation. He folded the paper and put it into his pocket.

'I'll let you get on with the work,' rising.

'I've been getting on with the work,' Maxwell said. They walked through to the front door. Maxwell held out his hand, as they were shaking he said, 'Sorry if I seemed a bit down on your man, I suppose to some extent it's sour grapes. I'd like to preach sermons like that, not like that exactly, but full of the sound of words.'

'Why don't you?'

'Oh, several things. I'm no great hand as a preacher really. And the congregation, well I'm not so sure they'd appreciate it. I wonder how many of his listeners, or readers, understood.'

'There was me,' Moseby said, feeling defiant and a little foolish for doing so. Maxwell smiled and nodded.

'Oh, if they were all like you, John, it would make things much simpler. Harder, but simpler.' Moseby stood for a moment then went down the steps. The minister waved and went in. The west end lay closed and quiet in the late afternoon sun. He did not like the west end. The thought slipped in, well worn and practised. All the closed doors and muslined windows. All the empty gardens and the tulips, the thick, pervading stench of order, of the governed, regulated world of priorities. And in its midst, just down Forsyth Street, the special school where the mutations milled at playtime, filling the filtered air with their idiot gaiety. In its very heart the worm, the hidden obscenity, the maggots in a song-bird's breast.

Suddenly the thought of what he was doing with Cathie overwhelmed him. Terror at the havoc it held, like a madman loose in the suburbs, hacker in hand. Hide, Mr Hyde, don't let them catch a glimpse of you, for they'll recognize you or they won't and either way they'll scream. And first to scream would be Edna, for her world was a west end, the landscape of her soul where the ugly things were discreetly hidden, trundled swiftly through the careful avenues in a special grey bus, special so that if you didn't want to look you didn't have to but could attend to the tall slender absurdities of the tulips.

Hurry home, Moseby, he told himself. To your green room and your unwitting wife and your bonny daughter. Hurry home.

CHAPTER TWENTY-TWO

The 'Monaco' was crammed and full of noise. All the tables were occupied and they had to stand. There was a young man who knew Kimber with them. He came from Guildford and wore a beret. He was a poet and was talking to Kimber about poetry. His own work was post-apocalyptic. Did Kimber see any future for the socialist tradition in poetry? He, personally, could not. He discovered Gibbon's Scottishness and asked him if he had read Dunbar. Much finer poet than Burns. Gibbon explained he hadn't read either. This was astonishing, like an American admitting he hadn't read Whitman. Or an Englishman Shakespeare. Or an Italian Dante Alighieri. Switzerland seemed the only likely baulk to his Grand Tour. Gibbon said he was pretty ignorant about poetry at which Cuffee patted him fondly on the shoulder and went to get drinks. There was a girl at the bar with a snub boyish face and a crew cut. She looked at Cuffee as though she might know him, then looked away. Cuffee said hello. The girl looked back, an intent reassessing glance. She said 'hello' with an accent. Cuffee asked if she were French and she shook her head.

'Are you alone?'

'No, she's not. So you can scram.' A big blond American in an ivy league jacket. He had a beefy amiable face, smeared a little now with drinking. Cuffee looked from him to the girl. Her face was guarded and she looked across the bar.

'I said scram jewboy.' Cuffee laughed and turned away. The man reached across and bit his fingers into Cuffee's bicep. 'You laughing at me, yid?' The girl stepped out from between them, ducking under the holding arm. Cuffee let himself be pulled round to face the man. There was a space between and the American stepped back trying to make room for a short right cross and as he did Cuffee kicked up and caught him inside the groin. He screamed, a choked expulsive cry and almost fell, holding with his elbow on to the bar. Cuffee slowly and deliberately pushed the retaining arm off and the man slumped down into a pained squat. 'Joey, Zus. The bastard kicked me,' he ground out. They were behind him and were pushing through the people at the bar. One of them in a striped matelot jersey swung from a long way out, a lunging right that caught Cuffee high up on the cheek and spun him round to the bar and he took a double-handed smash on the back of the neck which put him on his knees. As he went down the American managed to straighten up but before he could gather himself for a punch his other friend put the boot in only low and catching Cuffee on the hip. Then the American clubbed him on the side of the head and bounced his face against the bar. 'Come on boy, get up and take your stuff.' And they stood round, the striped jersey prodding Cuffee in the kidneys with his toe. Gibbon caught him by the neck of his jersey and pulled him back and as the other man turned butted him between the eyes and holding his lapels went on with the head until he was holding him by the coat front. Released he sank slowly reaching up for his bloody face, making a whimpery, snottering noise. The matelot stripes was coming in again and Gibbon took a slack-handed blow across the mouth before he could get set and then he hit him left hand right hand left hand to the body and the man stopped, a sick stretched look on his face and there was a pause and Gibbon hit him right handed to the open body and he went back, twisting himself away from the hurt. There was a space around them now and the patron was shouting for someone to get a gendarme. The American in the ivy league jacket back handed him across the mouth and made for Gibbon. Cuffee straightening up reached behind him and swung the bottle fluently, almost casually against the thick, chubbed neck and he went down in his stride and looked up glassily in time to be hit on the top of the head, the bottle breaking and wine and blood running down his face. There were two of them on the floor now, one of them on his knees with his face held cupped in his hands. The other, hit by the bottle was on all fours and was crawling slowly towards the door, the crowd opening up for him. The striped jersey was standing looking at Gibbon.

Cuffee came round unsteadily and shook the bottle neck at him, Gibbon held out a warning palm.

'You'd be better staying there, Jack.' The crawling man fell over and lay still. Gibbon took Cuffee by the arm and began to lead him away only for the patron to come over the bar and round in front of them talking loudly in French and holding out his arms to stop them from leaving. Gibbon pushed him back towards the door and he put his hands on their chests and pushed. Before Gibbon could pull him aside Cuffee had hit him in the stomach and he stumbled back, sitting on the edge of a table. His wife behind the bar stopped phoning and screamed. They broke out on to the street, a few half hearted clutches slipping off. Cuffee walked away from Gibbon and Kimber pushed through to join him. The bottle neck in Cuffee's hand dropped and smashed with a thin cruel noise. Cuffee began to run, bumping off walls then steadying up. Kimber held Gibbon back from following.

'Let's pick up a taxi and we can catch him up. The gendarmerie will be here shortly.' Gibbon nodded and watched Cuffee run out of sight round the corner. As they walked across the street the patron came out and looked up and down the street. Kimber hailed a taxi and they ran for it. Somebody shouted but they didn't look back.

He ran for a bit then turned left and walked. He went into a small bar, dark and empty save for a man and the woman who was serving playing dice and scoring on a cribbage board. He ordered a cognac. The woman scarcely looked at him and went straight back to her game. Cuffee felt his mouth. The bleeding had been from a cut inside and seemed to have stopped. There was a swelling on the side of his face from the big American's swing and a lump on the other side where he had bounced off the bar. His hip was throbbing. He let a little of the cognac into his cut and rued. The dice chuckled nimbly and clippered across the counter. The man tutted at the woman's luck. She mimed irresponsibility. The wood of the bar was smooth and grainy. It had a knot hole like the centre of a vortex. Cuffee fingered it. Like a blind eye it was. When the woman put

266

her hand over the cup the shaken dice made a knucky sound, dim and neat, then they came scampering. He swilled his mouth with the cognac. It stung and fumed. A man came in and handed over a parcel which the woman put under the counter. He had a glass of wine. The girl from the 'Monaco' came in and stood beside Cuffee. He ordered two cognacs.

'Hello,' he said.

'Are you fine?' Cuffee nodded gravely.

'Yes. Very fine.'

'Did they hurt you?'

'No. Not a lot.' She was very serious, the boyish small face intent on his. She looked very young.

'They were bad men. They hate all Jews, I am sure of it.'

'What age are you?'

'I am old. I am sixteen. I know about such things.'

'You're not French.'

'I am Israeli. Have you ever been to Israel?'

'No.'

'You must come. All Jews should come to Israel. Once in life. There it does not happen as tonight.'

'What were you doing with them if they hate Jews so much?'

'I was not with them. He talked to me and I talked with him and then you came.' She made a little fluttering movement with her hands, upwards around her face. 'I do not look very much Jewish. I am sorry. I am very proud to be Jewish.'

'So am I.'

'Do you speak Hebrew?'

'No.'

'You should learn. It is good that all Jews will speak Hebrew and come in their life to Israel. Your friend, in the fight, he is not Jewish.'

'No.'

'He must like Jewish people to fight for them.'

'He does. He is very fond of Jewish people. What is your name?'

'Sara. What is yours?'

'Peter. Are you going to stay with me tonight?'

'If you want.'

'You are living in Paris for a time?'

'For a year. Then I go back to Israel.'She had not touched her cognac. Cuffee ordered another for himself. He raised his glass.

'To Israel,' he said.

'Yes. To Israel' – and said something in Hebrew which she told him meant 'with all my heart'. She taught Cuffee to say it and they toasted Israel again, in Hebrew this time.

The room was almost dark and Kimber lit the lamp on the desk. The carnation green shade made a great turnip jewel. Through the windows the sky banked violet and the tops of the trees rippled and shifted. It had been a long time in coming to dusk but the lamp made it in a moment a finality. Gibbon sat on the desk and looked out.

'Funny feeling Paris gives you.' Kimber was at the gramophone.

'Funny?'

'It's got a mood hasn't it?'

'It's got a lot of moods.'

'It's got one now,' Gibbon said looking out into the dark, darkening trees. 'Wonder what it feels like to go to sleep in a tree. Like a bird.'

The room was sudden with sound. The piano a simple marching figure echoed gravely by violin and 'cello. The trees moved independent of the music, yet related in the context of the night and the night's mood, moved random against the ordered onwardings of the trio. The tenderness of two restrained implorations from the 'cello upon the high sweet violin voice. The trees were still, dark macy hushes, church. In them the 'cello pled with the violin, pleaded and was disregarded by the piano in its percussive pursuit of anthem. The trees twitched dimly in the soft splats of rain. Then quieted then quivered afresh in the wind. The second movement danced, lyricism pierced by wit. Kimber followed the invention closely, moving his head in time, the green light making the room mysterious in the corners, an oval cave, smaragd dim. And the music found itself unerringly and celebrated itself, celebrated its dexterity and its grace in succeeding measures, music heard at distance, of gaiety made abstract, a scherzo of thought. Gibbon no longer watched out, the night having swallowed the trees, the green lamp now holding the world in its hue.

When it ended the silence was like a kind of music, an original, pristine music.

The concierge's voice called Kimber from downstairs. He smiled at Gibbon and went out. Gibbon looked at the sleeve of the record. Beethoven. Trio No. 7 in B Flat Major. ('Archduke') Opus 97. First Movement: Allegro moderato. Second Movement: Scherzo (Allegro).

'Harry, it's for you.'

'For me? Who, is it Peter?'

'No, it's Annie. She wants to know where he is. I told her we lost him after the "Monaco".'

The phone was in a little glass partition cubicle. Annie's rather nasal, emphatic voice twanged in the receiver.

'Harry? Look Harry, it's about Peter, I mean I just don't know where he is, I haven't seen him for three days I guess. Do you know where he is?'

'Did Norman tell you about the fight?'

'Yeah, but you don't know where he is?'

'No. I expect he's getting drunk somewhere.'

'Are you sure he isn't with that German girl, Uta?'

'I don't know Annie. I don't know where he is.'

'Look Harry, look I know this sounds really bitchy and all that but you ought to warn him about that German dame. She's no good to somebody like Peter. She's dikey you know.'

'What's that?'

'She's les, her and that little dark girl that's always with her.'

'Well, Cuffee'll find out he's barking up the wrong tree.'

'Yeah but she goes both ways. Honest Harry, you ought to warn him.'

'Annie, he's a big boy. I can't go warning him about women. Anyway, I don't know that he's with her. I don't have a clue where he is.'

'When you see him, Harry, you'll tell him I want to see him?'

'Sure.'

'Okay. Thanks Harry, you're a pal.'

'That's me. See you.'

'Ciao.'

When he went back up Kimber was making coffee. He called out from the kitchen.

'About Peter, was it?'

'Aye. She's stuck on him.'

'She's a sad little cow.'

'Is she?' Kimber appeared with the coffee. Gibbon was looking out of the window.

'In her way. American girl in Paris, losing the sense of reality.' Gibbon turned and looked at Kimber, serious, almost doleful.

'I've just realised what it might be like to be stuck on Cuffee. For a woman.'

'There is something a bit terrifying about him. Like in that fight, he was the one who frightened me. You were, I don't know, animal, you seemed to be just acting spontaneously, but Peter, there was something cold about him.'

'He's a real fighter is Cuffee,' Gibbon said. 'He hates.'

'Does that make a good fighter?'

'Makes a good winner.'

'I would have thought you could take Cuffee in a fight.' Gibbon smiled.

'Sure, I could, first six seven eight times, I outweigh him a stone and a half, I'm built solid, I hit harder. But he'd take me in the end, when he'd worked up the energy, the hate, the need. He'd cut me up in little bits.'

'Why are you with him, Harry?' And Gibbon shrugged and walked, holding his coffee cup under his chin. He stopped and looked into the darkness of the guitar, the silent belly of music.

'I'm learning, I suppose,' sipping his coffee, 'learning.'

'Learning what?' Kimber under the lamp, the face modelled boldy by the shadow, suddenly a bared face, open and close to commitment.

'My grand-uncle said "if you don't go you can't go back". Only there must be some reason for the journey. I suppose it must be what you learn that makes it necessary. I don't

270

know what you learn. Peter is different from me, that seems a good reason for being with him. The more he is him, the more I am me.' Gibbon turned round and found Kimber watching him. They stared at one and other until Kimber, reaching up, switched off the light. For a moment dark, close warm dark and then the light went on again and Kimber was sitting, his face composed again. Gibbon sat down and looked at the floor.

'The trouble about queers Harry is that they have to rationalise what men and women can accept as the gilt on a relationship. That kind of chemical fever that passes between people who are in the position to say Thou to each other.' Gibbon looked up. Kimber wasn't watching him but had picked up a pencil and was holding it between his two index fingers. 'It's not so much that sex between men isn't natural, it's surprising just how acceptable it can become, no, it's that there is set in motion a whole process of articulation to explain and make intellectually comfortable what is after all a genuine feeling, a genuine emotional event.'

'Do you think I'm queer, Norman?'

'No.'

'I don't think I am either. But I expect it's one of the things I'll learn.'

In the morning the girl Sara woke him and said she loved him. She had made love many times in Israel with boys but she had never been to bed with a boy naked, in the kibbutz there were dormitories and they made love outside. He must come when she was in the army and they would have a wonderful time and he would like it. They would go to hotels and make love in the hotel beds. She had never said to anyone that she loved them only that she liked. Did he like her?

'There is something to tell you. I am not Jewish.' She didn't understand for a moment and then she did and her face grew grave and small. She got up out of the bed and asked him not to look. Then she put on her clothes and Cuffee lay with his wrist over his eyes watching her. When she was dressed she turned and looked at him. She was ready to cry. Cuffee watched her, his face without expression.

271

'You lied,' she said.

'Yes.'

'To get love from me.' Cuffee sat up and rubbed his nose.

'I felt very Jewish at the time' – which she did not understand. She looked at him then went. Cuffee lay down again and closed his eyes.

It was raining when Gibbon came down. He stood on the steps looking through the trees. The rain was steady but not heavy. He turned up his coat collar and went across the 'place' and through the trees. The rain made a noise in the leaves. There was no wind and the river was smooth and dull, marked everywhere with the rain ringlets, a mesh of brief expansions. He stood at the point and watched the thick slow run of the river. It bore a bottle, neck angled up, down towards a grey bridge. He watched it. The rain fell wetting his hair, cool on his face when he looked up. Then he was shivering and he left.

The streets were busy and black with rain. He walked through the morning throngs, his jacket collar still up. The dark blond growth made his face seem dirty. People going to work, the rain, the city noise.

The 'Monaco' wasn't open. The chairs were on the tables and curled on an inverted one the black and white cat slept, its head lost in its midriff. He went round the corner and up the street. The house smelt of cabbage water. He went up the stairs quietly but the concierge noticed him and called 'monsieur'. He went back. She recognised him, faintly and without affection.

He knocked the door and went in – Cuffee was in bed. When Gibbon came in he rolled over and opened his eyes.

'How are you, Harold?'

'Fine. And you?'

'Bit stiff. My mouth's swollen.'

'Where did you get to?'

'Oh, I got into a bar and got drunk. What did you do?'

'Stayed over at Kimber's.'

'He's queer isn't he?'

'Yes.'

'Did he make a pass at you?'

'No. Not yet.'

'Don't fancy it much. Not your style either. Would you say I was a bastard, Harry?' Gibbon sat on the foot of the bed.

'I might. Some ways yes. You're bastardish.' Cuffee got up and went to the sink where he urinated.

'Sometimes,' he said midway through, 'I feel like I'm a knife.' He looked down at himself. 'Funny, you'd have thought that'd be the first thing one of them would have noticed.'

'Annie phoned Kimber's last night.'

'What did she want?'

'To see you. I think that girl's stuck on you.'

'Harry, will we not talk about anything like that. You have an accusatory non-committal look all over that great coupon of yours. Let us talk of the fight last night, exchange accounts.' Gibbon got up off the bed, Cuffee fell into a crouch and jabbed the air severally.

'All right.' Cuffee straightened up and in annoyance said, 'Look, Harry, it'll never be so consequence-less again. Why not float with it?'

'You're just making her into a sexual thing. Making her the same as Gerda, or Gerda the same as her.'

'They're all different Harry. You want them all to be the same, all jellied up in love. A fuck's a fuck, and they're all different.'

'Okay, Peter, let's go and eat.' Cuffee began putting on his clothes.

'Ach, you. Now you've made me feel like some kind of animal.'

'Come on,' Gibbon said, 'Let's have some scoff and you can tell me all about her.' Cuffee looked at him and smiled. 'You're a shrewd kind of a big bloke, aren't you?'

They sat inside and watched the rain and the people. Cuffee drank two cups of coffee and ate several croissants. Gibbon had coffee. Sitting at the window, dark head arched towards fair, antithetical faces. A young girl in a transparent plastic raincoat went past. Her face was wet from the rain and there were raindrops on the coat. Under it she wore a coral sweater. It shone dimly in the dewy translucence. She glanced in, a quick creature look. Cuffee kissed the window pane, his lips pressed pink. The girl smiled and put a finger where her mouth was and went on. When he took his face away the mark of his lips could be seen inside the condensation of his breath. It faded away, from the outside in, until his kiss was swallowed again by the glass.

Gibbon smiled at him. Cuffee smiled back then shook his head dismissively.

'Oh Harry it's sore, they're so beautiful, aren't they? and I'll never know any of them, one, two, twenty-two, a hundred.' He shook his head again. 'All over the world they are, beautiful beautiful women, and I'll never touch them. Oh, it makes me want to cry. I love them, really I do, women . . .'

'On the hole,' Gibbon said. Cuffee laughed.

'Yes, on the whole.'

'What's happening about this Uta?'

'That's very trisical that is. Can't be rushed. She's a professional, I mean the skin game is what she does. Everything has to be won. There's no gifts with that one.'

'Will she hump do you think?'

'Oh, she's capable of it, and I've no doubt she has, but I'm not sure she will for me.'

'I can't believe that.'

'No seriously. You have to be determined and willing to spend a lot of time, and you might have to beg.'

'She's just a prick teaser then?'

'No, it's not that. She knows she's beautiful and that's for sure, she is. And she knows you want her, and you do. So that's the basis of the game, you want her and she wants you. But not sexually, she wants power over you. She wants to dominate you and she can because you want her sexually, that's her lever.'

'Annie says she's lesbian.'

'Annie hates lesbians. She'd say that of Uta out of sheer bitchery.'

'Do you think she is?' Cuffee looked reflective, fishing the scum off his coffee.

'She might be. She's certainly got enough hold over that poor little bugger Yani.'

'Do you think you can win then?'

'Oh you can't win, Harry. But it may be possible to make considerable inroads into the enemy position.'

'When are you seeing her?'

'Today. What are you going to do?'

'I'm going to write some letters, then take a walk around.'

'Harry, why don't you get yourself a woman? Don't you fancy anything here?'

'It doesn't bother me a lot Peter. Anyway, I haven't got the chaff necessary.'

'You worry me sometimes.'

'Likewise.' Cuffee smiled his crooked smile of affection and pressed Gibbon's nose flat to his face.

'Do you think I look Jewish?' he asked.

Ruth,

I hope you don't mind me writing to you. I had thought of doing so a few times since we left Manchester but each time put it off because I wasn't sure what I could say in a letter to you. I did start one a few days ago but never finished it and now I can't find it. I suppose I should tell you what has happened and what Paris is like but it doesn't seem very important. I don't think I can be very observant because Paris seems just as I expected it. No surprises. It's all the films you see.

What is most on my mind in writing to you is the feeling I have that I miss you, only of course that can't be true because I don't know you. Can you miss somebody you've never known? Maybe you can. Perhaps I'm reminded of you so much because I'm with Peter. Or maybe I'm just making a person up and thinking it's you. I feel strange these days, just ever so slightly ill, delicate I suppose you might say if I wasn't thirteen-odd stone and ate as much as I do. I find myself in moods, not sad, and not happy, just moods and things all feel sort of odd. I don't know what it is. Sometimes it's quite pleasant.

I've thought quite a bit about you and I would like us to meet again. I know you were very close to Peter but I feel from you both that it is in the past. For me almost everything seems to be in the past, that is one of the problems. I hope you will not mind all this stuff and I hope to see you when we get back. I don't know quite when that will be. Money goes fast in this town. Peter will be writing soon and should you wish to contact him our address is 29, rue Monsieur le Prince, Boulevard St Michel.

So look after yourself. Yours, Harry Gibbon.

Uta and Yani had a large studio room with polished wood floors and Scandinavian furniture. There were a great many books and several paintings, one of Uta in a black tunic dress. The room was the top floor of a building and was divided by a folding partition. The windows went almost the full length of the wall.

'Nice place you got here.'

'That is what they say in American movies. Talking of Americans how is your little piece?'

'Talking of little pieces how can you afford this?' Uta spun round, her hair flaring out around her head. She slowed down so that it was over her face.

'Yani's father is a very rich man. Very, very rich. He is almost as rich as anyone in Germany.'

'What did he do during the war?'

'He fought for Germany.'

'Was he a Nazi?' Uta stood before the mirror combing back her hair. Cuffee watched her reflection.

'You do not like Nazis?'

'Not from what I have heard.'

'Herr Zimmermann is a very intelligent man. He was much too intelligent to be a Nazi. But he understood what Hitler believed in, only he did not think it could be achieved in Hitler's way.' She turned. 'You would like him I think. Would you like to meet him?'

'No.' Uta frowned quickly.

'Why not?'

'I don't want to meet anybody like Herr Zimmermann because I am not interested in him.'

'What are you interested in?'

'Sex, painting' – he searched – 'that's about it.'

'You are a barbarian. I think that is why I like you.' Cuffee went over to sit by the window. There were pigeons on the coping outside. A cock swole and advanced, trailing

276

his fan, the female lifted into flight a few feet and landed again. Uta was beside him. 'You are watching the pigeons. Do you feel like him?' – pointing. Cuffee caught her wrist and twisted it, slowly.

'No. I feel like me.' She tried to hold against the tortion but he made her turn away and bend back with her arm. Then he let her go. She came round and slapped him hard, the noise and the movement frightening the pigeons. Cuffee watched her and rubbed his face. Uta went across to the other side of the room. She sat down, looking small against an expanse of empty wall. For a moment there was silence. During it the pigeons came back.

'You are very crude. Really you are. You will have to vary your approach. Twisting arms, it will not do. You have this way with you of not explaining anything, of presenting this inscrutable mask, hinting at how ruthless you are.'

'Many a true word spoken incest.'

'And really you are just a common or garden boor. I heard about your fight in the "Monaco", over some little tart. And this manner, it is too much out of a second-rate film. You are a very handsome young man and I think you may be more intelligent than you pretend but you see yourself in an adolescent way.' She stood up abruptly. 'Always the pose' – and she mimed Cuffee's stance, one knee bent, one shoulder high, thumbs hooked behind him. 'Always the careful composition,' and sitting down she hung an arm across her knee, the hand open, palm downward. 'You really think you are beautiful, don't you?'

'I'm a nice-looking boy, yes.'

'Why do you not want to meet Herr Zimmermann?'

'I have a father, I don't want to meet anybody else's father.'

'That is stupid. You are being particularly stupid today.' Cuffee came over and squatted down in front of her.

'Can you hear things when they are said to you. Listen while I say something to you. I can go now and get me a woman, I will be sorry not to have handled that splendid body of yours but you can't win them all. You are playing it tough too early. I'm not hooked.'

Uta stared back at him. She knelt before him, leaning her

277

face close to his. Her mouth yielded a small rapid kiss. 'You think you are strong, don't you?' Cuffee nodded. 'You are ready to take on the world. Are you?'

'If needs must.'

'You think you will win this with me?'

'No, I don't think that. But I know the rules and you can't touch me until I am hooked.'

'What do you mean by hooked?'

'Until I want you, not just your flesh. You, your very essence.'

'I knew you were a metaphysician under all that. Very essence' – and she sat back up on her seat. 'How predictable you are.'

'And I am taking care not to get hooked.'

'I could hook you if I wanted.' She was almost angry, stood up and walked across the room, stopped in the middle of the floor, turned, 'I could make you beg me, make you plead. Do you believe that?'

'Sure I believe it, only . . .'

'Only you are afraid.' Cuffee got up and came up to her.

'Only I'm afraid it might not be worth it.' She was against him and straining the long mould of herself to his body.

'Oh yes, it would be worth it. I am not your little American nymphomaniac, not a pick-up in a café brawl. It would be quite different with me, you would remember that we had been lovers all your life.' Yani came in and said something in German. Uta laughed and kissed Cuffee on the mouth.

'Yani, we are going to Bonn, to visit your father. Peter is coming. It will be a wonderful journey and Peter will meet your father. Aren't you glad Peter?'

Cuffee looked down at the gay, mocking face, seeing the scars running into her eyebrows and the faint line on the bridge of the nose.

'Sure. Sure I am. Who wouldn't be?'

Cuffee took him to the café where the girl had found him. The same woman was there, reading a paper this time. They had two beers. Gibbon drank his in one gulp almost. 'I was ready for that. So how long will you be gone?'

'About a week.'

'It's just we don't have an awful lot of money left.'

'I told her that. She says I don't need any money. Yani has a car and money. So it won't cost.'

'What's the purpose of this then? Not to see this Zimmermann is it?'

'That's part of it, only I think she's trying to take me where I'm completely on my own. I'll be dependent on her, in her country and I should be boiling with lust by this time. So she'll make me dance.'

'And what do you think?'

'I can accept or I can back down. If I back down she'll drop me. I've got a simple pick. Left hand, right hand. If I want her I have to go.' Gibbon frowned and shook his head.

'Seems a bit nutty to me.'

'No Harry, this is it. This is the thing you can feel with them all, this is it naked, with no appearance. All the women who are choking all the men to death in all the suburban houses in the world, all the silent struggles that go on in all the bedrooms for supremacy. This is it. Reduced to its very essence. And it's exciting. And I want her, Harry. That body she flaunts, I want to hear her begging me not to stop. No, Harry boy, this is it.'

'Well just look out for yourself.'

'What about you?'

'Oh I'll be okay with Kimber. Maybe move over there and save the rent.'

'Yeah, well you watch your brownie, boy. I don't want your aunt blaming me if you come home poofed.'

'What are you going to do this evening?'

'I thought we might have some scoff and then a drink and then before the fray I'd get me a nice bit of commercial, honest to goodness paid-for pussy. Keeps your values straight, going to the lodestone now and again. Let me know how much advertising this fraulein's doing.'

'Peter, you're a long way away?' Cuffee looked at Gibbon strangely, fiercely almost, a hawky scrutiny that relaxed slowly until he smiled.

'What was it that relation of yours said, "if you don't go you don't come back"?'

'Something like that,' Gibbon said.

279

Kimber was working at his desk, the adjustable lamp coned down on his hands. He sat up and stretched.

'Am I interrupting?'

'No, I was just finishing. Sit down, I'll put the water on for more coffee.' Gibbon sat in the wicker chair and Kimber put on the green lamp. The room drew closer in the jade light, the guitar torso dark on the wall, the bookshelf inlaid with backs of mocha, orange, purple, and cerise. The windows stained violet from the ebbing light.

'Reminds me of a lamp in Greenock.' Kimber couldn't hear in the kitchen.

'What's that Harry?'

'Your lamp, the green one. Reminds me of Greenock, there's a lamp, up where Moseby stays, in a tree almost, green like that.' Kimber came in.

'Come again, I didn't catch it.'

'Really I was saying I feel far from home. Not lonely, just far. I can feel the farness of it. You never feel that about America?'

'No, not any more. I think after Sam died I stopped wanting to live in America.'

'Why was that, because he killed himself?' Kimber put a cigarette into his mouth and held it there for a moment, then he flicked it out with his finger, knocking it to the floor.

There he let it lay. 'Yes, I suppose that had a lot to do with it. Although he wouldn't have lived another year. It was as if a door was closed, the only door there could have been for me, being homosexual, and a poet.' He picked up his cigarette and tapped it on his thumbnail. 'The thing about the American dream is that it resurrects itself over and over again in different forms. The country has a national myth and its people embrace it. Usually it's the country itself, the size of it, the great prone mass of it. Our literature is full of odysseys, *Moby Dick, Huck Finn, Catcher in the Rye, On the Road*, from masterpieces to mediocrities it's the same. The same theme, the journey, the search. You can't do it in Britain, drive for twenty-four hours and you're in the sea. In America the country awaits its travellers and those travellers set out with a naïveté which is almost incandescent, a true bravura of innocence. And somewhere between Morgansfield and Butcher's Ferry, between Green-castle and Taos, it tarnishes and the life models for the American hero emerge, the chain-smoking young man with the hurt eyes, the tawdry ex-blonde who knows a line from Emily Dickinson, which usually serves for the title of a play in which she meets the chain-smoking young man and gets taken, *en passant*, to their mutual disadvantage. And she goes to San Francisco and he to Chicago and never meet again. That's the way I saw it, that's the way I was going to go, one morning in the early summer I'd come down and cut some rye bread sandwiches and leave a note and pack a bag and turn the car towards the West and off I'd go. If I'd known what I was about I'd have just driven Polly right out of that left-wing vaudeville act and raped her all the way to the coast. But I didn't, I did what I did and by the time I got to New York I couldn't do that any more, the trans-continental dream is heterosexual by definition. That's where Sam came in. He made it possible to think of poetry and poetry-writing as an essential activity, not just the activity of a resident professor or an act of social protest, but the manufacture of new objects, new experiences. But as well he showed me how it was possible to live as a homosexual, not happily mind you, but with some dignity. Then he died and I waited until he was buried and then I cleared out. That was four years ago and I haven't been back since.'

'And will you go back?'

'Oh sure, I'll go back, when I'm ready for it again.' He got up and went out to the kitchen. Gibbon sat on, brooding in a green light.

At the end table in front of the café there was a woman in a grey sweater with a sling bag. With her sat a man in a raffia hat, wearing dark glasses. Cuffee caught her eye and went on past. When he looked back the man was leaving the table. He went to the corner and stood for a moment, then he went back. The woman smiled and he sat down.

Between his atrocious French and her American slang they came to terms. She was a biggish woman with broad rather coarse hands and a wide, badly finished mouth, the upper lip of which curled markedly when she smiled. She said it was too early for an all night, except at special rates. Her 'maquereau' would not allow it. Cuffee said he would come back at midnight. She said she would speak to her 'maquereau'. She had a sauntering stroll down to the other end of the café and then she came back after a moment or two and gave him a new modified price, which Cuffee, smiling, accepted.

The room seemed clean and smelled of furniture polish. There was a light over the bed which she switched on. Then she turned and put her arms round Cuffee's neck. They stood a moment and kissed. Then she stood back and started to undress. Cuffee stood at the window and looked out as he stripped. It was dark and the street lights were on. Someone laughed down below the window, a man and then a woman. The sound drifted into the room and dispelled. She touched his shoulder and motioned him to the bidet. Her washing with the big capable hands was brisk and almost devoid of sensation. Only at the end when she dried him did she allow herself a squeeze and a comment of what presumably was appreciation. She took off her shift and lay down on the bed making a sound of comfort. Cuffee stood by the window and watched the people in the street. The light above lit her like an abstraction, bright on the knee-caps and on the tops of the thighs but between shadow thick to her crutch, then the white bar of her body, her breasts almost under her armpits. The lampshade cut off her face at the mouth. The tops of her feet caught the light, the mark of shoes across the instep. He came down and sat on the bed. She turned, a swift reassemble of shadows and her breasts together like a great toothless shark. From her shoulder to her hip was a sea shape. As he turned to her, he noticed she had a varicose vein behind the right knee, a blue knotted lump under the skin. He touched it gently, and she smiled, saying something in French which he understood to mean 'a hazard of the profession'.

The third movement of the Beethoven trio unfolded itself, a slow ponder of protestant thought, reaching in layered reachings towards a final, finite moment of emotional surety and conveying in the process the splendour of evanescence, shaped so that the end is implicit in the beginning, the sweet brave counter melody of the strings a last poignancy on the downward iteration of the great hymn.

'Have you ever noticed,' Gibbon said after it had closed, 'how all your thoughts come from your, well your background. When I was listening to that, well all I could see was Union Street in Greenock, that's one of the West End streets, it goes out, slopes up a bit, and I could see me walking along it and then that quicker bit was the river and then at the end was just me on a boat telling myself it would be all right.'

'Emotions can't live by themselves, they need images to hold them. "An image clothed with emotion is a poem." One of Cleeve's aphorisms. He was interested in "haika" for that reason' – Gibbon's vagueness showed. 'It's a very rigid form of Japanese poem, short, with a set length for each line and really as he said, an attempt to create a verbal object, not so much descriptive as evocative. Blue room, green fire, gold eyes. He wrote an essay on them comparing them with Rorshach tests, no, you don't know what Rorshach tests are.'

'No, I'm afraid not.'

'Ink blot tests, used in psychiatry. Anyway it doesn't matter about that, in his last few years he was writing poems more and more to that definition, trying to make a new set of objects, yet objects that would serve complex emotional needs. Would you like to hear one of his poems?'

'I would. Only I'm not very good about poetry, I mean I don't know anything about it.'

'That's as it should be. Here's a nice short one, called "unnecessary words at the right time".' Kimber laughed at Gibbon's slight flinch to the title. 'Yeah, the titles tend to put you off, but Sam had a theory about titles too. Anyhow, listen.

> "As hawks in their cages
> dream of hills in the morning
> so the mind yearns for freedom.
> Implacable imaginer, yearning.

283

The rarest imaginings are poems,
poems of the captive mind.
Hold them to the light, crystallines,
their transparences reveal the world."

That's a classic example of his later poems, evocation changing to metaphor, metaphor concentrated into a definition, then argument and ending with exhortation. His last book consisted of fifty of these, they have a tremendous cumulative power, it takes a couple to get you into the way of it and then they have you and you can go on into the book becoming more and more responsive to them. And they were planned as a comprehensive experience, not simply a collection of poems. I'm sorry, I tend to get carried away when I start on about Cleeves.'

'No, I like to hear you talk, honestly . . . Only as I said I'm not much good about poetry. Actually when I come to think about it I don't see quite what I am much good about. I feel everything is inside me and I don't know what everything is exactly, things, moods, feelings, well for instance I feel I have a great capacity for love, since I met you and really could focus on being homosexual and all that, I feel it even more strongly.'

'I don't understand, about focussing on homosexuality.'

'Well being able to meet you and talk with you, tell you about Moseby and what I felt, I mean that time in the hills, yet not have to think I'm queer, before anything that wasn't man and woman was queer, now I know it's not so straightforward as that, that a lot of my feelings, like for Moseby and to some extent for Peter, they don't commit me, I'm still floating. Well, I mean everything is all in here and it's looking, I suppose it's looking anyway, for a way out, out into where all the people are. Only I'm no hawk, that's Peter, I don't know what I am.'

Kimber had watched him as he spoke, the thick shoulders urging his thoughts out, the blockages when the words jammed and the sudden surge when they cleared.

'Oh Harry,' he said, 'dear Harry, no you're no hawk. "Out where all the people are." That's when the trouble starts. Have you ever been in love Harry?'

'No, with my folks, my mother, I loved her, and my father. But I don't think I've been in love, not the way you mean.'

'But you believe in it, that it exists, love?'

'Yes. I could love somebody. I know I could.'

'And someone could love you, but love is more than just two people who can love, it's the effect of those two people one upon the other.'

'I know it's not easy . . .'

'I don't think you do, Harry. Because I don't think you know the loneliness from which one tries to escape through love.'

'I've been lonely. I was lonely when my father died.'

'Being lonely is not the same thing as knowing you are alone. When you know that it doesn't matter whether your parents are dead or alive, whether you're married or a hermit, then you need love like an addict needs his drug. Because love offers the only form of annexation, of incorporation in yourself of another person that will suffice, and once that starts then you begin to know about love and how hard it is. For soon you realise, unless solipsism has you completely, that the "other" you are pursuing, is pursuing you, you are "other". From your commingling should come "that abler soul" which "defects of loneliness controls", but for some the metaphysics of this prove too unsubstantial and you are faced with Buber's conclusion, "it is the exalted melancholy of our fate that every Thou shall become an it", and if you accept this all that is left is the way Peter appears to behave, treating the whole world of relations as a competitive sport in which the aim is to come out unscathed having satisfied your sense quotient and your ego in the process. Isolation leading to insulation. Or else you go in for a kind of crypto Christianity that extends to the "others" the recognition of their reality, "love thy neighbour as thyself", in the hope that they in turn will recognise you, a sort of mutual admiration society of the soul.'

'What if there is a God, doesn't that change things?'

'Oh, indeedy, yes,' Kimber said. 'Oh it certainly does.'

In the daylight the room looked smaller. The wallpaper

had flowers, pale blue small flowers, repeated endlessly. There was a tall dark wardrobe with a long mirror in its door. The table was bamboo and wicker. The sun lay in a deep solid bar through the window to stencil the flex and shade on the far wall. In the sunlight there constantly moved minutiae of dust and the occasional doodling of a fly. Above the bed there was a picture of the Sacred Heart of Jesus. The street noises were distinct. A clock, unseen, was ticking. In the middle of the floor a small spar-backed chair held on the seat a woman's clothes, folded, and under it a pair of shoes, one of them lying on its side. Over the back two stockings wet with sunlight. The bottom of the bed was cast-iron with four spars vertical to a horizontal and above that a cupid's bow shape. The prostitute was still asleep turned to the wall and almost but not quite snoring. Cuffee lay smoking, looking at the ceiling, waiting for her to waken.

The sun gathered green from the trees and hued the roof most delicate lime. Gibbon woke and went to see the weather. It quivered. The river glinted gay little gaws all over.

'He's got a good day for it,' Kimber said from the door.

'He has, hasn't he' – turning.

'Coffee.'

'Great.' A scrinch of grinding augured the reek of fresh crushed beans. Gibbon remained by the window, his face and hair pallored from the light, looking down on the trees.

'Greenock's not called after a green oak you know.'

'What?'

'No, Gaelic for sunny bay or something it is.'

'Sorry I couldn't hear you Harry. What'd you say?'

'Oh just that there isn't a real green oak, it's just in a song.'

'Most of the best things are. Coffee's ready.'

'Fine.' Gibbon came through looking thoughtful. Kimber poured him his coffee.

'Something wrong Harry?'

'What. No, not wrong. I was just thinking about Cuffee. About where he's going.'

'You mean Bonn.' Gibbon frowned and shook his head.

'No, I mean, where's he really going.'

'Ah well now—' and Kimber sat himself in '—"You will not find it down in any map, true places never are".'

'Oh I see. Big kinda symbolic guy' – making Kimber smile.

The roads went long and straight, marked off by trees. The fields were flat and men stooped in them. The villages had a casual squalor and few people were to be seen but dogs barked at the Fiat as it puttered along, Yani driving, Uta beside her and Cuffee in the back with the luggage. Uta was in a gay mood and had been from the start, talking German and English alternately, saying Yani didn't have to concentrate if she spoke German and could give all her attention to the road. She had her hair up and a few delicate tendrils had escaped which Cuffee, wetting his finger, pasted down to the back of her neck. In the breeze from the open window they dried and came free again. Uta talked of the Black Forest where she had lived when the war was over.

'Have you ever been in a pure forest, where all the trees are of the same species? It is very awesome, very beautiful and solemn, it is like a cathedral, all the columns standing straight and still and the sun coming down at a certain angle and so quiet to walk there, no sound anywhere. Trees must fall in such forests and no one to hear or see them. I used to walk in these forests and listen in case a tree were falling and I would hear it. For a tree to fall and not be heard, that is very sad. But, I had a pony and I used to ride and my hair was long, much longer than it is now, all the time I was in hospital they did not cut it because it was the most beautiful thing I had for my face was ruined and after when I was in the forest and the scars were going away very slowly I used to ride on my pony with my hair loose to my pony's back and think I was Brünnhilde waiting for Siegfried to return and race my pony through the trees in and out of the sunlight calling out . . .'

There was a small, dull thud against the car on the near side.

'What was that?' Uta said. Yani braked and looking back through the rear window they could see the cat, black and white, lying at the side of the road and as they looked it jumped up into the air and fell down again. Cuffee got out and went back. The animal was unmarked but seemed hurt in the back legs. It tried to stand up and couldn't and it pulled itself along a short way on its fore-paws. Then it flopped forward and blood came from its nose in a little rush, out on to the gravel. It made a sound, a moan with a deep harsh purring in it. Uta came down and stopped about five feet away from the animal. Just then it squalled and jumped again and fell on its side, blood coming out of its mouth and the noise rising until it gurgled and choked off. 'Kill it, kill it, oh kill it kill it,' and she turned and ran back to the car. Cuffee caught it behind the head and bit his fingers in feeling for the cortex then lifting it, threw his wrist over so that the cat's body flipped up as far as it could before the neck broke. It hung, dead and slack and hanging so the bowels voided in swift bloodied purge, a violent stench rising from it. He threw the body into the ditch with a shudder of nausea and went back to the car.

'Is it dead?' Uta asked, in a small, pale voice.

'Yes, it's dead.' They got in and Yani, who appeared not to have taken her eyes off the road ahead, started up the car and they drove on.

They stopped early as Uta had a headache and wanted to bathe and get some air before retiring. Cuffee sat in his room and noticed blood on the cuff of his shirt. He changed it for a clean one and went downstairs. After their meal Uta said she would like a walk in the garden behind the hotel. Yani said she would run a bath. They went out.

The garden was L-shaped and at the bottom had some twenty pear trees. They walked down and through them. There was an iron garden seat beyond them against the wall. They sat down. He put his arm around her and she came in to him slackly. Her mouth was sour and she withdrew it in distaste. A bat was hunting in the still evening air, zigging ceaselessly through the trunks.

'I am frightened,' she said.

'Why?'

'Do you never become frightened?'

'What of?'

'This,' and she gestured to the grove of small trees and the swift dark plot of the bat.

'Was it the cat, did it upset you?' She shivered and drew into him.

'Do you never become frightened?'

'Sometimes.'

'What makes you frightened?' and she was watching up from the crook of his arm.

'When there is nothing to be done, when you are impotent . . .'

'Well we are. No it was not the cat. I have seen many animals die. I go hunting with Herr Zimmermann, it is not death or the blood.'

'What is it then?'

'It is when it happens without reason. But no reason, I hate for there to be no reason.'

'Why do you want me to meet Herr Zimmermann?' She did not answer.

'Uta, answer me, why do you want me to meet him?'

'He lives in a castle. Not a very big one but with a moat around it and a drawbridge. Have you ever lived in a castle?'

'That doesn't tell me why you want me to meet him.' She stood up and stepped away, turned and held out her hand.

'Come. I have no reason, except you will like him. I am sure you will.' He got up and pulled her to him. She came but would not lift her head. Close to her ear he whispered, 'Uta, what is it, Uta? Uta, tell me.' And then he saw Yani, standing silent among the trees and around her, darting skein, the bat. She spoke in German.

'The bath is ready,' Uta said, her voice relieved and recitative. Cuffee let her go and she followed Yani back, Cuffee bringing up in the rear.

'I've always been kinda precocious,' Annie said, 'in that particular way. Even when I was little. I used to come in and say to my mother "momma, I'm ravished", meaning I'm ravenous, and my mother would say "don't cry wolf dear" and laugh and the thing was I knew what she meant after a while and I used to say it just to make her laugh. Then there was the music teacher, he was a kinda old guy, well when you're a kid everybody was pretty old if they were adult but he was about forty and all the kids from my neighbourhood used to go to him for piano lessons, Mr Tolamer his name was and he used to stand behind me and stroke my hair and once when I didn't know some piece he said he'd spank me and I said you're a dirty old pervert and ran out. He was too. I never went back there and he got had up for interfering with a little girl, not in his music lessons though. Then in high school, is this boring you, all this stuff?'

Gibbon said no, not at all.

'Well at high school they all did this heavy petting, you let a guy go almost all the way, and some girls did only the boys usually spread it around. So you stopped just before and that meant you were still a virgin or something, well I didn't go for that, I used to write poems about love and how love was this and love was that and I wanted some guy to come along and take me away to the coast, I didn't care much which coast, I'm from Minnesota and the coast's the coast. There was this girl, Jewish she was and I hated her, she was a real big deal she thought and at our college there was this thing "Miss Five Occasions", it was sort of the best all-round girl each year, social, cultural, athletic, domestic, academic. Pretty corny but it was big stuff then. Well this girl she just knew she was going to win it and she had this boy, Lawrence Sturges and he was really cream, he went to Minnesota University and she made this big thing about free love and they loved each other and I hated her, I don't know why, because she was a phoney, I didn't believe Lawrence Sturges was giving her a lay and I met him, kinda by accident when he was home and I made him notice me, I was like that, I could do that and he took me out for a malt and he asked me all about myself and I knew he was giving me the eye so right in the middle of all this casual kind of line he had going I said, just like so, I said, "you're giving Becky Myers a lay aren't you?" Boy you should have seen his face when I said that. Well what happened was that he got stuck on me, you won't believe me but he didn't get any encouragement from me, not at first, but then I saw he was really stuck so I began to think I was too. And then Becky Myers won this "Miss Five Occasions" and at the dance she was giving out about how Lawrence hadn't been able to make it. So next day I spoke to him on the phone and told him I wanted to go away with him and he came over for me in his car and we got in and this friend of his at University his father had a beach house on the Monterey coast at a place called Moss Landings and he gave Lawrence the key and it was, holy God it was fifteen hundred miles away and we just drove straight out of the town and headed for it.' She looked at Gibbon and around at the busy evening street. Shook her head, puzzled almost, smiled and put her hands over her ears.

'What happened?'

'Never got there. Got stopped on the state line. Minors, see. They had news out about us too. And I kept making him stop every twenty miles so he would lay me. I was pretty sexy all right. Anyway they took us back home and my folks they wanted to press charges only I said I loved him and he sort of said he loved me so we got married. And we didn't go to Moss Landings for our honeymoon, we went up to his aunt in St Paul and she used to listen outside our door and when we were right in the middle of doing it she'd sing out "good night Mr and Mrs Sturges". He was studying a lot and I didn't love him any more so I asked my mother what I should do and she was pretty easy about a lot of things my mother so she said leave him, come home and live with us again. So I left him, only I didn't go home, I sold everything I could and drew out the money we'd got at the wedding and I got on a bus and went to San Francisco. Two hours after I got there I had a job as a cashier in a self-service and inside a week I was living with a drummer out of a little combo that played the beat places. Harry his name was, same as yours.'

'And did you ever get to Moss Landings?'

'Moss Landings? Never. Looked it up once when I was in New York, waiting for my sailing to Europe. Looked it up in the reference room. Population two hundred and seventy-one. I remember that. Why?'

'Sounded nice.'

'Moss Landings, yeah, it's a nice name.'

From below came the sounds of an accordion and people dancing. The accordion made soft blarings, yellowy swung lanterns in the dark room where Cuffee lay, half drunk on brandy. Behind the inn there was a large wooded hill, he could see it upside down out of the open window. Uta had been in a commanding mood right from morning and had driven the Fiat herself, saying they would drive straight through to Bonn but just before the border at Aachen she stopped and said they would spend another night in France. After dinner an accordionist had started to play and Uta tried to make Cuffee dance but he wouldn't and bought a half bottle of brandy and came upstairs to his room. Outside an owl had been sounding his soft, concentric hoots, sometimes nearer, sometimes further away. Cuffee had tried to see him and once the blurry grey float had passed down behind a copse on the edge of a field and a small death occurred, the outcry brief and needling.

The accordion ended with a little flambeau and there was a rattle of clapping. Cuffee balanced the brandy on his chest and tried to see how much there was left. The owl hushed the night with his furry hoos. Cuffee got off the bed and went to the window. The accordion commenced, squeezing and pleating the air into sound. Outside it was almost dark. There was a knocking at the door.

'Come in.' It was Yani.

'Uta wishes for you to come down.'

'Does she?' Yani stood just inside the door, holding it open. The sound of the accordion and the dancing was louder. 'Shut the door.' Yani waited a moment then did. The music dimmed and the owl trebled. Yani started and came several paces into the room. Cuffee looked out but there was nothing to be seen. 'Out there all the little mice are crouching in the grasses, their bright eyes shining with terror.' He looked back at Yani and beckoned her close. She came, slowly, round the end of the bed up to the window.

'Uta says . . .'

'What is your father like?' Yani shook her head.

'I do not know.'

'Uta says I will like him. Will I?' She looked out of the window, her face glowing pale in the last light, her eyes dark and hidden in their darkness, she looked out and the owl sounded again, Yani clasped the sill so that her knuckles glinted like little teeth.

'My father, he hunts.'

'I know, Uta told me.'

'With a falcon.'

'With a falcon.' She turned to him.

'Do you love her?'

'Uta? I don't know. Why?'

'Because I love her. Why do you not leave her to me?'

'If it isn't me it will be someone else.'

'I know.' Cuffee offered her the bottle. She shook her head. 'There will always be someone, but I know.' She was trembling slightly and he could hear her teeth chitter softly. When he put his hand on her she stiffened and then slowly relaxed.

'What is it between you and Uta, how did you meet her?'

'She will destroy you.'

'Tell me about it Yani.'

'She wants you to come down.' He put the bottle down and pulled her close. She came in, very small and unresisting. Her face looked into his chest.

'Tell me about it.' Uta came in and walked to the window. Yani slipped out of Cuffee's hold. Uta looked at her then spoke in German, in a quiet conversational tone. Yani replied and then left them, closing the door.

'Now,' Uta said, 'what were you asking Yani about?'

'You two. How it came about.'

'How what came about?'

'Your friendship.'

'Yani and I are old friends.'

'From before your accident?'

'No, after.'

'How did you meet?'

'Why do you want to know?'

'I just want to know about you. Yani said you would destroy me. What does that mean?' Uta laughed and seeing the bottle took it and drank from the neck.

'Yani has seen too much killing. She thinks only in the terms of hunting.'

'What did she mean, you would destroy me—' Her hand came out quickly, flicking at the wrist, slap against his face, and she danced back smiling.

'You try, slap me, come on,' and as he stretched with his left she swayed away then coming in caught him across the mouth so hard that tears came to his eyes. There was blood in his mouth and he stepped back, touching at his lip.

'That is what she meant. I am very quick you see.' Cuffee took a drink to find the cut. It rawed in the spirit.

'You think you can beat everybody, is that it?'

'No. Only the people I am interested in.' Cuffee had her by the throat, one handed, throttling her back till she met the bed with the back of her knees and fell, still held and trying to pull his hand away, he on top of her. Her eyes stared and she made torn sounds in her throat. He held her for a moment and then let her go, pushing up and standing away. Uta lay there, her hands going up to touch her neck and moaning.

He looked out into the night where the owl was making its slow plundering flight over the rustling earth. He looked for it, listened but only the faintest strains of the accordion. She was still lying on the bed when he came in and didn't move when he sat down and turning, leant over her.

'Uta. Why? Why is it like this? You are very beautiful, we could be happy, you and me. What is this thing you must do, this conflict you have to make—' She turned to look at him and she had been crying. He kissed her and she let herself be kissed, then as his hand went under her dress and found the vivid warm turn of her thigh she kissed back and put an arm round his neck. The owl hooted and he was touching her gently, wetly, warmly when the door opened. He turned to see but Uta had him round the neck. Yani lifted her arm and Cuffee tore himself up in time to see he was being hit with a poker. The arm he tried to raise was held back by Uta. The blow caught him above the right eyebrow and the second on the left temple.

*   *   *

The weather was cloudy and bright and it had been raining. Gibbon walked, without intent, letting the streets choose him, threading through the back ways. The sun came and went, a raw strong yellow, fraying the edges of buildings and drying the streets for a moment. He walked and looked at things, into courtyards and alongside streets, at people and potted plants and the interiors of houses. It began to rain and became heavy. He stood in a metro entrance and when it showed no sign of slackening he went down and got a train, taking the first one in. He rode three stations and got off. In the street the rain had slackened but had not passed. In a café he had a glass of beer and a truncheon of bread and cheese. At another table a man read a newspaper and held a girl round the waist, occasionally turning to kiss her. He had a large ring on his pinkie. Gibbon left his tip and went on and came down to the river. It was a quiet stretch and he went down the steps and slowly along the quay. Trees on the street above overhung, dripping now and making a high-up sound of rustling. There was a smell in the air, of rain and trees and the sun and a smell of wet distant earth coming in across Paris on a small wind, a damp, drying smell, of the river and the buildings and the steaming pavements. He spat a fat spittle into the pinquid flow and watched it carry. On the street the black trunks of the trees were wreathed in vapours and the stones dried first in the centre and then round the edges so that the street was scattered with dwindling rings of wet. Passing a girl, sitting outside a café reading a book, she uncrossed and crossed her legs, a smooth at once over shuffling, showing silkings and above paleness and then crossed abstractions of curvace and surface, limbs. It was darkening over and this time the darkness grew lurid, a purply dull. He stood inside the awning to see how it would go. A few large spots fell and the girl closed her book and stepped inside. A wind gust drove a newspaper skidding and flapping across the street, then in over the roofs it came and the air was suddenly opaque as the street danced under the lumming shuttles. The girl crowded back close to Gibbon, turning to smile and apologize. Gibbon smiled back. Her coffee cup, left out, began to fill up, the water at first discoloured but soon clearing and running over into the saucer, the rain pistil spatting in the calyx of the cup. Her hair smelled cool and dry and faintly dusty. She turned to smile at Gibbon and at the rain's assault, raining now a full limpid abandon, falling swift simple fall, teemings of wet, germinant in briefest upblossomings, petallations that flowered and faded as the eye tasted them in the mercurial light, a mood of release, an exhilaration of jettison. The girl said something in French and gazed back out at the street.

'I love Ruth Cuffee,' Gibbon said, making her turn and shake her head in non-understanding.

'Yes, yes I do, here, now, in the rain, in Paris. Yes;' and the girl smiled, puzzled, and looked at the rain.

When he woke there was far behind his sight a blurry throb, pain that made him feel sick when he tried to sit up. The right side of his face was stiff and cold, touched, it had a rough grainy feel and was his blood dried and shelled. One eye did not see very well. He got slowly off the bed and heard himself moan and told himself to get a grip. In the mirror was the carnival of his face, painted black on the right side, the nose swollen and on the side of the forehead a large long lump. There were threads of congealed blood from his right eyebrow to his cheek. He brushed them away and they yielded then broke. He felt cold and sick and sat down. On the table in the room there was an envelope with his name on it.

My very dearest Peter,

I may not ever meet you again and will never know what you mean and what you wanted from me. But I will watch from the battlements of my castle for the glimpse of your armour coming through the forest. I do not want to leave you here, bloody and pale, I should stay here by your side until you wake and then bathe your hurts, I should tell you that I love you only I am not sure that I do, and worse I am

not sure that if I did it would matter. Love is a sweet singing bird and life is a hawk. Now I am becoming sentimen-
tal. I hope you will forgive or try to understand. I know you
won't be able to but I hope you will want to try. Good-bye
perhaps my dearest Peter, Uta.

When he washed his face he could see the cut, short and
wide and in the eyebrow itself, dark and splayed at the
edges. The eye was totally bloodshot, an awful maroon
goggle and when he closed the left eye everything lurched
and darkened. The lump was long and shiny and going
blue. He pressed around it gently, curiously soft it was and
not painful to touch. The pain came from bone above his
eye, a steady ache that winced occasionally at the turn of
his head.

There was blood on the bedclothes and on his shirt. He
changed into a clean one and packed his things, slowly,
holding a wet handkerchief to his eye. Then he read the
letter again and tore it up, putting the pieces in an ash tray.
He went downstairs. The proprietor looked up from the
desk and nodded. Cuffee nodded back.

'They have gone?'

'Very early this morning Monsieur. I am so sorry about
the injury, I only hope it will not ruin your holiday.'

'No, I shouldn't think so.'

'Your account has been settled of course. If you should
wish to see a doctor there is one in the village, two kilometres on the road.'

'In the direction of Paris?'

'Paris, not so, Paris lies the other way.'

Cuffee nodded and went out. It was still early and there
had been rain and now the sun was shining and the landscape looked newly painted, the pigment still wet and
gleaming. Away up the road heat waves made the surface
tremble and waver. Towards this mirage Cuffee set off.

They had a meal and then sat outside. The evening was
yielding graciously to night and in the street nobody
hurried. Kimber ordered lagers and lit a cigarette. Gibbon
hummed the opening theme of the Beethoven Trio.

'Music attaches itself to places,' Kimber said.

'Yes. I always remember the Army through "the Blue Tango", that was all the rage. I just have to hear that and I'm at the Saturday dance in the Drill Hall.'

' "We perish by imperceptible degrees, knowing no demarcation of decease".' Gibbon looked askance.

'Cleeve?'

'Yes.'

'Why now, I mean why perish?'

'Hearing you saying about the Army, the Blue Tango, just made me think on all the trivial things that come to signify epochs, whole eras in our lives.'

'Does he really mean what I think he means, that we never know what is happening to us, because' – and uncharacteristically he went on over Kimber's proffered explanation – 'I feel, for the first time in my life I think, I feel I know what's happening to me, and why.' Kimber watched him with an interest that bordered on apprehension. 'In a way it's been you, Norman, that's made me realise it. I mean about, about homosexuality. Before I got to Paris I was starting to worry about it, about how I didn't really bother about women, whether I had them or not, and how I was attracted to Cuffee and about Moseby, and I was just sort of open to any sort of suggestion. And when I met you then I realised that for some people there is a choice, a genuine choice, I mean Peter has no choice, he's male and even if he had it away with men, well he'd still be normal and heterosexual, and those boys you see with no hips and mascara, they've got no choice, there's nothing they can do. But you had a choice and you chose, I don't think you are very happy about it but you chose. I'm one like that. I can choose, and that is something I never really had clear before. I want to go back to Manchester and see this sister of Peter's, see if I can make it work with her.'

'When are you going?' and Kimber's voice wobbled between casual enquiry and panic.

'When Cuffee decides to quit tailing about.'

'This is the sister with whom he had the affair.'

'He's only got the one sister.' Kimber sat up and stubbed

out his cigarette and took another from the pack, offering Gibbon one then remembering he didn't smoke.

'Aren't you a bit worried about your motives in pursuing Peter's sister, considering their relationship and your feeling for Peter?' – lighting up as he spoke then looking at Gibbon through the smoke.

'How do you mean, my motives?'

'Well, I mean doesn't it strike you that this may be just a way of getting closer to Peter?' Gibbon looked troubled and shook his head.

'I think I love her, I don't know her or anything so I suppose I must be in love with an idea but I think I know what idea it is, and it's not Peter.' Kimber agreed and drank his lager.

'It was just a thought,' he said.

They sat on for another twenty minutes watching the passers-by then Kimber called a taxi and they took a drive. 'Parisian taxis, they've seen it all,' Kimber said. Later he gave the driver an address and they went to a house behind the Notre Dame.

'He's my literary agent,' Kimber explained. 'Knows everybody in Paris who's worth the knowing, his is the kind of place where you drop in one evening in mid-week and you find Orson Welles, an ex-middleweight champion of the world and Lord Something-or-other arguing about the weight of a gorilla.'

They were greeted by a small darting man with a subtly disproportionate head, just sufficiently over-large to excite a vague uneasiness and not enough to make specific the cause. He shook hands with them both swiftly, putting his hand out straight from the hip and notching into the guest's grip. He led them through into a large, severally lamped room to a group of people, all of whom, with the exception of a tall languid woman whose left eyelid drooped half closed, were men. The host, whose name was Vaubon, introduced them without formality and left to get drinks. Of the four men three were middle-aged and conventionally attired in lounge suits and stood one by the mantelpiece the other by the bookshelves and the third by the chair of the woman. The other man was young and seated. He wore pale blue slacks and a dark blue wool shirt. He had dark smooth hair and an effortless tan. He knew Kimber and seemed to be called Lotte.

Gibbon sat himself in a deep chair and replied to the woman's question that he did not know French. Despite her disapproval she went on in English to ask Gibbon what he was.

'A carpenter.'

'I beg your pardon.'

'A carpenter.' Gibbon began the motions of sawing a piece of wood then stopped.

'Carpenter,' the woman said. 'You are not a painter or a sculptor—'

'No. I'm a time-served carpenter.' She conceded this and turned to talk to the man beside her. Lotte watched Gibbon with an open appraisal, head turned in three-quarter profile, one knee drawn up and a wrist crooked over it, the long slender hand limp and palm down. The conversation in the room was going on again, in French. Vaubon came back with drinks for Gibbon and Kimber and enquired tenderly of Lotte if there were anything he would like. For a moment he went on looking at Gibbon, then looked up.

'A party. Let us all go to a party. Yes, Maurice, a party.' There was a muted mutter of disapproval from the three men and the lady. Lotte looked round at them and said something that amused Kimber and outraged everyone else. Vaubon, with the air of a tired and tried public relations man, shot a look at Lotte of weary annoyance and turned to placate his guests.

'A party. Where is there a party, Norman?'

'I don't know, not offhand.'

'Don't be offhand then. Find me a party.'

'Do you mind if I use the phone Maurice?'

'Of course he doesn't, he's too busy apologising for me.' Kimber went to phone and Lotte got up and stretched, hands above his head and fingers laced together, showing his slender long body and at the extent of his stretch looking at Gibbon and smiling, a girl's smile, coquettish but genuine, almost shy, the lashes folding down on the cheek and his body turning away from Gibbon. Vaubon had come between them and said something in a low voice. The others in the room were watching the scene with unconcealed relish. Lotte turned from Vaubon and went out to Kimber. Gibbon sat looking into his drink which he had not tasted. Vaubon stood a moment, his shoulders slumped and in that moment looking deformed, his head suddenly seemed enormous and the rest of him tiny. He sat down as though exhausted at the pretence of appearing ordinary and he was still sitting, his hands hanging between his knees when Lotte came back with Kimber and said something in French. Vaubon stood up and reassumed his disguise. He took Lotte by the arm and walked him to the door, talking to him earnestly in an undertone. Gibbon got up, drank his drink, which was brandy and which stunned him, bowed to the others and said good night.

The three of them, Vaubon, Kimber and Gibbon stood outside whilst Lotte got the car out of the garage. Vaubon said something intense to Kimber, his large pale face glistening in the lamplight and Kimber squeezed his shoulder and sounded reassuring. Lotte came round in a new-looking Renault. Kimber and Gibbon got in and Vaubon waved. Looking back Gibbon could see him waving after the car, a little big-headed man. Lotte was saying something to Kimber who was beside him in the front.

'Maurice is a good man, you want to be careful Lotte, you'll lose him.'

He laughed, midway between a shriek and a giggle. 'My dear Norman, you underestimate me, I know just how much that little freak will stand. But of course you are right, he is a good man and I treat him abominably. It's the only way he can be made happy,' and Gibbon found the long-lashed eyes caressing him in the driving mirror. He looked back but Vaubon was long since lost to view.

He walked the last five kilometres into Nancy in a steady straight rain. His head was very painful from the jolting on a lorry and as he held his face up into the cool rain he swooned and staggered, going down on one knee by the side of the road. By the time he came into the town it was nearing midnight and he was wet through. The grey cubes of French provincial buildings, battened in upon themselves, the walls showing the wet and the trees dripping sadly. A large empty square guarded at each corner by a general on horse-back. A dog ran across it as Cuffee passed, barking sharply. Down by the station there was a café, the windows steamy and the menu written on them in chalk wash. He had soup and a cognac and five Gauloises, leaving himself seventy old francs, and he got himself over against the radiator and changed his socks. Outside the cobbles shone and the gendarmes passed in bands. There were a great number of Algerians on the streets and here and there American servicemen. Cuffee sat on for almost an hour and slowly the café began to empty out and the waiters, when a table went vacant, put the chairs up on it. There was an old man in an army greatcoat sitting hunched over a drink. A waiter put the chair up above his head and he sat on unmoving. The waiter said something to the others about 'arc de triomphe' and they all laughed. The old man sat on. Cuffee went out. It was still raining. Standing up made his head ache and for a moment he felt himself about to be sick. It passed and he went across to the station waiting-room.

It was long and brightly lit and with benches round the walls and seats down the centre. There were a great many people and much baggage, most of them slept and a child cried, sitting among some baggage while its parents drowsed against each other. It was hot and fetid and Cuffee's head tightened and throbbed. He found a place between a woman in a fur coat reading a magazine and a small, dark, reeking little man who, just as Cuffee settled himself, farted a garlic fart that brought the woman's head round in a censorious disgust.

'Don't look at me,' Cuffee said, getting his bruised face gently cradled in his hands. The pain had changed since his waking in the morning. Then it had been on the bone, behind the gash. Now the whole right side of his face felt swollen and ached and the swelling on his temple seemed to have stretched the skin of the scalp taut. He held his head and waited for sleep to anaesthetise him.

The ticket inspector wakened him for his ticket. He shook

his head. There were two gendarmes with him. When they found he was not French one of them led him down the waiting-room and handed him over to another at the door. He put him into the police van. There were two men already inside, young, Algerian, who looked at him and talked one to the other without taking their eyes off him. He lit up his second Gauloise. One of the Algerians held out his hand. Cuffee smiled and shrugged.

'Only three. Trois, seulement.' The young man grabbed his collar and pulled him across. He said something into Cuffee's face, keeping his voice low. Cuffee struggled and the other one grabbed him trying to get the cigarettes out of his pocket. For a moment they were all on the floor wrestling around then the doors opened and the gendarme grabbed one of the Algerians and dragged him out. Cuffee looked up in time to see him being batoned. The other Algerian jumped out and ran for it, away across the square. The gendarme looked after him and hit the man on the ground again. When they got him back into the van he was sick with pain and sat holding his neck and breathing in short rasping releases. The gendarme looked at Cuffee and smiled, saying something friendly and closing the door. The Algerian looked at Cuffee as though afraid he might be beaten up. Cuffee found his Gauloise and relit it and on the first draw almost passed out. His head beat wickedly.

In the police station he had to wait until an interpreter was fetched. He was allowed to sit down but not to go to sleep. While he was waiting he began to sneeze and the pain was so severe that he had to clutch his head and brace his elbows on his knees. The interpreter was a bald young man with a tic that worked when he spoke English. Cuffee told him he had been travelling to Germany with friends and they had quarrelled and he was hitch-hiking back to Paris. He had no money. His eye had been cut in a fight with his friends. The fight had been over a girl. His friends would be in Germany by now. Their names were Harold Gibbon and Michael Stolleman. They were English too. He did not know the girl's name. He would hitch-hike to Paris. No, he did not know hitch-hiking was illegal. He would walk then. Yes, he knew it was a long way.

303

They examined his passport and copied down the number and then gave it back. The interpreter advised him to go out on to the Paris road now and hope to get one of the camions going through to the morning market. Cuffee asked if they would not keep him in the cells overnight but the interpreter shook his head and after a violent spasm of twitching said it was impossible as he had not committed any crime.

Outside it had stopped raining and there was a scud of moon. The town lay in its scant gloss, bleak, unlovely, its streets leading into silent little squares, the creak of shutters in the rising wind and flapping posters on the 'rotondes'. A clock struck a single blow. Cuffee was racked by another bout of sneezes that left him leaning against the wall, shivering and weak.

The waiting-room was locked from the outside and the only means of entrance was from the platform. The station hall was large and high. There were no seats and a wind skirled across it, carrying scraps of paper and chilling the legs. Cuffee walked round looking for somewhere to sit out of the draught. The best place was behind the end telephone booth, in the corner and the old man from the café was there, sunk deep in his greatcoat, asleep on his feet. From him came a smell, of feet and sweat and neglect. Cuffee went on round by all the places against the wall seemed equally exposed. He sat on his bag some twenty feet from the old man, just out of range of his fetor. He was very tired and his head ached in time with the rest of him, his back and his thighs and his feet. So far there had been no more sneezes but squatting now with the chill of the circular wind stiffening him he began to have regular, convulsive shivers which threatened each and every one to end in a head-wrenching sneeze and for which he prepared himself by cushioning his elbows in his stomach and his face in his palms. It was almost a relief when they started and the acute discomfort was transcended in the violent, buckling contractions. They seemed to ease when he stood up and started walking so he walked round the hall counting the steps. There were two hundred and ninety-one and he went round five times then sat down to work out how far he had walked. As he was sitting two gendarmes came towards him, stopping at the telephones and moving the old man on. He scarcely straightened up, lurching forward and walking across the hall, a slow stumbly walk. The gendarmes came down towards him but he sat on, looking after the old man. They passed, barely glancing his way. The old man reached the other side, turned and came slowly back, never looking up, settled into his corner and appeared to go immediately to sleep. Cuffee smoked his second last Gauloise and then walked around the hall five more times. When he sat down next time he was very tired and went to sleep. The gendarmes woke him and, looking past them, fuzzy and startled from sleep, he saw the old man making his drugged way to the other side.

Five times between half past two and six o'clock they moved them. Between short cold naps and these interruptions Cuffee walked round the hall another forty-three times and suffered occasional spasms of sneezing. It was as he arose to escape from one of these that he noticed the glass roof of the station was grey. The hall was completely empty save for himself and the old man. He stretched, the chilled limbs threatening cramps, his eyes red and watering. His head was sore now in a muffled hot way and he could feel a weight in his chest that sneezing disturbed. The old man stood as he had all night when he had been in his corner, hunched in his greatcoat in derelict sleep. Cuffee picked up his bag and went down and out through the swing doors. It was barely light and everything was a grey that defied the possibility of colour. Coming across the square towards the station, talking quietly, slow in their pace, the two gendarmes. They came at a casual copper's saunter, the ruthless disinterest of their approach, caped and draped, boots clacking and voices conversational. He watched them a moment and then went back in.

The old man snored a little and under his snoring there was a moan, a whimper of unmade protest and his stance was not as immobile as seen for a distance. He twitched and trembled almost continually and his legs jerked every few seconds threatening to collapse him. And close to he smelled very badly indeed, a smell that went further than

Cuffee's previous analysis, a complex evocative smell of rot and neglect, of empty houses and old newspapers pissed upon by cats, of underground and mould on bread, the gangrenous odour of life becoming unlife, of vegetable reclaim.

'They're coming,' Cuffee said, putting his hand on the shoulder. The old man started off without looking at him, seeming not to hear the words or even feel the touch but simply to be triggered once more into his trek. Cuffee watched him, shuffling away, going in order to come back. 'Poor old bastard,' were the only words he could utter, the trite commiseration coming most easily for his numbed pity.

Gibbon woke with the sun on his face. He still felt drunk and lay for a moment sucking his furry teeth. He was in the big room on a camp bed. He got up for the toilet. Coming back he looked into the bedroom. Lotte and Kimber were still asleep, at opposite sides of the bed, Kimber curled and grabbing the clothes. Lotte on his back, snickering a little in his nose. Gibbon went and put some water on for coffee. He sat on a stool and looked at Kimber's tidy, planned kitchen. The row of spice jars, the place mats, the vitreous-finish casserole dishes. The water began to murmur in the kettle. Someone got up and went into the toilet. The cistern sounded and Kimber came in wearing his white towelling robe, dishevelled from sleep.

'Hi Harry' – yawning, sitting on a stool, rubbing his chin ruefully.

'How are you feeling?'

'Not too bad considering the skinful I had. You?'

'Oh I'm all right. Got a bad taste in my mouth though,' Kimber checked on Gibbon's expression at this.

'Yeah, well get some nice strong coffee brewed, the kind you can trot mice on. That water's nearly ready.' He got the coffee mill down and attached it to the table then filled the cup with beans. Several fell on the scrubbed boards and lay like brown little bugs. Gibbon picked one up. Kimber ground slowly, tamping the beans down with his forefinger. Gibbon, looking at the bean:

'Used to be a kind of biscuit when I was a boy, split biscuits they were called and they looked like this, with a sort of cut on the biscuit and jam in it and it looked like we imagined a woman's thing to be. Split biscuit. Used to go in, about four or five of us and ask for a split biscuit and everybody would snigger. Don't suppose the baker ever knew what it was about.' When the coffee was ground Kimber made the milk hot and poured. They sipped for a time without words, Kimber watching him from time to time but Gibbon deep in his thoughts.

'You mean what you said last night about going back to England?'

'What? Oh, yes. When Cuffee's ready.'

'I suppose you know I'd like you to stay.'

'Wouldn't do, Norman. Really it wouldn't.'

'You angry about Lotte?'

'Don't be daft.'

'You know why we went over to Vaubon's I suppose.'

'I had an idea. But I don't see the point.' Kimber put his coffee cup down with a small uncontrolled clatter.

'The point was we're all the same damn us.'

'Who are?'

'We are, queers. We're all the same when it comes down to it. We can't leave anybody alone. Me giving you all that chat about Cleeve not influencing me, implying I wouldn't influence anybody. Like hell I wouldn't.'

'Did Cleeve influence you, I mean did he try to?'

'Of course he did. He couldn't help it I don't imagine any more than I can.'

'What did you think would happen with Lotte?'

'I thought you might go for him, end up in bed.'

'Proving what?'

'You'd be compromised, partially committed, I know it wouldn't be to me but I would be able to use it, turn it to my advantage, tell you not to worry it was a momentary aberration and at the same time be making you realise that you were, for what one toss in the sheets with a trollop like Lotte is worth, queer, and that I was queer and that we were queer together.' Kimber hadn't looked at him as he spoke and he now poured himself another cup of coffee and drank it without lifting his eyes. Gibbon sat still, pursing his mouth and occasionally shaking his head, not a negative gesture but a little turn to the side and back.

'Well,' he said after a moment, 'it's all very complicated. I mean last night when I was getting drunk I could have had it away with, what's his real name anyway, I feel a right mug calling him Lotte—'

'Walther Latham, he's French-Rumanian.'

'Walter, Walter, lead me to the alter,' and Gibbon laughed. Kimber glanced at him then away. 'Come on, Norman, where's your sense of humour?'

'It's something I find difficult to be humorous about.'

'Anyway, I could have been up Walter and probably not felt so badly about it, only I figured he was yours for the night, that was why you had gone along to Vaubon's . . .'

'You figured he was mine, so you left him alone—'

'It wasn't any great strain, mind you, except when I was drunk a bit I thought, well they did it in Greece and all that, what's so funny?' Kimber was laughing, silently at first then aloud, laughing close to hysteria and making all the gestures of mirth. When it eased he said,

'You figured he was mine and left him alone. That's rich, that really is. It's got all the hallmarks of a really funny anecdote. Oh, I must tell Lotte this.' And he went out of the kitchen and Gibbon waited to hear him go into the bedroom. Instead he went into the toilet, where Gibbon could hear him trying to be sick.

He got no lifts that day and around ten o'clock the rain started and showered heavily, interspersed with hot bright spells that steamed the road and his clothes. He walked doggedly along, thumbing only the lorries and the single drivers but by midday he had almost given up these attempts and his pace had slowed. He was getting dizzy spells that caused him to wobble out into the road and pains were seizing his back and shoulders and in his chest. Most disconcerting was his right eye which would not stay open, crunching closed, the sound clear in his head and the eye watering constantly. He stopped to rest a lot, sitting on his bag. Once when he got up to go on he forgot the bag and was nearly fifty yards on when he noticed it. He looked back and could see it and he began to cry, standing looking back, unable to move. His sight blurred with tears and he swayed, almost falling.

'It's too far,' he said and turning went on, leaving the bag by the roadside.

With the loss of the bag he walked completely turned in upon himself, an insulation of fatigue and illness and the pitying self-disgust of the castaway. He walked blindly and without making any effort to attract a lift.

The lorry did not hit him but the trailer came so close that its passage brushed him and stepping back he stumbled and fell. The grass was long and wet and he could see the stalks up close, smooth yellowy green and the neat ridges of the joints. They looked like a forest, a forest of tall high trees. He looked into it, waiting to see the rider coming galloping towards him, hair streaming behind her.

'Like a cat,' he said, mouthing against the ground. 'Like a cat'; and tried to raise himself on his forearms but the effort started him sneezing so he lay down again. This time the forest was grey with fog, swirling darkening grey.

A shoe. With a strap. The stocking was dark green. The boy's face seemed a very long way above. Very high. 'Like a cat,' he said; 'pardonnez-moi, comme un chat,' but the boy was running away down the road. His legs were cold and stiff behind him. He moved one and pushed down on the ground with his hands. It wouldn't move. He moved his leg further and found the edge of the ditch, slipping down and pulling slowly his body after it. He fell on his side into the ditch. There was water in it and his whole left side was soaked through. The sun was shining and on everything beads of moist sparkled. He began to crawl along the ditch but it was too hard and he lay down on his side, putting his arm under his head so that his face wouldn't go into the water. He could see quite clearly now with both eyes, see his arm and the water in the ditch and the sodden grass. He could see very clearly and he felt his body to be a peculiar angle. All the time he was weeping his eyes remained open and he could see everything perfectly clearly.

Food had been eaten and wine had been drunk. The evening sat replete, rising in vaults of drugged blue, clouded in wisps and heavy with the smell of trees and dust and the river and the slow cooling of stone. The houses had their shutters open and out of their interior the ribbons of radio and the occasional rag of laughter. Dimly at one of them a woman, pale in a shift or a white dress, passed to and fro. There was a cupola of sloth and ease over the mid-evening. In the tree above the tables the small wind sought separate speech with each leaf, making orchestral susurr.

'This was the café Peter and I came to the first day we really met. Do you remember? I mean we had met before but this was the first time anything happened between us.' Gibbon nodded.

'Yes, I remember. We were outside the "Monaco".'

'That's right. We sat here and the sun was shining and he just looked at me and I remember I thought you are a beautiful creature and I'm going to be in bed with you pretty damn shortly. Do you think that's awful?' – a small anxious child's look. Gibbon smiled.

'Do you care whether I do or not?' She tossed her head and looked serious.

'No, but do you think I'm, well a kind of nympho or something, honest I worry about that sometimes.'

'I think you just like it a lot,' smiling.

'Well, I do but is that not being a nympho?'

'I don't know. Do you like the people you do it with?'

'I try to, I mean I don't go to bed with guys I don't like. I liked Pete. I like you Harry. I think now I picked wrong between you and Peter. I should have picked you. Save you getting mixed up with Norman Kimber.'

'Kimber's all right.'

'Yeah sure, but he's fruity. You're not queer are you Harry?'

'No, I'm not queer.'

'Well, what gives, I mean how come you don't go for women? I mean there's plenty of tail in this town.'

'I don't know Annie. I've thought about it and I don't know. I think I want to be in love with whoever it is.'

'Christ, that's the way a woman's supposed to feel about

it. We've got it all mixed up you and me. I should feel like you do and you should feel like I do.'

'I wish you'd gone to Moss Landings.'

'Moss Landings, how did Moss Landings get into it?' Gibbon put his arm round the girl's shoulders, squeezing her affectionately.

'Oh I just thought if you got there things would have worked out better.'

'What the hell's in Moss Landings for Christsake? Two hundred and seventy-one. And all the moss you can eat?' Gibbon laughed. 'Harry stay with me tonight, will you?'

'Annie, I don't love you.'

'Oh I know you don't. Look just stay. You don't have to lay me or nothing, it's just I like you, I'm liking you this minute and I don't want it to stop. Will you?'

'I'd be honoured.' Annie stood up and kissed his forehead.

'You're great, you really are. You know we could be brother and sister, not in looks maybe but in colouring. Maybe if I'd had somebody like you for a brother everything would have been different.'

Gibbon laughed again, getting up and leading her away. Annie persisted.

'But mightn't it?'

'I'm sure it would have, Annie,' laughing.

'Oh you're joshing me.' They passed the tree. Annie stopped him.

'Listen to the tree, put your ear against it.' Gibbon stood close and listened. He could hear the tree singing, hear its thousand voices raised and woven in a great polyphony of woodwind, a murmurous choral, bass-rooted, treble-twigged, making high hosanna.

'Oh I wish I was up there, in that tree.'

'Yeah that's right, you are a kind of monkey aren't you?'

The room was white and large and high and there were beds and the smell of warm antisepsis and in the middle of the floor a black stove sent a long slender chimney to the roof. A woman in a pale blue habit passed smoothly down the floor, a gliding motion, looking neither left nor right.

He tried to call her but his voice would not emerge and he lay back in the bed exhausted by the attempt.

After he had been fed, a large mannish nun spooning soup for him, another nun came and spoke in English. Her name was Sister Thérèse. She explained she had been brought up in Sussex during the war. Did he know Sussex? Cuffee shook his head.

'You were brought in yesterday evening, a small boy found you and ran to tell his father but when they went back they could not see you and the father did not believe his son had seen you at all. But the boy went back later and found you in the ditch. You must have been there for six hours or more. If the boy had not gone back to look for you it is probable that you would have died. When they brought you to us you were suffering from exposure and you had a high temperature. The doctor says you have a single pneumonia and you will be in bed for some time. God was good to you when he made that little boy go back and search in the ditches.

'When they brought you in you were shouting out and in a fever. They did not know what you were saying because you spoke in English except you kept saying "comme un chat"! "like a cat". Very strange.' She smiled, a white smile in a pale cowled face. 'Now you must tell me who your friends are and we can send to them. You can write down the name and the address.' Cuffee wrote on the piece of paper. 'No one will be worried about me. I do not want to see anyone for a time. I will tell you later.' Sister Thérèse frowned at this but finally nodded.

'Very well, you can tell me when your voice has returned,' and she left. Cuffee lay for a time watching the sun moving across the opposite wall. When he woke it had gone completely.

He was in the Poor Hospital of the Convent of the Holy Mother for almost a fortnight. Sister Thérèse came to speak to him each day for a short time and for the rest of the day he lay quietly in his lukewarm bed feeling the fleshy growth in his chest slacken and shred and looking with horror at the brown fibrous sputum he hacked in his basin. The effort of passing these glutal curds through his mouth made

312

him sweat and sometimes in an overwhelming revulsion he swallowed them.

There were five beds on either side of the room and all but one were occupied. On the end wall a large crucifix, almost life-size, the cross black and the figure of the Christ white like the wall. It was quiet except for some bed to bed talking and the occasional moans of a man in the bed on Cuffee's side at the top of the room. The men looked curiously alike, dark weathered faces with thin noses and deep lines. They did no more than nod to him as they went past to the toilet, convict-like in the off-white bed smocks, their heelless slippers slap-slapping down the floor.

On the fifth day he had been there the man in the end bed died and they brought him down on a trolley that squeaked slightly, his bare yellowy feet showing like two old tusks. He had been in that bed for nearly two years and he was over eighty. Gaston Rieux was his name and Sister Thérèse told Cuffee that he had a medal for bravery from the First World War.

For the next few nights he didn't sleep very well and lay awake for long periods watching the lamp on the night Sister's desk and the pallor it cast on the crucified Saviour. Finally he would go to sleep, to dreams shot through with terror and loneliness and repetitive images of death.

When he wakened in the mornings the sun shone down in four steep rakes that during the day swept the room from end to end like great galley oars, rowing him slowly towards night. He woke early with the dawn birds and watched the nuns in the pearly morning light, pale blue shapes against the white walls, their skirts scliffing faint and cool, their voices pitched low grey stevenings and over them the chaunt of matins from the chapel. He felt well in the mornings. But by midday his bed irked and he had spat some of the stuff up and his temperature rose a little. The sweeps of the sun were almost stationary and the afternoon lay becalmed, even the Christ seemed to droop more hopelessly in his agony.

The nuns moved in the powdery dusk, blue dim shapes against the dove grey walls, skirts chaffering chaste and smooth, voices riffling quiet silver. Evensong plainted the hushed air and a slackening was everywhere, in the firm mouths of the nuns, in the talk of the patients, in the bird song, in Cuffee's clotted tubes and the rigorous tortions of Jesus on the cross.

In these parentheses, the ceramic mirage of morning and evening's gauzy carbon, time was the only true dimension and he lived totally in its density, a sensuous experience that left him exhausted when the dark finally came. Then in a trance he would watch the moths fuzz the sister's lamp and hear the sounds of the room, breathings and turnings, and catch the white-eyed glaze of the icon.

The first time he was allowed up he went down the room to the crucifix. Seen close up it was rather a botch, ill-proportioned and wrongly muscled, but the face had an idiot sanctity, a long cadaver with the great popping eyeballs blind as pebbles.

'Do you admire our crucifix? It was made by a local carver. Many years ago of course.' Sister Thérèse stood behind him.

'Yes. Very much.'

'He has done other carvings for the convent. There is a Pietà which you must see before you leave.'

'When will I be able to go?'

'In a few days the doctor might be willing to let you leave.'

'Will you write to my friend in Paris and tell him?'

'Yes. But would you not rather write to him yourself?'

'No. I have nothing to say.'

He went back and sat on his bed. Two men were playing draughts and opposite him, lying flat on the bed so he made hardly any shape through the clothes a sallow-faced man looked up at the ceiling. Sister Thérèse was talking to a man sitting in a chair. A cloud passed and the light thickened in the room. He felt tired from his walk down to the end of the room and his chest ached as though tightly bound. He moved very carefully so as not to disturb its inflamed membranes. He lay flat and looked at the ceiling. High above and white. He closed his eyes for a moment but when he looked again it was still there, blank as his mind.

Gibbon came down the day before Cuffee was to be discharged. Sister Thérèse was at the village to meet him and they walked out to the convent slowly, she pushing her bicycle and Gibbon carrying some groceries she had bought. She asked him about Cuffee, saying that he had made a good recovery but seemed melancholy, given to brooding silences and enigmatic turns of phrase. Was he always like that? Was he a happy young man? Gibbon answered as best he could and tried to find out what had caused the collapse in the first place. They reached the convent and although it was not a visiting hour Sister Thérèse allowed him to go straight in.

Cuffee was lying on his side, his back to the door, an arm under his head. Sister Thérèse told him he had a visitor. He looked round and got up, came round the end of the bed and held open his arms. They embraced. Sister Thérèse smiled and stood by. Cuffee said nothing, holding only close and hard to Gibbon. For a long moment they remained clasped together, when Cuffee released and withdrew. 'How are you feeling, Peter?' He looked pale and thinner and his eyes had marks under them. The cut on his right eyebrow had healed but left a path through the eyebrow which gave the impression that it was raised in a kind of surprise. His hands seemed very fragile and the large blue veins shone through the pale skin. He sat down on the bed and waved Gibbon to him.

'Am I happy to see you.'

'Well, tell me what happened.'

'Monsieur Gibbon, I will come back for you in fifteen minutes. And you don't have to tell him all at once,' she cautioned Cuffee. 'There will be plenty of time for that.' And she went. Cuffee waited until she had gone then lay back on the pillows.

'Oh Harry boy I thought I was a goner, I thought, until Gibbon walks in that door then I'm not safe.'

'Why didn't you write to me earlier?'

'No, I couldn't, I had to see what happened.'

'And what did happen?'

'Nothing, Harry, nothing at all. Time passed. I didn't know anything about time before. Time could wear down a mountain. I just waited, and it passed.' Gibbon shook his

315

head, uncomprehending, Cuffee caught his arm above the elbow and squeezed. 'I did, and it passed.' His hold slackened and his face settled out of its brief exhilaration.

'I've never been like this before Harry, ill, on my own. I tell you Harry they nearly got through to me this time.' And he lay back and closed his eyes. Gibbon sat on the edge of the bed and stroked the hand that lay, invalid, on his knee. Then remembering,

'Oh, there's a letter for you,' and he passed it over. Cuffee opened it and sitting up began to read. Gibbon looked around the ward until he was finished.

'Ruth?' he asked.

'Poor old Ruthie,' Cuffee said, handing him the letter.

'What's wrong?'

'Nothing. Life is getting to her. Life means none of us well Harold, I'm beginning to think. Go on, read and be illuminated.' And Gibbon, at this more characteristic bidding, read.

CHAPTER TWENTY-THREE

She looked into the Lyons Corner House that wasn't on the corner half thinking she might see someone she knew. But no. There were a few student types reading the *Observer* and the *Times* but for the most the customers were non-descripts, hovering between seediness and eccentricity, the quiet middle-aged men whose hands fingered everything, and self-conversant women with cloth flowers pinned to their coats; the fugitive and the distraught.

She ordered a coffee and took it to an empty table. The sugar chute emptied three small hisses into the cup. The spoon was so light as to be awkward, she moved it in the coffee, half convinced it did not exist below the surface. In the next cubicle a man was watching her. As she met his eyes he smiled, a small spreading grin. She blinked and looked away. Looking into her coffee she knew he was still watching, with his grimace ready for ingratiation. She put in sugar and stirred. The spoon floated well. It was of dull grey alloy. She remembered the pink plastic one in the coffee bar on Oxford Street. In her mind she concocted a romance in which they met each other and were married. But how would she find the plastic spoon, recognise it among its identical fellows. No, it was doomed before it began. She put the spoon in her saucer. It would exist here, weightlessly, in Lyons Corner House, until someone, in a small frustration, snapped it.

The man was still watching, his smile keeping him bent company. Ruth looked away and tried to think of something outside Lyons, outside Manchester, outside her life. Gibbon's letter was in her raincoat pocket. She took it out and read it again. 'For me almost everything seems to be in the past, that is one of the problems.' Snap! she thought. His letter had been unexpected and then on reading, rather surprising, not the kind of letter she would have imagined him writing. There was something almost fragile about him, she thought, something at odds with his solidity and those large, work-roughened hands. What would she do if he came back. Would he want to make love to her? Could she let him with Peter around? 'But I feel from you both that it is in the past.' Was it? Would it ever be in the past, not part of the present. Would she not always yearn for him, shackled by memories, memories of desire slaked, feelings like blue smoke in a pink jar, blue smoke in pink glass, delicate blue expansions in the pink amphora of remembrance.

She looked up to see the man nod and his smile twitch alive. Ruth had a curious sense of his thoughts, of his hopeless dream. Of her underwear and her postures at toilet, of her body's foldings and liquid recedings. Had he already unclothed and possessed her in one of the waiting bedrooms of his mind? Why had she come here anyway? Lyons was where the lonely came, where they drifted on Sunday mornings when the current of the week slackened, into this eddy, to sit over spinning cups and wait for someone to notice their existence. How desperate would she have to be before she welcomed that gaze across the partition. And how before she allowed him to sit opposite and press bony knees through his suiting. Before in the oppressive room with the paper roses writhing on the walls she let his fondlings cover her. How desperate can you get? Looking round she remarked that it was possible to get quite desperate. And the more desperate you got the more you needed the desperate for help.

'My name is Feeley, Mervyn Feeley, excuse me for troubling you but I couldn't help noticing you appeared to be in some distress.' He stood over her, bowing a little, 'May I?' and he did, his smile still withering on his mouth. 'And I thought maybe I might help in some way, we're all friends in the Lord Jesus you know, and that's one of the things wrong with the world today, nobody wants to help anyone else, don't you find? I do, I find that, everybody is too busy passing on the other side, going their own merry' – and at the word 'merry' his smile twitched in empathy – 'way, not really caring. I come here every Sunday just to study human nature, I like to think of myself, in a very modest way you understand, fascinating thing human

318

nature and seeing you in some kind of distress I felt maybe I could help, come over and help.' He had a thin face with patches of high colouring on the cheeks in which puce capillerings twisted, and when he spoke it was through his smile as though it grew, fungular on his lips. 'I said to myself that pretty young woman is in some trouble and I'm rarely wrong and I wondered what a pretty woman like you might be worried about, maybe a quarrel with her gentleman I thought, a tiff, a lover's tiff, but then I thought maybe something more serious maybe some kind of trouble and need a bit of help or just lonely perhaps, looking for a bit of cheering up. When you're lonely you need a bit of cheering up. This isn't much of a place for cheering up a pretty girl like you, oh goodness no' – and some of his mirth escaped in a little tittering giggle which he restrained by quickly licking his lips, obliterating the smile in the process, but it immediately grew again, clammy from the tropic of his mind – 'but I know a few cheery places, our Lord was not against being happy, oh no, and I thought maybe after introducing myself we might take a stroll and become better acquainted with each other and go to one of these cheery places I know or maybe just stroll and have a talk' – and his knee shifted so that its bony cap pressed between hers, slow carapace prising her open, and she tranced by the feeling that there was no real reason why she should not permit it, allow it, welcome it. Or perhaps it already had happened and she was recalling its inevitable sequence – 'or maybe we could just sit here . . .'

She rose abruptly, hitting the table and jarring the cups, slipped out past the upturned, surprised, smiling face and at the door looking back he was still looking after her, smiling, and she ran, ran until people turning in the street and her lack of breath made her stop and she slowed to a walk. She remembered she had left Gibbon's letter on the table but she didn't go back.

The city was everywhere, brooding with Sunday. She could sense it going out and out in houses and streets, in a great still vortex and she at its centre in a suction of boredom and fear and loneliness. The city breathed its arid breath, a great exhalation of emptiness and her heart fluttered in terror. Fly little bird, fly as far as you can.

She took the train to Altrincham. Sometimes she and Cuffee had walked into the pictures from Knutsford. The smell of the cinema and the noise the projector made came back to her vividly. She remembered a fight Cuffee had with a boy sitting behind them who had stuck chewing gum in her hair and Cuffee had caught him by the jacket and pulled him over the seat. She could see Cuffee's face, lit on one side from the screen pulling the boy over and kicking him when he was on the floor and in the middle of it looking up at her and smiling, quite pleasantly. She walked out along the Warrington Road thinking of her brother and the terrible, controlled savagery of which he was capable. There was a text on a church board. 'God loves every one of us though there were but one of us to love.' It did not give chapter and verse and she walked on trying to place it.

The houses stepped back and the country encroached. Memories came to her, grassiness and smells and the shapes of trees and the tint of flowers. The sun strained through the clouds. She walked down the left turn to Knutsford beginning to feel warm and relaxed and glad to be here and herself. About two miles down in a field on the left was the island. They had called it the island. It was a knoll, swelling and distinct and firm, planted with a dozen or so tall straight trees, a little atoll on the land. It was where, when she had tired or had been separated from Cuffee on their forages, she would come to wait for him. Snuggled down against a tree listening to its woody drone and watching for his figure, come suddenly running, moving certainly across the fields.

She went up the steep swell of the ground, using her hands in places. The trees rose around her, unbranched, columnar, Scots pine she thought, or is it fir. Looking up she could see in the high foliage needlings of brighter green. A bird was singing, the notes spiky, and in across the fields came the soft spaced caw of rooks. She could see where Knutsford was behind trees and as she was settling herself a clock floated two chimes faintly to her. It was warm, down close to the ground and against the tree,

320

rough and comfortable at her back. She closed her eyes and heard. There was the same noise she remembered, the same moan in the wood and above it a high feathery brushing through which the bird stitched bright tines. Beyond these foresounds a heavy thrull, a nearly unheard roar of grasses grinding and butterflies beating, like the sea on some far shore. She listened and felt in her, diffuse and drifting, a vague expanding, green smoke in yellow glass, a happiness, a pleasure. In it she could detect shapes and textures, of the promise of her body and the flavour of her mind, the richness of the waiting world and her love of it, her sworling, unfocussed love and its certain, uncertain future.

The sun came out and warmed her into a drowse. She dreamt of things, of swimming under the sea and the colour the light was through the water and of fishes, blue fish and yellow fish, swimming cloudy shoals, swimming inside her as though she were a transparent creature, swimming single file fish, delicate vulval ravishers and she could see them this way and that within her and then she saw a big scaly fish came swimming up from down and in panic she fled and coming up there was a raft floating in the sea and she climbed on to it only to find it was an enormous school photograph and she crawled along the rows and rows of faces looking into every one but they were all empty and she came to her own but instead there was a hole and as she fell there was a voice crying but she knew it was herself and she looked into all the lighted windows as she fell and saw people shake hands, clean shoes, tear up newspapers, pour tea, lick stamps, lay carpets, do exercises, change shirts, point upwards, scratch their knee, break sticks, polish mirrors and she saw them all as she fell and it always seemed to be somebody she knew, maybe all the same person but familiar anyway only she fell so fast and now she wasn't falling but was in a train rushing past the houses overlooking the railway and just before she went into the tunnel she saw in a window or was it a mirror two people making love and she knew them only with a great roar the train went smoking into the tunnel and it was all dark and coming out of it she was wakening up.

She had a headache from sleeping in the sun and she

walked down through the fields looking for a stream to drink and bathe her face. The dream was still with her and thinking on it she felt disconcerted by the two people who had been making love when the train went into the tunnel. The rest of it she could accept without comprehending anything very much about it but the two bothered her because she knew she knew who they were only their identities remained hidden. Stopping a moment she closed her eyes and thought back, trying to re-run the dream like a film and after a moment of seeing different, unrelated things it unwound itself again and this time she saw or knew or decided that the girl was her but the train kept going into the tunnel before the man came clear. The only additional information she noted was that both of them had their clothes on. For some reason this depressed her.

On the other side of the hedge she could see a cornfield and through a gap caught sight of the milky red stains of poppies among the coarse upstanding stalks, kisses in yellow rain, and touched her mouth with reminded fingers. She went through the gap and to the edge of the sown. A poppy trembled as she parted the corn to touch it, fleshest tissues cool on her fingers. The delicate cling ravished her, a sensuality so fine yet so intense and she brought her face down to it, the rank venereal odour and its membrane on her mouth, the kiss of a daemon lover, of some old earth god, taking her from behind with a quick brute thrust, seeing not his face but the hot of his pant on her back and the smell of the ground in her crushed nostrils. She lay there nursing the soft throbbing wish for sexual release, not the turmoil of a girl for her dearest but the dim pulse of waiting womankind, the nymphomania of priestesses in temples, of reapers in harvests, a single-minded yoni yearn for some priapic agent, some ritual rapist. Behind her eyelids the red blaze of the sun and the dark opius whirl of its centre, to her lips the silken stink of a poppy. A young woman mouthing a poppy in the hot summer sun.

She stood up and the bruptness dizzied her, for a moment she could not focus and everywhere before her eyes red blotches on a tawny ground, becoming common poppies in a cornfield.

As she went in the sound of her father's voice, raised to make a point in some discussion and she could hear Robert Eldman saying 'yes, I'm sure that's so', and the rattle of crockery. Sunday evening tea. Like a taste in the mouth the memory of them, those countless long since Sunday tea-times, with Mrs Cuffee futtering about getting the table laid and 'Children's Hour' on, always something about saints or explorers who were Christians and competitions she never entered and Uncle Mac saying 'good night children, everywhere', and it was always cheese for tea or cold meat with halved tomatoes and Cuffee would be upstairs and she would half help her mother and half listen to the wireless and Mr Cuffee would be in the garden smoking a pipe and listening to the evening birdsong.

Before going in she stooped to catch her eye in the mirror knot-hole. 'Ruth through the looking glass' she thought and smiled affectionately at the unchanged distortion. Then she went into the sitting-room. Mr Cuffee was standing before the fireplace and Robert Eldman was in his usual easy chair. The familiarity, fraught for her by its new dimension, was disconcerting. Somehow she felt her entrance was like the introduction of some fresh constituent, rendering a hitherto stable compound instantly volatile. It made her tense and ill at ease and she felt her greetings to be hysterical and patently a façade. The discussion, on the deficiencies of the secondary modern school, went on however, seemingly impervious to this chemical development. She watched Eldman as he nodded to Mr Cuffee's words and wondered what emotion circled behind his acquiescence, was he hating or scorning, or merely irritated. He looked at her and smiled. For a moment she felt conspiratorial and following upon, the thought that perhaps Mrs Cuffee might have told him. The discomfort of such a possibility sent her out to the kitchen where her mother was making Welsh rarebit. The sight of the melting slabs of cheese in some way reassured her, an irrational, nostalgic comfort that dispelled as she had another comprehension of the objective, still incredible fact of her mother's adultery. Anger, almost immediately extinguished by a sense of the ridiculous that made her want to shake Mrs Cuffee, shake her until it came home to her the total absurdity of the situation, of the two men talking about secondary education and herself making Welsh rarebit.

'Cheddar or Wensleydale?' Mrs Cuffee asked at that moment, and Ruth realised sharply that she was hungry. She settled for the Cheddar which was mild, Mrs Cuffee assured her, and went upstairs to wash her hands.

Her mood was one of complete confusion, any feeling which achieved definition was almost as quickly cancelled out by its reaction. The initial concern she had felt for her mother on discovering her secret had never reached the density of emotion, rather was it a scrappy sort of sympathetic amazement that had faded somewhat to leave her in the position of feeling she ought to have a feeling and experiencing thrusts of guilt at her inability to do so.

As for her father, she found it impossible to focus the matter so that all three figures were clear at the one time. She could see him and Mrs Cuffee, and Mrs Cuffee and Eldman, Eldman and Mr Cuffee, but never them all in their total interrelation. It was when she considered him separately that the deepest sense of concern was touched, to be played cuckold now, at this juncture, seemed a rueful accolade bestowed upon a blotched life.

The meal was a smooth enough charade. Ruth was certain now that Eldman did not know and almost the feeling that Mrs Cuffee had forgotten she did. Mr Cuffee chuntered on about school politics and made heavy sarcasms about the other masters. Eldman smiled at these and wiped the corners of his mouth and moustache from time to time after sipping his Whitbread's. Ruth scarcely listened after a while and was taken unawares by her father's question.

'Sorry, what did you say?'

'I said, where's our wandering boy tonight?'

'Oh, Peter. Paris I think.'

'Paris eh, well that's the place to be, up to the knees in "laissez-faire" and "ménages à trois".' Ruth told herself amid the deafening rush of blood to her head that it was simply a phrase, a cliché in conversation.

'Have you heard from him?' She glanced at Robert Eldman who was predictably engaged in napkining his mouth.

'No, from Harry Gibbon, that friend of Peter's who went with him.'

'Strange thing about our eldest, dear,' Mr Cuffee went on as though he were talking to his wife and she, seconding the pretence, switched on her expression of alert reception, 'he almost seems bearable at such a remove, which only goes to show the optical aberrations induced by distance,' and he chuckled at his verbal dexterity and drained his glass.

Her mother's complete calm led Ruth to reflect that three years of this sort of situation had probably insulated her from nervous apprehension. And yet her own unearthing of the secret seemed ridiculously simple. She had just known, and her mother had known that she knew and had asked her not to tell Mr Cuffee. But why had Mr Cuffee never suspected, surely three years of even the most lukewarm adultery must leave some traces, some clues. The telephone ringing when he might have answered it, something of Eldman's in the bedroom. Perhaps he did know. She looked at him, he was carefully buttering a cream cracker. Perhaps he knew and was waiting his moment. What moment, for what? No, it was too foolish to think of him behaving like that. But how would he behave if he knew? What could he do? She then became aware that conversation had ceased and they were sitting in silence. Somehow such a state seemed especially dangerous, as if out of it might come something as shattering as that last silence in Coleman's Coffee House, as though silence, if protracted long enough and as they sat there casting through their minds for some gambit, might lead them to discard all the frivolities of talk and each according to their need, say the words lying closest to their heart.

'I was wondering if, if any of you might know this quotation, "God loves each one of us as though there were but one of us to love". I saw it on a church text board but I didn't think it was Biblical somehow.' Eldman looked at Mr Cuffee and frowned.

'I'm not so sure—' he began but all the time waiting for the other's voice.

'Saint Augustine I think.' Eldman mocked surprised enlightenment.

'Do you think so?'

'Exactly the sort of thing he would say. Can't swear to it mind you, but it's got the kind of paradoxical flavour he went in for.'

'You may be right Peter, you usually are' – still playing the reluctant second opinion.

'Simplest way to settle it;' and Mr Cuffee got up from the table.

'Oh don't bother, it's not important,' she said only to see immediately that for him it was important. He went out of the room and they could hear his steps going up to the study. Ruth was left looking from Robert Eldman to her mother. For a moment they all sat then he stood up and out from the table.

'Very tasty, Daisy,' he said and placed his chair neatly in. 'Can I help you clear?' But his mistress waved the offer away so he sat down and turning to Ruth said,

'Shouldn't be at all surprised if your father's right about that quotation, he's very good on that sort of thing, retentive memory. Me, I can't remember a thing.' And she hated him for being able to say that, in that tone, to her. Since there were no words for the occasion she remained silent, seated at the table and presently Mr Cuffee came down again bringing with him a book of quotations.

'Yes, that was it, Saint Augustine all right. Spot the old rogue a mile off' – and gave Ruth the book, pointing out the line. She managed to say 'thank you', casually enough but to fix the shimmery print in her wet eyes was more than she could manage.

It was just beginning to get dark as she got back to Manchester. She passed down the street where Cuffee had jumped into the hedge and tried to remember which one. And where Harry Gibbon had gone right through and into the flower bed. She smiled, thinking how long ago it seemed. At her gate as she was going in she started to search for the key, wondering whether or not she had remembered to bring it and just as she found it a voice,

'Excuse me but you left this when you went out, I thought you must have been taken queer, the one moment we were sitting there and the next you were gone so I thought she's been taken ill or something so I waited for you to come back and then I brought the letter over here but you weren't in.'

He stood under the lamp and the light was behind him and his face was in shadow so that she couldn't tell if he was smiling. He held out the letter with his left hand and the other was in his raincoat pocket.

'I didn't want to put it through the letter box it being open and not knowing if it might be private. I thought you must have been taken ill when you ran out like that.'

'Have you been waiting here all day?' And she came forward to get the letter. As she took it, and before she could step back he had opened his raincoat and with his left hand began to masturbate. For a moment Ruth neither moved nor made a sound then lurching back and making a noise, disgust and fear, she turned and ran to the door. The key stuck in the lock and then went in and the door opened. Looking back she could see he was still there, seeming not to have moved, doing it to himself. She ran up the stairs, stumbling and only at the top of her flight did she realise she was sobbing heavily.

Inside, with the light on she didn't want to cry any more. She sat on the bed and looked at her name on the envelope until the name became a clueless cipher. Ruth Cuffee. Ruth Cuffee. ruth Cuffee. Ruth Cuffee. ruth Cuffee. 'God loves each one of us as though there were but one of us to love.' Does he now. She opened the envelope. Gibbon's letter was gone. There were two sheets of ruled paper, torn from a loose-leaf notebook. One of them had drawings on both sides, clumsy graffiti.

The other contained a clotted, obscene message, in her frantic sight a jigger of promise and threat, plea and demand that escaped a full comprehension, bringing only an acute sense of vulnerability to such enactments.

She felt very tired and nerves were fluttering in her stomach. For a moment she thought she was going to be sick but it passed. She put the two pages and the envelope into the grate and lit them. Then she sat on the bed again, looking at the floor. She wasn't anything now, except tired.

327

Not frightened, not disgusted, not even sad. She thought of him, the pathetic cringing manner and the bravura of his obscenities. He had waited there all day, all day for a once seen girl to grant that he exists. Poor Mervyn Feeley, but the thought was a mere husk and she let it drift away. They were all in it together she was beginning to see. Herself, Ruth Cuffee. And those three at Knutsford. And Miss Armitage, and Maureen next door. And Mervyn Feeley and if you could see it almost everybody else. Her dream and the thoughts in the cornfield should have told her to be prepared, for her no-face man, for her daemon lover. When you get desperate the desperate seek you out. She really did not know why she should object to his attentions. The garbled recall of the note itched in her mind, obscene really in that it stemmed from the poor crippled creature outside, not in itself obscene, at least not to her for she knew now as she had never known before that she was desperate and that she needed to escape, to fly this town, and these people, these monstrous other beings. It was not simply sex she craved but what sex augured, the closeness of another. But if they were all monsters like the ones she knew. What then?

But her tiredness made this an unnecessary question. She abdicated to its compulsion. She was very tired. She locked the door and took off her shoes. Then she got into bed.

CHAPTER TWENTY-FOUR

The sky was low, hodden with cloud, and the morning had been flecked with intermittent rains. Moseby had spent it in the Art Galleries, walking through the quiet rooms, looking aimlessly at the model steamships, the stuffed animals, the samurai swords and the plaster casts of the family of man. The assembly of objects and facts depressed him, or maybe it was the louring Glasgow day through the windows. Or MacIndoe. Or the fact that he hadn't answered Gibbon's letter. And it certainly was Cathie. Life, he told himself, life is getting wired right in.

This morning, for a short time, he'd thought that it was all over, that he wouldn't be able to get up. He'd wakened before the alarm and thought of rising and putting on his clothes and making the tea and brushing his teeth, thought he would never, never in the creation of Christ, make it. He must have been only half awake for the thought hardened into conviction and he lay back and considered the vistas ahead. He would never leave his bed, become a kind of Saint Inertia and people would pilgrimage along Dempster Street, past the window and there would be a set of mirrors angled so that the faithful could see their prophet in kip. And outside the window a banner, bearing the legend, 'come unto me all ye that labour and are heavy laden and I will give you rest'. Before the fancy cloyed the alarm went off and Edna in a reflex nudged him. He tried in a half-hearted sort of way to make love to her but was of course rebuffed. Then Carol came galloping through and before he knew it he was up. But the feeling was still there, that he couldn't do it, not again. And it stayed with him on the 7.50, and through his chat with MacIndoe who virtually nailed him down to a promise to come to dinner on Friday. Once it was done it wasn't so bad, really, except MacIndoe had been in a strange sort of mood and had talked about this girl he was having it off with and how it was all impossible. Moseby kept thinking he was waiting for a mutual admission of guilt so that they could breast-beat together but he said nothing, but on his way down to the Art Galleries he slowly sunk into depression at the thought of meeting Cathie.

The Art Gallery had been her idea, she wanted a change from the matinee and the neighbours, she thought, were getting a little suspicious. It had been years since she had been to the Museum and she'd never been where the paintings were. And he would be able to tell her all the things she didn't know, wouldn't he. There was a kind of cosiness in the air these days that he didn't like. In a ridiculous sort of a way she was setting up house with him. The melancholy of the early meetings had passed and in its place there was a certain domestic complacency. Once when he had come out without a handkerchief she had said it was his wife's business to see he had a clean one every morning. It had nothing to do, he knew, with Cathie being fastidious, it was simply a snipe at Edna, whom she never referred to by name but always as 'your wife'

Moseby knew it was going to have to end and end soon. He didn't think much about it, how it would be achieved, what he would say and how she would look because he was really hoping something would happen, like her husband would come home or she would get knocked down. He didn't know whether he wished that or not but it was in his head often enough so he must not be totally averse to the idea. And yet there was something about her, a bleak sort of charm. 'The full gloom of her youth' he remembered and smiled. If only she had had children then none of this could have happened, she could have become one of those nondescript women who sit beside you on buses a lot.

He sat in front of the Dali Crucifixion and hoped a nutcase would come in and throw a brick at it. Two middle-aged ladies in heather mixture tweeds and ribbed stockings were standing looking at it and saying nothing. Then one said 'very impressive' and the other nodded vigorously and said 'yes, most impressive'. Dali's Crucifixion thus assessed they moved on. He felt rather embarrassed for them, their serviceable suits and thick legs, clad for survival against the Scottish summer.

330

Might not Edna get like that? Certainly that would be the kind of stuff she would go in for. It was no good imagining her suddenly becoming a beatnik. For a moment he saw it from her angle, or what he imagined hers to be. She probably felt that slowly they were going where she had always planned they would go. Towards comfortable, middle class well-being. And why not, they were both equipped for it, accustomed to it. Only in his case there was this trap door that he might choose to open and enter. But wasn't that all kind of a dream thing. He wasn't going to go looking for his mother, not now, not now he knew he wouldn't find her sad-eyed in the walled garden tending the wistaria. And he didn't need her now, not really. And most like she was dead or untraceable. So he wouldn't open that trap door. He would go on and become what he was to become. In some ways he was resigned to this evolution, that had something to do with why he hadn't answered Gibbon's letter. In a way it annoyed him, to hear him speaking of discovering his identity, and the sense the letter gave of a kind of slow inevitable expansion, a coming to fruition; he just didn't want to know, it was petty and unpleasant but he didn't want Harry Gibbon to make it out into the world. Not while he remained bound to his stereotype. Yet what would he want to be, or do, how could he make his escape, not by leaving Edna, that would only make the whole thing a shambles. Cromwell's words about the value he placed upon tradition, how he would pursue it 'were but a hare upon the water'. Order is your hope, the only freedom possible lay in order. Maybe when he had gotten through University he might settle down to do some writing, that would help. If he could write, that is, what if he couldn't?

The hell, he thought and got up and went out into the corridor. It housed a collection of Russell Flints. There were about forty of them, all ravishing surfaces, a hermetic world of the senses, untrammelled and unexperienced, the haughty torace nippled and tawny, the draped haunches and the laughter that echoed under the simple arches. All a dream, a sweet fantasy, slates and cinnamons and dull rich browns, and greys, the whole exquisite range of greys. They were the colours of Greenock he noted, the Greenock of his mind's eye, unpopulated, in autumn weather, the river seen down the swift streets, the hills on the other side, long bulks in the cool sun. And at night? What about at night. Did a small hunchback man hirple between the moon-cast buildings, longing for a glimpse at a high window of a woman in a silken shift. He looked at one of the gouache gipsies. How sexless they were he thought, and it gave him a small surprise that he could think such a knowing thing. Just like that. Oh you're a smart apple Moseby, no mistake.

He couldn't be all that smart or he wouldn't be waiting for Cathie in the Glasgow Art Galleries, would he? Certainly it would have to end. And in a way it was only when it was over that it would really have happened, only then would it be a piece of the past, be history, something about which it was possible to have definite opinions, not the vaporous crypto feelings of the present. What did he feel about her? He must feel something. The question, once articulated, remained starkly in his mind as he groped around for something that might pass as response. He liked her didn't he, cared? There was a moment when he didn't know what he thought and then there was a moment when he did. No. He thought away from the denial with a little twitch of the head and was surprised to find himself remembering the funeral of his aunt, if she was his aunt, in Glasgow all those years ago. One of the mourners, a woman in a black dress with small black sequins on the shoulders saying to his mother who was seated with himself at her knee 'she looked so very like herself' and the smell, that sweet, covering-up smell everywhere.

All right, he shouted in his head, so I don't love her. I never said I did. It was Edna he loved, Edna he had always loved. He remembered the first time he had seen her, at a staff dance, in an evening dress, and how unattainably ordinary she had seemed, rather good-looking, rather enjoying herself. She had been escorted by a tall young man going bald on front. Walter Kinneard his name was. Once when he went to get drinks he had asked her to dance, and for five minutes had savoured the illicit firmness of her and her warm fleshy smell through the perfume. While they danced

332

he talked the clipped incessant patter he reserved for such occasions and wanted this conventional, attractive girl with a rapacity that told him it was quite impossible.

In a way he'd never really stopped feeling like that. Once, before they were married, he had told her about wee Joe Moffat and Mary Agnew and she had said she was in favour of sterilising deformed and defective people and his heart had sunk in him though then he hadn't known why. He knew now though, had known for almost all of their married life. It was simply that he wanted the beast in her to show, to break through that overweening propriety and make her deformed like him. And bed was the only place where this might happen, once out of her clothes and in the dark, it might. He had a lurid, yet dim, vision of some apocalyptic sexual event in which he and Edna would participate and at the end of which they would have achieved some obscure cathartic regeneration.

What form this might take he could not really envisage and he knew if it was necessary then it was only for him and not for Edna. So where was it all going and what was it all for? And now quite without warning he had a sore head, a down pressing pain above his eyes. Yes, he thought, life is getting the boot right home.

He could see out over the parked approach to the building, the damp gravel paths and the ornamental flower layout and beyond it the buses running green and red against the dark band of the tenements. And it rained, dejected, wet-making Glasgow rain. Cathie, in a white raincoat, was coming up to the steps. He turned and went along the corridor and then down the stairs into the big hall with the glass cases around it with animal tableaux. It was here they were to meet. She had come through the doors and stood in the foyer. Then even as Moseby went towards her she turned to her right and went through into one of the other departments. When he got to it, it was the family of man one, she was just going through an open arch and into the engineering hall. By the time he had got to the entrance he had decided to give Cathie the slip. Not just as flatly as that or he would have turned and gone out, but the idea had come and not been put away and was being held now and

Moseby looking carefully into the hall, feeling as he did so like one of the models in the evolutionary exhibition he was leaving and in a curious self-mockery that was at the same time an attempt to excuse his behaviour as a joke should Cathie spot him, he slumped forward letting his arms dangle and prognathing his jaw.

Cathie was looking rather emptily at the central cases with the Chinese junks and the Arab dhows. Moseby scuttled in crab-legged and calipered round and up the stairs, near the top of which he began, almost involuntarily, to make ape-like 'hgu hgu hgu' noises which made Cathie look up but he was out of sight. The upstairs gallery was empty and in a little panic of hysteria he went jigging and grunting along the corridor only to meet the two Scottish ladies emerging from yet another aesthetic experience. He was almost disassociate in his reactions at this point and without a pause changed his anthropoidal canter into the ruffianly stroll of a seven-foot sailor, saying in passing, 'good morning to 'ee missis', to which the matrons exchanged glances and increased their pace. Moseby felt himself about to laugh and he restrained it by clapping both hands over his mouth. The mirth involved was of no such volume and petered out weakly against his palms. Suddenly depressed he leant on the cool stone balustrade and looked down into the engineering hall. Cathie was still there, examining the cross section of a connecting arm. She was almost underneath him, turning away from the case now and looking around her. Was she thinking about Tom, among all these marine reminders. He couldn't see her face and realised that if she looked up she would notice him, and he didn't care. He would go down and talk to her, tell her about Dali's Crucifixion. What did it matter. She walked slowly down the hall and once near the bottom looked back and up. She did not see him although he smiled a bit, but went on and out.

Moseby put his face down on the stone. Its coldness made his cheek sore. It hadn't meant anything, he'd never promised her, never said the word; what would she do with love anyway? The stone ached against his temple. He would miss the sex he supposed, catching her still in bed, with a

334

bad breath and warm yielding limbs. She wasn't like Edna, who basically thought sex was wrong, in a thin, tepid way. Cathie just didn't care. No matter how tender or careful you were with her still you had used her because in her mind she was a thing, and things got used. Surely somewhere he thought there was a woman who wanted it, really wanted it so you didn't have to worry if you were doing them down. His sore head had gone away. It must have been the stone. He straightened up. West Coast women, they all had this kink about it one way or another. On their honeymoon he remembered Edna saying once when they were up on a headland, lying looking over the water, 'oh outside is so much better than inside', and then having to put her face down on the grass because she was suddenly aware of what she meant by it. Dirty men, with their nasty sticking-out things. He came slowly down the stairs, expecting Cathie to come back in. She wasn't in the next section and he walked through into the foyer. Cathie was looking into one of the large side cases. He felt he loved her then, love like a white worm reaching out between the lid and the edge. Hopeless, pale, doomed feeling. He went the other way and out the front doors. It was still raining. It was too early to go home. He turned up the hill to the University.

MacIndoe was marking papers. He called 'come in' and went on working, a frown of intent between his eyes. 'Sit down' he said without looking up, doing his big dedicated lecturer unable to break train of thought bit. It comforted Moseby to see him in an identifiable role and he sat down to wait for recognition. MacIndoe did look up, blinked, smiled and swung his seat round once completely.

'I'm a busy man, John. Reading some opinions on what the Stuarts did for English constitutional development.'

'I'm very happy for you.'

'Well, what can I do for you?'

'Nothing. I just came in to kill a few moments before going for my train.' MacIndoe looked at the heap of unmarked papers, shook his head in despair, whether at the work ahead of him or the quality of the essays Moseby couldn't be sure. He got up and, stretching, went to the window.

335

'Did you never have any religious background?' he asked, his voice pitched deliberately casual. He always felt embarrassed about these questions, Moseby thought.

'Church. Nothing very intensive. Why?'

'Why?' And he turned on Moseby, pausing a moment then coming to his desk. 'Why, because that's the other basic component of the Lowlands, West Coast male. Along with sex. What people don't realise about us' – it gave Moseby a strange feeling to hear the pronoun – 'is that we are existentialists, classically so, and that the twin pillars of our existentialism are religion and sexuality.'

'That makes our basic emotion guilt then.'

'My wife calls it "geegs". I think that's better, it's a more existentially expressive phrase I think. Do you know it?'

' "Geegs". Dirty things, spittles in the dust, that class of item.'

'Yes, Nancy is very sensitive to the geegs, in other people too. She says it's the hallmark of a metaphysical revulsion against our fleshly existence.'

'Does she?'

'You don't agree.' Moseby shrugged elaborately.

'I don't know. Really I don't. I think we are all a bit sex-obsessed because we've all got the feeling it's dirty, we're all a bit pervy.'

'But that's simply the eschatological emphasis of Calvinism being denied by a positive like force. It is a metaphysical assertion.' He smiled, jerkily and got up from his seat, going back to stand at the window. 'I've decided to give up this thing with Jennie,' he said.

'Where does that put your metaphysical assertions then?' Moseby said, annoyed at this having come up again.

'Within religion there is room for the mortification of the flesh.' It all seemed a bit unreal to Moseby, whose sore head was inching back. He said nothing, knowing not what to say. MacIndoe was leaning on his palms, arms straight and his head dug in between his shoulders. Moseby remembered how they used to make themselves dizzy by doing that between the desks and would get taken down to the Matron's room. 'If you don't mortify the flesh then it will mortify you,' MacIndoe said. 'It will ruin everything for you, it is in its unbridled appetite the agent of chaos. And the only freedom is in order. You know that of course' – turning to ask. Yes, Moseby thought, I do. I thought that today, didn't I? Did I believe it when I thought it though?

'That's what Oliver said.'

'Did he?' MacIndoe advanced and with a deliberate clumsiness howked open a cigarette packet and took out a cigarette, bent in the process. This he placed in an awkward part of his mouth and lit. 'Your admiration for Cromwell does your sentiments credit but your intelligence less than justice. Never mind. What steps are you taking to put your life in order?'

'Oh I'm praying for inner peace.'

'How was it your man put it, "teach me Lord to sit still".' Whose book of quotations have you got MacIndoe, and at the same time he remembered the little Dutch couple taking their delfen ease under the toothbrushes. Oh shag it, he thought, time to get out of here.

'I'll be getting along, let you get on with the constitutional Reforms under the Stuarts.'

'Beginning to get to you where you live, eh,' and he adopted an American accent to deliver this. Moseby grinned and went to the door. 'Don't forget Friday now,' in an ordinary tone.

'No I won't.'

Outside and in the corridor he remembered Cathie looking into the stuffed animals. That was the solution, he thought, taxidermy. Most of us wouldn't even know the difference.

Edna went to visit her mother after tea and Moseby put Carol to bed. After he had told her a story he sat beside her, holding her hand and answering her questions.

'Daddy does Princess Serendipity have, does she have a, a mammy?'

'Yes.'

'Where does her mammy live?'

'In a palace with Princess Serendipity's father the King.'

'The King?'

'Aha.'

'Is he a bad King?'
'No, he's not exactly a bad King.'
'Is he a good King?'
'Kind of.' A pause. Much thought.
'Yes, well he isn't wicked?'
'No, not wicked.'
'Does Princess Serendipity love him?'
'Oh yes.'
'Even when he's bad?'
'Aha.'
'She doesn't skelp him.'
'No.'
'Does he skelp her?' Moseby grinned and kissed her eyes.
'No, he doesn't. Now go to sleep.'
'Abut Daddy . . .'
'No abuts, get you down to sleep.'

There were sounds of children playing on the street and the light was slowly draining from the evening. The blind was drawn in Carol's room and it made everything yellowy and dull. Carol lay back thinking about the story and holding her father's hand. He watched her, feeling soft things in him, moods of tenderness and a sadness too, sadness for the simple separateness of them, linked by her small soft hand in his. Her thinking had dimmed and she was nearly asleep. He could see it come over her, a smooth onrush of oblivion leaving her breathing quietly, her mouth a little open, a hand lying on its back, fingers curled. She was another life, launched by him in a distracted myopic moment. He wished now it could have more purpose, more intent. They should have prepared themselves as for a rite, bathed their bodies and anointed their parts then taking each other close made the motions that led to life. It should have been a holy thing. Then he would have been more truly her father, there would have been a mite more order, and perhaps, a little more freedom. But you know nothing. He had known nothing then and he knew very little more now. Ask me it and I bet I don't know it, and he rose quietly from Carol's side and went into the kitchen.

He sat up on the dresser and looked down into the allot-

338

ments. There were only two of the plots being tended. A train went through the Wemyss Bay line, sending up great grey spumes of smoke, they drifted over the allotments, and rose, thinning. Beyond its veil the town lay spread to the river's edge, roofs and chimneys and the steeples of the churches, the town hall tower. He thought of the lamp on the stairs that would soon be lit and thinking of it he had a sense of the town, extended along the coastal plain, a sense of her all at once waiting for a lover to discover in her topography his own erotic intent, and this sense became a longing for a woman, and he saw himself vividly, running in the way he had in the Galleries, through the empty streets of the town, looking for such a woman as would liberate him. Funny, to feel trapped and yet never to have been free. How else would he know he was trapped then. Yet he was, he felt it on nights like this, watching the river over the roofs, could feel the slow run of the water tugging at him, pulling him out of himself. The hills, the stars, the moon. A fox that ran barking.

He watched, one man at a window, one town in the world. The evening closed down and the lights began to come on in the houses, patching yellow the dark.

CHAPTER TWENTY-FIVE

Kimber got their tickets and saw them down to the station. Cuffee wasn't very well and sat in the corner seat looking flatly out, the flesh on his cheek bone pressed in a white disc against the glass. Gibbon stood on the platform with Kimber waiting for the train to start.

'Thanks for all this Norman, and for everything else.'

'I'm pleased to be able to help, and the money is nothing. I owe you something anyway.'

'I owe you a drink.' Kimber looked surprised, Gibbon nodded towards Cuffee.

'Oh, you mean Uta. Ah well, even I didn't think it would come to that.'

'She's a strange one.'

'She's all of that. Here—' and he called to a porter and spoke to him in French. The porter took some money and went off briskly.

'What was that?'

'I sent him for a drink. Will you be back Harry?' – looking at Gibbon in a way that was almost pleading. Gibbon returned the gaze until it became an embarrassment, then put his hand on Kimber's elbow.

'I'll be back Norman, sure I will.' Kimber looked around, as though for the porter, speaking as he did so.

'This time it was all a bit of a ballsup, I mean I tried too hard to, well to pretend I was something I wasn't.' Turning round, 'Look Harry, I know it's all impossible to predict but I'd like us to try again, without me trying to run it all from the sidelines, d'you know what I mean?' And there was something naïve and self-convincing in his voice, reminiscent of Annie almost. Gibbon nodded in response to this. Kimber went on: 'Us queers, we're always talking about how we want a real thing to happen and then when it does, or it might, then we just go and screw it all up by playing it queer. I'd like us to be friends, whatever that entails.' Gibbon didn't have to answer immediately because the porter came back with a bottle of brandy. Kimber stripped the paper and tore off the tinfoil. Uncorked he offered it to Gibbon, who nodded and raised the neck. 'Well here's to us.'

'To us.' As he drank there were a series of shouts and whistlings. Kimber took a swig and gave the bottle back to Gibbon.

'It'll keep Peter warm on the way home.' Cuffee's face was twisted against the window, the mouth pulled open in a snarl and his large canine tooth showing. Gibbon got on the train which began to move. Kimber walked alongside then they shook hands.

'Look after yourself Harry.'

'You do the same. I'll write when we get in.' Kimber released his hand and stopped walking. He waved. Gibbon waved. The train gathered speed and curled away until they could no longer see each other. Gibbon turned in from the window and Cuffee was beside him.

'I thought you had passed out.'

'No, just giving old Kimber a snarl of discouragement.'

'Ah come on, he's all right.'

'But he's after your bakey old son and I'm saving your bakey for myself. Give us a bash at that drink.' While he was drinking Gibbon looked out of the window but the station was left far behind. He made a mouth of resignation and came in. Cuffee put his arms around his neck and gave him a reeking brandy kiss.

'Harold, it's a life of poovery from here on in.'

The trip back tended towards the hectic. Almost right away Cuffee started an argument with a German student who was coming to holiday in England. Cuffee told him there was a rabid anti-German feeling in Britain and the German student begged leave to disbelieve this. Cuffee insisted. Werner asked to be given some instance of this. Cuffee said that 'The Magic Mountain' had been serialised under the title 'Tuber, Colossus of Rhodes', the German smiled broadly and said 'ah, a choke', whereupon Cuffee grabbed him by the throat and shouted 'ja, ja, a choke' until Gibbon and a man in the carriage got him off. Cuffee subsided in the corner with the bottle and made faces while Gibbon apologised for him. The man who had helped save Werner turned out to be English and his wife and daughter came in after freshening themselves up. The mother was a compact, attractive woman of about forty-five to whom Cuffee immediately addressed a long lecherous smile that she didn't quite know how to deal with. Her daughter fell into conversation with the German lad whilst Gibbon and the man surveyed all apprehensively. Cuffee offered the woman a swig from the bottle which she unhesitatingly refused.

'Madame this is a love potion. It was purchased by my friend's lover in order to stimulate his ardour to such a point that he would not leave Paris, but remain, the plaything of degraded passion. Is that not so Harold?' Gibbon smiled and nodded in placation. Cuffee urged drink on the lady who smilingly refused.

'I will have some, thank you very much,' Werner said, forgiving all.

'Will you fuck, kraut head.' The carriage was now united against Cuffee, and the man said he would report it to the ticket collector. Gibbon sat amongst them, embarrassed and on the verge of hysterical laughter. Cuffee curled his feet under him on the seat and looked cunning and without warning commenced a song, 'nothing could be finah, than to be in your vagina, in the mo-o-orning'. The rest of it fell upon appalled ears and at its closure he rose and bowing asked them to excuse him, if he had in any way troubled them, it was owing to the peculiar circumstances in which he found himself, and left the carriage.

'Is your friend ill?' the German student asked with great tolerance for the insults he had suffered. Gibbon nodded. 'I would say it was a form of mental trouble. Psychology is a special interest of mine and I find his symptoms very interesting. His abnormal violence and the desire to be always the centre of the limelight, it is all very characteristic.' The man muttered something about a young hoodlum but Werner, who had suffered most, disagreed and went on to discuss Cuffee further, occasionally asking Gibbon for some information, saying yes, he thought so. From time to time

Cuffee lumbered along the corridor outside, once miming urination into the brandy bottle. Gibbon excused himself and went outside. Cuffee was by the window.

'You want to get a grip of yourself,' Gibbon said angrily. Cuffee turned round and changing the bottle from his right hand to his left hit Gibbon between the eyes with a long straight right which jolted his head back and made him stagger. By the time he got upright Cuffee had opened the toilet door and gone in. Gibbon tried to open it but couldn't.

'Peter, what's wrong, what's up with you?' There was no reply and he repeated the question. He thought he could hear water running and then clearly the sound of Cuffee being sick. He opened the door and went in. He was being sick into the basin. After a moment he straightened up.

'That's better,' he said.

'Peter, what's wrong?' Cuffee wiped his face with a paper towel.

'I was just thinking about a lot of things and I got angry.'

'What things?'

'Oh, me, Uta, an old man I saw. Things. I'm sorry I hit you.'

'That's all right. You've got me worried.'

'Don't worry Harry, it's just something inside me. I've got it all up now,' and he ran the taps to flush away the basin. They jolted and rolled in the little compartment and Cuffee handed over the bottle. Gibbon drank.

'You should wipe the neck,' Cuffee said, 'that's what happened to Thomas Wolfe, he didn't wipe the neck and he got influenza and later he got tuberculosis of the brain and later he got dead. They trepanned his old nut and it was all little tubercles. Nuff said. I used to think about all that stuff growing in my chest, green foliage in my old ventricle tree. Horrid. You die. That is the conclusion I have reached Harold. You see before you a clear-cut case of a man who has reached his first unaided conclusion. The best left hooker since Charley White Ernest called him, you see I'm a literary sort of chap under this casual crude exterior. My trouble is I'm too sensitive for the brute it would suit me to be. Gaston Rieux his name was, got a medal in the First World War which was a tidy old knacker up in itself.

Here we are Harold, you looking at me with your intelligent homo sapiens sort of face and me sitting here and it's all very mid-twentieth sanctuary, genuine slip of the tongue that, by the way, and we don't have a chance, neither of us. I mean you don't believe in owt, do you Harold. Not in owt worth believing in.'

'Love,' suggested Gibbon. Cuffee considered, requested the bottle, drank, reconsidered.

'All right Harold, I'll allow you to believe in love. You have the temperament, I feel. But you must not only believe in it, you must practise it.'

'I do.'

'You cannot love me Harold. I do not wish to be loved. It requires of me an energy of denial I cannot always conveniently summon up. If you love me, then love Ruth. Let me be Harold, will you. Watch out for me, and all that, but dedicate not your little self to Cuffee. Squires are dead wrong this mid-twentieth century, and knights may even pursue nought but neuroses, nary a grail be there between here and Bonn.'

'Would you not say you were in love with her?'

'No, I would not. Before her I was a prince, I cut slices off the world for sandwiches, the sun rose so I would see where I had left my cigarettes. But she and all the things she caused to be was when the world decided to tell me a word. That is the bit of the world I am committed to Harold, that is my dragon.'

'And she is your Princess.'

'Harold, they have deceived you, that is the new catch. Princesses are no longer saveable, they are in with the dragons and the wicked Kings and the turreted castle. Knight's no job at all nowadays, they all need chopping.'

'That's against the rules.'

'Too true it's against the rules. But see who cares.' Gibbon looked around. There was but himself and Cuffee, swaying, jolting, bounced from one wall to the other.

'I care,' Gibbon said. Cuffee swayed towards him.

'Harry Gibbon for God, that's how I'm voting next time.' And the movement of the train heaved them back against the door and they went into a tunnel. They held each other close and Cuffee's face was against his and his lips against his ear.

'If you start loving somebody Harry, they'll never let you stop. It's like a drug, it is a drug, it kills the pain of being alone, and the people who love, Harry, they don't want to stop, they can't stop, they've got all that much love in them and they're going to get rid of it so some poor bugger has to get loved. Promise me you won't do it to me. Promise. Promise me.'

'I promise.'

'Good. Sealed with loving kiss. Swalk' – and it lasted until the tunnel ended, whereupon they drew apart and looked somewhat awkwardly one at the other.

By the time they were in London and had got to Gerda's Cuffee was unwell. His temperature had gone up and he had a couple of bouts of sneezing that hurt his chest and made him cower up in his seat and hug the brandy bottle to his chest. He finished it in mid-Channel and threw it overboard with a cry of 'excalibur' and a lunge which had Gibbon grabbing for his waist.

Gerda was in and seemed unsurprised at their arrival. She helped Cuffee up the stair and while Gibbon was making a cup of tea she got Cuffee undressed and into bed. Then she got several codeine down him and he went to sleep, wheezing a little. Gibbon told her about his illness. Gerda listened without saying anything and then nodded. She took him through to the end room and showed him the bed. Suddenly Gibbon was very tired. He sat down and took off his shirt.

'Has he changed do you think, Harry?' She was a large, waiting woman, standing at the door looking at Gibbon as he removed his shirt. He looked up.

'I think he has Gerda. I don't know in what way, but I think he's changed.'

'I love him.'

'Yes. I hope it goes well.'

'Yes. You will be comfortable there. I'll see you in the morning, Harry. Thanks for bringing him back.'

'That's all right.' He lay for a while thinking before he

345

went to sleep, concentric, self-annihilating thoughts, bruising his mind into a dull ache which sleep when it came covered and no more.

When he woke the doctor had been and taken blood tests from Cuffee. Stolleman was in the kitchen with Gerda drinking coffee and smoking a panatella. Gibbon looked but Cuffee lay with his back to the door so he came out without saying anything.

'He's got some kind of virus the doctor said. We'll know a bit more after the blood samples come back.' Stolleman regarded him quizzically as he sat down.

'How are you, Harry. How was the trip?'

'Oh it was fine. I'll tell you all about it.'

'When I'm out of the way, is that it?' Gerda said from the stove. Gibbon smiled.

'No, not really. Just so much of it I can't fit into any sort of, well, doesn't make a lot of sense.'

'It doesn't make sense, Harry,' Stolleman said, 'not most of it. Come on, let's you and me go and have a drink, leave Gerda to wallow in domesticity.'

'Wait until he's had his breakfast can't you. You're a vicarious sex maniac.'

'Nonsense, I never touched a vicar in my life.' Cuffee's voice from inside, said,

'Oh yes, very droll, very droll.'

The Tavern was empty and dark after coming out of the sun. Stolleman had a lager and Gibbon a tomato juice. They sat up at the bar and Stolleman lit a cigar.

'You always smoked cigars?'

'When I could afford it. You never smoke?'

'No, my father was against it.'

'Show me one who isn't.'

'He said it was profaning the temple of the body.'

'Did he now?'

'Yes.' Looking at Stolleman, 'I'm worried about Gerda.' Stolleman did deft things to his cigar ash and drew on it.

'She's a big girl, Harry.'

'But she's in love with Peter.'

'So?'

346

'It can't be done, I mean he doesn't want to be loved.'

'Maybe he just doesn't want to be loved by you, or the people he's known up until now.' Gibbon seemed impressed by this.

'Maybe so. I just wouldn't like to see her get hurt.'

'Shut your eyes then. Go away. Gerda's been getting hurt all of her life. That's what makes her what she is, that's what gives her resonance. That's what makes her so good in bed. She's been hurt, and hurt again and again. And in between all those hurts she's been happy. She's a great woman. You let her get hurt, because there's nothing you can do about it anyway.'

'I suppose not. It's just, well Peter, he's strange.'

'Sure he is. He's not fit to flush her cistern. But like you were saying, things don't make sense. What else didn't make sense?'

'Nothing really. Oh that's daft really, I just met some people and felt things I'd never felt before.'

'You met Kimber?'

'Yes.'

'And—' Gibbon looked at him but Stolleman only nodded that he should reply.

'And, and I found out that I wasn't queer. Only I didn't find out with a great sudden kind of certainty. I just sort of came to the conclusion that, after all, I didn't think I was.'

'Better'n a poke in the eye with a sharp stick. So what are you going to do now?' The question brought Gibbon's head up again.

'Why do you ask that? I mean, should I do something now?'

'If you've something to do. Me, I'd paint. Cuffee, he'd screw something, which if he only knew it is the same thing. What will you do?'

'Yes. Well, I'll go and see somebody I know.'

'A girl?'

'Yes, and if that doesn't work I'll go back to Greenock.'

'You've just come from there.'

'I have to go back some time.'

'Why, I thought your folks were dead.'

'They are, but Greenock's where I come from. I have to

347

go back there. Don't you ever feel, well lost, because you don't want to go home? I mean that's how you know where you are isn't it, because you know where you come from.'

'Some accident of geography you're talking about, any-place, sometown. It's what you do, what you make, that's the thing.' Gibbon was silent for a moment, then he smiled, without looking up.

'Well, everybody sees it different ways, Michael,' he said.

After dinner Gibbon went on the Heath. A great field, bubbed and bronded, dotted with folk. A small wind ac-complished fluences of green, running swales, glossal licks, sent the spinnacles of dandelion drifting above the con-versations in the grass, sibilants and labials, vegetal and human. Bent stems rank with sap, close askings, sunitch on a vernal crust. Bright fritillary flutterbys pursued by bark-ing dogs. On the hill kite fliers reached up into the sky with their taut trembling twine, watching the loft quivering frames, coaxing altitudes out of them. There was a tele-scope on a tripod looking away over the city, beyond which in a haze there seemed to be hills. To the left High-gate, a steep-roofed pitch, set with a pale green dome. Gib-bon watched the kites, some of them very high up, in their own domain of current and lift, almost free, like the thoughts of their owners whose faces Gibbon noted, up-turned, open with rapt care, self-transcendent, unwinding out of themselves the long bellying rise of cord, up, up, up to where their aspirations achieved precarious poist.

She lay on the bed and felt him moving on her, feverish and damp, her arms around his neck, holding him to her breast. His bare feet on the floor, toes spread straining, ten-don stretched and slack in a flexing pushup into where re-sponse thickened as he thudded home time and time and time again while she coddled and cuddled and clung in a waist high leg lock, allowing him no outcome from the crutch close morticing join at the delirial vulva, repeated sweet sheathing viscal lunges, she unseeing now blind to all but the innermost dark where shapes were summoned at each delve, short, shorter, shortening strokes and ignas-cent now a small seedling of distant light below and above and beyond her exfoliates, whitens at each injection of fuelling flesh, a light in which nothing is seen, a self-luminant expansion of sense as she waits hearing his thunderous effort of hoist, inth by inth, the normous load, leaden molten rising outblow that releases him in seizures, twitching in gorspasm he thrutched and splayed while in her, salmon live, his seed lept, shoaling upwards towards her welcoming interiors.

Gibbon lay in the long grass and smelled the smell of crushed stalks and of the earth. Over his shoulder, up on the hill, the kites were still in the sky. Earth dreams and air dreams. Gibbon looked through the grasses smelling the old, unchanged odour of growth. Above him, quivering frails, the kites reached blindly for zenith. He was torn by these old adversaries, stretched upon their antithetic urgings, the sensuous sluttish suck of the earth, draining him, prone old whore, short timing him into the green sloth of inertia; and the yearning, longing upward motion of the mind for some pinnacle of vision from which the manifold contours of the world will resolve into a pattern, a map of meaning whereon the traveller may plot his path to haven.
'You will not find it down on any map,' he said to himself, then aloud – 'True places never are.' And he rose and brushed himself off and started back.

Cuffee was asleep and Gerda bathed, standing in the bath and sluicing herself over, her hair caught up on her head and her shoulders and breasts confected with the soap sheen of lather. As the water flowed over her the flesh seemed to shimmer and melt and her nipples made little spigots that caught bubbles and dripped soapy drops. Her eyes were closed and as she put her head back a pulse fluttered in her throat. Satined with water she stood, the full body pendulous with pleasure and the knowledge within her of her lover's leavings growing up like a flower towards the sun.

'Do you mind?' Cuffee shook his head and smiled.
'Of course not. What did I tell you on that train?'
'Yes, I know, but this is different.'

'When will you go?'

'Tonight. Gerda says she can get me a lift.'

'You scared?'

'Yes.'

'I don't know what to say, Harry. I can't promise her to you, if I could I would.'

'No, I don't want that. I just want to know you don't resent me.'

'Of course I don't resent you.'

'You might be, well jealous, you know what I mean, your sister . . .'

'No, I won't be jealous. Maybe I'll get to know what Ruth's like. Lost a friend and found a sister. If it works out will you stay in Manchester?' Gibbon looked perplexed.

'I haven't thought that far. I wouldn't mind coming back to London. Oh, it's all in the air just now.'

'Well I'm pleased. You know, pleased. She likes you.'

'You're going to stay with Gerda?'

'That's what it feels like.'

'I'm pleased about that too.' And Gibbon held out his hand and they clasped.

Gerda's ex-husband was a rather short man with one shoulder, his left, carried slightly higher than the other. He had a pale diffident manner and stammered slightly in the middle of long sentences, to obviate which he tended to speak in a rather clipped way that made for an awkward military manner. Gerda had rung him up to ask him if he would drive Gibbon to Manchester that night and he seemed very pleased to be able to help, coming straight over in a small, off-white M.G. He was wearing a new suede jacket which Gerda remarked.

'That's new. And expensive, sold a Rolls have you?'

'Sold a damn nice Alvis though. Chap drove it out of the window. Straight to Aberystwyth. Sent me a telegram. Bloody good car.'

'You'll drive carefully tonight.'

'Course I will. Some nice stretches. M.1's bloody good road.'

'You're a sweet, Terry, to take him.'

'Pleased at the chance of a spin.'

Gibbon was ready and went in to say good-bye to Cuffee.

'And Terry.'

'Yes.'

'Be careful on the way back, won't you.'

'Of course, Gerda.'

'Well, see you do.' And she put her hand against his cheek tenderly. He smiled and touched her wrist lightly. Then Gibbon came out and they went down to the car.

After they had made love they lay, smoking, the room soft with light from the oil lamp.

'Are you sure it's good for you?' she asked him, 'in your condition.' He nodded without opening his eyes.

'I'm just beginning to feel right.'

'What happened then?'

'Oh, I'll tell you some time.'

'Do you mind if I get pregnant?'

'Not if you don't.'

'You won't feel trapped—' He looked at her.

'Not if you don't.' Gerda smiled and came closer.

'What will happen to Harry?' His mouth was into her hair.

'I don't know. He'll survive.'

'Is he in love with your sister?'

'He wants to be. Harry's a great man for love.'

'Yes, you can feel it?' She shifted round so that he could see her face.

'I wish you had known me when I was eighteen.'

'Why?'

'I was beautiful. You cannot imagine how beautiful I was. I was so beautiful that I used to cry sometimes to think about it. Can you believe that?'

'Yes, I can believe that.'

'You can't, I know. But it was true. It was the war. Everything became a little more so. I was a very pretty girl until the war, then I was beautiful. That's how it was. We lived in Southampton. I joined the WAAFS. Everybody joined something. War can be an idyll, you know, quite idyllic. I don't know why I joined the WAAFS. Not the uniform

351

anyway. I went to Sussex. To an air-field. I was there during the Battle of Britain. It was all quite unreal in a way. Rather beautiful, but quite unreal. That's when I met Terry. He was a fighter pilot. I can't describe those days, not so they sound real. Do you know Sussex?' Cuffee shook his head. 'It was in the summer. A hot summer it was, in Sussex. It's very rich down there, the country. Green and lush. The pilots used to sit out on the runways playing chess or cards or writing letters and the alerts would come and they would run to their planes and they were up in the air, all in minutes. Unreal it was, especially for them. And we would watch. And although you were frightened, because you knew everybody up there, it was beautiful too, looking up into the blue sky and the vapour trails and the distant noises they made and much louder than they were bees or a cow or "Music While You Work". And the kids from the French Convent School going along the lanes, all in those odd clothes French children wear. Oh it was quite unreal, made you feel funny. And for them after all that terror up in those little machines, to come down and the country just the same, quiet and green, and they talked that argot everybody made a fool of afterwards in all those rotten pictures that came out only it was easy to understand then why they talked like that because if they didn't then they wouldn't have talked at all, there wasn't ever anything like that, one minute at peace and the next at war, there is no way the mind can become used to that, can accept it as normal. So they became men who could live with it. Not real men, not real men in touch with real life, but unreal men in touch with the only life they knew. And we helped them. As I said I was beautiful then. I was glad I was so beautiful. I used to lie on my back in those Sussex fields and be grateful that I was beautiful. And those men, those unreal men, became a little more real every time it was over. I don't know how many men made love to me, if you want to call it making love, they just broke down on my body and if they wept we pretended it was because the night was beautiful or I was beautiful or we were in love. And we were, too, in a way. Not love with a capital but love of being here, alive. Many many men, some just boys not much older than I was, and
352

many of them died. I've held them close in the night and next day they were charred and smashed. When things like that happen you change, you can't help but change. I never slept alone in those days, I felt I was beautiful and my body was sane even though I certainly wasn't and I gave my sanity to every man who asked or hoped or wished. Then I began to get dreams, I dreamt I was holding a man and all of a sudden he was all smashed up and I woke up in terror. I think maybe I was going to crack up then only I got news that my parents had been killed in Southampton and that helped me in a way. I couldn't remember what they looked like, not for days, everything was so unreal, and I didn't cry or feel anything then one night I was at a dance and I went out with Terry and when we were making love I started to cry and I cried until I thought I would never stop, and Terry held me and he didn't say anything, not even "what's wrong", nothing, just let me cry myself empty, for every-body and everything. Then he took me back. I think that's why I married him. When he asked me I didn't really know what to say only I remembered the night I had been crying and how he just held me and rocked me back and forth, not saying a word, and I said all right. It was a mistake of course but how could it have been otherwise, there wasn't anything steady you could look at and say that will be there tomorrow. I could have married fifty men and they would all have been mistakes of one sort or another. Terry wasn't the worst, I liked him then and I like him now. But I couldn't love him. When you've loved a race, a species, it's hard to get used to loving just one member of that species.'

After a moment Cuffee said,

'Why are you telling me?'

'Just so you'll know, in case you ever wonder about me.'

The car ran in a roar of engine and wind and tyre noise, ran fast in the dark with the long probes of the headlights skimming ahead. The lane marks clicked past and the coun-try whirred dimly alongside, trees inching up then rushing past with a noise like all their leaves torn off, across the fields an occasional lighted window as the car sped low to the road and the wind drubbed in the canvas. It ran and ran and ran and Gibbon watching saw on the side the lights of the lorries and their great high squared bulks and Terry, lit from below by the small glow from the instrument panel, smiling a steady little smile of concentration as he drove. There were stars and away in front, low in the sky, a half moon that edged some slow clouds. The smell of the night land damp and cool, spread away on either side as they fled on through the enormous dark, tunnelling down through the cool night, their speed a live throbbing knowledge, their onslaught on time and distance an exhilaration, a joy.

'She's running well don't you think?'

'Like a bird,' Gibbon said.

'Damn good little car. Like a bird. Yes. Marvellous night for a drive. Drive yourself?'

'No. No, I don't.'

'No, some people don't. Even some who do. Know what I mean?'

'You drive well.'

'Yes. Always have. Best thing I do. Some people shoot, or play games. I drive.'

'Do you still fly?'

'Now and then. Not the same though. Flying's damn good. But it's not for the likes of me.'

'How do you mean?'

'Oh, a man flies he c-can't h-help feeling good. Can't help. Like a drug it is. When you have t-to c-come down. You have to. Life on the ground's n-not the same. Nothing like flying. Think I'd just d-damn well s-stay up. Till there wasn't any m-more gas. Then I'd come d-down all right. Have to, eh?' Glancing at Gibbon, smiling.

'Does it all make sense then when you're flying?'

'Better still. Doesn't matter. Doesn't give a damn. Like a bird. Shame to spoil it really.' Gibbon felt the wind on his fingers, like ten thousand yards of cold velvet. Terry urged the car forward and the noises heightened, lost their edges and blurred into the one triumphant roar, onward and ex-ultant, headlong, eight-five on the straight, winding up road and scattering the stars. Gibbon smiled into the dark and let himself go.

'Ruth,' he said into the wind, and the name flattened sweetly on his lips.

CHAPTER TWENTY-SIX

She wasn't asleep when the buzzer went and she lay for a moment trying to convince herself that it was Maureen who had forgotten her key. The buzzer went again and she got up. It was nearly half past one. She went out and knocked on Maureen's door. Again, and her buzzer sounded and at the same time Maureen called out sleepily, 'who's that?'

'It's all right, it's Ruth. Sorry to bother you,' and went into the kitchen. It must be him then. She'd seen him once since Sunday, standing across the road and she had wanted to go across and speak to him but instead had quickened her step and hurried up the stairs.

In the kitchen she put the kettle on, waiting all the while for the buzzer to sound again. Maybe it was her father, come up to say he had discovered Eldman and her mother together. Maybe he had killed them. The unreality made her shake her head. Poor Mervyn Feeley. Maureen's door opened and she came out, wrapped in a candlewick dressing-gown.

'What's wrong?'

'My buzzer went. I thought you might have forgotten your key.'

'It must be that sex maniac' – and Ruth regretted ever telling her. 'You ought to phone the police. You really should Ruth, he might be dangerous.'

'Oh, I don't want to phone the police Maureen. I'm sorry I woke you.'

'That's all right. I could do with a cup of tea. Will I get some biscuits?'

'No, not for me thanks.'

'Make it strong. Won't be a mo.' There was a strong dorm feast element in Maureen she was only beginning to notice. Now that she and Tom were lovers it had released in her a desire for the exchange of confidences and much talk of a technical nature which Ruth found embarrassing simply because Maureen refused to refer to specific parts or functions by names, but talked of 'his, you know' and 'that bit'. These conversations were taking place at night, over cups of tea and had already reduced Ruth to lies about her sexual experiences, attributing some of her sensations to anonymous lovers, lest Maureen take the bit in her teeth and describe her sex acts in detail all for the sake of her clueless friend. What she did glean, however, was not altogether comforting. Maureen spoke of her lovemaking in such a way as to remind Ruth strongly of something she knew about, without ever quite seeming to be the same thing. She realised that this was because Maureen still thought of it as something being done to her by another, strange person, while for Ruth the only intimacies she had ever known had been with someone whose identity scarcely seemed distinct from her own, indeed someone of whom she conceived herself to be the extension, the continuation. She could remember long periods of a certain 'rapport', usually when in the country, as they padded along, he ahead and her eyes rarely leaving him so that the sensations of walking and running, brushing through the grass, ducking under branches, all seemed his sensations and his awareness. His muscling in act of penetration was akin to this in many ways, a heightened experience which they had between them. It had caused her surprise to have to consider Maureen's point as to whether 'they got more out of it than we did', that perhaps a man's sensations were quite distinct from those of a woman, and once considered it seemed only too obvious that there must exist vast gulfs of feeling between going into and being gone into. The predominant impression she was left with was of herself lying encased in some kind of shell on the outside of which the male animal crawled, seeking the fissure through which he might goad her into response. It was a disturbing, insect-like vision of sexual relations to which Mervyn Feeley had added a dimension of horror. The thought of him waiting below was in itself a kind of erotic overture, for now that she had commenced to think of the sex act as an acquisitive, prying masculine event, the mere presence of men in the street with organs concealed in their trousers made the whole day a courting of violation.

The tea was that precious event, a perfection. Her absent-minded sugaring must have been accurate to the grain. She was grateful she had filled the largest cup. Maureen had come back with a packet of jaffa cakes and was going on about Ruth's duty in reporting this man who kept following her.

'He doesn't keep following me,' Ruth said and sipped her tea. Maybe he does though.

'Ringing your bell at one o'clock in the morning, that's following you.' She was suddenly curious to know what he would do. Would he exhibit himself again, or say something obscene. It was rather terrible to wonder about such things. Maybe she was getting 'kinky', as Maureen always said about Tom's several sexual fetishes.

'Let's go down and if he's there we'll call the police,' she said, not really intending to do so but wanting Maureen's company at the front door.

'Don't be daft Ruth, just call them.'

'They'd come over and get the whole house up, and maybe he wouldn't be there. Let's go down and see. He won't do anything if there's two of us.'

'What if he does that thing again?'

'You don't have to look.'

'All right then;' and immediately Ruth regretted it, felt she was somehow betraying the passion of Mervyn Feeley by this desire to titilate herself. At least he was risking arrest, disgrace, even imprisonment, while she was preparing for some little sexual thrill, safely protected from consequence.

'No, he'll be gone by now.' Before Maureen could speak the buzzer went again and Ruth's heart lurched in panic.

'That's him,' Maureen said in a whisper.

'I'll go,' Ruth said. 'You stay here.'

'I'd better come with you.'

'No, it's all right, I'll go. I'll tell him if he doesn't go away I'll send for the police.' Maureen was reluctant to let her go alone but was almost as reluctant to accompany her, so Ruth, finishing her tea, and without knowing quite why taking a jaffa cake, went out and down the stairs. On the way down she heard her buzzer again and the knowledge that even before she opened the door to confront him he was there, pressing his finger on her bell, real in his own world before it overlapped into hers, this made her suddenly excited, a kind of nervous sympathy with the fact of other people's lives, existing independent of her own. She opened the door almost welcomingly, eager to confront him, this figment of her mind who was at the same time perhaps the most positive admission of her own reality, this man for whom she had become an obsession.

Gibbon was just going back down the path. He turned and said,

'Oh, hello Ruth.' She felt faint and leaned against the door.

'Harry, is that you Harry?'

'Yes it's me, Ruth.' And she could feel the coldness of the night air and Gibbon had come towards her, bigger than she remembered him and he stood in front of her and there was a smell from him, a night smell and petrol and a faint sweaty man smell and she realised she was holding his hands which were warm, surprisingly, and large and which now took hers and he had kissed her knuckles, he had a small stubble and his lips moved against the back of her hand, quiet and strongly accented so that she had to put her head close to him and somehow that made it dark and he was saying,

'I've come up on my own because, this is something maybe I should wait to say but I want to tell you how I love you and if, well if I should have waited well I'll go back to London or something only I wanted to tell you as quickly, Ruth, Ruth do you hear me.'

'Yes Harry, come upstairs.'

'Wait, I have to tell Terry.' And he went down the path to where at the kerb a sports car was sitting. Ruth turned into the house, aware for the first time of the lateness of the hour and the dangers of awakening Mrs Pendleton. The car roared outside and she heard Gibbon call thanks and then he was in. She shut the door and said shush, then took his hand and led him up the stairs. Maureen was waiting for her and she looked at Gibbon in amazement. Ruth introduced them and they went into the kitchen. It was all very crowded and Gibbon's bag got in the way. He was looking at her steadily and she realised she was avoiding his gaze. She took his hand again and he followed her into the room.

'I'm glad you've come Harry. I've been wanting you to;' and thought it was true in the very heart of things, maybe she hadn't known it but she had because when you came to think of it who else could have come. She took his face in her hands and drew him down to her mouth. He did not hold her until they were kissing then his arms tightened and pulled her up and she felt her feet come up almost clear of the floor. His mouth on hers was firm and unmoving and she had the sense that he held her awkwardly. All this re-assured her, made her feel in control, older and more ex-perienced and about then she realised that they would be lovers that night, which didn't frighten her but made her see herself from very high up and him too, big, slow, ten-derly clumsy Harry Gibbon and only then did she feel affec-tion for him and the first tremblings of happiness and his hands were cupping her now purposefully and she spoke his name, still against his mouth.

It was all rather strange. Nothing was said but he sat on the edge of the bed and undressed, slow, habitual move-ments, while she much more quickly was naked and under the clothes. His back was to her, broad and smooth and he took off his shoes and socks and then his trousers. He didn't wear any underpants she noticed. Who was he anyway, this big slow person who was preparing to come into her bed.

'Do you mind if we leave the light on?'

'I'll light a candle.' And she got up and put on her robe and looked for the candles. They were in the drawer with her skipping ropes. She touched the candles and thought 'phallic' and smiled. He was in bed, sitting up, his arms folded, slightly ridiculous. She lit a candle and put it on the chest of drawers and another on the table. Then she put the light out. He was looking away so that she could get in un-witnessed.

'Harry.'

'Yes.'

'I don't mind you seeing me' – and she saw that the tears were running down his cheeks and his mouth had to be held by his teeth, all the while he was sobbing quietly.

'What is it Harry, oh Harry, darling. Harry, what's wrong?' and she pulled him down to her shoulder and felt warm, then cooling, his tears find between her breasts.

'I was thinking, thinking about everything and I just couldn't help it, I just couldn't help.' And his sobs prevented him from going on, she wiped his face with the sheet and he said thanks several times and then lay back looking at the ceiling, every now and then gulping. After a moment he began to shiver and she pulled the bedclothes up and lay down close to him. For a time he remained silent and she could feel him tremble against her.

'I'm sorry,' he said finally, 'I couldn't help it. I was just thinking, oh about hundreds of things really, trying to see how I came to be here, and it all seems so, oh, so accidental.' And he shook his head with a kind of dismay at the haphazard of it all.

'But you are here Harry, that's the main thing.'

'Yes. Yes I am, amn't I.' And to her curious realization he was actually asking this last so that she put her hand on his face and said,

'Yes Harry, you are.' He closed his eyes at the touch and brought his face close to her shoulder so that her hand went round on to his back, where by some instinct it began to clap him, just behind the shoulder blade, a slow heartbeat clapping that comforted her as much as it appeared to comfort him.

'I can remember my mother clapping me like that,' he said, 'anyway I can remember the clapping even if I can't actually remember her doing it, but it was her and when she was clapping me like that it seemed all right. Do you know what I mean?' All without opening his eyes and she nodded and he went on. 'It all seemed safe, and when I used to wake on a Sunday morning I would lie in bed and hear them at their breakfast in the kitchen, their voices and the noises of the dishes and the knives and it all sounded far away though it was just through the wall and that all seemed safe too. But after my mother died nothing ever really seemed safe again, not like it had been. Do you think that's silly, Ruth?' And he opened his eyes to ask this.

'No Harry, I don't think it's silly. It was the same for me,

360

only it was my skipping ropes. Things happen, that's all. Things happen and everything changes.'

'I suppose so.' They lay on a moment and then his next movement, casual though it was brought them flat together and asserted in a whole host of pressures and yields their respective polarities. He was big and smooth and his body had no joints or muscles or features, a large limber bulk, rounded and warm and heavy that she set her small open palms against in tentative zones of discovery, the hub of his shoulder, the boss of his breast, a mounded hip. She wasn't excited and she could feel no current of excitement from him, instead she was calm, calm and waiting and thinking all the things about a man doing it to a woman only detached and calm and she waited for him to begin the possessive movements of man-sex but his face was in her neck and his arms around her and he seemed to be speaking against her flesh or kissing her so she reached down, long smooth sculpts of flesh and found him, oddly lolling, improbably lax.

'Harry,' and he clasped her tight. 'Harry, oh Harry love.' And her words and her hands upon him brought a sigh from his mouth against her neck and a swift tumouring from which in decorum she withdrew her touch.

Now she thought of her brother and their lovemaking in the gone ago unrecallable past and of her mother's and Robert Eldman's in the lost, hopeless present and of Harry Gibbon and hers in the immediate, distant future and the terrible compulsion of this act, this many-motived ritual, assailed her, of the people all over the world who were assuming these ungainly shapes to force through the flesh some ache of love or wince of loneliness, some tortion or surrender, some demand or compliance, grappling together as the world spun through space, clinging close for fear they fall for ever through loveless night, and in the midst of his fumblings she took him and placed him and in a low throbbing voice 'there' and 'yes there' and 'there' and 'there' and 'there', the demonstrative adverb of her love repeated again and again in a syntax of rarest compassion.

And afterwards they talked, or rather he talked and she

lay close to his heart, hearing in one ear the deep blood thuds while into the other fell, scattered at first, then becoming richer and more certain, his recall: of taking his father's tea to the shipyard in a blue enamel can with a sock round to keep warm and they sat in the sawmill on the big sliced logs and the smell of wood and saw-dust and resin and when his father took off his cap there was a mark from it around his brow as though his head had a lid on it like the blue enamel can from which his father poured into the lid for me and drank from the can himself strong tannic golden-bronze milkless and ate rolls with wersh penny-tasting tomatoes and told him as they shared the different kinds of wood, oak and ash and maple and spruce, larch, beech and the different sorts of pine and mahogany and teak, which his father called 'tick' and that would not burn, and greenheart, which he never heard of again, and when he asked the undertaker if it could be made in greenheart he said he'd never heard of it but oak was excellent and he could have it fumed which gave a nice effect, so maybe there wasn't any such wood or such tree, like there wasn't any green oak tree and he smiled at that, saying blessed are the green in heart for they shall not pine nor oak, as in a kind of joke, and went on about it being a sandy bay or a sunny knoll though the song claimed its roots still lingered by the square but that must have been a long time ago for his grandfather couldn't remember it and he could tell of when the James Watt Dock wasn't built but went in green meadows, cow browsed, to the river's edge.

The words, rolling together with the accent, and the images evoked, and the unfailing strophe of his heart drugged and dimmed her mind into a luminous certainty of his nearness, however fleeting or fragile it might be.

In the morning he was still there, a large sleeping man in her bed. As she lay beside him quietly, not long awake, she tried to find if in her something had changed, if she was reborn or liberated. All there had been was, just before consciousness claimed her, one of those tinges of well-being that as a child had been engendered by Christmas or the first day of holidays or sometimes even the sense of the morning bedroom floating with motes and golden light, a thereness seen with a single eye, not yet shattered into the multiple fracture of the mind, looking a long look until, inexorable, the room crackled and wrinkled and with a noise of names splintered into fragments.

Her alarm clock tried to brazen her out of bed but she cut it off in mid clangour. Gibbon however had come awake and rolled over on his side, pressing her in the narrow bed.

'Hello,' he said. 'You all right?'

'Yes, Harry, I'm fine.' And in the midst of his embrace thought that she was, if not fine beyond the dreams of avarice, at least no longer empty, no longer threatened by the migraine of empty aching boredom. Now something, something at last, after all the nothing, was going to happen.

They spent the morning in bed, talking. She got Maureen, who was avid with curiosity, to phone Miss Armitage and plead illness for her. Then after breakfast she got back in beside him and he talked about the trip, mainly about how Cuffee had affected him, and a bit about an American writer and about Gerda with whom, as he put it, Cuffee was now lodging. She found nothing about Cuffee's activities really troubled her, she wasn't jealous in any way that she could recognize, perhaps only that she had been left out of so much.

She decided to spend the afternoon in going over to Salford and enquiring for Miss Patricia Mullen. She still had a strong curiosity concerning the recipient of those weekly ten bobs. Harry knew nothing about it. Cuffee had never mentioned the girl to him. It was bright and rather blowy and she took his hand and walked very quickly, stealing quick looks at him in the light and space of outdoors to get that sense of him in proportion, that awareness of his body which a room obliterated. His movements she noticed were part of a continuum, one action blending into the next through a kind of slow dissolve, letting the edges of a particular motion blur and fade while the subsequent statement evolved. He handed her on to a slowly moving bus and she

363

dropped her glove. Picking it up he seemed to move very slowly only when he straightened up he was already running and his jump on to the platform let him go inside without checking his momentum. She was delighted with this gratuity and covered her smiles of gratification by putting her head on his shoulder.

They asked in the Post Office for Patricia Mullen and were directed to a rather severe-looking lady in a flowered smock. She was rather hesitant about divulging information but Ruth explained that the weekly payments were due to stop soon and she would like to make some new arrangements.

'Well, all I can tell you is that Patricia comes in to collect it on a Friday, about half past four usually, after school I suppose.'

'What age is she?' Gibbon asked.

'About eleven.' They exchanged glances and Gibbon went on.

'There's no other way we could contact her?' The lady assessed his facial character, then Ruth's. She debated a moment with herself before saying,

'Patricia goes to St Theresa's school on Mount Vernon Street. You should be able to contact her there. Or perhaps you'd like to come back tomorrow.' They thanked her and said they would try the school.

St Theresa's was a large blackened building with netting round the playground and courts marked for ball games on the speckled asphalt. High up in a niche on the face of the building a whitened icon of Our Lady. They went in and across the playground. A girl in a royal blue cardigan and red stockings ran out and nearly bumped into Gibbon. They asked her if she knew Patricia Mullen. The girl nodded and then ran off into the school. Inside there was a smell of disinfectant overly diluted in water and a multitudinous hum of voices and desks and feet and doors. They stood at the foot of a flight of stone stairs and looked about for someone in authority. Ruth thought it strange they should be here, in this school, standing feeling slightly odd and ill at ease. Surely two lovers of such brief duration should be lying alone somewhere telling each other mutual delectations. It seemed somehow apt and moving that they were in fact doing nothing of the sort. She stopped a little closer to him and noticing he winked and put his hand on her shoulder.

'Are you looking for me?' And the child, the straight fair hair and the quick scrutiny of her strange violet eyes, stood on the flight above them.

'Are you Patricia Mullen?' The girl nodded, looking steadily at Ruth.

'I'm Peter's sister, Ruth Cuffee.' She almost took a step forward but checked herself and said,

'Is he back yet?'

'He's in London,' Gibbon said. 'I was with him, we're just back.'

'You're the one from Scotland, you sent him the letter.'

'That's right.' She looked at them a moment longer.

'Wait and I'll get my books.'

'Can you come right now, I mean is that all right?' Ruth asked.

'Yes, that's all right. She won't miss me,' and she was gone up the stairs, to reappear in a moment and come two at a time down, carrying her books in a belt. She ran past them and beckoned to follow. They went quickly after her and out into the playground. Here Patricia took their hands and walked demurely across the open space, looking up at Gibbon once and saying in a grave voice,

'School is a bastard.'

Patricia took them down the canal and they sat on a bench. She asked several questions about Cuffee, how long he would be in London, where he had been, was he worried about the cats. Then she said,

'Did he tell you much about me?'

'A bit,' Gibbon said.

'Like what?'

'Well, about how you looked after the cats and you were friends.'

'We're engaged,' she said.

'Oh, he didn't tell me that.' Patricia looked down, frowning.

'No. Well he doesn't know, not exactly that we're engaged. But I've got a ring.' She fished inside her dress and brought up a string with a ring on it. It had a small diamond type stone set in a claw. 'That's a real diamond,' she said, and untied a knot in the string and put the ring on the appropriate finger. She looked at Ruth. 'I know it isn't official until he asks me,' she said. Ruth smiled and looked at Gibbon.

'Well, he will, once he knows you've got the ring.'

'I'm not so sure. I don't think I'm his type,' and she took the ring off and put it back on the string.

'Is that skipping ropes in your books?'

'Yes. You want to skip?'

'Please.' Patricia pulled out the rope which was knotted at each end and shook out the kinks in it. Then she gave it to Ruth who said thank you and stood up.

'It's years and years since I've skipped,' she said to Gibbon and she took a few paces from them.

'It's all changed,' she thought. The grey canal and the bare earth and that serious little child and Harry and these ropes with no handles. It's not the same. You can't expect to skip now, not here with everything changed. But the rope when she twirled it made that same light, firm 'thwick' on the ground and she found herself lifting her feet exactly as she used and walking then a little quicker going down the tow path and although everything was different it was the same feeling as she danced on one foot then the other, the whirr of the rope around her and the regular 'thwick' on the earth beneath her.

They looked after her as she went spinning away along the canal, her reflection keeping her company and occasional little ripples spreading out from pieces of grit flicked into the water by the ropes. Patricia watched her critically for a time then said, without looking up,

'She's good for her age,' and Gibbon smiled and leant forward on his knees, bringing him level with Patricia's face.

'I love her,' he said. The girl looked at him steadily and then away. Then she nodded,

'She's a good skipper.'

Ruth when she stopped could see them, heads together, talking. She skipped back towards them, at the centre of her turning world.

CHAPTER TWENTY-SEVEN

MacIndoe had a shooting brake that immediately bore witness to his status as a family man. Moseby sat on a small teddy bear with chewing gum matted on its chest. There were comics in the dash-board shelf and on the floor. The *Beano* still seemed concerned with all the creatures Moseby remembered from his own days. He browsed nostalgically, thinking at the same time that children take in a lot of old rubbish. MacIndoe drove with the concentration of the unconsolably nervous motorist, talking to himself about his fellow road users. Moseby watched him and wondered how any one man made such a compound fuck up of life in such a short time. MacIndoe was thirty-ish. He must have done most of the irremediable work in the last ten years. For some reason the *Beano* reminded him that he wasn't exactly without problems himself. A reassuring glance at MacIndoe however calmed the dis-ease.

The house was biggish, pseudo Adam, with Tuscan columns, painted all over battleship grey and the door which was open led into a large tessellated hall in which stood a small and unkempt girl child with a loosely pinned nappie. She saw MacIndoe and ran, knock-kneed and screaming into the back of the house.

'That's Sharon,' MacIndoe said.

'A daughter of yours?'

'Oh yes. Only have the one daughter.' A cat came downstairs and hesitated on the bottom step. Then noises from the back decided it and it went needling out past them. There was an odour Moseby detected, partly food and partly children and part cat and then something else which bound them together into this distinctive aroma. MacIndoe was calling 'Nancy' and a voice answered from upstairs and then a cistern sounded and Nancy MacIndoe come downstairs, drying her hands on her apron. She was not tall and had longish browny hair that was almost to her shoulders and curled slightly at the ends. He noticed as he shook an undried hand that her legs were wide calved and short and had black scrollings of hair. She wore a grey cardigan buttoned back to front and from the location of her breasts seemed not to use a brassiere. As he followed her into the kitchen Moseby thought that when they go to seed the bourgeoisie really make a job of it.

Three of MacIndoe's five children were not yet at school. Sharon had mounted a high chair and trapped one of her legs below her, causing a low quiet whining. There was a muffled infant in a pram and sitting on the floor was a boy of about five, without trousers, who appeared to have wet in front of himself, where a number of toy soldiers, engaged in bayoneting and grenade throwing, dripped urine.

'He does that,' Nancy MacIndoe said, 'pees all over them. Says it's raining at the war.' His father smiled rather wanly at this instance of his son's imaginative flair and waved Moseby to a seat. Getting as far away from the boy as possible brought him close to Sharon who was augmenting her generally revolting appearance by allowing two clear drools of snot to reach her upper lip, whereupon, checking her crying for an instant, she licked swiftly up, from right to left and partially cleaned herself. Moseby tried to straighten out the leg she was sitting on but Sharon screamed so he let her be and sat down. MacIndoe was rubbing his hands together in the manner known to indicate relish and asked what was for dinner.

What was for dinner was stewing steak, done in the time-honoured manner, about an hour too long, and which immediately became string in Moseby's mouth. The gravy was viscous and brown and tasted of oxo burning. As he made the motions of eating and swallowing, an elaborate facial mime under guise of which he choked down the fibrous gobs, he stole an occasional glance at the cook who was listening to her husband who was talking to Moseby. She had a long nose, slightly flared at the nostrils and this and the somewhat protuberant eyes gave her a lacklustre agog look, a kind of constipated zest. Below these features her mouth was a different creature, a long thin upper lip and an absurdly pouting lower which established the rapid curvature of her chin. If it hadn't been for this curled lower

lip the face would have been a top-heavy, rather febrile, in-
tellectuals and Moseby would have thought her a totally
unattractive woman. As it was the mouth introduced a
further element, not in itself particularly fetching, but
making a simple reaction impossible.

MacIndoe was talking about the basic empiricism of the
English and how Cromwell was perhaps the best historical
example of it.

'His detractors call him an opportunist when in fact he
was merely embodying the deepest characteristics of his
race. You see it immediately if you compare him with
Charles, the man was the worst kind of metaphysician, the
hereditary kind. I'll bet you anything you like Charles the
First aroused in Cromwell exactly the same kind of feelings
as *The Sunday Post* does in me.' Moseby could see that
working its way into one of MacIndoe's lectures, all part of
his 'hip' approach to history. Since it was his turn to say
something he leaned forward so that Sharon was out of
vision and said,

'You don't think of Scotland being an empirical nation?'

'No, never. Existential mystics. Passionately concerned
with the world as our domain yet obsessed with the dream
of transcendence. That's what causes all the conflict about
the flesh, just the fact that we are so committed to our
bodies. Only all our avenues of transcendence have been
calvinist. That's why there's Scotsmen "doing" things all
over the world, because existence is so real to us. A York-
shire man's thrift is conservative, it's the preservation of
energy against some possible crisis or need. The Scotsman's
meanness is essentially dynamic, it's the world of things
savoured, possessed, controlled.' Very good, Moseby
thought. A right load of old rubbish. All that kind of chat
was a waste of energy. To keep the onus of comment from
himself, and also to see that fabulous lower lip in action he
turned to Nancy MacIndoe.

'I heard you had some rather original opinions about the
Scottish existential character.' She shook her head and
made a quick bite at her lip, releasing it to talk.

'No, Mac has a tendency to make theories out of quite
specific comment. I just said I thought the purest emotion

370

known to people like me was guilt. Only I call it geegs. But I never said people like me were Scottish or anything like that.' MacIndoe put in, eager to adjust this partial point of view,

'But that is very Scottish, guilt, wouldn't you say so John? Would he say so. Did he know. Edna didn't have any guilt. Harry Gibbon didn't. Balls, what did it matter what you said.

'I don't know. I don't know enough Scotsmen.' Then without knowing why he went on, 'but it's true for me.'

'Well there you are,' and the conclusive, proved right tone somehow seemed to lock him out of the glance of recognition that passed between Moseby and Nancy MacIndoe. It isn't, he thought, that she's giving me the eye, or is it. He wasn't sure that he wanted to be given the eye by Nancy MacIndoe. She had risen and cleared the table, putting out dessert bowls. Sharon had stopped crying and Moseby suddenly wondered at the silence of the boy on the floor.

'The boy's very quiet,' he said.

'Oh Donald doesn't speak,' MacIndoe said. Moseby didn't quite see what he meant and looked at him enquiringly. Nancy put a large bowl of chopped oranges in the middle of the table and turned to look at Moseby.

'He's deaf. He doesn't speak.' And again the look, whatever it was, between them.

'Oh, I'm sorry.'

'Yes, at first we thought he might be defective,' MacIndoe said. The oranges tasted, unbelievably, like oranges.

'How long have you had this house?' he asked.

'MacIndoe's folly? Oh, we bought it about four years ago. Never really got round to fixing it up properly. We thought about letting rooms but it's more trouble than it's worth.'

'Would you like to see the place?' she said.

'Yes, yes I would.'

'Mac, will you feed Sharon, there's a tin of baby food there on the dresser.' MacIndoe nodded and looked at Sharon who began to cry again. Her father looked at his wrist watch.

'I'll have to be starting back shortly,' he said. His wife turned back from the door and Moseby was rising for his place.

'My God man, it's only an eight-room house.' MacIndoe looked immediately abject.

'No dear, I didn't mean that, I was just saying . . .' but she had gone. He looked at Moseby and smiled, an unsuccessful affair. Moseby did a kind of shuffle with his eyes that let him look across MacIndoe's face without meeting his gaze.

'Won't be a minute,' he said.

She was waiting at the foot of the stairs and as he approached she went up. He followed, the wide heart-shaped calves filling his vision. She had a small branching of blue veins behind the knee. There was a worn red carpet on the stairs, which rumpled where the rods were missing. The wallpaper was painted over boss, brown cloacal paint with a dull shine as though the walls were wet. At the landing she stopped. He came up and stood beside her. The smell of oranges clung to her.

'Spacious stairways,' she said and turned up the stairs to the first floor proper. The landing window was in tinted glass and the light on the first hall had a diffuse, uncertain quality in which her face seemed suddenly softer and calmer. There was a large square hall and five doors opening off. 'This is the playroom,' she said, her voice flat and non-committal. She opened the door into a large bright room in which newspapers and bricks and bits of wood lay all over the floor. The wallpaper hung down in great peeling shards and here and there the lathe and plaster showed. There was a distinct smell of ordure and the dry dusty smell of broken mortar. Moseby looked and waited for some comment, some explanatory note on the advanced rearing of children. None forthcame.. He found himself nodding foolishly.

'Yes,' he said and stepped back. She moved to the next door.

'This is the children's bedroom.' There were two large beds in the middle of a green linoleum floor. Round the walls were heaped toys and books and children's clothes.

At the window, on a tripod, was a telescope. The room had been painted white. The effect was in its way rather impressive. Up to a height of about six foot there was a panel of smearings and scribblings, of daubs and marks. Moseby, old graffiti expert that he was, could pick out a few likely-looking images. He nodded and stepped back, this time looking at her. She seemed withdrawn, as though this were a chore forced upon her and not her own idea. The room directly facing the stairs was the bathroom. Moseby made no attempt to look in. There was that distinctive smell cigarette smoking in a toilet always leaves.

'Our bedroom.' Looked as though it had come straight out of the window of one of the big hire purchase firms' windows. A lilac carpet and a bedroom suite in pale wood covered with little eyes, two easy chairs with the great swollen lines that conjure up elephantitis of furniture. There was a standard lamp with a great pleated coolie hat shade. On the wall was a Gauguin reproduction.

'And this is Mac's study.' The books made it almost normal, only the waste paper basket was on the desk and its contents scattered over it. Moseby felt he was being kidded. She was playing some kind of game with him. He stepped back and smiled wryly.

'Nice place you've got here.'

'There's the attic.' My God, the attic. Just what this house needs. The stairs were steep and there was a handrail. He could see up her clothes. He was surprised that she didn't smell badly. She had opened the door to the back attic and switched on a light. It was nothing really, just a lot of old respectable attica, trunks and cases and an old chair and wicker baskets. She left him and went to the other. It was locked and there was a pause while she produced the key.

'This is my room,' she said. It was a long low gallery of a place, running the width of the house and obviously the centre partition had been knocked away for there were two fireplaces. The floorboards were showing and there was nothing in the room except an old chaise longue placed between the windows and a few feet out from the wall. She went now and sat on the end of this, feet apart and knees splayed. Moseby looked out of the window. There was a house directly opposite.

'Cuts off the view.' he said.

'Of what?' Moseby smiled.

'Yes, well that's a point.'

'Geegs Castle. What do you think of it?'

'Takes my breath away. I'm not sure I understand.'

'I'm sure you don't.' She got up and came over. For the first time he caught her scent, it came up to him as she stood about a foot away, looking round the corner of the cami-ceiling and out the window, a smell that was many smells, baby sick, the smell of milk, and of cooking and the smell of her body, with its folds and secretions and un-washed fragrances, a rich thrilling smell that he wanted to wallow in and breathe deeply, a smell he knew, the smell of his cabbage soul riddled with the maggots of imagin-ation. He reached for her but she stopped his hand and glanced at the door. The boy stood there, his baffled face set in a frown of incomprehension. With his left hand he plucked at his small drooping penis.

'Don't worry, Donald knows what's going on. Don't you pet?' and the child ran to her, burying his face in her lap.

'I wish I did.'

'Mac tells me you have a girlfriend in the city. Is that right?' Moseby nodded. 'Well, when you're through with her, and there's no rush mind you, I'd be pleased to see you some afternoons. I think we have a lot in common. Don't you?'

'I don't know.' She led the boy towards the door, holding his head close to her leg. Moseby followed her.

'Yes I think we have. Anyway it would be something to find out.' She stopped and looked at him. 'You're not like Mac at all. He thinks you are. He thinks you and he are of a kind. But it's not so. There's a kind of anarchism in you. I can feel it, waiting for a chance to blow everything up.'

Moseby preceded her down the stairs. MacIndoe was waiting in the hall.

'I really must get back. If you don't want to walk you'd better come along.'

374

'Sure, fine.' He said his thank-yous and good-byes to Mrs MacIndoe and shook the soft damp boneless hand again and she said it was nice to have met him and perhaps he would come again. Moseby got into the car and wondered how he could tell MacIndoe. Your wife's a nympho. Your wife's a nutter, and while he was thinking he realised that MacIndoe must know, there was no other way it could be, and he had to have brought Moseby along deliberately, for his wife to appraise and proposition. He got into the car and started it up. As they moved off he waved. Moseby didn't look back.

'Well,' MacIndoe said, 'what did you think of the family?'

He wouldn't go home immediately. He wanted a little time to think. Time to see it all clearly, get it all sorted out. His head was thick, congested with the commerce of thought, the breeding and bartering, the exchanges and usury of his rife rank imagination. The hills would be the place and a memory of them came to him, their arrested silences, the calm of the great land billows. Yes, the hills would do it, only he couldn't go there. That he couldn't only depressed him, yet it was his beckoning salvation. He was coming from the Central Station and not the West, going up Trafalgar Street and glancing in through the close there was framed in the cool deep stone a patch of green. Jesus ducking under the clothes ropes. He went in, not knowing why, then on impulse up the stairs, up to the top flat. There was a skylight but he couldn't reach it. He put on his spectacles and made prominent his briefcase and knocked on Duffy's door. After a moment a small woman with her arm in a sling came. Moseby excused himself for bothering her and explained that he was from the air-pollution department and he wanted to go on the roof to collect soot samples. Mrs Duffy was deaf and called out to her neighbour, Mrs Keogh to find out what the young man wanted. Moseby regretted the notion. Mrs Keogh, however, understood perfectly and brought him out a pair of step-ladders. He thanked them and climbed up and into the loft, urged by the women to watch himself. He stepped carefully across the joists to the roof skylight. It was heavy and had a long cleek to hold it open. He put his briefcase down and his glasses on top of them. Then he climbed through on to the roof. The ridge was about eight feet above and he stretched out, grasping the zinc spine and pulled himself carefully up, getting his right leg over and then slowly bringing himself upright.

The roofs, slate blue slopes, everywhere; and chimneys crowned and capped with cans, coloured lustrous bronzes and yellow orange and mocha and cream, soot layered, rust red and out of them lunting up in duns and greys and dimble blues, uplanguors of slow emotion, colly-spindills, culmes of soft ruth, smoke psalms, lum plumes, purled prayer drifts, and everywhere enormously high the great azure pend of heaven in which with its golden effulgence unimpaired by cloud the sun shone magnificent, heraldic blazon of day's dominion.

Dazzled and dazed he clung to the roof, assailed by the jewelled immediacy of this world of rooftops, the splendour of form and colour, a fabled landscape on which the sun seemed an intimate source, not the loft orb street-dwellers know. He was close to prayer, close to some evocation of the world as revealed to him, close to worship. He sat on, entranced, looking across a Greenock he had never guessed existed, not even from his window, high up as it was. It was the light, the overwhelming access of light. He was a dweller in darkness, in the most literal sense of that expression. His life seemed to be a set of dim interiors, the house of his parents, Joe Moffat's stick factory where so much of his obsessed sexual life had its roots, the dusk of that drawer with his hidden birth certificate, the escape into the dark of the old Central, the twilight between Edna's thighs. And now the inevitable corollaries finding a purest conclusion in Nancy MacIndoe, the black bloom of his guilt-ridden urge to nadir, to the pit, where surely some peace must wait the damned.

The only light in his life, light that shone across time undimmed, was the light of those bare, sun prone hills and that moment when, pulling her behind him, the headland had yielded vision of the sea, sown with light, stretching into the farthest distances of his yearning. And now, on top of Greenock, stunned with the volume of illumination, seeing in a hallucinatory clarity the meaning of his life and its inevitable outcomes, knowing at last, in that simple way that things come to be known beyond all dubiety, that he must leave, must go, escape, fly, find that freedom in which all life must be lived. Had not the town urged this on him without respite, like some great metaphor of the mind, the world beyond the province of the self, the true idea of transcendence that MacIndoe had garbled in his notions of national men.

Life as lived is allegory for life unborn, the mind in its embryonic dark is being born each maieutic moment, each time an external reference is made personal, real. The mind is articulated through the world, in the beginning was the world and without it no word was. The mind is God striving to create Eden in order to live there. Some day the cripple God will walk his cripple walk, feeling on misshapen feet the cool of Paradise.

The house was empty when he got in. He looked in the room and went back into the kitchen. Edna must be at the park, she didn't go to Mrs Davidson's on a Friday. How would he begin to explain what they must do. How would Edna whose world was this, was balance and order, how would she respond to what Nancy MacIndoe had spotted, his true anarchy. A remarkable woman that in many ways. He hoisted the window and looked out. Friday evening, a great relaxation in the air, men home from the yards with money in their pockets, feeling the rhythm of their lives lift at the end of a measure. Their Greenock was a different place, a geographic location, gazetteered and national gridded. He wished Edna would come home so that he could begin explaining. Maybe he could see Maxwell, get him to help in convincing Edna that he must go, leave Greenock, try to be whatever it is he was.

It was as he came in from the window that he saw the

note, where it had fallen from the mantelpiece on to the hearth. It said, 'John', and was unsealed.

John, I have gone to my mother's. When you are ready to explain the enclosed letter I will be ready to see you. Until then Carol and I will remain here.

your wife, Edna.

The enclosed letter was written on lined paper in an open, childish hand. It was quite short.

Mrs Moseby,
I'm sure you would like to know that your husband has been seeing a lot of me in the past few weeks and we have been intimate. I knew him long ago before you did and we were the same then only now he has decided he is too good for me. I thought you would like to know of this no matter what you may think of me.

Yours, Cathie Pollock.

He sat down in the chair and put both letters on his lap. Cathie. He'd almost forgotten all about her. She must have been alive all this time. Poor Cathie. Poor Edna. It must have just come in through the door and she would dry her hands and open it and Carol would say 'what is it mammy?' and Edna would sit down, and then she would cry. People don't really vanish when you're not thinking of them. All over the world they're living away like mad. What would he do. Go down and see her. And say what. What was there to say? I love you. John Moseby loves you. Yes, that's what he'd say, she'd like that. He got up and went into the room and then back into the kitchen. She was sitting down there in that well-groomed room wondering why she had been kicked, thinking back over everything, seeing it all with a pale, sickening clarity, hating him. And why not, you have to hate somebody. Who did he hate?

His mind twitched this way and that, trying to find some avenue of escape from the slow spreading ache of his guilt and its useless gnawing remorse, until he knew there was none, the novelty of his shock wore off and it felt all so inevitable, right from the word go, from birth, 'history is inevitable because it has gone to the trouble of happening'. He was here and looking back he could see no other way it could have been. And once he had seen that there was nothing left to do but suffer, to sit quiet and let it happen. He thought of those two patient sufferers, sitting down there in the bathroom. Go in, look at them, Edna. Pray to the Great Anaesthetist. Sit quiet. If you could find some, consume drink. He was quite surprised at the amount of stuff they had. A bottle of white wine, a half of a half of 'Cointreau' and four bottles of Tennant's stout. He drank the 'Cointreau' in two large shuddering glasses and felt his stomach coil and fume. Then he started on the wine. Maybe when he was drunk he would go down to Gourock and see Edna. Maybe he would gas himself, walk before the Great Umpire raised his finger, maybe he would go next door and rape Mrs Allen. That thought touched the dormant erotic nerve and as the drink began to get to him he became, quite ridiculously, randy. Fine time, he thought. You're scrubbed on that count for a few thousand years. You pathetic little prick Moseby. True, but he hadn't been, not a few hours ago, perched on his rooftop, seeing it all, the world and his way in it. But he was, sitting here rolling his testicles in his pocket. He looked with interest at his erection. Surely in drink you couldn't get a hard on. Blindly, hurtfully, he wanted Edna, wanted her willing or unwilling, wanted her to surround the stiff little digit of his egomaniac identity, soften him, absorb his self-assertion, let him forget the ache of being John Moseby, on his onan.

The window was still open and he went to shut it. The town was all street lamps and dark, diced bulks. The river ran pale and silky. The West Kirk Clock looked four ways at once and saw nothing. Moseby could feel no feeling nor think any thought that related the landscape to his plight. He shivered, afraid, emptily afraid as night covered the land from end to end in pure dark, faintly stained by towns and cities but rising always above their yellow scars into the regions of silence and still, the high hang, the vast vault of other than earthly space, where the moon does not shine to light nor guide but in purposeless perpetuance exists, where stars no longer twinkle their blinter to yearning watchers but burn aeon-old holes in time. Where no birds fly and prayers do not reach and the dawn flood rising foams against no sight but sweeps its sweep across the deserts of the endless air.

The City and the Pillar

by Gore Vidal

Jim Willard was naive enough to believe that love never changes. And determined enough to search from Virginia to Hollywood, from Mexico to New York for a childhood friend and for a kind of love which society condemned. *The City and The Pillar* is an uncompromising novel of the homosexual underworld which scandalised America on its first publication. Gore Vidal has now substantially rewritten his explosive early novel, a book which won praise from critics as discerning as Thomas Mann and André Gide and which was widely acclaimed in the British press.

'A serious work of literature. The theme is most sensitively handled.'—*Spectator*

'A wise and sober book. . . . Mr Vidal tells a good story and his narrative is charged with imagination.'—*The Listener*

THE NEW ENGLISH LIBRARY 5s. 0d.

In a Yellow Wood

by Gore Vidal

Twenty-four hours.

One whole day in the life of a young stockbroker executive in New York City. A man who has lived life to the full and is already, at twenty-six years of age, beginning to feel disillusioned.

This is the New York City of the rich business man, the society hostess, the decadent fast set.

'The account of a single day in the life of a young man who has experienced too much, given too much of himself to conventionality, and who realizes too late that revolt, even for love, is impossible. . . Sex, for Vidal's young man, is not automatic nor is it tawdry. It is a living force of great beauty and perhaps it is the truest means of escape from the prison of the self into union with another in love. Vidal sees that love is the single unshakable truth left to us, the only condition in which beauty and decency have a chance of survival. And, for a world bent upon suicide, it is the only chance.'—*Harper's Magazine*

THE NEW ENGLISH LIBRARY 6s. 0d.

The Injustice Collectors

by Louis Auchincloss

The world of the neurotic—frustrated, embittered and disillusioned people. The rich, time-wasting society of the American seaside resorts, the dilettante Americans of Paris and Venice.

These are the injustice collectors—as seen by Louis Auchincloss, internationally acclaimed author of *The Rector of Justin* and *The Embezzler*.

'Mr Auchinloss' stories, like Mr Angus Wilson's, succeed best when they are nastiest . . . *The Injustice Collectors* is the best-written and most original collection of stories that has been published for a long time.'—*New Statesman*

'Brilliant'.—*Daily Mail*

'. . . a born storyteller who is wise as well as highly intelligent.'—Raymond Mortimer, *The Sunday Times*

THE NEW ENGLISH LIBRARY 5s. 0d.